MW01145955

French
Fried

A NOVEL

Stephen Lewis and Andy McKinney

authorHOUSE®

AuthorHouse™
1663 Liberty Drive
Bloomington, IN 47403
www.authorhouse.com
Phone: 833-262-8899

Published by AuthorHouse 12/14/2021

ISBN: 978-1-6655-4735-2 (sc)
ISBN: 978-1-6655-4734-5 (hc)
ISBN: 978-1-6655-4736-9 (e)

Library of Congress Control Number: 2021925191

CONTENTS

PROLOGUE

Haifa Military Hospital
2007

Ariel Garon gripped the French - designed Prostar Laptop Core 2 and navigated through the motley group of television reporters coalesced at the hospital's portal. The spectacle was reminiscent of Jerusalem's Old City's active Christian and Muslim Quarters, verbal and physical engagement echoed in an amalgam of languages.

News that all crew members who had survived were being treated for various degrees of physical ailments, including radiation exposure and physical trauma, had yielded to even more explosive headlines about the near nuclear miss and suggested conspiracies. In one French newspaper, the front page began with "Conspiracy Over Pakistan," and plastered on the front page of an Italian newspaper was the heading "What Went Wrong Over Pakistan?" And overnight countless blogs of conspiracy theories appeared on the Internet.

Ariel flashed his ID for security and took the stairs to meet Shimon in the basement cafeteria. During the last three days, the two Israelis interviewed Sanjay and Alexander, listened to every song on the mp3 player, deciphered all the cellular-phone calls, retrieved emails, and reprinted Ari's manuscript and Sanjay's diary. After lunch, Shimon and Ariel planned to interview Andre before submitting their final report to

Israeli Prime Minister Olmert. Sanjay's diary had been most revealing and helped establish a profile of the Frenchman.

"Not a bad chicken sandwich," Ariel opined. He had taken a few bites when his phone rang. He glanced at the caller ID and swallowed quickly.

"Shalom, Dr. Wasserman."

"Ariel, we need you upstairs."

"What's the problem?"

"We have two French visitors demanding to see Andre,"

"Be right there," Ariel responded. Within three minutes the two Israeli interrogators walked off the ninth floor elevator. Dr. Wasserman had placed himself between the door and the disagreeable Frenchmen. Shimon and Ariel approached them.

"Hello, I am Shimon Levi and this is my partner Ariel Garon. Can we be of some assistance?"

"Most certainly, Monsieurs Levi and Garon, allow me to introduce myself. I am Antoine Giroux, adjutant to the French Ambassador Michel, and with me is Inspector Jean Gallant from Paris.`` The inspector spoke in accented English calmly but confidently.

"Messieurs, we are conducting an investigation of a priest who we believe died under suspicious circumstances. Perhaps you may have seen him commit suicide on national television," the inspector added.

"I did," Shimon replied.

"I see you are carrying a French manufactured laptop. I must assume it belongs to Andre Dubois," the inspector noted.

"You are very perceptive," Shimon added.

"It is in my job description, Monsieur Levi. Perhaps we will find communications that will help us understand why a man of the cloth willfully defied God by committing suicide. An act of a crazed individual as his church superiors would have me believe, but nothing I discovered suggests this priest was agonized. And to televise his own death suggests there may have been hidden meaning in what he did. Did he sacrifice his life to save others, like our Lord and savior, Jesus Christ?"

Shimon was not humored by the pompous, short and stocky, bulbous faced Frenchman with the oversized head and wavy white hair.

"Presently, Inspector, our government is conducting its own investigation into the descent of the capsule. When our investigation concludes, and if Andre consents, we will be happy to consider your request. In the meantime, you might be better off to recover Father Gothier's laptop," Ariel advised.

"Unfortunately, Father Gauthier's laptop has strangely disappeared."

"That is indeed unfortunate," Shimon said.

"Monsieur, Levi, I must insist that we be allowed to question Andre," Antoine interjected.

"If Andre is willing, I am willing. Let me ask him." The two Frenchmen were visibly upset but agreed. Ariel and Shimon walked into Andre's hospital room and closed the door.

"Good morning, Andre. I am Agent Shimon Levi and this is Agent Ariel Garon. On behalf of the Israeli government I want to extend our appreciation. The warning shots you fired at the Russian helicopter certainly avoided what would have led to an international incident between our countries. And due to satellite interruption, the news agencies never knew of your accomplishment. How are you feeling today?

"How am I feeling? Excellent and good enough to go home, which is exactly what I want to do now."

"We're good with that. Dr. Wasserman says you are fine medically. Outside your door two French officers are eagerly waiting their turn to see you. One is the adjutant to the French ambassador and the other is a Parisian police inspector."

"A police inspector you said?"

"Yes, Inspector Gallant wants to ask you questions concerning the death of your priest, Father Gauthier."

"That is good. I have much to say."

"I am sure you do, Andre, but church officials and the Russians will only deny your allegations. "They'll say you are mentally unbalanced from living in space."

"But I have the emails to prove my case."

"On this laptop I am holding?" Shimon queried.

"Yes, my laptop."

"Unfortunately for you your emails are now the property of Israel. But possibly some good can come from this. We might be able to blackmail the Russians into behaving well."

"Monsieur, Levi, please don't use the word 'we.' I am not interested in Israel's welfare. I am a citizen of France, an orphan whose father was killed from an unprovoked bombing raid at Osirak."

"Andre, your father wasn't supposed to be working that weekend. Noone else was at the reactor. I am sorry for your loss but we were able to destroy the reactor before it had nuclear fuel and avoid nuclear fallout. I understand why you don't like Israel, but you are not an innocent man, though you have a chance at some redemption."

"Unless you can bring Father Gauthier back to life, I will have no chance for redemption in this life."

"We can't bring your priest back, but with your cooperation we might be able to get Alexander's brother, Yuri, out of the Russian prison. Would that be important to you?" Ariel inquired.

"Of course, he is in prison because of me."

"Then tell these Frenchmen you know nothing, and let our government handle this delicate situation. Will you agree to be silent until we can free Yuri?

"Yes, I can agree to that."

"Andre," Ariel continued. "An Israeli named Ari Davidson was killed by a Hezbollah sniper near the Lebanon border."

"The only Ari I know is Ari Ben Ora," Andre responded,

"He was an archeologist at a dig near Ashkelon," Shimon added. There was a moment of silence. Andre took a deep breath.

"I believe he was in a relationship with my ex-fiancee. Michelle must be devastated.

"Two days ago she sent you an email. I took the liberty to read it because it's my job to go through all communications," Shimon revealed. "Would you like to read her email, Andre?

"I would." Shimon sat on the edge of the bed and opened Michelle's email on Andre's laptop.

"Can I reply?" Andre asked.

"I'd rather you not," Shimon said. "Your laptop is still part of our investigation. Why don't you see her? I can take you to Ashkelon whenever you want."

"I am ready now." Shimon opened the door.

"Gentlemen of France, Andre will see you now."

CAST OF CHARACTERS

FRENCH CONNECTIONS:
Michelle Dumas foreign exchange student
Lucille Dumas, Michelle's mother
Andre Dubois, astronaut
Louis Major, Andre's friend,
Henri Bettencourt, news reporter
Antoine DeGaulle, aide to Archbishop Clement
Archbishop Clement,
Father Martell
Father Scarpone
Shai Tanger, waiter
Jean Gallant, lead detective
Detectives Blanc, Francois, and Claude
Nate Gottschalk, criminal
Phillippe-Zoran, criminal
Sasha Andreev, criminal

THE ISRAELIS:
Ari Ben Ora, astronaut
Shimon Levi, interrogation agent
Eshkol Rosenbaum, Israeli Embassy, Paris
Gideon Asher, Israeli Consulate, Los Angeles
Izzy Rothstein, criminal

THE AMERICANS:
FBI Special Agent Woods, San Diego
Detective Ryan, San Diego
Eric, Bette, and Z Miller, Scottsdale
Jaime Gonzales, confidential informant

MEXICAN CONNECTIONS
Alfred Diaz Chief of Police, Tijuana
Fernando Valenzuela, drug dealer
Helena Valenzuela, wife
The Muslim Brigade: Rashid, Gamal, Sammy, Amir Delshad
Hezbollah: Ali Chaboun, Ibrahim, Anwar Saba, Farouk Hussein, Faisal,
Karim, and Yasser

Chapter 1

BEN GURION INTERNATIONAL AIRPORT

2009

"Kidnapped" read the headline on Le Monde. Person or persons unknown had snatched French astronaut Andre Dubois. Naturally agent Shimon Levi knew about that incident already. He even knew the victim. He combed his fingers through mushroom brown, wavy hair in an attempt at taming it. He had once again not found time to visit his barber. A good looking enough man with bright blue eyes, a strong nose, and a good chin, he might have been taken for a taller version of Prime Minister Benjamin Netanyahu. Women found him attractive and his training as an interrogator made him easy to talk to, if not easy for them to get to know.

They had three hours until their flight for Paris departed. He watched the March rain cleanse the air through the terminal windows and pondered his travelling companion as he waited. Michelle, the beautiful French archeological post-graduate student, now living in Ashkelon, Israel. She had given him the news of the kidnapping of her fiance in a call the previous day. She asked the agent to accompany her to Paris.

She had met him the year before at the welcome home party for fellow astronaut Ari Ben Ora, the Israeli member of the international foursome on an ill fated space mission. Shimon had certainly noticed and remembered Michelle, not a surprise. Michelle did not have just a beautiful face and form but had the grace and feminine presence that French women had by reputation but often lacked in reality. As he did as a matter of habit with women who held his interest, he had slipped her his card at the party, not in an aggressive way but as a matter of polite interest to someone new to his country.

Sometimes it worked for him.

"I am glad to hear your voice, Michelle. But why do you want me, of all people, to go to Paris with you?"

"Shimon, I do not trust the French authorities," she replied. "I do not know who took Andre. It may even turn out that the government has some twisty involvement. I trust you, your abilities, your instincts."

She brightened. "I will be staying with my mother. She has a room for you too if you would like a place to stay. It might be convenient for us to stay together."

"For the sake of appearances, thank you but no. When I received permission from my boss to leave Israel, I had the office make arrangements for me. You are right about it being convenient for us to be close together, but it might be better if we're not associated too closely until we find out more about Andre."

He briefly thought of the ironies of life sometimes sent his way. He knew her fiance. Shimon had been the interrogating officer when the space capsule had landed on the sea near Israel and the crew rescued. More irony, Andre deeply detested Israel but was saved from death by Israeli airmen, healed by Israeli doctors, and in the Jewish homeland, he and his lost love Michelle found each other again.

For Shimon, things had changed dramatically in the fifteen months since he had first met Michelle at the party for astronaut Ari Ben Ora. Most dramatically, his divorce had finalized, making him a free man romantically and a poorer man financially. His emotional discipline and his former wife's natural good nature had prevented the horrors that too often submerge couples in a divorce. The former pair could and did communicate without rancor. He had the boys on weekends.

When he spoke to his former wife about his sudden trip to France, she had a helpful, cooperative attitude. She understood the nature of his work. He had a few moments to speak to his boys and say goodbye.

Then he called Michelle back with the information on their flight arrangements. His office made things go smoothly.

The chances for peace in the area had depressingly diminished in the time since he and Michelle had first met. A glimmer of hope for an agreement between Israel and the Palestinian Authority had vanished in the wake of a civil war between the PA and Hamas. Hamas, an even more dedicated enemy of Israel and of Jews generally, had driven the PA out of Gaza. The ones they caught out in the street were shot dead on the spot. With blood in the street, the PA and Fatah had little time or interest in patching up some kind of permanent peace with Israel. Those who could escape from Gaza did so to the areas of Judea and Samaria that the PA still controlled.

When Hamas immediately began to fire rockets into peaceful neighborhoods in Israel, the IDF invaded. That put a near-total stop to the attacks, but at the cost of near worldwide condemnation of Israel. The world tsk-tsked at Jewish homes being blown to bits but the very idea of Jews defending themselves drove the world wild.

And in southern Lebanon, Hezbollah, the Party of God, continued to build up its already vast arsenal of rockets, safe behind a screen of UN troops. Hezbollah had pledged to divest itself of its deadly horde of rockets, but had not done so nor had the UN insisted that it do so. Iran kept pushing more, better, and more deadly sorts of rockets into the terrorists' hands while at home it continued to work on building an atomic bomb. Iran regularly threatened to incinerate the entire state of Israel.

Russia had promised to sell Iran first-rate radar and anti-aircraft missile systems to protect the nuclear program development sites. And in a major bit of good news, Russia had not delivered the new systems. Iran did not suspect the reason for Russia slow-walking the transfer was a deeply secret quid pro quo between Israel and Russia.

Following the landing of the space capsule off the coast of Israel, the laptop of French astronaut Andre Dubois got scooped up by Israeli agents. That began the quid pro quo. The laptop revealed the Russian-Iranian conspiracy against Israel, and a plot by Russia to intentionally destroy its own International Space Station, along with the crew. Also uncovered were emails implicating the Vatican in a blackmail for a silence scheme against Russia in exchange for Russia's return of confiscated church property. Now Israel, Russia and the Vatican all had good reasons to keep the vile and the murderous plans of Moscow under wraps.

Former tank commander and astronaut Ari Ben Ora was another of the quartet of space men. Slowly recovering from both radiation exposure and a knock on the head, he initially suffered from retrograde amnesia. Russian astronaut Alexander bounced back from his radiation exposure but his brother Yuri, the source of the deadly information, now sat in a Russian prison. Alex expected to find out at any moment that his twin brother reached the business end of a Russian rope. Only Sanjay, the astronaut from India, felt safe. He rested at home in India.

Some tense dickering between Israel, the four astronauts and the Russian government allowed Yuri to join his twin in Israel. Each of the four astronauts agreed to maintain silence in return for Yuri's release and relocation to Israel.

Shimon thought for a good long while about his emotional reaction when he met Yuri and the mother of the twins, also released to travel to Israel. How, he wondered, could he, a cynical secret agent and hard bitten Israeli Defence Force veteran, feel such a lump in his throat about people that he had never met before.

Now, fifteen months later, Andre could not stand it any longer. Upon his return to Paris, he contacted those he knew in the French media. He out right accused Catholic officials, very publicly, of trying to cover up the suicide of his father-like-mentor, French priest Father Gothier. The late priest had filled the paternal space left when the Israeli 1981 airstrike on the French built Iraqi nuclear reactor inadvertently killed Andre's dad, leaving him an orphan to be cared for by Catholic agencies.

For Andre, first the Jews had killed his God, then his father.

Shimon took a seat at the Starbucks after he passed through the security lines. He recognized Michelle at once when she took her place in the long line in front of the security station. He took a moment to just look at her, to enjoy the intense femininity she presented.

She wore a pair of designer jeans, not the $20 sort a woman might buy at Wal-Mart to cover her legs but rather a $200 pair of jeans that molded themselves to the lower half of her body, showing the best aspects, her legs and adjoining parts. A black leather jacket in a fashionable cut covered a crisp white linen shirt. She tucked her long, lustrous brown hair into a cap fashioned in Milan and costing a week's grocery bill for a family. Shimon didn't mind the expensive clothing. Michelle looked like a million bucks, like a movie star from Hollywood or a fashion model that came to do a film shoot.

He watched the beautiful young woman as she passed through the security line. She removed her ankle high 'Elf' boots and placed them in the security basket along with her purse and hat. She had nothing in her pocket to unload. Pocket items would ruin the flow of the jeans. After showing her passport and student ID card, a female agent took her aside, gave her a thorough going frisk and began asking a long series of questions.

"Enough" thought Shimon. He quickly approached the security agent and flashed his badge.

"This woman is with me. Let her through," he commanded.

The guard, deprived of her chance to abuse an infinitely more attractive woman, motioned Michelle to be on her way. She graced Shimon with a glare.

"Thank you," Michelle said as soon as she had her little boots back on her feet. She stuffed her cap into her purse and gave Shimon a quick hug. Up close, Shimon could see that even her expertly applied make-up did not hide her puffy eyes.

"My pleasure, Michelle," he replied as they found seats. "We are very security conscious here. Can I get you something, a drink or something to nibble on?"

"Just a coffee for me, please. Large and black." She dove into her purse for some money.

"No, allow me, please," Shimon insisted

She smiled her thanks. It was not the first time in her life that she had traded a smile for a drink or a better place in a line outside a club, a cocktail or some other favor that men offered a beautiful woman.

She sipped her coffee with demure grace, even in that simple act. Shimon noticed that she left a scarlet, lip shaped imprint on the paper coffee cup.

"Michelle, I am glad you called me but I admit I am surprised that you had my phone number."

"At Ari's homecoming party, Andre introduced us. You gave me your card and I kept it." She gave him a look that Shimon could not interpret and held it for an extra heartbeat. "You wore a wedding band when we met, Shimon."

He felt his ears heat up but his training kept his face calm and bland. "Indeed I did. I am recently divorced." He gave her a level gaze, direct without being impolite. "You are very observant."

"Oh, I am sorry. I didn't mean to be too forward."

"No reason for anyone to feel sorry, Michelle. I would say parting was wanted by both of us. We can maintain a cordial relationship, both for the sake of the kids and because we do not feel any rancor for each other. We just could no longer be happy in our marriage."

She looked interested. "Do you have children? Boys or girls or some of each?"

"Boys, one nine and one seven. But enough about me, tell me how you found out about Andre's abduction?"

She might have lost her composure but didn't. She took in a shallow breath and said. "My mother called me. A few hours later I got a call from a policeman, an inspector Gallant. He has the case."

He nodded at her words. "I know the man. I met him in Israel a couple of years ago. He visited Andre at the hospital then, he and an adjutant to the French ambassador to Israel. At that time both of them had the task of the investigation of the priest's suicide."

Michelle looked even more somber and distressed. "Andre believes that someone in the Vatican caused his mentor, Father Gothier, to kill himself."

"Michelle, please understand, I have no jurisdiction outside of Israel. Gallant had no reason to think kindly of me or to cooperate with me. I am happy to accompany you to Paris but my usefulness might actually be less than you think."

"I understand. I also know you will do your best and that your best is quite good. You rescued Yuri and his mother from the Russians, from prison even. You brought that family together. Andre told me that. She smiled but in a neutral way, not coy or flirtatious at all.

"Where will you stay, Shimon?"

"My office has arranged for me to stay at the embassy." He offered a small Italianesque shrug. "I work for the government and the government has a list of rules so long as to be incomprehensible, except to clerks."

"But you will be with me when I see the inspector?"

"Yes, of course, if you wish." He glanced at his watch.

"Should we walk to the gate?" Michelle asked. Shimon agreed.

Michelle left the remains of her coffee, grabbed her purse and stretched her legs, moving quickly. Shimon guessed that she stood about five feet eight inches with her high heel Elf boots. He liked women, he approved of this woman and wondered if he might approach her as a man does a woman he finds attractive. Did she sense his attraction? Probably, he guessed. A woman with her wonderful good looks no doubt assumed that any healthy male would find her attractive. She would be right.

Yet he had a difficult balancing act ahead of him. If Michelle thought of him as a good Samaritan, she would be wrong. The safety of her fiance had a place well down his list of concerns in this regard. If Andre shot his mouth off too much, he could jeopardize Israel's complicated three corner bargain with both Moscow and the Holy See. Better that the kidnappers should murder Andre than Andre let the cat out of the bag.

But he did have a morsel of pity for the Frenchman. Andre's mother had been struck and killed by a drunk driver when he was still small. Then Israeli bombs had blown his father, a nuclear engineer, to bits, leaving him an orphan. No wonder Andre hated the Jews.

They passed a newsstand and Michelle bought a copy of Le Monde, a French newspaper. She read the paper as she walked, linking arms with Shimon for guidance so she could concentrate.

"Oh, Shimon, here is the interview that Andre made with Henri Bettencourt just before his abduction. I can translate into English as we walk, if you can keep me from stumbling. Shimon had her arm through his and thought that was just fine. Michelle read on.

7

"Monsieur Dubois, you are returning as a French astronaut and hero. Two years ago, you piloted your escape capsule through unfathomable searing heat and force of tornado driven turbulence generated by the Pakistani atmospheric nuclear detonation that threw your spacecraft off its gravitational course. Instead of landing at your intended landing strip, your capsule landed hard but safe on the Mediterranean Sea on July 20, 2007. By most accounts the velocity and angle of descent and landing should have blown your capsule and occupants to shreds."

"We were blessed by God," Andre said.

"However, it seems lately you are remembered more for what some say is a concocted story which disparages the Roman Church. Your detractors claim your constant exposure to a micro-gravitational environment in space contributed to a deterioration of your acuity and mental faculties. How do you respond?"

"My faculties are fine. I was checked thoroughly by the doctors in Haifa."

"Well then, please tell us your story."

"Let me begin by acknowledging my unlawful misappropriation of another crew member's private email. The crew member whose privacy was violated was Alexander Kafelnikoff from Russia. While Alex was asleep, he received an email and attachments from his brother, Yuri. I stole, copied, pasted and forwarded the message to my own email account, after which I forwarded this email to the late Father Gothier without Alex's knowledge. I then attempted to destroy evidence of that email."

"Before I ask you the contents of that email Monsieur Dubois, how did you happen to discover it? Bettencourt probed.

"Alexander had been suffering from radiation sickness and forgot to shut down his laptop. His brother's email was in full view."

Shimon grimaced. Andre peddled an egregious lie. Shimon had interrogated the Frenchman after the space capsule had landed on the sea. At that time, Andre admitted that he had hacked into Alexander's laptop while the three astronauts slept. Why did he spin this fantasy to the press? What did he hope to gain?

Michelle continued reading.

"What was in that email Monsieur Dubois?"

"Henri, very few people in France knew that my father, an engineer, was the only casualty of the Israeli airstrike on Osirak that destroyed the Iraqi but

French built nuclear reactor. Thankfully, the construction of the reactor was in its early stages and there was no nuclear fallout. By Israeli standards, I surmise the mission couldn't have succeeded better, except for the death of my father. My mother died the previous year and I became an orphan without siblings. I left Baghdad and lived in a Catholic orphanage in Reims. Father Gauthier was my mentor. I loved him as my father."

"Would you agree you were no fan of the Jewish state?"

"I was no fan of Israel, and Yuri's email described the machinations of a new existential threat to Israel by Russia and Iran. A myriad of thoughts entered my mind. Should I wake up Alexander, should I inform my Israeli crewmate, or should I inform French Intelligence first? So I asked Father Gauthier for guidance?

"And who was Yuri?" Henri inquired.

"Yuri Kafelnikoff, Alexander's twin brother, was a foreign policy advisor to Putin," Andre replied.

"And that response begs the question why Yuri would share opinions of state secrets with his brother?"

"The two brothers were Christian Zionists," Andre answered.

"So the brothers' loyalty and love for Israel trumped their loyalty to the country that rewarded them with positions of power and prestige, a charge that historically had been leveled against Jews in France, even as early as the late 19th century with a false treason treason conviction of the Jewish Captain Alfred Dreyfus. Apparently Christian Zionism is not just an American phenomenon," Henri posited.

"I don't believe Israel existed until after World War 2," Andre responded.

"Ancient Israel existed during the first millennium, but the Zionist push for a Jewish homeland in the 20th Palestine seemed to have started soon after Dreyfus was improned on Devil's Island until his pardon, exoneration and reinstatement into the French Army. I believe that was in 1906. It was a fascinating case involving French author Emile Zola, who came to Dreyfus' defense."

"Back to the Russian, Yuri. It seems that Yuri's intent was to have his brother Alexander warn the Israeli astronaut Are Ben Ora so he could notify his government of this existential threat."

"Correct," Andre replied.

"Tell us of this alleged plot against Israel," Henri pressed on.

"*There were attached photos of an Iranian oil tanker docked at Jakarta that showed Russians boarding from a dinghy. Yuri believed a Pakistani nuclear bomb was secretly transferred to Iran through a structured lend-lease program that provided below market priced oil to Pakistan. When Ahmadiniejad became Iran's president and threatened Israel's annihilation, Pakistani president Musharraf got nervous and demanded that Ahmadinejad immediately return the nuclear bomb. Ahmadinejad balked and sent Rafsanjani who sought Putin's assistance. Rafsanjani convinced Putin that the one million Russian emigrants to Israel after the breakup of the Soviet Union, often credited as the engine of Israel's technology boom, could be in play.*"

"*What do you mean, 'could be in play?'*"

"*Rafsanjani convinced Putin he could reclaim the majority of Israel's Russian Jews after the crisis,*"

"*What crisis?*" Henri asked.

"*Russian nuclear experts were secretly placed on an Iranian tanker to engineer that Pakistani nuclear bomb onto an Iranian missile. The missile launch and detonation was to happen high above the Indian Ocean. The strategy was to mislead the world that Iran had joined the exclusive club of nuclear nations, and would not back down from a nuclear exchange with the Israelis. By observing the United States engagement with North Korea, the Iranians concluded that no country would dare attack a nuclear armed Iran as no country had dared to attack North Korea. And North Korea is without the leverage of petroleum.*"

"*Oil and nuclear missiles are a powerful deterrent to U.N. interference,*" Henri declared.

"*Yes, the entire theory was predicated on the fact that Israelis were still traumatized by the thousands of Hezbollah rockets that reigned down on them during the 2005 Lebanon war,*" Andre stated.

"*Fascinating, how many Jews did Putin expect to repatriate?*"

"*Eventually, hundreds of thousands from the nearly one million who immigrated to Israel within the last two decades, most of whom were not considered political Zionists, but rather political refugees who fled a failed Soviet system that was unable to protect them. Estimates were that thousands of them had questionable Jewish bloodlines. Thousands more were considered Jewish by marriage only.*"

"Interesting, but Israel has a formidable nuclear deterrent itself, even the ability to obliterate Iran in a nuclear exchange?" Henri asserted.

"Supposedly, but would tiny Israel mount a preemptive strike if their leaders suspected Iran could retaliate in kind? Iran is geographically many times larger, and Iran would only need one nuclear strike to destroy Israel in my estimation. Israel is geographically very small," Andre opined.

"Let me repeat," Henri requested. "By launching and detonating a borrowed nuclear bomb above the Indian Ocean provided by Pakistan and with the help of the Russsians, Iran believed it could achieve strategic regional dominance and begin to disassemble the state of Israel."

"Constant Iranian threats of nuclear annihilation were intended to demoralize the Jews, sink their economy, dry up investment capital, engineer a brain drain, and send back to America companies like Israel Intel and Microsoft Israel. If successful, that pressure, coupled with Russian financial incentives, intended to precipitate an exodus of Russian Jews and perhaps many thousands of others that would shrink an Jewish majority to a minority one," Andre explained.

"Extraordinary, one can only imagine Arab citizens of Israel becoming the majority. That is something that this reporter has read could happen far into the future, and could very well mean the end of the Jewish state and a win for Palestinians," Henri surmised.

Michelle paused in her reading when the attendant announced that the first class passengers could now board. Shimon stood up, touching her arm in the process to cue her to rise as well. Michelle lifted one perfectly sculptured eyebrow in surprise and inquiry. She had no reason to suspect they would be flying first class.

"For the cost of my ticket, Shimon, what do I owe you?"

Shimon noticed his reaction to the sound of her voice, a clear, sweet soprano. He, a trained agent, analyzed his reaction and told himself to calm down, step back emotionally and pay attention to his business and only his business. He had a hard time with that self admonition.

"Nothing, Michelle. My government picked up the tab for the both of us. Obviously, they are interested in Andre's welfare." They boarded and found their seats, side by side in the forward section, nearest to the cockpit.

"Shall I finish reading the article, Shimon?"

"Yes, please. We need to know as much as possible when we get to Paris if we are to be of any use."

He did not mention just how much he liked to watch her lips move as she read the newspaper, translating as she read.

"Monsieur Dubois, even had this alleged crisis materialized, that these Russian Israelis would not so quickly forget their very bad history under the Czars and later Stalin. They would have to be concerned that a future repatriation could be political fodder for Russia's anti-Semites. And any economic inflation or stagnation would surely be blamed on the Jewish arrival."

"Putin's primary concern was that the intended Jewish repatriation to Russia would immediately offset Russia's annual endemic population decline, which last year exceeded 700,000: a dangerous trend which if not reversed could portend a diminished role for Russia on the world stage," Andre responded.

"Indeed, France and much of Western Europe are dealing with their own population declines," Henri averred.

"With a Jewish population infusion, Putin envisioned Israeli technology and business development coming as well, and eventual job creation and bigger families would follow," Andre added.

"Who was to finance the Jewish repatriation?" Henri asked.

"Iran would contribute," Andre answered.

"And what would Pakistan achieve from this?"

"A civilian nuclear assistance program patterned after the U.S. assistance program for India," Andre responded.

"I remember that was in the news two summers ago."

"As were discussions of Vatican property claims against the Russians," Andre added.

"Andre, in your opinion, was the offer of the restitution of Catholic Church property from Russia and Russian nuclear assistance to Pakistan linked?"

"Yes, undoubtedly. Both of these schemes were withdrawn at almost the same time. Clearly they were linked."

"Those events undoubtedly pleased our French intelligence services. Getting back to Father Gauthier, did you ever receive a reply to your email to him?"

"I received a reply time stamped several hours after his death."

"That is amazing," Henri replied.

"It would be amazing that a dead man could reply to an email."

"Can you tell me and my readers about the contents of that email from beyond the grave?"

"It was a terse reply, Henri. Father Gauthier intended to consult his superiors."

"Do you have these emails, Andre?"

"No, all of my emails which could prove my allegations were in my hard drive on my laptop. Israeli intelligence services confiscated my computer and changed my passwords."

"And Andre, what happened to Father Gauthier's computer?"

"It seems to have disappeared within the Vatican," Andre opined.

"Vatican representatives claim they don't have the computer."

"I don't believe them, not for a minute," Andre exclaimed.

"Who within the Vatican do you believe had access to Father Gauthier's email?"

"I don't know for certain. Perhaps Archbishop Clement?"

"And you think they would conceal it because the publication of your correspondence would present a dark side of the Vatican? Did you finally tell your crew mates what you had done?"

"Yes. After hearing about Yuri's arrest and Father Gauthier's suicide, I came clean to them about everything," Andre admitted.

"How did you first hear of Father Gauthier's suicide?" Henri asked.

"When our phone communications failed to recover after Yuri's arrest, the Russian techies of Central Command said the breakdown was weather related, but the report of Father Gauthier's suicide came to us through the internet services. We suspected the Russian Central Command interdicted all communications going in and out of the International Space Station, but the Russian techies could not successfully jam all the satellite network signals."

"You must have been upset when the news of his suicide broke."

"Yes, at first I denied to myself that he had done such a thing. Then, I realized he had some purpose in mind, a purpose that he would trade for his own life."

"What purpose?" Henri asked.

"He wanted to warn me that we would all be dead men if we stayed on the ISS. Because our emails were screened, Father Gauthier had no way of warning me of the pending danger. Because he tried to warn me, he became a liability to the Russians but also to the Catholic Church."

"*That might explain his sudden transfer to South America,*" Henri affirmed.

"*Yes, he knew he was a dead man. When Father Gauthier saw the film crew at the Basilica de Sacre Coeur, I am certain he took his own life to save mine.*"

"*It kind of parallels Jesus' life, doesn't it? Giving his life for the benefit of others? Why did you believe you were facing danger?*"

"*In order for the Russian-Iranian scheme to succeed, the few people on the outside who knew about Yuri's emails had to be taken out. They arrested Yuri. Father Gothier had already sacrificed his life. That left me and the remaining crew to deal with, to cover their tracks.*"

"*Fascinating. Let's recap. While up in space, you received Yuri's email which you forwarded to your lifelong mentor, Father Gauthier in Reims. Then the Russians soon after arrested Yuri, and soon after Father Gauthier commits suicide in front of a camera crew to warn you of pending danger. Yuri's email allegedly reveals a sinister Russian-Iranian plot against Israel. Your suspicion is that Father Gauthier passed this information about this plot contained in Yuri's email to his superiors who then allegedly approached the Russians with threats to publicize the emails. The Russians subsequently offered once owned Church property seized by the Communists back to the Vatican in exchange for their silence. Wow.*"

"*Examine the trail of evidence, Monsieur Bettencourt. Who was at the crime scene when Father Gauthier died?*"

"*The Archbishop of Paris Clement and Archbishop Lajolo from the Vatican foreign service,*" the journalist replied.

"*Why would Father Gauthier require such a star-studded send off, after all he was only a monsignor?*" Andre asked Henri.

"*Now that is an excellent question, Andre. At the time of his death, the two archbishops only revealed that Father Gauthier was suffering from depression. Was that truthful?*"

"*No, there is not a shred of truth in their false statement. If I could get the church to release his medical records, I can prove that their charge is spurious. If the depression allegation was true, why transfer him to South America where he knows no one? It doesn't make any sense, as anyone can plainly see.*"

"*Monsieur Dubois, for the record, how did your crew mates react when you told them you had stolen the email?*"

"*They were angry, of course, as anyone would be angry. Alexander was especially angry. He blamed me for the arrest of his brother at the Kremlin. Ari lost an opportunity to warn his country of the nasty plot against Israel. It was then that I revealed my reasons. I told Ari that my father was killed by an Israeli airstrike."*

"*In Iraq in 1981,*" Henri reconfirmed.

Shimon displayed little reaction to Andre's revisionist account and selective memory. In reality, when Sanjay loaded software to retrieve Yuri's missing email, he discovered it in Andre's email account. Andre was restrained and injected with a sedative. He denied any involvement with the email and only came clean upon hearing the news if Father Gauthier's suicide. The truth was quite different from what Andre told the French journalist.

Even as he absorbed this faulty information, Shimon had an acute awareness of his seat partner, of the sound of her voice no matter the words and the gentle waft of her scent.

He refocused as she continued to read.

"*Yes, but we refocused and came together because our immediate survival was at stake. In order to fool the Russians, we created an incident on the ISS. We radioed in a story that we were hit by space junk, a punctured hole too large for us to repair. I was the one who punched the hole discreetly during my final space walk. Discreetly, because I knew the Russians were watching us.*"

"*How did you make the hole?*" Henri inquired.

"*I fastened a blade to my flashlight. When I placed the flashlight near the surface, the blade slid through. Our life support systems began to deteriorate. I helped the others with their space suits. Then we had to tell Central Command, the Russians in other words, that we had to bail because we couldn't fix the problem. They were quite upset because the resupply shuttle was due to arrive within two days. We believed the shuttle was rigged to explode upon arrival, and that is how we were supposed to disappear.*"

"*The capsule was pre-programmed to land at a strip in Russia. As pilot, I reprogrammed our flight plan and assumed manual control. Just before the incident, Ari was able to alert the Israeli authorities of the plot and our intention to land the capsule at an airstrip in the Negev.*"

"*If you believed the ISS communications were interdicted by the Russians, how was Ari able to alert the Israeli authorities?*"

"Lyrics from Beatles' songs mostly, and a few others," Andre admitted.

"Are you serious?"

"Yes, Ari chanced that an email to his wife would not be interdicted. Central Command apparently thought it was harmless and let Ari's email though and his wife's reply also coded. The truth was that each placement of each song title was in code."

"Forgive me but this sounds like a John Le Carre novel," Henri replied.

Michelle stopped reading and peered out the cabin window. Below her as the plane lifted and turned into the clear, soft blue sky, she could see the Mediterranean sparkling and dancing below her. The engine noise and the pressure pops in her ears prevented any conversation for a little while. She spent a few minutes taking in the beauty and worrying about Andre.

Shimon, on his part, pondered the omissions and falsehoods in the newspaper story. He leaned back, closed his eyes and reviewed those things that he knew Andre did not know.

Andre did not know about the last hour before Father Gothier met with the high church officials. The Father had printed out the email in question and placed a copy, folded vertically, in the inside pocket of his windbreaker. Andre did not know that Gauthier had taken his bicycle to his usual and favorite cafe that morning. He intended to take a cab to Paris to the Israeli embassy. If the cab had arrived just five minutes earlier, he would have missed the fateful limousine ride with two archbishops that quickly led to his suicide.

But the archbishops' limo did arrive first. Father Gauthier calmly walked to the car with his laptop, but carefully left his windbreaker folded over the back of his chair. As the archbishops' limo left, the taxi arrived and pulled into the same spot, now vacated and available. Shai, the waiter, approached the cab driver and apologetically explained the monsignor's absence and offered the driver complimentary croissants and coffee. And over coffee, the driver revealed to Shai that the monsignor's destination had been the Israeli embassy in Paris, a very good fare for the cabby.

Later that day, gthe tragic news of the suicide of one of his best and favorite customers came over the TV. Shai eventually discovered the printed version of the email. Shai knew at once the importance of the papers and took them himself to the embassy. He at a stroke fulfilled what he thought would be the intention of his customer and friend, and he helped the Jewish state.

Shimon had enough brain power left as he reviewed these things in his mind to focus some of it upon his seatmate. He had an acute awareness of her, not as a part of an investigation, but simply as a woman. He admitted to himself that she was a particularly beautiful woman. He could feel his attraction to her, powerful and primal. The trained agent shook a mental finger at himself in warning. Stay away, beware, this is not the correct thing, to be entranced by this woman, the agent in him warned.

His maleness just told his agent-self to shut up.

"We can hear again, Shimon. Shall I continue to translate the newspaper for you?" Michelle asked.

"Absolutely." If she wanted to read him the entire phonebook, that would be just fine and dandy with him, as long as he could hear her voice and watch her lips form the words.

"When we landed hard on the Mediterranean Sea, a Russian naval helicopter soon found us. I used the on board emergency micro-Uzi submachine gun to spray a few rounds at the chopper. I don't know if I hit it, but they flew off. If we had fallen into Russian hands, I am certain we would all have been killed on the spot. They would have simply told the world that we had died on impact. Who could say otherwise?"

"You had a weapon in your survival kit?" Henri asked, in astonishment.

"Yes, the smallest sort of Uzi. It isn't much larger than a handgun. Personal protection details, even in major countries, use them because they can have a fully automatic weapon that fits into a shoulder holster. It is a standard part of the survival kit in the escape capsule. There have been other space shuttles that have landed off course. There are hostile territories all over Asia. It makes perfect sense. I can personally attest that the Uzi saved our lives that day."

"Monsignor Dubois, I've rechecked the video and we witnessed only an Israeli rescue copter at the scene of your landing, not a Russian one."

"The Israeli copter arrived moments later. Monsieur Bettencourt, do you recall prior to our landing there was a communications blackout?"

"Now that you mention that, I do recall a temporary blackout. The

Pakistani atmospheric nuclear detonation resulted in electro-magnetic pulses that caused disruptions to our normal satellite feed."

"Were there any witnesses to the Russian helicopter, perhaps from another vessel?" Henri asked.

"None have come forward so far. The Israeli chopper pilots could have had a visual sighting of the incident."

"Alright then, you and your crew mates get rescued by Israel. Will they confirm your account of the landing?"

"You will have to ask them, Monsieur Bettencourt. Sanjay has returned to India. Ari has recovered and I have heard he is on a book tour in the United States."

"Of course, Ari authored "The Palestine Exchange" while he was aboard the ISS. I understand it is a novel created during the British Mandate period in Palestine. In the book you four astronauts got blasted back in time to 1939 from our present era. I hear he pokes a jab or two at the French during their mandate in Lebanon, but he really goes after the British. Have you read the book, Andre?"

"Not yet, Henri. Certainly, I intend to read it soon."

"Perhaps we can send a Le Monde correspondent to America to track him down. He may verify your account. Do you know where we can find your fellow spaceman, Alexander?"

"He lives in Israel. I promised the Israeli interrogators that I would say nothing about the emails and Father Gauthier's suicide until they were able to bring Yuri and his mother to Israel. I have kept my promise, my end of the bargain. Yuri, Alexander, and their mother are now safe in Israel. The two brothers are affiliated with the International Christian Embassy in Jerusalem."

Shimon cringed at the thought of the French or any other media descending on Ari or the others. The embassy staff in Paris must have read this and reported to Jerusalem. He certainly hoped the embassy had been quick to notice the article and take action.

He allowed himself a quick glance at Michelle and caught her looking at him in what seemed to him to be a speculating way. He turned his head and closed his eyes again. Safer that way.

Michelle continued to read and translate the lengthy article.

"That explains why you didn't come forth with this information sooner. Monsieur Dubois, we have contacted the Russians. They deny that Yuri was

ever harassed in Russia. The Russians acknowledge that Yuri and Alexander are Christian Zionists and granted them visas to leave Russia for Israel."

"Monsieur Bettencourt, do you really believe the Russian government would allow one of its citizens with high security clearance and access to the Kremlin entrails to move to Israel? Do you not think it strange that Alexander never returned to Russia for a hero's welcome like I received in France?"

"I do think it is strange. But permit me to get back to the capsule landing. You were able to escape the Russians, and there was no Iranian nuclear launch in the South Pacific. What do you think happened, Andre?"

"I would speculate that the Iranian launch was scrubbed. Their bluff was over. I can only imagine the Israelis would have their pretext to destroy Iran's nuclear facilities had Iran been stupid enough to detonate their only nuclear weapon during a test launch. The Israelis would have had a great legal case, after all, Ahmadinejad frequently threatened to wipe Israel off the map. Intent with means could constitute self defense in the world court."

"I'll have to verify that with our legal department. Some of your detractors say you are using your celebrity status for a future book deal, like your Israeli comrade Ari Ben Ora. What do you say to them, Monsieur Dubois?"

"I would say that I don't intend to write a book. But to those who conspired against Father Gauthier, they should know I will never give up until I can prove their culpability in his suicide."

"And when you find that proof, Monsieur Dubois, this reporter would appreciate being contacted first, Merci."

Michelle folded her newspaper on her lap and became very teary eyed. Shimon gave her his handkerchief. She wiped her cheeks. Even in her distress she seemed perfect to Shimon, perfect tears on perfect cheeks.

"He was expecting me to return to France with him at the end of my semester, but they accepted me into the doctoral program at Tel Aviv University. I couldn't turn that offer down. After I told Andre about the offer, Andre left. I feel so responsible."

"Hey, you are too hard on yourself," Shimon responded gently but reasonably. "Your life is in Israel. He could have stayed but he chose to leave. I believe you French had a term for this, Michelle c'est la vie. It is life. And believe me, Michelle, it is not your fault."

"We also have a word for guilt," she replied, giving him a shy look from under her brows, her big eyes still moist but with a hint of a smile.

"Hah! Thank God you French have only one word for guilt. We Jews have created a whole dictionary based on guilt."

They both laughed. Like her tears, her laugh too was perfect.

When she handed his handkerchief back, he noticed that she was careful not to actually touch his fingers. He wondered what that meant and despaired at ever understanding women, even a little.

Chapter 2

PARIS

On his next day off from his waiter job at the Cafe Voila, Shai bicycled to his bank. He retrieved an envelope from his safe deposit box and tucked it safely inside his jacket. Next, he peddled to the train depot, padlocked his bike against thieves, and bought his ticket to Paris. The trip from Reims to Paris was less than an hour, hardly enough time for him to fret about his mission. At the station, he caught a cab. Twenty-five minutes later he walked into the building housing the office of the archbishop.

Shai cleared electronic security, the familiar scanning array known to all who traveled by air. A prim, middle-aged woman stopped him at the security desk.

"How may I help you, Monsieur?" The receptionist's harried expression belied her greeting.

"I would like to see Archbishop Clement."

She swiveled slightly to her right in her chair and placed her lit cigarette in the ashtray. Now, she gave the young man her full attention.

"Is the archbishop expecting you?"

"No."

"Monsieur, Archbishop Clement is available only by appointment.

Perhaps it is a matter that I can help you with? What is the nature of your business?" She asked with brisk efficiency.

"I don't think you can help me, but why I am here concerns the suicide of Father Gauthier. He was my friend and I was with him on the day he died."

"I see. What is your name, Monsieur?"

"I am Shai Tanger."

That name registered with her. She dialed her desk extension. She spoke a few words, listened to a few more, and hung up.

"The archbishop is not available, but the vicar general, Antoine de Gaulle will see you momentarily in his place. Please have a seat."

The narrowly built, swarthy, complexioned Moroccan sat down in a waiting chair and began to read through a month-old Vatican newspaper when the elevator doors parted. A tall, a youthful, vigorous man strode rapidly into the reception area. The man had black trousers and a black priestly shirt with a white clerical collar. He came close to where Shai sat.

Shai stood as the man approached

"Monsieur, I am Antoine de Gaulle, the vicar general, and assistant to the archbishop. Would you follow me please?" On the elevator, they remained silent and avoided eye contact. Shai barely stood five feet five inches tall. The big, robust seeming vicar-general dwarfed him. The doors opened into a private office on the ninth floor.

"Come in and sit, Monsieur Tanger. I understand you were a friend of Father Gauthier."

"Oui. I was his favorite waiter at Cafe Voila. On his final day, I served him breakfast and then watched him leave in a car with Archbishop Clement. I don't believe Father Gauthier was in a state of depression. He was always upbeat and friendly at the cafe." Shai began in a straight-ahead fashion.

"Antidepressant medication can be a wonderful cure for depression, but sometimes the relief is only temporary." de Gaulle replied.

"I don't understand why he didn't tell me he intended to leave France for South America on that very same day. He would have mentioned it to me. After all, Father de Gaulle, I had been serving him for years. I have confided in him. We were that close. We were friends for a long time, speaking of many things and speaking nearly every day. Father de Gaulle, I cannot believe he would leave Reims and not tell me, his friend."

Antoine de Gaulle waited for several seconds before he replied to this sally. Then, with calm politeness, he continued. "I am sorry, Monsieur Tanger. I have no explanation as to why he didn't tell you."

"Your two archbishops could have let him finish his breakfast," Tanger spat out, anger clear in his voice.

"I understand you are still upset, Monsieur, but arrangements were made to pick up Father Gauthier at Cafe Voila."

"Apparently Father Gauthier was unaware of those arrangements. He was waiting for a taxi to pick him up at the cafe."

"An easy explanation, Shai, may I call you Shai?" The waiter nodded his assent. He had no need to be rude. It was the two Archbishops that held his anger, not this church flunky.

"One of our employees mistakenly told the monsignor to take a taxi to the airport, but Archbishops Clement and Lajalo decided to honor his wonderful service to his church and the community and personally escort him to the airport. I believed that the archbishop called the monsignor a few minutes before his arrival."

"He did call," Shai affirmed. "Father Gauthier instructed me to offer apologies and payment to the cab driver. He left with his laptop and placed his bicycle in the trunk of the archbishop's limo before he departed. That was the last time I saw him. I was in shock when I saw the replay of his death on the television."

"We all felt that same shock and all of us were very saddened," Antoine continued with a calm, deliberate tone. Shai listened carefully, more carefully than it seemed. At the mention of the laptop, the priest flinched away, just a little. Shai concluded that this churchman was a dangerous man, but he suspected that all along.

Shai resumed speaking, now watching his opponent for any sign, any hint. "Father Gauthier insisted I keep his windbreaker, the one he left folded on the seat of his chair. He said he didn't need it anymore. As it turned out, he didn't need anything anymore, nothing at all." Shai now nearly choked on his words.

"How fortunate for you," Antoine responded with kindness. "Father Gauthier gave away many of his personal items in preparation for his new assignment in South America. The jacket will make a reminder for you of your friend and the friendship you shared."

"Monsieur de Gaulle, can you imagine my confusion when the taxi driver arrived and told me that Father Gauthier's wish was to be driven to Paris, to the Israeli embassy?"

"I am certain that the cab driver was mistaken, he must have been mistaken, don't you think?" The Vicar-general asked, his face a bland mask.

"Perhaps so, perhaps not, Antoine, you don't mind if I call you Antoine do you?" Shai asked, turning the tables on the priest. "That windbreaker hung in my closet for a few days until I took it off the hanger to send it to the cleaners. His jacket would become my family heirloom, cleaned but never worn again. I emptied out the pockets and discovered an envelope in the inside pocket, an envelope placed there by Father Gauthier and left behind for me to find." He looked directly, boldly at the Vicar-general without a trace of either deference or fear.

"And what did you find?" Antoine asked, prepared for the worst possible news.

Now Shai had the advantage. "In the envelope, I found a computer printout. The printout held the emails between the astronaut Andre Dubois and his mentor, his protector, Father Gauthier. I know about Andre's kidnapping, the disappearance of Father Gauthier's computer, and the emails." The slight little waiter now had a voice of iron. He removed an envelope from an inside pocket in his jacket and handed it to the Vicar-general.

Antoine took his time and examined each page with care. He gave particular attention to the sequence of the dates and times attached to each entry.

"Who have you shown this to?" Antoine asked, his voice no longer as firm and decisive as it had been.

"The Israelis have a copy, and I have a few also."

"You are a Moroccan Jew, no?"

"Oui, that is true. Maybe the Israeli government has a reason for not publicizing Andre's e-mails, but I am willing to do so and prove Andre's case against your church and your archbishops. Because of Andre's untimely disappearance, this will be very bad for your church, no?" Shai said with a sharp tone to his words.

"Are you an Israeli spy? I am aware that Mossad is very clever and wants to discredit the Holy See in order to stop the beatification and eventual sainthood for Pius XII," Antoine replied with deliberate sharpness, implying that the waiter had motives beyond friendship for his words and actions, and false motives.

Shai had prepared for this conversation. He spoke rapidly, not bothering to disguise his loathing. "Pius XII was not even a priest, even I know that. Eugenio Pacelli held the office of Vatican Secretary of State before becoming Pius XII. He was in fact only a lawyer who attained the Papacy and then granted formal recognition to Hitler's Nazi party in 1933. You know this. And you know that he recognized the Nazis so as to destroy the German Catholic political opposition to Hitler and to centralize the authority of the Pope. In exchange, Hitler got a green light from the Vatican to go after the Jews, which as we all know, he began to do immediately. Father Antoine, don't you think it is about time your church excommunicated the Fuhrer?"

Antoine recoiled. "You have a sharp tongue, Monsieur Tanger. I am a busy man. Now, tell me exactly, what do you want?"

Now Shai waited before he spoke again. Now he had the Vicar-general where he wanted him. He let Antoine stew for a few more seconds, then he spoke with clear, strong and precisely modulated words, words that permitted no mistake in his meaning.

"What I want for my silence is simple. I want a million euros wired to my bank." Shai stared at the priest and placed a deposit slip on the Vicar-general's desk and slid it across. "You have four days to wire the money."

De Gaulle gave Shai a hard look, a look that did not seem right on the face of a priest, not at all. With quiet malice he said "Monsieur Tanger, you must be aware that France is a very dangerous place for Jews these days. Not a day goes by when there isn't some kind of attack on a synagogue, or a Jewish school or center, even the statue of Alfred Dreyfus is continually defaced."

"Enough of your merde, priest. Your kind blessed the torture and expulsion of my ancestors from Spain during the Inquisition. You stood by and watched as Hitler murdered millions. Know this-if anything happens to me or to anyone in my family, I have made arrangements that these emails will be delivered to the media, and not just to any media. I know which reporters would gleefully spread any news that harms the church. Then, Monsieur de Gaulle, you will have a mess to deal with that is more important to you than just money, much more important." The little Moroccan Jew had a spine of iron.

De Gaulle paled. "What assurances will we have that you won't resort to additional blackmail or approach the media with your, ah, fables, Monsieur Tanger?"

"You have my word." Tanger replied with simple directness. He showed no sign of weakness to the Vicar-general.

Now de Gaulle dropped the mask of civility and gentle humility entirely. "Monsieur Tanger, your ancestors from Spain discovered the Church can be a powerful adversary. Even if a worse case arises this episode will eventually be forgotten. The Church never dies, because the Church is truth. But you, Monsieur Tanger will not be forgotten. Remember, we have tentacles that reach around the globe."

"You have four days, Monsignor," Shai stood his ground.

"Monsieur Tanger, give me a phone number. I offer you no guarantees, but I urge you to think about the consequences of your actions on you, on your family, and on the entire community of Jews here in France. Think long and hard, Monsieur."

"My cell number is written on the envelope. Good day, Monsieur de Gaulle."

Tanger had vacated the room for perhaps fifteen seconds before the vicar-general connected to his superior, the archbishop.

French police senior inspector Jean Gallant checked his caller ID and answered.

"Bonjour Henri, tell me something I don't know." Gallant smiled as he spoke.

"Inspector, in two hours Andre's fiancee is expected to arrive at Charles De Gaulle on El Al flight 232 from Tel Aviv. Did you know that?"

"Henri, give me credit. I am an inspector of police. I have reliable sources, too, you know. Thanks Henri, but I have to go. I am on the way to the Basilica Sacre Coeur in Montmartre."

The newsman hung up wondering what else the policeman knew that he didn't know, at least not yet.

Gallant did indeed have a' reliable source,' eye witness, a long time friend of Andre Dubois named Louis Major. Major had been with Andre at the moment of his kidnapping. Andre finished his interview with Le Monde while his friend Louis waited in the car, playing games on his smartphone. Louis reported to Inspector Gallant that Andre exited the newspaper building, began to cross the street to return to Louis's car when a dark blue Renault pulled up next to Andre in the middle of the street. One of the men in the Renault aimed a pistol at Andre and forced him into the back seat. Then the blue car sped away, taking his friend. Totally alert now, Louis counted four kidnappers in the blue car. He also managed to snap a photo of the license plate with the phone he held in his hand.

The Renault driven by the kidnappers was registered to, of all people, a priest. Monsignor Antonio Scarpone owned the car. Scarpone served at the Basilica of the Sacred Heart, the Sacre Coeur in Montmartre.

Louis also alerted Michelle in Israel about Andre's kidnapping, and arranged to meet her at the airport upon her arrival. He naturally had concerns about her safety after the abduction of her fiance. He convinced Inspector Gallant to keep her under surveillance for her own safety.

Louis was not only an excellent 'reliable source' but a good friend to both Andre and Michelle.

Chapter 3

PARIS

From somewhere unseen a nun appeared, quickly, silently crossing the nave with that odd, floating sort of gait that some nuns had. She seemed to be on wheels rather than feet like the rest of us. She looked at the pair of policemen with a disapproving appraisal.

"Welcome to the Basilica Sacre Coeur. I am Sister Amorette. Did you come to pray?"

"No, sister, I am afraid not. Allow me to introduce myself. I am Inspector Gallant and this man with me is my colleague, Detective Blanc. We have come on police business. May we have a word with Father Scarpone?"

"I am sorry, inspector, but Father Scarpone is out of the country. He is not in France at the moment."

"Out of the country," the inspector affirmed.

"Oui, he has been gone a week to the day to visit his family in Italy, in Tuscany."

Inspector Gallant had a severe expression on his face, a no-nonsense police business expression that overcame the Nun's expression of disapproval. "Sister Amorette, it is very important that we can verify his itinerary," Gallant said.

"I will find his travel log and show it to you, Inspector Gallant. Monsignor Scarpone is not in any trouble I hope?"

"Does he own a dark blue Renault?"

"Oui, he is lucky to have a car, a gift from his extended family in Italy. They gathered the funds to buy the car from aunts and cousins out to the second and third degree. Italians, even now, have close families, no?"

"And Sister Amorette, does he live in the rectory?"

"Oui. Why do you ask all these questions?"

"If Father Scarpone did not drive his car recently, he is in no trouble at all. But somebody drove his car late in the afternoon. Felons used the blue Renault in a crime." Blanc interjected, his rough voice and hard words shocked the nun.

"I think this is a misunderstanding. You see, detectives, Father Martel received permission to drive Father Scarpone's car while he was on vacation," Sister Amorette replied with a sigh of relief.

"Sister, would you be so kind as to take us to Father Martel?" Gallant requested.

'Certainly, please follow me. The rectory is across the yard."

They walked through a courtyard, passing by a three-hundred-year-old marble statue of the Holy Mother and a fountain that danced merrily with tinkling water. The petite nun repeated her nun on wheels trick, seeming to float across the courtyard. Sister seemed delicate and middle-aged but her skin was smooth, wrinkle-free, flawless as the face of a younger woman. A wisp of hair stuck out from under her habit, showing a trace of gray. When they came to a closed-door she stopped and knocked.

"Father Martel?"

"Sister Amorette?" A voice from inside replied.

"I have two gentlemen here, an Inspector Gallant and Detective Blanc with me. They would like a moment of your time."

"Invite them in, sister."

Father Martel opened the door to a small room, suitable to the diminutive stature of the priest. The room was furnished simply with a cot, a desk, and a wardrobe. The priest wore a T-shirt over long, black slacks that reached the arch of his feet, clad only in socks. "Excuse the messy desk. Come in, please. Thank you Sister Amorette, you may return to your duties."

He ushered the two policemen into this room. The three of them filled the space to capacity and perhaps beyond. With only a single chair, the trio stood.

"Detective, did you find the car?" Martel asked.

"Is it a dark blue 2005 Renault?" Detective Blanc verified.

"Yes. I was going to call today and report that the car had been stolen. It is registered to Father Scarpone but I have been driving it the last few days."

"When was the car stolen, Father Martel?" Blanc asked.

"Two nights ago. When I looked for it, it was not where I parked it." Martel said.

"Why didn't you report it stolen sooner?"

Martel shrugged in the Gallic, nonchalant way. "I hoped the car would show up. It belongs to Father Scarpone and I wanted to avoid an embarrassing situation, as you might imagine." He gave a small, rueful smile.

"An embarrassing situation?" Blanc inquired.

"You see, I was dining at Cafe Rousseau at 24 Rue Grenata and met someone. Has there been an accident? Was anyone injured?"

"Father Martel, the car was used in the kidnapping of the Astronaut, Andre Dubois. The whereabouts of the blue Renault is unknown".

"Oh my God," Father Martel covered his face with his hand and sat heavily on his bed, the picture of despair.

"Who did you meet?" The inspector asked.

"The person I met there called himself Philippe. I don't have a last name." He cast his eyes up to the policeman, shame clear in his face. "Inspector, I don't even know if Philippe is his real name but it is the name he used."

"Was the nature of your meeting official business or private pleasure?"

Father Martel looked with tragic eyes, seeking some measure of understanding or forgiveness. "It was not official business," Martel replied quietly.

The inspector correctly suspected that the priest was involved in a homo-sexual, one-night stand.

"How did you and Philippe make contact? Did you know him prior to that evening, Father Martel?" The inspector wanted to know.

"He came into the cafe right behind me, inspector. Now that I think about it, he might have followed me. Of course, I didn't think about that at the time. I had just sat down at my table alone. He came right up and asked if he might join me, as we both seemed to be dining alone. I said yes. You must think I'm terribly naive, inspector."

Gallant did not respond to that but continued his questioning. "Can you describe your dinner guest, this Philippe?"

"Philippe was younger than me, younger by at least two decades, and nice enough looking. His eyes seemed to me to have a depth of understanding and kindness. A young, nice-looking man and me, that should have been a warning to me, inspector, wouldn't you think?"

"Father Martel, did this Philippe steal the Renault?"

"He must-have. Inspector, may I go off the record?"

Gallant nodded his agreement. "Until I object, father, you are off the record."

The priest continued resolutely but in a quiet voice. "Philippe and I took a room at the Hotel Vallee in the red light district. He must have put something in my drink. I don't remember anything after dinner. When I awoke hours later, the keys and the car were gone."

"I see." The inspector replied. "Father Martel, we will need you to give a detailed description of Philippe to our sketch artist back at the precinct. Your cooperation may be just what we need to solve the case and return the astronaut to freedom. Do you understand how important your testimony is, Father Martel?"

"Inspector Gallant, I have a picture of him on my cell phone." The dwarfish priest displayed Philippe's picture.

"I think this will be good enough, father," Gallant judged.

"I don't think he ever knew I took his picture," Martel said.

Using the cell phone's email function, the inspector forwarded the video to his computer's document file.

"Once we corroborate your story, we can begin to clear you of suspicion, but you'll need to surrender your passport and remain in Paris for the time being. Is that clear?"

The small priest looked both guilty and stricken. "Please don't reveal my true identity inspector. I don't want the church to suffer for my sins."

"As long as you remain innocent, we will do our best to shield your identity," Inspector Gallant qualified. He could see no good reason to doubt the priest and no good reason to allow Martel's identity to escape into public view and humiliate him.

Chapter 4

PARIS

The flight from Tel Aviv screeched to a landing, bringing Michelle and Shimon safely to rest in Paris. The pair came off before the bulk of the passengers, a perquisite of their status as first class passengers. While the herd of ordinary travelers still crammed the aisles, stretching and fetching their carry-on bags, Shimon and Michelle had already left the aircraft. With no checked luggage, the two avoided the baggage area entirely. Michelle spotted a waiting Louis Major about the same time that he spotted her.

Behind Louis a less welcome Henri Bettencourt and his photographer lurked in the crowd.

Michelle introduced the two men.

"How did they know when I would arrive in Paris, Louis?" Michelle asked while kissing him on both sides of his face.

"I am sorry, Michelle. I asked the police to provide a protective escort for you, under the circumstances. That Inspector Gallant must have leaked your arrival time to the press, the bastard."

"I know him, this inspector." Shimon told the others. "He came to Israel to interview Andre a couple of years ago. He has a forceful personality, no?"

With only their hand luggage to impede them, they fairly quickly made their way through the airport crowds to where Louis had his car parked. Shimon climbed into the back seat of the little two door auto. Michelle sat in front as they crossed the Paris traffic to deposit Shimon at the Israeli Embassy. Upon arrival, Shimon retrieved his travel bag, little more than the sort of thing a man might carry his gym clothes in.

As Michelle had to get out of the car to let Shimon unload, the two stood on the sidewalk facing each other, suddenly awkward.

"Thank you for the lift, Louis." Shimon called as he ducked down to have eye contact with the other man. "And Michelle, you will hear from me in the morning. Good bye for now."

She nodded and offered her hand for him to shake. "Thank you for coming with me, Shimon. I feel better knowing you are around to keep me safe."

He didn't know how to respond to that. He just nodded, turned and entered the embassy grounds.

Louis could sense something between Michelle and Shimon. Affection perhaps? He hoped so. Michelle was a good and close friend to Louis, a good person who had not been lucky in love. One fiance, Andre Dubois, had drifted away from her and she from him. She broke off the engagement after meeting someone else, an Israeli archaeologist, had later been murdered by a sniper as he worked a dig. She deserved happiness.

As they left the embassy, Louis caught sight of Henri Bettencourt driving a large sedan a few cars behind them. The reporter obviously thought that Michelle had some part to add to the story of the kidnapped astronaut.

A further few cars back and unnoticed by either Louis or Bettencourt officer Charles Beauline followed in an older, nondescript van. He continued to track their progress until Louis dropped Michelle safe and sound at her mother's apartment. Then he parked where he could watch the entrance to the building and settled in for a long wait until his relief showed up at midnight. Inspector Gallant might well be a bastard, as Louis said, but in this case he kept his word to watch over Michelle.

But neither Louis nor Michelle knew this nor could they credit the inspector's good intentions.

The following morning Michelle and her mother Lucille slept in to give

Michelle the best possible chance for a good rest. When she arose, Michelle wrapped a robe around herself and went into the kitchen where she put the morning's coffee beans on to roast. She could hear the comforting sounds of her mother getting ready to shower in the bathroom. While the coffee beans roasted, she went back into the bedroom to dress. She slid into a pair of jeans and wiggled into a black top with a sparkly depiction of the Sphinx on it. Fashion and archaeology met in a way that made her look great. She looked at herself, gave a tug or two to the shirt and brushed her hair one more time. Ready, she headed back into the kitchen. The noise told her that mamam had moved into the shower.

She took the now nicely browned coffee beans and slid them from the roasting pan into the grinder. Seconds of whirling blades had them at the right size. She then dumped the fresh grounds into a French press and put a kettle on to boil.

Looking at her work, she issued a congratulatory nod to herself, happy to be home, doing familiar things.

She stuck her head into the bathroom and shouted over the sound of running water.

"Maman, I am going down to get a newspaper and a pastry. Do you want anything?"

"Cigarettes, the American kind in the red box, since you are buying."

"Maman, I thought you quit?"

"I did. Now close the door, Michelle. You are letting the cold air in."

Michelle smiled as she shook her head and closed the door. "The coffee is ready to go when you are. I'll be right back."

She locked the apartment door behind her and gracefully descended the two flights of stairs. She exited the building and turned sharply to the left to the corner grocery. A rested and refreshed Officer Charles Beauline had just gotten settled in for a day of observation. He enjoyed the view of the stylishly clad, oh so attractive young woman as she walked the short way to the corner store. He thought she moved like a dream, or perhaps a model on the catwalk.

Moments later Michelle sprinted from the store, a paper in one hand, a bag with a couple of pastries and a red box of cigarettes in her other hand. Charles wondered what was up.

Vicar-general Antoine de Gaulle dreaded the inevitable phone call from his superior, the archbishop. Sure enough, the phone on his desk issued a demanding sound, pick up, pick up, it seemed to say.

"Bonjour, de Gaulle, here."

"Antoine, did you read the front page of Le Monde this morning?" The familiar and noticeably irritated voice of his superior asked with none of the usual polite back and forth.

"Oui, I did, your Excellency."

"Well, what are you doing to contain the situation?"

"I am trying to contain it, your Excellency."

"The car involved in the Dubois kidnapping is registered to Father Scarpone, but he was in Italy at the time of the incident. You must tell the press and demand a printed retraction. Will you see to that, Antoine?"

"It is not quite as simple as that, your Excellency. It is about Father Martel. He had the keys to the car. Father Martel had been driving it."

"You do not suggest that Father Martel was a part of this mess?" The Archbishop snapped in outrage. "I know him personally. He is a wonderful and caring priest."

"The car was stolen from Father Martel the night before the kidnapping."

"Why didn't he report the theft?" The archbishop sputtered.

"Father Martel was embarrassed, your Excellency," Antoine grimaced into the phone. "He was duped at the Cafe Rousseau and drugged at the Hotel Valle."

"Father Martel did not even know the car was gone until the following morning."

"Ah," the Archbishop grunted. "Father Martel, in the red light district? Please spare me the details, Antoine."

"Gladly, Excellency. We did manage to keep the sordid details out of the papers, at least for now." The vicar-general replied.

"Thank God for that." The archbishop said with relief.

"The police are investigating, and eventually, Father Martel will be fully cleared," Antoine surmised.

"Many Parisians already believe that we organized the kidnapping to silence Dubois. The press will have a field day with this one. Imagine the glee the reporters will have, a high profile kidnapping linked to the Catholic

Church. The Godless atheists in the press will be beside themselves. This will cause a firestorm that will not go away in a hurry, Antoine."

"Eventually this will pass. But we have an immediately pressing problem to deal with. What shall we do with our Moroccan blackmailer?"

"Our less than resplendent Jew, Monsieur Tanger? Rome has approved a wire transfer from a Swiss account," the archbishop informed.

"And if he should make additional demands?"

"Make certain he doesn't, Antoine." The archbishop killed the connection with a bang. Antoine swiveled in his chair as he reread the headline in La Monde, hoping to discover a 'silver lining' in a very dark cloud that hovered overhead.

Beneath the headline was a related story that included a photograph of Michelle Dumas, the former fiancee of Andre Dubois. The photo showed the attractive young woman at the airport in the company of two men. An additional photo showed one of the men just entering the Israeli embassy in Paris. Antoine had an idea. He dialed for Amelia, his assistant.

"Oui,"

"Amelia, can you place a call to Henri Bettencourt at Le Monde for me?"

In a moment she connected to Antoine again.

"Monsieur Bettencourt doesn't answer. Shall I leave a message to call you back, sir?"

"Yes, Amelia, please do just that."

"So Jean, you think the Roman Church was framed?" Reporter Henri Bettencourt jabbed at his breakfast partner. He allowed himself a bit of a smile as he said the word 'framed,' thinking of how quaint and archaic it sounded in the current age. Across from him sat his sometimes friend, sometimes foe, but always interesting and lively Inspector Jean Gallant of the Paris Metro Police.

"I think so, Henri. This is off the record? I can give you background but everything I have for you this morning is just speculation." Gallant took a sip of his coffee and waited for a reply.

"Jean, you are one of my most important sources of information and information is my stock in trade. Without you and those like you, I have nothing to tell my readers. If you want to play the sly fox with me, it is all right. I hope that you will let me know, promptly-before the other jackals of the free press get a whiff of the news- what you can when you can."

"Our investigators have confirmed the priest's account. It must have taken some courage on his part to admit such a tawdry affair. We found witnesses that place the priest and this Philippe at the Cafe Rousseau and at the Hotel Valle. It feels like a setup to me, the handsome stranger, the drugged priest, the stolen car. We think that the key to finding Andre Dubois is to find this mysterious Philippe."

"So Father Martel went out for a night on the town to have, if you forgive my pun, a gay old time." Bettencourt enjoyed his own use of language. Gallant just found it irritating.

"It is the twenty-first century for goodness sake, Henri. Grow up. Martel can choose to be as gay as he wants with a consenting adult." Gallant very nearly harrumphed in disapproval. As a policeman, he saw the worst of the human condition on a daily basis. A priest caught out in a sexual sin with another adult did not come up to the top one hundred tragedies that he had seen even in the current month.

Bettencourt slathered his croissant with orange marmalade. "Are you prepared to say that the priest is not a suspect? Can I at least say that?"

"He never was officially a suspect, only a person of interest. As you know, a person of interest can mean whatever we need it to mean. But no, he is not a suspect. He is certainly a victim in this case. I don't think your readers need to know the details, Henri. Something like this will cause Martel unlimited problems if it comes to light, no? But we still have a lot to discover, which we will. Kidnapping an astronaut, a national hero, focuses the attention of the state. I have resources that I have never before in my life had to work with."

"Of course, I understand. I can assure you that this Philippe person's photo will headline tomorrow's edition if that is his real name-which I doubt. We will publish your police hot-line phone number as well. The press stands ready to help the French nation in this sad hour." He said this last with a perfectly straight face. Both men knew that the journalist and the policeman had long ago had their devotion to the government of France pushed aside by their intimate and cynical knowledge of how the government actually operated. That did not dilute in either man their devotion to the ideal of France, her people, and her culture.

Bettencourt felt the buzz of his phone in his pocket.

"Excuse me, Jean. I have to take this call." Henri left the table and lit a cigarette as he walked outside. He saw the missed call on his phone. He hit the button to return the call to Vicar-general Antoine de Gaulle.

"De Gaulle here," Antoine's voice answered.

"Father de Gaulle, Henri Bettencourt from Le Monde returning your call."

"So glad you called Henri. Do you remember when we met? It was two years ago at the archbishop's birthday celebration."

"Oui, of course, I remember."

"A lovely party it was, his excellency, the archbishop, warmly recalls it. It seemed like all the dignitaries in Paris were there. Members of the press like you attended, the chief of police, Christians, Jewish leaders, artists, scientists, and Muslim Imams. I could continue to reminisce, but I have important business to discuss with you, Henri. To begin, Archbishop Clement would like Le Monde to post a one hundred thousand euro reward from his office for information leading to solving the Dubois kidnapping."

"I will print it, Father de Gaulle." He jotted down a quick note, 'Church reward to solve astronaut's kidnapping.' That alone should be good for forty centimeters of print."

"Merci, Henri. I am most appreciative. I happened to see in Le Monde some photographs of Andre Dubois' fiancee and two male companions. One of the men with her is an Israeli. Do you know him?"

"I do not know him personally but I know of him. His name is Shimon Levi. He is an investigator with the Israeli government but of which agency I do not know. That is what I have been led to believe."

"An investigator, how interesting. A policeman, do you think? I wonder why he is in France just now and why he seems to have arrived with Andre Dubois' fiancee?"

Bettencourt thought and spoke rapidly. Things, thoughts at least, were moving. "We know that Dubois spent some time in Israel. As to Levi working as a policeman, now that you mention it, I think not. I would bet he is an agent of their intelligence services. Could he have met Dubois at the time of the capsule falling into the sea? That would make sense. He might have known Dubois, he might have been sent here by his government to help recover the kidnap victim."

"How can you be so certain that Dubois' disappearance was a kidnapping, Henri?"

That startled the newsman. "Monsieur, the Paris police believe it's a kidnapping."

Antoine de Gaulle, vicar-general to the archbishop of Paris, tapped his big forefinger on his desk, thump, thump, thump. The noise was audible even over the phone. Then he said with conviction "Monsieur Bettencourt, I think Andre Dubois staged his own kidnapping in order to discredit the Catholic Church. He has no evidence and his allegations are all over the place, especially his accusations of a Vatican conspiracy to depopulate Israel of its Jews. Henri, as you attested in your interview, his account reads like a Le Carre novel to you, but more like a Dan Brown novel to me. Henri, do you honestly think we would use a vehicle registered to a priest in broad daylight had we wanted to kidnap Monsieur Dubois? I think not. Maybe there is an Israeli connection to his disappearance?"

"Father de Gaulle, with all due respect, you have two suppositions, which like chewing gum you are throwing against the wall, hoping that at least one of them sticks. The first of your suppositions is that Andre Dubois staged his own kidnapping, but there is no proof, and your other superstition is that the Israelis are involved. Again, without proof your superstitions are meaningless."

"Could it be so unfathomable to you that Dubois is an Israeli pawn? He wants to embarrass the Church and so do the Jews."

"Which is it, Monsieur, Jews or Israelis?" Bettencourt bit back, a bit of anger getting loose into his voice. The conversation had reached an absurd place for him.

"Is there any difference between them, Henri? Don't you know that the Jews want to stop Pius' beatification? And while Dubois remains a kidnap victim, the French prelates will have their honor and reputations stained. Conspiracy charges will take on a life of their own and will penetrate to the bowels of the Vatican. I am simply bearing upon you to keep an open mind, and that is all."

"I just will not go down that road. I do not wish to be part and parcel of another witch hunt, another twenty-first century Dreyfus Affair."

"The dishonor from the Dreyfus exoneration and pardon enabled the imposition of crippling sanctification upon our Church," Antoine spat.

"You refer to the separation of church and state and the Third Republic's revocation of the privileged status of the Catholic Church within French society, right?"

"Of course I am." Antoine replied.

"In my opinion Monsieur de Gaulle, and in the opinion of the vast majority of French citizens both then and now, the punishment of the Church for leading the charge against Dreyfus simply because he happened to be a Jew was and is entirely justified. Even after the Dreyfus exoneration, your Church, your Vatican newspaper, in fact, insisted he was still guilty and accused the free press of selling its 'conscience' to the Jews. Atonement came in the form of a revocation of the Church's privilege in French society, which I for one, Monsieur, do not regret."

Bettencourt had about all he could take and still retain some gloss of politeness.

De Gaulle continued in a more conciliatory tone. "The Dreyfus trials happened over a century ago, Henri. The world has changed since then, as has France, as has the Church."

"Not so much that I can see, especially from your insular, clustered and hidden world."

"Ah, another conversation for another time, Henri. Perhaps we will have another opportunity to speak again on the history of the twentieth century. I must say au revoir for now." With that, the churchman broke the connection.

Fuming, Henri took a final drag on his cigarette and crushed the cigarette butt on the cement of the sidewalk. He returned to the cafe. He saw Inspector Gallant complacently buttering a croissant. Gallant looked up at Bettencourt expectantly.

"I got a call from the vicar-general." Henri revealed.

"Vicar-general Antoine de Gaulle, what is he doing getting his oar in these turbulent waters? I would think he and the other prelates would rather have a low profile just now."

"Among some foolish bombast, he wanted to know the name of the Israeli agent who came back from Israel with Michelle."

"Antoine could have called me. His name is Shimon Levi. He is a cool customer and a tough one. He totally stonewalled me in Haifa last year when I went there as part of my investigation into Father Gauthier's suicide. He denied me access to Dubois's laptop at the time. The fucking Israelis are sitting on information that I need to solve that case. I have a reputation as a man who solves cases, Henri. They make me look bad by withholding information from me." Gallant said grumpily. He reached for a dish of plum preserves, until then untouched. He needed a little sweet comfort and his waistline be damned.

"So why do you think this agent, Monsieur Levi, has come to Paris? And why did he specifically come with Dubois' fiancee? Obviously, you didn't invite him, inspector."

"Of course I didn't invite him. If our paths should cross, I plan to give him the same treatment he dished out to me in Haifa. I honestly don't know why he came to Paris. Maybe his government sent him or maybe she asked him. He might even be her lover. She is fantastic looking, any man would be attracted to her." He wiped a bit of plum preserve from the corner of his mouth. "I am damn sure going to keep my eye on him."

Chapter 5

RIVE GAUCHE, LEFT BANK

They hadn't removed his wristwatch. That made things worse. He could track the time. It seemed to him that an eternity had passed, ticking off slowly, slowly, maddeningly slowly. Andre had been alone and imprisoned for two endless days. He had not eaten. His leg had a chain connected to an ankle bracelet on one end with the other snapped to an iron bedstead. His captors had said not a word to him in two days but had removed his blindfold and duct tape, along with his shoes and socks.

Prostate, famished, groggy, and terrified, he spent his hours on a soiled mattress covered by a cheap ruin of a blanket. He could reach the toilet, thankful that his captors had provided a roll of toilet paper, the scum, the bastards. He could barely drag himself back and forth to the toilet or to the sink where he could splash water on his face or drink, filling his belly against hunger.

The large, empty warehouse existed in a sort of dim twilight, the windows stained against the sunlight. A few occasional streaks of sunlight slipped through a filthy skylight at the far side of the warehouse, near the exit door.

The abdication happened so fast Andre was still confused about it. With a gun on him making him frightened and making him shut the hell up, his captors stuffed him between two rough men in the back seat. They handcuffed him, blindfolded him, and wrapped duct tape across his mouth. He couldn't see and could barely breathe.

The last thing he remembered was the smell of ether and the rag held against his face until he knew no more. He could tell that night had fallen. The ominous silence of the warehouse broke with the footfalls of two men. He caught the silhouettes of two men heading straight for him, and he still had a chain on his leg. The men wore the robes of Franciscan friars. One monk carried a satchel. The other carried a pistol, open in his hand for all to see. And fear.

Would they execute him on the spot?

"Remove your shirt and put on this cotton pullover." The gunman ordered brusquely. He held the gun on Andre. He stood outside of Andre's reach, so this was a professional thug and not likely to be some random monk conscripted for special duty by the church. Every bit of information that came to Andre's trained eyes, senses, and brain, he stored for sifting and evaluation.

Andre sat back on his bunk and removed his shirt, now rank after days of continuous wear. He seemed small and pathetic to the gunman as he slipped the shirt over his head, over his thinning blond hair, over the gray creeping onto his temples.

A two-day growth of stubble made him look shabby without making his soft features seem tough. At five foot eight, he did not seem formidable. Now, chained, dirty, and scared, he seemed even less so. He certainly felt as helpless as he looked.

But Andre paid attention to every detail that came into his ken. He noticed that the gunman, the supposed monk, held a Russian Makarov pistol, a common enough gun but one used in France mostly by criminals from the Balkans.

"Good, now lie down on your stomach." When he complied with this indignity, the second man unlocked his ankle chain.

"You can get up now and put on fresh underpants and this pair of sweatpants."

Andre did as bid, happier to have something clean against his skin than he was ashamed to be naked before these kidnappers. They hooked him up again to the iron bedstead, leaving him with clean clothing but still dirty and no better off than before. He had not been shot. Maybe he would not be shot.

"Who are you?" he asked, almost in a whisper.

"Your saviors," replied the man with the satchel. He slowly emptied out onto the mattress a bar of soap, paper towels, and toilette paper. He revealed a baguette with sliced Beaufort cheese, a chocolate bar, a Bible, and a pen-sized flashlight.

Andre tried to gauge the accent the man had, without success.

"We have provided you with nourishment for your body and your soul. Bonsoir."

"I have questions," Andre begged.

The man chuckled. "I am sure you do. Your questions can wait."

The two men left and Andre turned his reading light to the bible. Embossed on its inside cover he fingered the letters SSPX which stood for the Society of Saint Pius X. Once considered too radical and anti-Semitic, the bishops of SSPX had been treated as persona non grata by the official Church. Many of their bishops had been excommunicated half a century ago. But during their banishment by the Vatican, mysteriously, their theological writings still found their way into the basilicas and abbeys of the Catholic Church.

This very year the Pope lifted the excommunications and welcomed the Society back into the fold, even though the bishops of the Society remained bitterly opposed to Vatican II. One bishop in particularly, Levesque even went on record as a Holocaust denier. Andre was no stranger to SSPX. As a young boy and orphan of the church, he had been influenced by some of the writings of its founder, the late Archbishop Lefebvre.

Andre put all the facts in a row after the 'monks' departed. Why would Catholics give him a bible marked with the letters SSPX? Not likely. Would a monk have a pistol usually, in France at least, found in the hands of Slavic criminals? Not likely. Would Catholic kidnappers wear clerical clothing, giving themselves away? Not likely.

Even if he could not name the accent of the false monks, he found it off somehow. It was as if the speaker had lived in Paris for a long time, years or decades, but had started somewhere else.

Chapter 6

PARIS

"Ari, you need to return to Israel now. You may not be safe," Shimon pleaded and ignored an incoming call.

"I'll be fine," Ari demurred. "I've been in the States for two weeks, and nothing has happened. There are only two more signings, one today in Newport and one tomorrow in San Diego."

"And you will return after San Diego?" Shimon queried.

"Yes, yes. Tomorrow night I will drive up to Los Angeles, go to LAX and catch the midnight El Al flight to Tel Aviv. There. Are you satisfied now, mother?"

"Don't be cute. You call me when you get to LAX. We can't be certain that Andre's kidnapping isn't part of something bigger. Alexander and Yuri have already returned to Israel. Sanjay is hiding in India, but safe enough for now. We have serious people to deal with, Ari, people who have serious stakes in play. We know they have tried to kill you and the other astronauts before. Now Andre has been taken at gunpoint in broad daylight. Do not let your guard down, please." Shimon pleaded, his voice without a trace of levity.

"I will call you when I get to the airport tomorrow night. I hope someone finds Andre soon, safe and unhurt. The longer he stays gone, the

46

worse his situation gets. Do you know who kidnapped him yet? Have they issued a ransom demand, anything like that?"

"I don't know yet, not even enough to speculate. We know the vehicle used in the kidnapping is owned by a local priest."

"What are your thoughts? Did the priest do it?" Ari asked.

"I just don't have a sense of this right now. I don't have enough in the way of facts to work with. But how do your book sales go?" Before Ari could answer, Shimon lost the connection. He checked to see who had called while he was on the phone with Ari. It wasn't Michelle, which disappointed him.

Eshkol, one of the embassy staffers, came in, bringing a newspaper.

"What have you got for me, Eshkol"

"For you, my friend, I have today's edition of Le Monde, fresh off the press. Shimon, take a look at the front page."

"So, this is what Philippe looks like. Now maybe the French inspector will be focused on him instead of me, now. Good."

"The French consider you a suspect?"

"I think he does, at least he thinks I may be involved somehow. I, of course, was still at home in Israel when Andre got snatched. I met with him yesterday and informed him that I was in Paris as a favor to Michelle. The inspector reminded me very pointedly that I was way way out of my jurisdiction. He intimated that Andre's disappearance might even be part of a love triangle. As if."

"A love triangle? Shimon, you dog. What have you been up to?"

Shimon waved him off. "Honestly, nothing at all. Well, nothing beyond longing. She is a beautiful woman and smarter than the both of us together. Not likely she would be interested in an old shoe like me."

"Well, never mind that then. You did stymie his investigation when he was in Haifa. Do you think this Inspector Jean Gallant might just be settling the score, giving you your comeuppance for your encounter in Israel?" Eshkol asked. "You should have heard the women here gossip after Michelle came to the embassy yesterday. They don't think you are an old shoe, Shimon, far from it."

"Crap, don't they have better things to do, Eshkol? If not, we should fire the whole bunch of them and send them to the unemployment line in Israel." he retorted.

"You are too touchy, Shimon. After all these years, you still don't understand women? Shame on you," Eshkol replied, smiling at Shimon's discomfort.

"If I understood women, wouldn't you think I would still be married?" Shimon would dearly like to have heard what the female gossip was. Instead, he listened to his voicemail. He heard a message to call the vicar-general, the adjutant to the archbishop of Paris. Shimon returned the call and was offered an invitation to tour Paris.

Curiouser and curiouser.

"Yes, thank you. I can be ready in an hour," Shimon answered.

The morning started out sunny but brisk. By early afternoon, the sky turned dark and overacted. Rain began to fall, slowly at first and then in torrents. The official archbishop's limousine parked in front of the entrance to the embassy. The uniformed driver stood beneath a wide umbrella waiting for Shimon to come out. A hat-less Shimon dashed from the embassy doors to the large, luxurious vehicle. The driver opened the door for him as he climbed aboard and then closed the door with a heavy thud behind him.

Shimon avoided eye contact until after locking in his seat belt. Antoine sat comfortably on the opposite seat in the private compartment. Antoine's big frame settled well into the beautifully crafted leather seat, as it sagged beneath him. Seeing that Shimon had settled himself, Antoine greeted him.

"Bienvenue to Paris," Antoine smiled and extended a handshake.

"Thank you, Father de Gaulle."

Without taking his eyes from Shimon, Antoine knocked twice with the back of his hand on the small window that separated them from the chauffeur's compartment. His driver placed the car in gear.

"Have you seen Paris, Monsieur Levi?"

"Very little, I am sorry to say," Shimon admitted.

"We shall drive to the Eiffel Tower."

"Vicar-general, I sensed plangency in your voice, but I could not begin to fathom why you, a high official in the Catholic Church, would want to meet with me. There are diplomatic channels to my government that are available to you, available quite easily to a man in your position."

"But Monsieur Levi, you are no ordinary citizen. You are an Israeli interrogator, perhaps even a Mossad agent. I read Le Monde. You are as connected to Andre Dubois as I am and also to his fiancee. I will be blunt. Do you know a man named Shai Tanger, a Jew of Moroccan descent?"

Shimon paused for three heartbeats. "I have met many Jews of Moroccan descent." He replied in evasion.

"I forgot to mention that he is from Reims, France. He serves food at the Cafe Voila. Is his name familiar to you now?"

"It is possible."

"This man has engineered a scheme to blackmail the church. He claims he has email communications between Andre Dubois and his friend and mentor, the late Father Gauthier."

"I wondered if those emails were real," Shimon sallied.

"Please, do not be coy with me, Monsieur Levi. We know Israel has the identical communications because your government confiscated the laptop that Andre Dubois used during his voyage in space. These communications are as detrimental to Israel as they are to us, no? Do you think that we do not know about the quid pro quo between you and the Russians?"

"What do you mean? What quid pro quo?"

"That Russia has continually delayed shipment of the S-300 and the Tor-M1 missile defense systems to Tehran, the missiles that are absolutely vital to the protection of the Iranian nuclear reactors from attack."

"I see the quid but not the quo. Please make your point, Monsieur de Gaulle," Shimon replied with an edge to his voice. Shimon was indeed an intelligence operative and not a diplomat.

"Your country, my church, and the Russians, we are all on the same side on this one. We all stand to lose if these emails go public," Antoine de Gaulle stated.

"Let us assume for the moment that what you say is true. What would you have from me? If you want me to eliminate this Moroccan blackmailer, the answer is no."

"Oh please, Monsieur Levi, we are not about the Inquisition anymore. This Moroccan wants to extract a million Euros in blackmail money from the Church." Antoine sighed, a sound that seemed tired, sad, and world-weary all at once. "We will pay him for his silence. We don't want to kill him. We want you to convince Tanger to take the money and make no more financial demands upon us, no more blackmail, not ever."

"A million Euros will be deposited into his account tomorrow. But," Antoine lifted one of his big fingers for emphasis, "if he continues with any more threats we will make life miserable for the Jews of France. The French are known to be quite visceral to charges of Jewish treachery."

"I am well aware of that, Monsieur de Gaulle, as disgusting as it is to have a senior churchman use such a vile threat," Shimon replied with venom in his voice.

Antoine let the tone and the words roll off him. "And can you imagine stoking the ever-present anti-Jewish passions of several millions of Muslims in France?"

"I can imagine," Shimon responded dryly.

"Then you realize that France will be a very dangerous place for Jews if this problem is not contained?"

"You, obviously, have a plan in mind. Tell me." Now Shimon was terse to the point of rudeness, and no wonder.

"Very perceptive, Monsieur Levi. We would like you to visit Monsieur Tanger. You can find him waiting tables at the Cafe Voila in Reims." He smiled a professional if false smile. "Tomorrow will be a good day to visit Reims. The weather is supposed to be beautiful, the rain will have gone away, the sun will be out, bright and cheerful. Are you free?"

"I have an engagement in Paris tomorrow evening." Shimon had accepted a dinner invigoration from Michelle and her mother.

Antoine had made his preparation and plans. He advised "You can leave the train station as early as 6 AM tomorrow morning. You can be back in Paris by early afternoon."

"Even if I plug this leak for you, this won't solve your problem with Andre." Shimon pointed out the obvious.

"Dubois is not my worry right now unless he reappears. Incidentally, nobody from our church kidnapped him. Our priest will soon be exonerated."

Traffic suddenly came to a halt a mile away from the Eiffel Tower. There was a demonstration. A traffic cop, frantically redirecting automobile traffic, yielded to hundreds of Parisians marching on both sides of the boulevard carrying signs and chanting for Archbishop Clement to resign and to set Andre Dubois free.

"Excuse me momentarily."

Antoine pulled out his cell phone and hit the speed dial for his assistant. She told him that a similar demonstration noisily crowded the street in front of the archbishop's residence. Antoine closed the call and sat for a moment, pondering.

"Monsieur Dubois must be very popular among some of the French citizens, or could the problem be that your church is less popular?" Shimon posed the question in a flat, neutral voice.

"I take your point, Monsieur Levi. Only fifteen years ago, 80% of the French people identified themselves as Catholic. Today, just over half do so. And even among that half, only 10% regularly attend church services. And as terrible as it sounds, only half of the French people who identify themselves as Catholic believe in God. To them, being Catholic is nothing more than a cultural identity, not a religious conviction," Antoine said in a matter-of-fact way.

"If your church is alienating its flock, it needs to change or risk becoming more insignificant as Islam becomes more significant. And, Monsignor de Gaulle, your church needs to stop alienating the Jews," Shimon responded sharply.

"The Jews are meddling in church affairs and impugning Pope Pius " Antoine came back just as sharply.

"I don't care if you make him a saint. That is your business."

"What do you care about Shimon? What is Pius to you, to your country?"

"I care that this Pope remains silent when Iranian leaders call for the annihilation of the Jewish state, just as Pius XII held his condemnation from the Nazi regime. He did not publicly condemn Hitler for his genocide against the Jews. What is the only country in the Middle East where the Christian population is safe and growing, Monsignor?"

"I suppose it is Israel," de Gaulle responded listlessly.

"And when the Holy See does not publicly oppose or rebuff Ahmadinejad when he calls for the destruction of Israel, the silence of your pope is as reassuring to Ahmadinejad as it was to Hitler," Shimon lectured with fervor.

"Unfortunately Monsieur Levi, I cannot speak for either of the Popes. Pius is no longer alive and I am only the deputy to the archbishop."

"A soldier who follows his orders," Shimon retorted. Antoine ignored his insult.

"The rain is hard, and it will be difficult to park near the Eiffel Tower today. Perhaps another day," the clergyman said. Then he stayed quiet, looking at the rain and thinking who knew what kind of thoughts. Then he stirred again.

"What time shall I send a car for you tomorrow, Monsieur?"

"Don't bother. I will arrange my own transportation in Paris and in Reims."

"Very well, it shall be as you wish. I trust we will be in touch, Monsieur Levi." Antoine slid open the cab window and instructed his driver to return to the embassy.

Assigned to monitor the Israeli's activities, Detective Balnc watched the travels of the limousine about Paris with avid interest. He phoned Gallant when Shimon left the embassy and phoned him again when the vicar-general dropped him back at the embassy.

"So, they finally did meet. The Israeli agent and the vicar-general, very interesting. What do you suppose they had to discuss, Blanc?" The inspector asked his minion.

"Did their meeting surprise you, inspector?" Blanc asked. Nothing surprised Blanc. His years as a detective had taught him to gather facts, to assemble clues, anticipating nothing, remembering everything until he understood what was what.

Gallant did not answer the question. Instead, he issued another order. "Put a tail on the vicar-general as well. Let's see where he goes, if anywhere. But you, personally, stick with Shimon. Keep in mind that he is a trained agent. You must be at your best."

"Got it. Right away, sir," Detective Blanc responded. He did allow himself a speculation or two, but he kept that to himself.

Chapter 7

INTERSTATE 8

"Don't you ever get tired of driving?" Bette inquired.

"I like to drive in the desert," Eric replied.

"It's still a boring drive from Scottsdale to La Jolla, and you need to download some different songs, something newer. I'm tired of hearing the same CDs."

"These old songs relaxe me, and I don't like the new songs, no catchy melodies to them, just a lot of noise and lousy lyrics for the most part. Remember the old country crossover songs by Patsy Cline and Skeeter Davis? When I was growing up, they got radio play alongside the Beatles and the Beach Boys way before radio programming became genre segmented. I can't stand talk radio, so depressing."

"But if I fall asleep, wake me up at the Yuma Starbucks, and don't forget to take exit 8 or you'll miss it like last time," Bette snipped.

"So I took the next exit and backtracked. It took an extra five minutes. Do you think Z would know who Patsy Cline or Skeeter Davis was?"

"She might recognize their music but not their names. Don't forget our daughter belongs to Generation Y, and doesn't live in your past."

"I'm not so sure," Eric noted. "You remember after my colonoscopy she insisted we go to a free concert at the Indian Casino to see Gary Lewis and the Playboys."

"That's because you played the Playboys' songs to her when she was little."

"I did. There was something unique and pleasant about vinyl albums, a fragrance, and large covers of biographies and liner notes. It was cool watching the records spin around the turntable. Did you ever stack a bunch of 45s on the spindle?"

"I never bought records. I just danced to them," Bette replied. "Eric, you're still a child of the 60s. When are you going to grow up? When you live in the past, you get kicked in the ass."

"That is poetic. Did you make that up?"

"Eric, the past was never so good to you. You just choose to think it was. This is the best time of your life. Tomorrow we'll be the proud parents at our daughter's college graduation."

"Yes, we will, but this afternoon we might have time to go to the beach."

"And do what? The ocean's still too cold. I'd rather go shopping," Bette insisted.

"I like to look at it."

"You should have stayed in Maine. I don't know why you ever moved to Arizona."

"Because of the promise of you," Eric quipped.

"I'm going to take a nap."

Eric marvelled at how quickly his wife could go to sleep after she adjusted the incline of the passenger seat slightly backwards. Even with music playing softly and his vocal contributions seemed not to interrupt her slumber.

Soon she was asleep, and he once again began to reflect on life's unpredictable twists and turns which transplanted him from Maine to Arizona by way of Denver. He listened to the music and it triggered a memory of Maine.

Chapter 8

REIMS

ynical cops and life-saving EMTs alike called them floaters, bodies
that for one reason or another found their way into the river Seine
as it flowed through Paris. The body that firemen fished out of the
chilly waters on the morning following the conversation between the Israeli
agent and the French churchman had belonged in life to a man known to
the newspaper-reading public as 'Philippe.' No one knew his actual name,
of course, but the police certainly didn't think his name might really be
Philippe, anything but.

The true identity would be difficult to discover. Without his fingers
and thumbs to match against recorded fingerprints, the police would have
to fall back on dental records or to fall even further back and try their luck
with DNA samples. Some bad actors had used tin snips to remove the
murder victim's digits. Gangsters sometimes took the trouble of obscuring
the identity of their victims, making difficult police work even harder.

Inspector Jean Gallant examined the evidence at the crime scene, that
is the body and clothing of the victim. He didn't get much, to his disgust
but not to his surprise. This certainly looked like a professional hit. His
cell buzzed.

"Gallant here."

"Blanc here, inspector. I just watched Shimon get on the train for Reims. Shall I follow him all the way?"

"Yes. Don't miss the train."

"I have a couple of minutes. I will continue covert surveillance."

"We just pulled 'Philippe' out of the river. He doesn't have his fingers anymore."

"Kidnapping and now murder. This case keeps getting worse."

"Oui. Keep me informed."

"Yes Chief."

While on the train, Detective Blanc carried a shopping bag, full of snacks, supplies for the trip as well as a simple disguise. No one would suspect a man with a mouth full of breakfast to be a cop. He wore the sort of warm clothing that any man might wear against the early morning chill. He looked a lot more like some random citizen than a policeman. This was not his first job at tailing someone. He sat in the same train car as Shimon but behind him, in the last seat in the car.

He could easily see his subject but remain anonymous as he sampled a soft roll and some smelly cheese and read the morning paper.

At the station, he watched Shimon enter the first taxi in the line outside. He noted the cab number and hit the speed dial for the taxi dispatcher, a prearranged phone number in his cell.

Blanc needed no special permission in France to conscript the aid of the cab company to help him.

"Detective, your subject is approximately ten minutes from arrival. He is heading south on Boulevard la Paris, please remain on the line," the dispatcher said.

Blanc grabbed the next cab, sliding into the back seat, his phone still up to his ear.

"Where to, Monsieur?" The driver asked.

"South on Boulevard la Paris," Blanc replied as he fastened his seat belt with his free hand, still listening to the dispatcher.

"What address," the driver asked?

Blanc relayed the address as he got it from the dispatcher. "Take me to the Cafe Voila at 144 Rue Clovis."

"Oui." The driver replied.

As soon as Blanc ended the call to the dispatcher, his phone buzzed again. He heard the voice of Inspector Gallant.

Blanc, you do know my investigation of Father Gauthier's suicide began at the Cafe Voila?" The familiar voice of his boss came through the phone.

"I know, I know but I was not part of the Gauthier investigation," Blanc replied.

Blanc paid scant attention to his Tunisian driver. Joseph Taieb habitually eavesdropped on his passengers' conversations, but this conversation-or the half he could hear-touched a raw nerve. Taieb never came up on anyone's radar and for that, he gave abundant thanks. Still, he regretted not picking up the monsignor that fateful July 19th, 2007 morning. If he had arrived a few minutes earlier, he might have prevented the death of the priest. Obviously, the priest was on a secret mission to get to the Israeli embassy in Paris. It seemed like yesterday to the cabbie. Taieb parked in exactly the same space that the archbishop's limousine had occupied on that July morning.

Taeib recalled the friendly waiter who came up to his cab, apologizing to him and explained that Father Gauthier had been whisked away due to the unexpected arrival of the archbishop. Taeib told the waiter "No, I am to pick up a Bertrand here, Monsieur, not a clergyman."

"Oh, the father gave his first name, not his title," Shai explained.

"Oh brother, what a fare that would make? All the way to Paris, to the Israeli embassy! I can't Imagine a priest going to the Israeli embassy. The tip alone would make my workday for me."

Shai Tanger looked like he had been struck in the forehead by a mallet. He reasoned that the arrival of the archbishop may have been staged to prevent Father Gauthier from reaching the Israeli embassy. The waiter recovered quickly. He smiled at the driver and made him an offer.

"Please come in, the least I can do is offer you a complimentary bite of breakfast and a cup of our coffee."Where are you from?"

"Tunisia marginally, but I am French now."

"I came from Morocco. Come in for a minute. I can make you some coffee like we grew up with, coffee with some vigor!"

That made Joseph Taieb chuckle. Coffee in North Africa, their mutual homeland, came thick as tar and strong as night.

The two, the cabbie and the waiter, had exchanged names and phone numbers and now had become friends or at least friendly acquaintances. In later conversations, the pair concluded that the archbishop had intercepted Father Gauthier with deliberate intent. His attempt to reach the Israeli embassy had been thwarted. Then he died. He died in a spectacular, public and especially tragic way for a priest, a suicide.

A sharp voice from behind shook Taieb from his reminiscences.

"Can't you drive any faster," his passenger complained.

Taieb stepped on the gas.

"We are very close, Monsieur, only a block away," he said loudly over the sound of the now racing engine. A moment later he applied the brakes and pulled to a stop in front of the Cafe Voila. Blanc paid the fare, left a tip to cover his rudeness, and bounded out of the cab.

He entered the cafe and spotted Shimon sitting alone at a table to the right. As the cab headed off again, rain began to drop down, in defiance to the predictions of the vicar-general to Shimon the day before.

Blanc overheard a few words between Shimon and the waiter as the maitre'd escorted him to a table where he could see Shimon.

The middle-aged, balding detective didn't attract much attention, even from Shimon, a trained agent. His clothing had been wrinkled and rumpled on the train. He did not have a remarkable physique, if anything, he was of less than average height and bulk. Nothing about his appearance would attract anyone's attention. Blanc had worked surveillance for years. He could disappear in a crowd of two.

He could easily see Shimon from his seat by the window. Blanc had worked and worked with a deaf man until he could lip read conversations in both English and French. He asked for coffee and a menu.

"You asked to be seated at my table, Monsieur?" Blanc read the words of the waiter.

"Monsieur Tanger, do you speak Arabic?"

Shai switched to Arabic, which Blanc did not speak nor could he lip read. But police work often, in his experience, had downs as well as ups. He would at least enjoy a decent meal.

"Yes, I am from Morocco. I speak Arabic."

"Good," Shimon replied in that language.

"Now that we can speak more privately, Monsieur, tell me how you know my name?" Shai asked.

"I have been sent by the vicar-general to give you his assurance that you will be wired one million euros from the Vatican bank within two days. When you receive the money, you must move your family to Israel."

"Your Arabic is very good, Monsieur. You know me, you know a lot about me and the dealings that I thought were completely private and secret. But I know nothing about you, not even your name."

Shimon offered a wry hint of a smile.

"I am Shimon Levi, an Israeli intelligence officer." He dropped the words which sounded to Shai as loud as a slap. "What do you recommend from the menu?"

Across the cafe Blanc whispered into his cell phone.

"I can't make out their conversation. Shimon is talking to his waiter in Arabic. I think they are on to me."

"Arabic huh? Gallant replied." He must be talking with Shai Tanger. I once interviewed him, you know. Tanger was the last person to speak with Father Gauthier before the good father got swept up by not one but two archbishops. They took him to Paris and his death. Blanc, I got nothing at all from Tanger. He is a Moroccan Jew. I think I will call in a judicial favor and have a tap put on this Moroccan's phone line under our recent anti-terrorism law."

"Inspector, I wouldn't count on it. He is an Arabic Jew, not a Muslim," Blanc reminded his superior.

"You don't think Jewish terrorists exist, Blanc? All you have to do is ask the British. They had decades of bad experiences with the likes of the Stern Gang and the Irgun."

"Jesus save us! Inspector, that was seventy years ago. And in British occupied Palestine besides. You might as well remind us about Samson and the temple." Blanc was having none of his bosses blather.

"Look Blanc, I don't have to be right."

"Or honest?" Blanc asked.

"OK, OK, I just have to get the judge to go along with me. I think I can. I might not even mention that Tanger is Jewish, just that he is Moroccan and connected somehow to the kidnapping of a French astronaut. That might just be enough. If not, I'll think of some added details. Don't you think that there are too many unexplained coincidences all mushed together somehow? We have the suicide of Father Gauthier, we have the Dubois kidnapping, we now have some unexplained connection between this Israeli agent, Shimon Levi, and the Jewish waiter, Shai Tanger, and another unexplained connection between Levi and vicar-general Antoine de Gaulle. And we do not know what these connections are, Blanc. And Levi and Tanger are playing cute by speaking Arabic to each other. I need answers, Blanc. You will get them for me. Continue your surveillance on the Israeli, you hear me?"

"Yes, of course inspector." Blanc mentally made the arithmetic in his head. He had four years, three months, one week, and one day until he could retire with a full pension. He broke the connection and sighed.

As Shimon finished his duck in orange sauce, which he had to admit was exceptionally good and not something he would have ordered on his own, he glanced at the man they suspected of watching him and Shai. The assumed policeman had his phone to his ear, speaking quietly into the instrument. When Shai returned to remove the plate, Shimon spoke to him again, still in Arabic.

"Shai, the police are onto us but we can use that knowledge to our advantage. If I was a French policeman I would want to tap your phone and probably your computer as well. We can set them up to hear your alibi. I want you to call me in a few days. You will tell me you have decided to make aliyah to Israel. Mention our mutual friend from Tel Aviv. Call him Adam, that should be enough. They will think that all we had to talk about was your emigration from France."

Shimon tucked his payment into the payment folder, leaving a modest rather than a lavish tip. The tough little waiter now had more wealth than Shimon could muster in two lifetimes and a big tip just seemed silly.

He left the cafe. The earlier rain had stopped and the sun began to come out to play. The vicar-general's weather prediction had come to fruition after all. With the weather, as with many things, patience proved necessary to find the desired result. Shimon began a short walk to the Reims Cathedral.

His tail followed.

Chapter 9

------------- ◆~◈~◆ -------------

REIMS

Shimon phoned Michelle from the train station in Reims just as soon as the taxi dropped him off. She started right in, not giving him a chance to say more than 'Hello.'

"Shimon, did you hear the police found a dead body in the Seine? They think this man had a part in Andre's abduction."

"Yes, I heard the same thing."

"Oh, Shimon, is he dead? If they killed this kidnapper does it mean they have killed Andre also?"

"I don't think so, Michelle. I believe that Andre's kidnappers murdered this man because his picture hit the front page of the newspaper and the TV news. Believe me, Andre is more important alive to the people behind this plot than he is dead, a lot more." He replied to assuage her anxiety.

"They cut the dead man's finger off!! Who would do such an awful thing?"

"Gangsters do that sort of thing, Michelle. It makes it hard for the police to identify the body. No fingers, no fingerprints. All we have now is a fake name and a dead body that we cannot yet identify. Try not to worry, worry will not help things nor bring Andre back."

She snorted. "Don't worry? Are you sure you are Jewish, Shimon?"

"Good point." He smiled into the phone. Michelle had switched gears, the hysteria had vanished.

"I will try not to worry. Can you be at Maman's house at six this evening?"

"It should be no problem. I am just about to get on the train from Reims."

"What are you doing in Reims? Does it have anything to do with Andre's disappearance? Or the dead man in the river?" Anxiety sneaked back into her voice, but less than before.

"No" he lied easily, professionally, even to this exquisite woman in whom he had a now undeniable interest. "I went to visit a friend of a friend. Afterwards I walked to the Reims Cathedral. There is a synagogue nearby barricaded with concrete blocks, a shouted commentary to our times to anyone who might listen to such things. Except for the Star of David, the facade is nameless. It does have a memorial with the names of Jewish children taken away to their deaths by the Nazis during the war."

"It was a very sad chapter in France's history, and the Nazis had many willing French collaborators," she said somberly. Then her voice brightened. "Call me when you arrive, Shimon. I'll take Maman's car to the station and pick you up."

"It is just as easy for me to take a cab," Shimon pointed out.

"I know, but I want to. So call me. Au revoir."

Well, that was settled and he noticed that he had no part in the decision. But having a beautiful woman collect him from the station was in no way a bad thing. Puzzling, confusing perhaps, but not bad. He made one more call before he had to climb aboard the train back to Paris. To Ari. Ari didn't answer so Shimon left a message for him on his voicemail.

"Ari, the French police pulled a dead body out of the river. They think the deader is an accomplice in the Dubois kidnapping. Get this, the guy had all his fingers snipped off, a nasty way to make identification harder. Call me."

With that, he boarded the train. He now had some down time to think through the latest developments from the angle of the French police, the Catholic Church and whoever the kidnappers might turn out to be. He also had time for a thought or two about Michelle, who seemed to be determined to spend time with him.

That evening at the flat where Michelle was staying with her mother, Lucille, Shimon had the dubious pleasure of the full attention of two women, mother, and daughter. He could put up with the women, it wasn't that bad, just predictable on the mother's part. The food was terrific.

"Do you like your veal, Shimon?" Lucille asked.

Answering honestly, as he dabbed a bit of something from his mouth with his napkin, he replied "Lucille, this is really very very good. Having a home-cooked meal is a treat for me, and to have a home-cooked meal by a Frenchwoman who is a wizard in the kitchen, well, I am glad you two invited me to dinner. Yes, Lucille, the veal is excellent."

Michelle glowed. "Maman cooks the best veal." She burbled.

"Michelle tells me that you were born in Argentina?" Lucille began the third degree. He knew this would be part of the dinner, his fee as it were, for enjoying a home-cooked meal in the home of a Frenchwoman. He would gladly pay the fee. The food was delightful. He got to look at and listen to Michelle, which while dangerous to his emotional well being was equally delightful.

"I was born right in Buenos Aires. I suppose that is about as Argentinian as I can be." He smiled. The inquisition would continue, he knew.

"And your family moved to Israel when.....?"

"We made aliyah in 1973. We moved to Jerusalem just before the October war."

"Well, that was a long time ago, wasn't it Shimon?" Lucille continued, a pleasantly determined expression on her face.

"Yes, it seems so to me too. I was only four when we moved to Jerusalem. I have only bits of memories of Buenos Aires."

"What of your family? Do you have any brothers and sisters? Are there little nieces and nephews in your life?"

"Here we go." Shimon thought to himself. *"Next comes my kids and the divorce."*

"Two of each, two brothers and two sisters but I am the youngest. I have a whole circus of nieces and nephews, an even dozen, and at least one more on the way."

Michelle, as aware of the interrogation as Shimon, interjected "Some more wine, Shimon?"

"Yes, thank you. In France, the wine is so good that it is even money each way if the wine compliments the meal or the meal compliments the wine. Either way, this is the best dinner I have had in some time, Lucille. Thank you for inviting me."

"It is good for me to cook for a man who enjoys his food, Shimon, and who appreciates the entire experience. You could almost be French."

He lifted his glass. "High praise indeed, Lucille. Thank you."

"Do you speak Spanish?" Lucille continued, a relentless smile on her face.

"I used to. I haven't had much chance to practice. I wonder how much I can still remember? It is probably just kid stuff if I can remember much at all."

Blanc reported in.

"Inspector, I have followed him to the apartment of Lucille Dumas, the mother of Michelle."

"Fill me in on the rest of his day, Blanc." Gallant demanded.

"Nothing too eventful, inspector. After the suspect left the cafe he walked around and toured the Cathedral at Reims. After that, he stopped at a nearby synagogue."

"Did he enter the synagogue, Blanc?"

"No. He just looked at the monument dedicated to the Jewish children taken by the Nazis. Then he walked back to the intersection and grabbed a cab back to the train depot. I followed and sat behind him, out of his direct sight but in the same train car. He knew I was there. We were both polite about it. In Paris, Michelle picked him up at the station. She drove him to her mother's apartment, where they are now."

"Thank you for your concise report, Blanc. Now I have some good news for you. I convinced the judge to grant a phone tap on Tanger's cell phone and computer. It turns out that the Tangier family no longer has a landline."

"Fewer and fewer all the time, sir."

"True. His wife doesn't have a cell phone, so it is just the one and the computer connection."

"Can your friendly judge give us a tap on Shimon?"

"No, too much to ask for. He is not a French citizen and he also has the complication of having diplomatic status while he is here, even though we know he is a spy of some sort. An agent at any rate. So, no tap for him."

"Shall I continue the surveillance on the Israeli, sir?"

"Not you Blanc. You have been compromised. Francois is on the way for the hand-off. He should be there anytime. You have been compromised so we will have a fresh set of eyes on him. It has been a long and productive day for you. Go home, get some rest, eat a good meal, and make love to your wife. You deserve it, my friend."

"Merci, Inspector. I will make love tonight but not to my wife," Blanc quipped.

"As you please, Blanc. Drop by the precinct tomorrow. We still have a case to solve." Gallant briefly pondered what the mistress of a man with Blanc's looks, crazy hours, and marital status might be like. Then he shook his head to clear it of something that was, after all, none of his business.

Chapter 10

PARIS

"Thank you for a lovely dinner Madame Dumas." Shimon checked the time and rose from his chair, heavily, reluctantly. He was happily full of the best food, wine, and company that he had enjoyed in quite some time. "I should probably get back to the embassy." He reached for his cell and called Eshkol.

Michelle protested.

"No, please, Shimon, let me drive you." She clutched the arm of his coat for a fleeting instant, just for emphasis. She wanted to drive him.

"You have schlepped enough for me today. I have summoned Eshkol. He will be here in just a few minutes. But thank you for the offer."

Lucille chimed in. "No more of this Madam Dumas nonsense, Shimon. You will call me Lucille. You are welcome back here any time, whether Michelle is here or not. Understand?" She offered him the glance of a severe third-grade teacher, no-nonsense indeed. She did it with a smile.

Michelle however, pouted.

"Thank you Lucille. I will take advantage of your hospitality as often as I may. Honestly, this was a wonderful evening for me."

"I can at least walk you downstairs, Shimon." She attached herself to his jacket sleeve again but this time she did not let go. They took the elevator down to the lobby and walked outside. They sat on the steps to wait for Eshkol but mostly just to be with each other, to be each in the close presence of the other.

"Shimon, did I tell you that the police have men watching me? I usually wave to them," Michelle said, mischief springing from her voice.

"I have them watching me too. They are very polite about it when I catch them." He smiled a small rueful smile. He wondered if they had a hidden tail on him, the one he saw today was so obvious that a more careful tail would not be out of the question. But no, they just didn't care much if he knew about them.

"Shall we give them something to talk about, Shimon?"

"What do you have in mind?" he asked, innocent as a child.

She threw her arms around his shoulders and planted a firm, lengthy and sincere kiss on his lips. He did not push her away.

"What now, Francois?" Gallant asked his spy.

"She waved to me and now they are kissing," Francis reported into his phone.

"What? Who is kissing? What is going on?"

"Michelle and Shimon are kissing. They don't look like they are kidding around about it either. They haven't stopped."

"Ahh, he's playing me for a fool," Gallant snapped. "Pick him up and take him to the precinct," he ordered.

"Are you sure inspector? A car just pulled up. He's getting in."

"Are you driving a squad car?"

"No inspector. I have a car we took from some dope dealers, an almost new Peugeot. I was, or I thought I was, trying to be inconspicuous."

"I don't care. You have a portable light, I am sure. Pull him over and bring him to the station, right now."

"What shall I charge him with?" Francois was nonplussed at this break in surveillance prototypical and didn't like it.

"Anything, nothing, I don't care. Did the driver have his blinker on when he pulled away from the curb?" Gallant asked his minion.

"No, I don't think so."

"Just bring him in." Gallant was in a fury.

"Eshkol, any word from Ari?" Shimon asked his driver.

"Not yet, but never mind that for now. What was all that kissing about?"

Shimon waved a dismissive hand.

"Nothing, nothing at all, just theatrics. Michelle knew the cops had a watcher on her house. She just wanted them to know that she knew they were there." He smiled a bemused smile. Theatrics or not the interlude was quite nice, memorable even.....

His happy rumination ended with the blue flashing lights of a police car demanding them to pull over.

Eshkol complied and pulled to the side of the road. Detective Francois climbed out of the Peugeot and sauntered up to the driver's side. He bent down and showed his identification badge. Eshkol already had his window rolled down. Beneath his jacket his right hand finger coiled gently around a handheld small semi-automatic pistol, a French-made Ruby from the 1930s. The sturdy little gun fit easily in his hand, out of sight.

"Your driver's license, Monsieur," Francois asked the driver.

Eshkol released his pistol and rummaged around his pockets for his wallet. He pulled out his license and showed it to the policeman.

"So I see you are Eshkol Rosenbaum at the Israeli Embassy? Is that correct?"

"I am. What have I done that the French police have stopped me, a diplomat?" Eshkol responded testily.

"You left the curb without signaling, Monsieur Rosenbaum."

"But I did signal," Eshkol protested.

"Monsieur, are you accusing me, a decorated French policeman, of lying?" Francois asked, letting a bit of anger enter his voice. He was beginning to enjoy this even knowing it would be to no purpose save to assuage the flash of momentary anger in the mind of his superior.

"No, I am saying a mistake was made, officer."

"Monsieur Rosenbaum, you and your friend must come with me to the station house. Francois ordered and drew his gun. "I smell alcohol on your breath and you may be too intoxicated to drive."

"I had a couple of glasses of wine this evening with dinner but I assure you I am in total control. Besides, detective, you have no legal authority to take us in. Can't you see we have diplomatic license plates? Do you want to stop this charade now or create an international incident?" Eshkol responded, his voice rising in his irritation.

Francois strolled to the rear of the car and looked at the license plate. Seeing that it was indeed a diplomatic license, he put his gun away. He returned to the driver's window.

"You are both free to leave. Drive carefully Monsieur."

Upon returning to his undercover car, Francois hit the speed dial for his boss.

"Inspector, I think we have had too long a day. They pulled diplomatic immunity on me. I can't take them in."

"Son of a bitch," the inspector yelled and broke the connection.

Chapter 11

RIVE GAUCHE, LEFT BANK

A ndre awakened to the sound of footsteps and the sight of two light beams bearing down on the cement floor. He made a quick glance at the luminous dial on his wristwatch to read the time. The watch showed the hour and minute, one-ten AM. Night still ruled and a black night indeed inside the rough warehouse.

Andre forced himself into a sitting position. The voice rang familiar to his ears but not identifiable. He could see nothing of the advancing men in the darkness. He couldn't even tell what color their hoods were.

"Face the wall," one voice demanded. As Andre did as the hooded man ordered him, the men got busy with his badly needed food. One man spread a table cloth on the foot of Andre's bunk while the second man put out bread and some slices of cheese, good strong smelling French cheese. Andre could smell the cheese and the very odor of the food caused his mouth to water.

The pair stepped away from the cot.

"You can eat your food now." The same voice instructed him.

Andre quickly sought the cot and the food there. "Can I turn on my flashlight?" he asked his captors.

"Not yet. Wait until we are gone."

Andre said nothing for a moment. Instead, he stuffed bread and cheese into his hungry mouth. He couldn't say a word if he tried. It took him a minute or two but when he swallowed he asked "What are you going to do to me? Will you murder me?"

"No, we will not murder you. You will stay until you make peace with yourself and Christ and no longer than that. But not before that either." The hooded man replied in an even tone as if he talked of something of no importance.

"I am not the one who sinned here. I am the victim of the sins of others, of you men in fact," Andre said, surprising himself at his sudden boldness.

"I beg to differ." The same man responded, in the same even, neutral tone. "You chose to wage war on the Roman church."

"Someone inside the Roman church is responsible for Father Gauthier's death," Andre challenged.

"Your priest committed suicide. Suicide is a sin against God and one for which one cannot beg forgiveness nor can one make contrition," the same monk said. The other hooded man had not said a word.

"Father Gauthier sacrificed his life to save me." Andre would not be budged.

"He sacrificed himself to save a Jew and two apostates. You were not to be killed." The monk let that important information, or nasty falsehood, escape his lips.

"I don't buy your story. The Russians tried to kill us all at least two times."

"Andre, you are either in good standing in Christ's church or you are with the outcasts. Do you wish to throw your lot in with the Jews and other heretics who deny that the Holy See is the Vicar of Christ and the Vatican is God's holiest city? Your father was killed by Jews. Take a look at these Andre."

Andre reached under the floor for his light. The taller monk carefully placed two photographs on his bed and slowly retreated into the shadows. He still had not said a word. The photographs showed Shimon and Michelle standing in front of her apartment. They were engaged in a kiss, a real kiss not just a polite French smack on the cheek.

"You see Andre, not only did they take your father, they took your fiancee, too."

Andre remained silent. He turned off his flashlight and coiled underneath his blanket. His captors left him.

Chapter 12

LA JOLLA

Even in upscale La Jolla, properly named in Spanish 'the jewel', occasional days came along with a breeze and overcast skies. Eric and Bette Miller changed into more dressy clothing after a shower and a long long day in the car barreling across the desert from Arizona to San Diego. They planned to meet their daughter, just graduating from UC San Diego for a family dinner tonight at the Sushi restaurant in the UTC Westfield Plaza. The next night they would host a big affair with about twenty members of the extended family and friends of Z's. The big dinner would follow the graduation ceremony. With her graduation, Z would be off into the adult world, leaving them behind, proud but wistful.

Eric never did figure out what the UTC in the name of the shopping mall stood for. He supposed it didn't matter.

"Honey, we have an hour to kill before we meet Z. Do you want to go to Westfield now?" Bette inquired.

"Sure. We can wander around, look things over," Eric answered.

"Don't forget your windbreaker. It will get chilly here later on tonight." They left the hotel lobby, found their car, and headed for the mall. Eric carried his LL Bean windbreaker bought two years previously in a trip they made back to Freeport Maine, his old stomping grounds from the long past days of his youth.

Bette smiled at her husband, happy with Z all grown up, to have at least him to manage. By the time they began to stroll around the mall, the sunlight faded into dusk. The fog began to roll in from the coast a couple of miles away. Bette congratulated herself for having Eric equipped for the evening as she watched him slip into his windbreaker.

"Honey, I think I'll take a look at the shoe store over there. Do you want to come with me?" Better asked her husband.

He laughed. "No thanks. There is a book store around the bend. I'll see what they have to interest me. Want to meet at the fountain there in an hour?" He pointed to a splashing fountain in the open space of the Mall.

"Sounds good. Are you getting hungry yet?"

"Some. I am looking forward to getting some good sushi."

They both went their separate ways.

Out in front of Baker's Bookstore Eric saw a contraption like an artist's easel. On it the store people had placed a dry eraser board with a hand-drawn sign advertising 'Israeli Astronaut Ari Ben Ora, author of 'The Palestine Exchange. He also read the words 'Book Signing-1 to 4 PM.' Eric walked into the store just after 4 PM. He spotted a young guy with a name badge reading Bobby. The kid had bleached blond hair and a deep surfer tan.

"Bobby, where is the book signing?"

"Ah, dude, you just missed the space guy. He left about a minute ago for the parking lot."

"Can I still buy the book"?

"Sure, of course. I have some right at the checkout. Come on, I'll get you one." Bobby led Eric up to the checkout desk. "He gave a good talk, too bad you missed it. He had a rough time up there, with all that happened."

Eric slapped $30 on the counter and asked "Which way did he go?"

The kid pointed and said, "Hey, you have change coming."

"Keep it dude, and thanks." Eric hurried away, laughing as he went. Even casual Phoenix wasn't as casual as the beach community, dude.

By hustling Eric found the big covered parking area. He spotted a guy putting a couple of cases of books into the trunk of a new-looking four-door Prius. A two-wheeled upright carrier had one case left to be put away. The guy looked to be in his mid-forties. He was of medium height and medium build, but fit looking. He looked just like the guy on the book jacket, Ari Ben Ora, down to the salt and pepper hair.

"Hey, excuse me, are you Ari Ben Ora?"

The Israeli author turned toward Eric. "Yes?"

"I am sorry but I just missed the book signing. Would you mind signing my copy? I can tell all my friends that I met you. I am from Phoenix." Eric ran his sentences together quickly, thinking that a foreigner would better know Phoenix than Scottsdale, and it was close enough anyway.

The author smiled at this rush of words and the implied compliment. "Sure, I would be glad to. What is your name?"

"Eric Miller." Eric said as he handed the freshly bought book to Ari.

"Did you drive all the way to La Jolla just to meet me, Eric?" Ari kidded as he wrote 'To Eric, My American Friend' inside the front of the book.

"Not exactly," Eric chuckled. "My daughter is graduating from UCSD. My wife and I came for the occasion."

Neither Eric nor Ari noticed a brown Toyota Corolla as it slowly approached, just an anonymous car being careful in a place where people might be walking around going to or from their parking places. The driver stopped right at Ari's car. The olive complexioned man in the passenger seat flashed a Beretta. There were three other men with him.

"In the back seat Mr. Ben Ora, right now," the gunman growled. "Just drop your keys on the ground." Outgunned, Ari dropped his keys on the ground and slid into the back seat, one of the kidnappers making room by getting out the far side of the car, also holding a pistol.

Eric stood stock still, his book in hand, scared down to his bones. The second gunman came up to Eric, the Glock in his hand looking like a cannon to Eric.

"Pick up the keys, mister, and get behind the wheel. Don't try anything funny." The gunman jerked the Glock up a few inches for emphasis. Eric thought the gun now aimed right at his heart. He got behind the wheel as the gunman took the passenger seat. Eric did not try anything funny. It was all he could do to hold his water. The guy kept the gun on Eric but held it low, below the windows and out of sight.

"Take the parkway west and exit south on Interstate 5, understand?"

"Yes," Eric managed to say. He put the book on the seat divider between him and the gunman and started the engine. It switched on with only the smallest, quietest of sounds. Eric had not driven an electric car before and the lack of engine noise shocked him, but not as much as the big Glock shocked him.

The man in the passenger seat picked up the book with his free hand. By his looks and accent, Eric pegged him vaguely as 'Middle Eastern.' Eric grew up in Maine, what did he know about people from that part of the world?

"You bought this Zionist rubbish? You must be a Jew."

"No, sir," Eric managed to squeak out.

"No matter. Just shut up and drive. Whoever you are, you have no luck today. You came to be at just the wrong place at the wrong time."

Eric's phone rang from the front right pocket of his pants. The ring tone was "My Girl" by the Temptations so he knew it was Bette calling him. She probably wanted to know where he was. She finished her shoe shopping in record time. That thought skittered in and out of Eric's mind.

"Don't answer. I want you to be very careful. If I have to shoot you while you are driving you will die, which I don't mind, but it might cause a crash which might hurt me. I do mind that. Get it?"

"Yes, I am being careful. No need to shoot me. I will do just as you want, believe me."

"Take your phone and drop it in the back seat. Keep one hand on the wheel and keep your wits about you. You are getting on a California freeway in a minute. Stay in the slow lane but keep up with the traffic." The phone stopped singing and made the little noise that meant that a message had been recorded.

Eric complied as carefully as a human being could execute that small task.

"Where is your wallet?"

"Front left pocket."

"You carry your wallet in your front pocket?"

"Sorry, I don't mean to be difficult. I do that to make it more difficult for pickpockets. I read about it somewhere. So far I have not had my wallet lifted."

The gunman cracked a smile at that. "Well, take it out and hand it to me without wrecking the car, please. Give it to me slowly. These are times when things can go wrong, even father wrong for you"

Eric did as he was told, very carefully.

The gunman fished out Eric's drivers' license and credit cards with his freehand and read them aloud.

"Eric Miller, Scottsdale Arizona. What are you doing in La Jolla, Miller?" his captor demanded.

"A few days of vacation here in a beautiful place, a few days out of the desert. San Diego is like Hawaii to us in Arizona and close enough to drive." Eric responded with what he thought was a very reasonable tone of voice. His voice did not reflect the terror that he felt. And he did not want to disclose anything about Bette or Z unless he had to. No need to give anything away.

He had no importance to the terrorists, he had figured that out. They would do what they would do for their own purposes with not a thought of how it would impact him, the random victim. If they thought it would make their cause look magnanimous, they would release him. If they thought that his murder would give more publicity to their cause, they would kill him without a thought. He found himself in the hands of people who would stop at nothing and to whom he had not the importance of a date pit.

He resolved to be brave, alert, and to watch for a chance. He would not leave his fate in the hands of these creatures if he could help it. He felt a bit better with this resolve while still having the cold shock of terror running through him.

The terrorist's cell phone chimed. He spoke into the device in Arabic for a moment and then broke the connection. He did not look happy.

"Sir, you can let me go. You know where I live and you have my cell phone. I will not have the courage to say a word." Eric thought he was quite brave to admit his fear. The fear certainly was true enough. "I have my family to protect. I would not risk their lives to betray you. Whatever you are doing has nothing to do with me, nothing to be worth the lives of my family members. You can just pull over and let me out. You will not have to deal with an unexpected guest, so to speak."

"You make some very good points, Miller. I do believe you. If someone had picked me up by mistake or chance I would make the same argument and the argument would have the same truth to it. But I cannot release you. If I did, the others would kill me, just to encourage everyone to stick strictly to the plan, whatever it might be. In my line of work, the bosses do not like the workers making decisions on their own. We do precisely as we receive our instructions, no more, no less. So, we speak no more about it, OK? Keep to the speed limit. If we get pulled over, I must shoot you." He looked at Eric to judge if Eric understood and would not make a problem for him. He had long before sacrificed his own life for his cause, the date of his death in the struggle was not yet known. The inevitability of his death he did know.

"You may call me Rashid."

Eric kept quiet and drove. They drove along the freeway, leaving the La Jolla area and then passing by Mission Bay, a huge water playground for San Diegans and visitors alike. Eric wanted to be there, frolicking in the bay and not in this stolen car with an Arab with a gun. They left Mission Bay behind, then the airport. Next, they passed by the central part of the city with the downtown buildings on the left side and the harbor on the right. He saw a tall sailing ship and an aircraft carrier, both lit up in the dark for evening visitors.

He knew they aimed straight for Tijuana. Once in Mexico, he could vanish easily and completely. No one would ever know his fate. He didn't think anyone witnessed his abduction. He would become an unsolved case, a mystery, a man who disappeared for reasons that none could know. If there were security cameras, perhaps he showed up on them. But that was not a certainty in the parking area, far from it.

Or knowing the Israeli author vanished at the same time, maybe the police would put the two kidnappings together. He wondered what good that would do. Bette would go nuts with worry. Z's graduation would be ruined, her four years of dedicated study, the scores, hundreds, of evenings spent with books rather than boys would not be celebrated. She might forever combine his death with her graduation, a nasty burden to carry with her through life.

Eric had a boatload of gloomy thoughts. He began thinking about James Bond movies, reaching for some way out. He thought the Prius sounded weird, a little electric hum rather than the vigorous sound of internal combustion. He didn't want to die right now, not in some pitiful, grotesque, pointless way in some Mexican sand dune.

They came close to the border.

"Pull in here and park, Miller." Rashid ordered him. There was a vast parking lot where people conscious of the safety of their vehicles could leave them for a while as they shopped or boozed across the border. They had no sooner stopped than another man opened the rear passenger door and handed a paper bag to Rashid.

Rashid opened the bag and removed a syringe and a vial of some liquid drug. He inserted the needle into the vial and loaded the syringe. Then he turned to Eric Miller, a man whose eyes had grown large with terror.

"Don't worry Miller. This is just a mild sedative to help us get you safely across the border. It won't hurt you at all. If the bosses wanted you dead, we could have done it in the parking area and we would not have to bother with you anymore. Be at peace, Miller. You will be OK. It willg just take a little time."

With that not altogether reassuring speech, Rashid injected Eric with something or other. Eric didn't have more than a few seconds to worry about the sanitary condition of the needle or the medical purity of whatever this Arab terrorist stuck in him. He slumped in his seat. He could not focus his mind at all. His body did not properly answer the commands of his brain, such that his brain could command anything. Eric was out of it.

Rashid removed the magazine from his pistol. He wiped the gun free of fingerprints. He wiped the magazine as well. Then he slowly removed each cartridge from the magazine. He wiped each one just as carefully as he had the pistol and the magazine. He knew that each bullet had to be forced into place by a thumb. This made each bullet casing a prime spot to preserve a thumbprint. Rashid had undergone various training sessions from professionals who worked for intelligence services. He had paid attention.

He did the same with the syringe and medicine vial and put everything in the paper bag. Then he wiped down every surface he could reach in the front part of the car as his comrade did the same in the rear area.

The second man took out a half-pint of Old Granddad and sloshed about half of it over Miller's head. The bottle was wiped like the other items and put in the bag for disposal in a convenient trash bin near the entrance to the car park.

A blurry eyed Eric, more or less helpless, offered no resistance to his assailant. One kidnapper held him up by his left arm, the other by his right. The American border agents had no interest in people leaving the country. The Mexican agents had no interest in a couple of amigos who nearly carried a drunken gringo through the turnstile and into Tijuana. The three men didn't actually attract much notice at all, just more stories that crossed into Mexico every day.

Chapter 13

PARIS

U p early, still blurry from sleep, Shimon had started drinking his
second cup of coffee of the morning. He sat in his tiny room in the
embassy drinking decidedly substandard coffee-maker coffee. His
alarm went off. He beat the alarm in waking by half an hour. He pushed
the button to stop the unnecessary noise. Ari had not called. Shimon
prepared to call and leave yet another message.

He didn't have to.

"Salaam." A voice greeted him in Arabic.

"Who am I speaking with?" Shimon demanded, shaken to hear the
strange voice. He feared the worst.

"You can call me Rashid. You have been calling for Ari Ben Ora? And
who shall I tell him is calling him?"

"What have you done with him?" Shimon fought to keep his voice
calm. Over the years Shimon had dealt with men like the one on the
phone, that is, he had killed them. He wanted to kill his one.

"For the time being, we have done nothing. I am so sorry but Ari
says he cannot come to the phone but he wants to assure you that he is
comfortable and in a safe place."

Shimon could hear the snark in Rashid's voice. He made a point of listening very carefully to this voice. He fully expected that he would have a chance to meet Rashid in person. He wanted to be sure of him when they met.

"Where is Ari?"

"You ask too many questions, Shimon."

"What do you want for his release?" Shimon replied, sharply aware that he had never revealed his name to Rashid.

"Ari is the guest of the Muslim Brigade. We will soon have a list of demands which include the immediate release of freedom fighters that you hold in Israeli prisons." Rashid paused to take a breath. "Now listen carefully, Shimon. Henceforth, our demands will be made to the U.S. Consulate in Tijuana." The line went dead.

Shimon looked at the phone in his hand with fear and loathing. He reported at once to his superiors in Jerusalem. Then he placed a call to Rachel, Ari's wife.

"The Muslim Brigade? Who are they, Shimon?" Rachel asked, her voice filled with emotion even with these few words.

"We think it is a name for a patchwork of Hezbollah cells in Mexico. As you know, these names really don't mean much. The terror networks are all connected to each other to some degree, even if it is just swapping guns and gunmen or providing money from Iran to the fanatics on the ground."

"Shimon, do you think it could be one of the Mexican cartels masquerading as Muslims? It might be a simple kidnapping for cash," she suggested.

"Anything is possible, Rachel, and that would be the preferred outcome. Drug dealers want money. We could just deal with them. We give them the money, they return your husband to you. Then of course me or someone like me would track them down and kill them in some very public way so the next time some criminal gang wants to kidnap an Israeli astronaut they think twice about the long term viability of their business plan."

"Don't make jokes, Shimon. Not until we have finished and Ari is back with me where he belongs, OK?"

"Rachel, I am not kidding around. I would take some degree of pleasure and not just professional satisfaction in putting the men who took your husband from you deep underground. But I think they are not the hoped for criminals," Shimon responded.

"Well....well." Rachel tempered, not speaking aloud the words she undoubtedly heard in her head. "How can you be sure?"

"The kidnappers' demands include the release of Arab terrorists from jail. The narco-traficanties, the cartels, would not muddy the waters with a demand like that. They would stay strictly on point. They just want the money. So, I don't think the bad guys are simple crooks. I think it is Hezbollah, I am sorry to say."

Rachel accepted this latest ill-tiding with a steely resolve that was either part of her DNA or had been trained into her as a survival mechanism. Her husband took occasional walks in space, over a hundred miles above the earth. She had ample time to accustom herself to fearing for the life of the man she loved.

She did stand alone in this stoic stance, be it real or be it pretend. Israeli women had a toughness that their sisters in other advanced countries lacked. They know, every day and all day every day, that their husbands and sons either were or might become engaged in hostilities at a moment's notice. Not one of them ever got used to it but they did find a way to cope with it, to understand that danger lurked nearby at all times. It made Israelis different from the Dutch or the Icelanders. They recognized in an entirely different way that life had a fragility to it, that life lasted for only a while and for some too short a while.

They did their best, men and women both, to live every day as if it were their last, to love their best, to achieve their highest goals-if possible-and to appreciate each moment as a gift they must treasure.

Here today and gone tomorrow had been a reality all too common when Arab terrorists had been able to slip through the checkpoints and plant bombs on a Jerusalem bus or blow up a pizzeria full of teenagers on a Friday night. Israel had the best medical device industry in the world when it came to high tech artificial limbs. Israel also had the best trauma counselors in the world.

Rachel and Shimon had first met at the Haifa hospital where Ari was taken after the space capsule landed in the Mediterranean. The emergency landing had Ari suffering from radiation sickness and his bashed head gave him a concussion on top of that. The concussion left Ari unconscious and when he eventually awoke, he had retrograde amnesia. Rachel had dealt with all that and still had her emotions intact and under control. Not that any of it had been easy.

Remembering the attentive concern that Shimon showed to her and to Ari in the hospital, she had invited him to the homecoming party for Ari upon his release from the hospital. She thought of them, Ari and Shimon, as friends and she supposed they were. She certainly trusted Shimon in every sense of the word, emotionally, physically and in a real world practical way as as well. She knew that if anyone could return Ari to her, it would be Shimon. If.

They ended the call. Shimon looked at the closed cell phone for a moment and thought about his own life. He pulled it apart, briefly, for examination. He had not married a Sabra like Rachel. Instead he married Stacey, an American from Charleston, South Carolina. She was the mother of his children, a bond impossible to break or even fray, unlike the bonds of marriage which had snapped apart as if they had never existed.

He and Stacy had met a decade before. She, a Jewish brunette, had come with friends on her first visit to Israel, young and full of life. Shimon had been their tour guide, older, handsome and from her perspective, a trifle exotic. It didn't take long for fireworks to begin between them, loud, colorful fireworks.

He smiled at the recollection of their courtship. It had seemed like never in the world had two people loved so hard, loved so deeply. He smiled wider as he remembered. And loved so often.

But now he had the truly precious children and a woman that he dealt with in a friendly way but for whom he had no romantic interest whatsoever. How strange that such fire had turned into utter indifference.

Chapter 14

LA JOLLA

"Special Agent Woods here" the FBI man spoke into his cell phone.

"Special Agent Woods, Officer Ryan here. I work out of the La Jolla precinct."

"Kevin Ryan?"

"Yes sir, the same. We met each other last year at the chief's retirement party," Ryan reminded the FBI man.

"I remember it well. We gave old Charlie a nice send-off I think. Besides, there were no arrests and no injuries, a real bonus for law enforcement retirement parties," Woods snarked but with some truth. A fair percentage of policemen self-medicated to excess as a way of dealing with the day-to-day horrors they dealt with.

"Maybe you can help me, Agent Woods. Let me tell you the situation we have here at the Westfield UTC. I need to cover my bases. We have a missing person identified as Eric Miller from Scottsdale Arizona. He was last seen just after 4:30 PM leaving Baker's Bookstore and heading for the adjacent parking lot."

"Who reported him missing?" Woods inquired, all business now and sharply focused.

"His wife, Bette Miller, said that she and her husband had arranged to meet at the outdoor fountain in the Plaza no later than 5:00 PM. They intended to walk down to that sushi place to meet their daughter. She thought he would have gone into the bookstore just on the Plaza."

"Was he seen in any other stores in the mall? They have a million of them."

"No."

"Did you find anything out at the bookstore? Did he buy anything? Did the staff remember seeing him?" Special Agent Woods spat out questions, rapid-fire.

"Yes, yes, yes. Miller bought a book and got directions for the parking area." Ryan answered the questions in sequence, just as rapidly.

"Did he have a vehicle at the location?"

"Yes, but his wife sent her daughter to check the car. No Miller there."

"If he didn't go to his car, why did he go to the parking area?" Just then the cell vibrated with an incoming call, from FBI HQ in Washington. "Kevin, hold the line, please. It's Washington on the line. I'll be right back to you." Woods put the local cop on hold and answered the incoming call from the demigods in Washington DC.

"This is Special Agent Woods," he said on the new call.

"Special Agent, Director Brown on the line with you." Totally surprised to have the Director of the FBI calling him personally, Woods involuntarily stood to attention. This call totally violated the Bureau's procedures and the chain of command. An eleven-year veteran, Woods had never met or spoken to this director or either of the two previous directors that had served in his time. Talking to the big boss was ...eventful.

"Yes, Director, I am listening." Woods did the arithmetic to estimate what time it was in DC. It was well past time for the director to have gone from the office.

"Woods, I'll get straight to the point. Deputy Director Sanford told me to go to you on this one, that you were the man for the job. We have a situation. Have you ever heard of the Israeli astronaut Air Ben Ora?"

"If memory serves me, Director Brown, he is an Israeli astronaut, one who went up to the International Space Station. He was part of that bunch that splashed down in the Mediterranean a while back. I guess that's about all I know, sir. Do you have information about him that you think I should know about?"

"Yes. According to the Israelis, he disappeared shortly after his book signing at Baker's Bookstore around 4:00 PM today, your time. Baker's Bookstore is located at the Westfield Plaza Mall in La Jolla. I'm sure you know where the Westfield Mall is. We traced the GPS receiver on Ben Ora's cell phone to Tijuana at approximately 2100 hours. He has vanished and his phone is in Mexico, got it, Woods?"

"Yes sir." Woods responded. He waited to speak until he heard everything that Director Brown had to tell him. He could tell that exalted personage what little he had to offer at that time.

"I'm sure I don't have to tell you, Special Agent Woods, that this is a messy situation with international implications. It gets even more complicated. Get this, a French astronaut named Andre Dubois sailed? Flew? Soared? How do you term a time spent spinning around the Earth in a tin can? He served, I guess that will do, the two of them were both on the same team that landed just off the coast of Israel in their escape capsule. Well, this Dubois was the victim of a kidnapping in Paris three days ago. He hasn't been seen since. The other two astronauts, an Indian and a Russian, are now under heavy guard 24/7 until we figure this out."

"Do you think the two kidnappings are in any way connected, sir? The chances that two astronauts on the same mission get kidnapped within days of each other not having a connection seem pretty small to me. But we follow the evidence. I guess stranger things have happened."

"It is too soon to tell, Woods. As you say, we just don't have any evidence either way. Gather evidence, puzzle it out, solve the crime, that's how we work. But the Israeli Mossad and the CIA will try to be all over our turf on this one and the State Department too and who knows who all else. The only way we can keep their noses out of our business is to solve the crime quickly. You are the FBI in your district. You will take the lead on this, Special Agent Woods."

"Yes sir, I understand everything you have told me. If I may, sir? I have some information for you." Woods kept his voice calm. If he did well with this case he might become Special Agent in Charge years before his career calendar would normally have him make the jump. He thought he was up to the task and eager to prove himself.

"Yes, go ahead."

"I have Detective Ryan of the San Diego Police Department on hold on another line sir. He reported a missing person, an American named Eric Miller. Mr. Miller was last seen at Baker's Bookstore and has now vanished. With your permission, Director, I will connect to Ryan and patch him in so we can have a three-way conversation."

"Sure, go ahead, you have my permission, Special Agent Woods."

"Detective Ryan, I have you on speaker phone. Also on the line is Director Brown of the Federal Bureau of Investigation."

"Hello Director Brown," Ryan said respectfully. In general, he thought the FBI stood for Fumble, Bumble, and Incompetent but it never hurt to be polite to someone so high up the proverbial food chain.

"Director Brown," Ryan continued. We believe that Eric Miller was kidnapped at or near the parking area close to Baker's Bookstore. It may be that Miller was not intentionally targeted but was at the wrong place at the wrong time. The intended victim was Ari Ben Ora, an Israeli author, and astronaut. Ben Ora is on a book signing tour of the US, of California just now. Special Agent Woods can give you any additional details that you might need."

"Thank you, Detective Ryan. Special Agent Woods, are you still on the line?"

"Yes, Sir.

"Do you think this Miller guy was a witness to the Ben Ora kidnapping? He just got scooped up because he happened to see what was happening?" Brown asked, his mind hurrying to keep up with this new information.

"I do think Miller was as you say scooped up because he was in the wrong place at the wrong time based upon our current information," Woods replied.

Woods paused for a breath or two.

"Be sure to keep me posted, Woods," Director Brown instructed and hung up.

"Of course, Sir."

"So, Ryan, what do you think, in light of the new information?" Special Agent Woods asked.

"This Israeli author and astronaut, Ben Ora, has a high profile. Everyone in Israel will know about him like he was a movie star or something. He might have been grabbed for ransom. Or, and I think this is more likely, he could have been grabbed by one of those terrorist groups, you know, the Palestine Front to Avenge the Dying Martyrs Brigade or something like that. They might want to swap him for some high-level terrorist that the Israelis have in jail. Or they might just kill him and brag to the world that they can kill any Jew they want to, any time. Or it might be something entirely else. The French guy getting grabbed in Paris might not be related," Ryan responded.

Woods chuckled. "We have to detect, right detective, before we make a judgment? Do you know anything about this Miller?"

"A little. He and his wife are here from Scottsdale Arizona. They came to La Jolla to celebrate the graduation of their daughter from UCSD. As far as we know, there is no connection between Miller and Ben Ora or Miller and criminal actors, anything like that. He bought Ben Ora's book and we think he went to find the author and get him to sign the book," Ryan replied.

"Do we know his occupation?" Woods asked, getting the basics down so he could form an opinion of the victim.

"He is in the investment field. He handles retirement planning for people, pensions, 401K plans, and that sort of thing. I guess Scottsdale is sort of like La Jolla, with lots of high-income people."

"OK, what about his wife?"

"She is a retired teacher. We have called out to the cops in Arizona to get any information they have on the couple. They seem just like they should, just good citizens, no ties to drug traffickers or anything like that."

"So far as we know after, what, a few hours of investigation?" Woods had seen ordinary-seeming people before who had deep secrets.

"Yes, so far."

"I do have something for you, Kevin. We have traced Ben Ora's cell phone to Tijuana this evening."

"Do you have an exact location?" Ryan asked.

"We pinpointed the location near the border, but we don't know if Ben Ora is there or if it is just his phone. I am on my way down there as soon as we finish. My office has the exact coordinates. I can call back when we find the phone and let you know."

"Thanks, I appreciate that. Our two cases are connected in some way.

If I find out anything interesting, I'll let you know. If you need or want to reach me, go ahead. I keep my phone near me 24 hours a day so you can call anytime," Ryan offered.

"Same here. We might be able to help each other. And the French guy too. I have to go with the idea that all three of the kidnappings are mixed up together somehow."

"Yes, thanks for sharing your information with me, Special Agent Woods." Ryan thought briefly how the shock of 9/11 had changed the often antagonistic and superior attitude of the FBI to a more cooperative one. He liked the new FBI better.

"I'll be in touch." With that, Special Agent Woods broke the connection.

Chapter 15

PARIS

Paris police detective Blanc did not make love to his mistress after all. She said shehad a touch of the flu. He made sympathetic noises at her, wished her a speedy recovery, left the wine and flowers he had brought for her, gave her a friendly French smooch to each of her cheeks, and departed feeling disappointed. He was tired in any case and perhaps it was all for the best.

He did eat a late meal prepared by his wife, a woman that he considered one of the great cooks in Paris. He was fond of her and enjoyed his time in conversation. She listened to his tale of the long day of detective work, the puzzling case of the kidnapped astronaut and then went to bed. The absurd question of making love to his wife did not even come up. Bastille Day and the anniversary of their nuptials took care of that event for the year.

The next morning he arrived at the precinct much refreshed, ready for another long day of often boring, sometimes interesting and very occasionally terrifying police work.

His boss, leader, sometimes mentor and in a sort of sideways way, his friend, Inspector Jean Gallant had news.

"We got the real name for that deader in the Seine. Philippe was actually someone named Zoran Coldovic," Gallant revealed with a happy snap in his tone.

Blanc gave a little shrug. "He looked like a Serb, even wet and with no fingers. Who made the ID?"

"I have an informer inside the Pink Panthers. He said Zoran was used by them to fence stolen property. He, so far as anyone knows, was just a low level scum, just scraping by doing the odd job here and there. He robbed sometimes but mostly served as a go between, helping more accomplished robbers get rid of their loot. He had no history of assault, kidnapping or murder."

"Did Zoran have any particular ideological leanings? Was he an ardent Catholic or a communist or anti-communist, anything like that?" Blanc inquired.

"Or did he hate the Catholic Church? It is a good question but my informant says not. Most Serbs are Eastern Orthodox, so he might well be Orthodox himself. The Orthodox and the Catholics do not get along very well at the best of times. But so far as we know at this point, he was just a crook. I think, and the informant thinks, that someone paid him to snare a gay priest, lure him to a hotel room, drug him and steal his car. Parties unknown used the Renault the next day to kidnap Dubois, right off the street in clear view of anyone around. Bold of them but stupid."

"I agree. The kidnappers were too bold, too public. They left too many clues behind. We will get them, we almost always do," Blanc asserted with vigor. "Was this Zoran even gay?"

"Probably not. We know for sure that he wasn't a regular in the red light district. No one there seemed to recognize his face. But someone got spooked when his photograph appeared on the front page of Le Monde. I don't blame them. I bet they expected some anonymous Serb low life to remain anonymous."

"Can we tie the finger-less Philippe/Zoran to the Dubois kidnapping?"

"That could be challenging, now that he's dead."

"Or do you think the Pink Panthers had any connection with the kidnapping inspector?"

"The Pink Panthers, not according to my informant and I expect that he would have that information. Lucky for us, criminals are not nearly as smart or clever as they think they are and they talk too much. He told me that in his circles the talk is just as it is with us, speculation, theories and wild conspiracies. They don't know who did the deed but they know it wasn't them," Gallant said.

"Well, maybe your informant is wrong. Zoran, as we suppose, a member of the Orthodox Church might have gotten tangled up in some kind of an anti-Catholic hate crime. Dubois is quite devout, I have learned," Blanc suggested.

"You think Zoran had a grudge against the Catholic Church for the war crimes against the civilian Serb population in World War II? I don't think so, Blanc. This Zoran doesn't seem to be a big thinker, much less a historian. Besides, the French Catholics were not involved in that killing and slaughter in the Balkans. Even the Italian Catholics under Mussolini viscerally opposed the slaughter of Serbs and Jews. I think Zoran is as likely to be angry about the Christians who were fed to the lions back in Roman days." Gallant dismissed the idea.

"Maybe your informant is pulling your chain. They could be involved," Blanc suggested. He and Gallant had had similar conversations many times. It is how they worked through and through every possible aspect of a case, leaving no stone unturned.

"It makes no sense. The Panthers smuggle arms from the East. They bring in drugs all the way from Afghanistan. They bring in those poor girls from Russia, the Ukraine, Romania and who knows where else to serve as sex slaves. But killing? They reserve that for their business rivals. Like the Italian Mafia they will kill other criminals to protect their interests, to guard their own turf, their protection rackets or the numbers game. But to be so public as this kidnapping? It isn't how they do things. I don't know of anyone they have murdered who was not a crook themselves. No civilians like Dubois. Killing crooks doesn't excite us in the department all that much, as you know Blanc. Killing or kidnapping some honest citizen, that is another story entirely. Kidnapping, or even the very loud, public murder and mutilation of Zoran, does not fit the Panther's profile. For them, it would bring unwanted attention from us, the police."

"OK boss, I am just talking out loud here. Who could have hired Zoran? Who masterminded the kidnapping?" Blanc asked.

"Let me examine the sequence of events, my young Padawan. A few weeks ago Andre Dubois returned to France from Israel. He used his status as an astronaut and a nation's celebrity to level very loud and serious accusations at the Catholic hierarchy. He flat out charged them with a conspiracy, in league with the Russians, in a dastardly plot to destroy the International Space Station, kill the whole crew of international astronauts and conspire against Israel in a very very serious and fundamental way."

Blanc nodded. He had seen Gallant do this before. It often worked, often they had solved even sticky cases by careful analysis like this.

"Next, Dubois gets abducted in broad daylight, in full view of many witnesses, very public. The vehicle used in the snatch is registered to a priest, of all people. The priest is on holiday, so the owner of the car is innocent. But the innocent priest loaned the car to his friend, another priest. The second priest, as we know, sometimes visited gay clubs for personal reasons. The gay priest admits to an interlude with a man he just met that evening, a man who drugged him and ripped off the borrowed automobile. The gay priest gives us a photo of the man who drugged him. The photo appeared on the front page of Le Monde, and the next thing we know, the seducer of the gay priest ends up dead, floating in the Seine with no fingers. Do you follow me so far, Blanc?"

"Ah oui, inspector, I do follow you. But I don't know who killed Zoran or who kidnapped Dubois. Who can we rule out? That will make a good start."

"We can rule out Father Martel. The lab discovered traces of ether in his blood. He was drugged. His alibi stands up strong and proud. Well, not proud I suppose."

"The archbishop will be happy to hear this news," Blanc opined, his voice betraying nothing in its tone but he did allow himself a hint of a wry smile. It was as if he said 'What has the Church come to that having a priest seduced in a gay sting seems so much better than a priest suspected of murder.' He would of course be right to think that.

"For the present, we must keep Zoran's identity a secret. We don't want the Serbs to think they have a snitch in their organization. Plus, we have no physical evidence or fingerprints to establish the deadder's identity. In due time, DNA testing will confirm his identity and we can go public without compromising my informant."

"The press will want to hear something. Already the hounds are baying us for not solving the Dubois case."

"We can stall for a while yet, I think. We will say that DNA testing suggests a Serbian or at least a Balkan ethnicity. We explain that we must make a painstaking investigation into the Serbian community in Paris to track down all the leads. That will take time. Even the jackals of the press understand that."

Blanc snorted derisively at the sunny notion. "If it isn't the Panthers, we have to consider the Israelis and the Russians," Blanc asserted.

"Whoever murdered Zoran wanted us to believe it was a Panther hit," Inspector Gallant replied with confidence.

"Not that I think you are wrong, but how did you come to that conclusion, inspector?" Blanc asked politely.

"Tell me, young Padawan, why do you think his face was spared?" Gallant answered smugly.

"I hate it when you call me that, boss. But the question is a good one. The killers went to a lot of trouble to eliminate any possible fingerprints. OK, they made good murder craft there. But they left his face easily identifiable, bad craft there. They wanted us to know who the deader was, at least to narrow down his ethnic background. With a face, posters and the newspapers, we would track down the victim sooner or later. So they wanted us to discover who Zoran was. Am I right?"

"Excellent deduction, Blanc. And I won't use the Padawan crack anymore if it bothers you. It is meant with affection, no?" Gallant raised an eyebrow as a plea for forgiveness.

Blanc nodded.

"The perpetrator wants us to use our time and resources to investigate the Serbian community in Paris, our limited resources at that. A thorough investigation of the Serbs could not be complete without an investigation of the Panthers. So that is why we will conduct only a routine investigation of the Serbs and bypass the Panthers entirely."

"And we cannot investigate the Serbs without investigating the Russians, right inspector?"

"So very right, Blanc. They have been allies forever. Had the Russians wanted to silence Andre, they would not have allowed a dead Serb to surface in the Seine. By deduction, Andre's kidnappers and Zoran's killers are likely Israelis."

"Well, that does make perfect sense." Blanc agreed

"It's all in the timeline, Blanc. As soon as we found Zoran's body from the Seine, our Israeli visitor jumped on the train to Reims where he met with the Moroccan waiter, Tanger, who we know is also Jewish. I just have to prove they were involved."

A civilian police clerk rushed to attract the inspector's attention.

"Please excuse the interruption, inspector. This bulletin just came in from Reuters. You should see it right away." The woman waved a strip of computer paper.

The round, too stuffed face of Inspector Jean Gallant lost a bit of its ruddiness as he read the scrap of paper.

"Reuters reports that Ari Ben Ora was kidnapped in California last night. This is the second astronaut to be kidnapped in a week, and both of them from the same mission."

"Jesus, that news sort of muddies up our waters," Blanc opined.

"It is too soon to say, Blanc. It could be a copycat crime. Or it could provide additional clues for us. It does, as you say, muddy up the water for us. But be of good heart. In every rain cloud there is a silver lining." He gave Blanc a stern, resolute look.

"We are the finest detectives in France, Blanc. We will detect, we will solve the case, we will triumph."

Chapter 16

PARIS

The embassy operator, an eighteen-year-old Israeli girl named Naomi Roth, born in Trenton New Jersey and doing her military service, transferred the incoming call.

In a designated room at the Eighth Arrondissement Police Station, that of the Elysee, a recording device waited with its machine patience to document for history the incoming and outgoing telephone conversations of a humble Jewish waiter, Shai Tanger. It had just clicked on.

"Monsieur Levi, I have talked to my wife and she agrees with you and Adam. As soon as you receive the official approval, we will prepare to relocate to Israel. We are very excited," Tanger said, the excitement clear in his voice. He would be moving to a new land.

"Congratulations, Monsieur Tanger, this is wonderful news. I will call Adam and let him know you will be coming. He will be glad. The embassy staff will contact you to help with the paperwork and to give you a good feel for what will happen to you, when and how it will happen and everything you can expect. Israel is not like Holland or some other country where you just cross the border and sign in. You will have formal language lessons in Hebrew, for example. When you arrive, people will help you get a job, perhaps as a waiter, perhaps something else, or perhaps you will want to go into business. Israel is a small country but it has different areas, different topography, everything from the beach to the desert to the Golan which is a sort of an elevated plain. We have welcomed millions of new citizens, Shai, we do it better than anyone else, perhaps better than any nation has ever done it. People who care will help you and your wife get settled. You can count on it."

"And Shai, you have me just a phone call away. I will be back home soon, you have my personal phone number. I will be there to help smooth out any rough spots. I do not want you to hesitate about calling me if you need to. OK?"

"That is very reassuring, Monsieur Levi, believe me. When I came to France, the French had nothing as you describe. We were left completely alone to fend for ourselves. This sounds much better. My wife and I both thank you from the bottom of our hearts."

"You are entirely welcome, Shai. I mean that in every way. You are welcome to come and live in my country, to live and love there, to grow prosperous and happy there. I know that you will do well in Israel."

"If I need to, I certainly will call upon you, Monsieur Levi. Shalom."

"Oh, Shai, can we give you a lift to the airport? We have someone who can do that for you, a driver from the embassy."

"No thank you, Monsieur. We have that taken care of. Shalom."

"Shalom."

Blanc knocked on the inspector's door with his experienced police knuckles.

"I just pulled the tape of their phone conversation. It is brief, boss."

"Go ahead and play it for me. Brief I can handle," Gallant responded.

The two detectives listened to the tape, Blanc for the second time.

"So, Tanger is going to Israel. Who the fuck is Adam? Son of a bitch Blanc, Shai, and Shimon just created the perfect alibi. These guys suspected that we would tape the call, didn't they? Shai could have used a phone booth just as easily. They are onto us," the inspector railed.

"But for them to suspect us, wouldn't Tanger have to have something to cover up?" Blanc asked reasonably.

"Oui, exactly, so they concocted Adam, a mutual friend who doesn't exist."

Not at all convinced, Blanc decided to let his leader rant on. "What can we do, inspector? Tanger has no criminal record, not even a traffic citation to his name. I don't see how we can interfere with him at all."

"Merde', Blanc. We played the phone tape and it is we who got played. I am not happy about this," Gallant fumed.

Just then the phone rang on the inspector's desk.

Gallant picked it up, listened for a second, and said "Hang on. I'll put you on speakerphone so Blanc can hear you too." Then he mouthed 'It's Francois.'

"Go ahead Francois, we can both hear you now. How fares the lady Michelle this morning?"

The policemen surveilling the French woman reported. "A few minutes ago she picked up Shimon at the Israeli embassy. He carried a suitcase. It looks like she's driving him to Charles de Gaulle airport."

"Do you have Jean Claude with you?" Gallant asked.

"Oui, right here."

"If they split up I want you to stay with Michelle, Francois. Jean, if they split up, you stick with the Israeli. Carry on, you two," Gallant ordered his men. He put the phone down and turned to Blanc, right next to him.

"I have to call Adrian Goddard again. I have to beg another favor from him."

"What, what favor, inspector?" Blanc wondered.

"I will need a warrant to search Tanger's bank accounts."

"Do you even know what bank he uses?"

"Soon, Blanc. I am the head of detectives. Knowing the bank will be the easy part," he responded with a smug snarl. Gallant was not in his best mood.

Michelle stopped in front of British Air, signaled with her right blinker and waited for space occupied for the moment with a Peugeot to finish and depart. She watched the couple at the curbside. With arms enfolded, the woman kissed her man passionately before letting him go. The woman drove away, perhaps with a tear in her eye. Michelle slid into the open space and turned off her engine, encompassing them is a bubble of quiet.

"I might as well fly back to Ashkelon. I can't fathom all of this. First

Andre and now Ari. I don't know what is going on or how to think about it," Michelle complained.

"I couldn't agree more, Michelle. Everybody close to Andre is considered a suspect as far as the French authorities are concerned. You can park your car and go to Israel right now if you want."

"Not just yet, I think. But what about you? When will you return to Israel, Shimon?"

"I don't know. I do know that I will be thinking of you, no matter where I am. I will worry about you," he replied.

"And I will be thinking about you, Shimon. Please be careful. Be careful for my sake." She nearly whispered the last few words.

Michelle placed her hand in his and gave it a squeeze. She leaned in and kissed him warmly right on the lips. She took her time about it and did it right. It was the kind of kiss that a man remembered, perhaps for his entire life.

Then she hit the trunk release. Shimon scurried around and fetched his suitcase. He closed the trunk with a thump and hustled into the terminal. He was gone and she felt empty and deprived.

Detective Jean Claude pulled to a stop at the curb several cars behind where Michelle took a minute or two to say goodbye to Shimon at Charles de Gaulle airport. He left his car to follow Shimon into the terminal. Shimon paid no attention to any possible tail.

Either he didn't think the French would bother or with his diplomatic status, he just didn't care. Jean Claude had no trouble following his suspect, up until his suspect entered the security zone. He could no longer follow Shimon into the area served by British Airways. Shimon could take any one of a couple of dozen departing flights. Jean Claude wanted to know which one.

He waved down one of the horde of airport security guards.

"Bonjour officer, I am Detective Jean Claude of the Paris Metropolitan Police," the policeman announced in a friendly if somewhat imperious way. He pompously displayed his police credentials which held his badge and a photo ID.

The security guard, a thin young fellow, his face covered in acne scars from his teen years, looked up in earnest alarm. "Do we have a problem at our airport, detective?" The guard wanted to know.

"No Monsieur, but I need to ask you a small favor." Jean Claude identified Shimon as he made his way by jerks and fits up the line to the security checkpoint with its explosive sniffers and x-ray machines.

"This is part of an ongoing and very important investigation. I cannot say which but if I could you would know the case from the press reports. It involves both serious crime, the most serious crime, Monsieur, but also national security. I would ask you to help the Metro Police by following that man to his departure gate and then let me know which flight he is boarding.

"We may contact our colleagues in another country to pick up the scent there, but we need to know which country he is headed for, no?" Jean Claude offered the man a thin but serious smile.

"It will be my pleasure, detective. Please remain here. I will return in a moment or two, never fear," the young man enthused.

When the security guard returned a few minutes later he had a request of his own. "Detective, I would like to end my career as a security guard and join the police force, to upgrade my status from the lowest level in law enforcement to the highest level. Might I be so bold as to ask you to be a reference for me?"

"Yes, of course. You have proven that you are helpful and reliable. Please take my card. Feel free to list my name," Jean Claude said generously if fraudulently as he handed the young man his card. As if. No one got on the Metro Police rolls without some heavy inside help, brother, daughter or generations-long family ties to the department were common enough. "What flight did our suspect take, agent?"

"Our suspect even as we speak is getting on a jet for Los Angeles. You should have many hours to arrange an agent to meet the flight detective." The security guard had mentally moved already into a post with the Metro Police.

Jean Gallant scarcely controlled his steaming anger with the magistrate. He remained as impassive as he could as he listened to the man blather on.

"Inspector Gallant," said the magistrate, "I cannot authorize a warrant to search his man's bank records on hearsay. We must have some evidence of a crime. It is still perfectly legal for French Jews to immigrate to Israel, and you know it." He gave Gallant a disapproving eye which Gallant could feel even through the phone line.

"Your honor, I fully understand your decision. Thank you for your time with me today. Please give my best regards to Madame Godard." Gallant ended the call on the best terms he could muster, proud that he had not finished the call by screaming into the receiver.

He hung up and flipped through his Rolodex for another number, his one for his contact at the French Public Utility Commission, Frederick La Claire. As soon as he had the number, he dialed it.

"Fredrick, bonjour, this is Inspector Gallant. Comment ca va?"

"Bien, merci. How may I assist the Metropolitan Police today, Jean?"

"Frederick, I need a small favor, if you please. I need the bank and location for one of your paying customers in Reims. His name is Shai Tanger. He lives at the following address....."

Gallant had been a detective for a long time. He knew a dozen ways to skin a cat.

Chapter 17

MOSCOW

At the Kremlin, the imposing if ramshackle citadel of Russian power, Dan Rabin presented his credentials to the Russian President, Dmitry Lebedev. Rabin had just arrived as the Israeli Ambassador to the vast Russian state.

When the pair had exchanged handshakes and polite greetings, Lebedev smiled at his guest in an almost friendly way. He opened and offered to Rabin a mahogany cigar box cornered with gilded brass fittings. "May I offer you a smoke, Ambassador Rabin?"

"I rarely say no to a Cuban, Mr. President." Rabin responded, an almost friendly smile on his own face. The meeting was getting off to a good start on both sides.

"Let's proceed into the sitting room, Mr. Ambassador. I have drinks set up for us. We can get to know each other a bit and have some comfort as we do so."

Dmitry led, Rabin followed him into the next room. Wood paneling layered the walls. The ceiling carried a heavy load of gold leaf. Massive draperies parted the huge windows and sunlight filled the room casting reflections upon the brush strokes of more than a dozen works by the greatest of the French Impressionists.

Rabin had no claims as an art scholar. As a well educated man he did recognize the style of Manet, Renoir and Claude Monet. Others there he could not name by their style but at least recognized as being French and of the period. More than the imposing building with its heavy decoration, marble and gilt, the display of great art impressed him. And delighted him. He liked the impressionists a good deal, even if he had not made a study of them.

He gestured at the wall of beautiful paintings with his cigar and exclaimed, "What a lovely thing, to have such exquisite work to see every day. It must give you a good deal of pleasure, Mr. President."

"Yes, in my position, I can have works brought from our famous museums and put up here. If I tire of them, which I doubt, I suppose I can have them traded out for something else. The Czars did manage to collect a vast trove of the greatest art in the world while they wrecked the country. But to the drinks. What will you have?"

"Vodka, Mr. President."

"An excellent choice." Lebedev turned to a servant. "Anatoly, make us two vodkas on the rocks, please. Let's try Moskovskaya Osobaya today, shall we?"

The sitting room soon collected a haze of fragrant smoke from the very finest of Cuban cigars. The two men, the President of Russia and the Ambassador from Israel, puffed away, seated in elaborately overstuffed and over-decorated chairs. They clinked the heavy-cut crystal glasses in a mutual toast by reaching over a low coffee table, also antique and over-decorated in the heavy-handed Russian style and each wished the other good health.

Dmitry took the first gulp.

When he had absorbed the shock of the vodka blast, the President of the Russian Federation looked directly at Ambassador Rabin and without a preliminary thought asked, "Are you going to kill the Frenchman?"

Rabin didn't turn a hair. "If I had him, I would not have him die a martyr. Someone would take up his cause. I actually thought you had him, Mr. President. The list of possible suspects is pretty short, I think you will agree."

"I never said that we had him. The important thing for all of us is that Dubois doesn't talk. I concur with your position. Like you, I think it would be counterproductive to have him killed. We can permit no leaks, Ambassador Rabin. You have Dubois' computer, the Catholic Church has Father Gauthier's computer, and I have Yuri's computer. We can allow no leaks." Lebedev swirled the ice and vodka around in his glass. His voice had a measured tone to it as if he were explaining some intricate process to a boy, how to fix a running toilet or what spices to mix in an omelet. He did not have a tone that was especially pitched to discuss the life or death of a human being.

Lebedev had to presume that the Israelis had recovered the information about the plot from the hard drive on Andre Dubois computer they recovered from the capsule. The Russian still didn't know that the Israelis had known about the plot from their Paris embassy well before the doomed escape capsule fell to earth in the Mediterranean Sea off the coast of the Levant.

"Ambassador Rabin, this agreement we have is costing Russia millions of dollars. I could send Iran the missiles, get the money from them, and be forgiven for diminishing Israel. Beating up on Israel is generally accepted in Europe, South American, Asia and Africa."

"So, what is stopping you from selling your weapons to the Iranians?"

Beyond a first polite sip Rabin had not touched the liquor in the expensive glass in his hand. He just held the cut crystal like a stage prop.

That got a reaction. Lebedev's face took a fast rush of color, and he barked out.

"What is stopping us? I will tell you. We don't want millions of our people to even consider the possibility that Russian leaders, me in particular, could order the death and destruction of our own space station and our supply ship. We don't want them to believe that we ordered the Pakistanis to launch their nuclear missile into space in order to destroy the escape capsule on its descent to earth. No one would forgive us."

"Mr. President, if you sell Iran the missile systems, you would leave us with no choice, as you can well imagine. We would have to release the Dubois e-mails. You know that you would do the same if the shoe were on the other foot. But, Mr. President, Israel is not without empathy." He graced his host with a small smile that seemed genuine but of course was totally phony. "Our economists are formulating a ten-year economic plan to allow more Russian exports into Israel that can replace the lost Iranian revenue. We will provide you with a list of products. Your government simply needs to approve the export of those products."

"Excellent, excellent, the prime minister will be delighted to hear of your proposal. Another glass of vodka, Mr. Ambassador?"

"No, thank you, Mr. President. I have reached my limit," Rabin graciously declined. He placed his heavy glass, still mostly full, on the coffee table as a signal that he was finished with it.

"Mr. Ambassador, you have not mentioned the Ari Ben Ora situation," Lebedev probed his guest.

"You see, Mr. President, this is what too much vodka can do to me."

Lebedev could barely contain his laughter. He could easily see how little the level of liquor in the diplomat's glass had gone down.

Rabin looked the Russian right squarely in the eye.

"Mr. President, the kidnappers have made contact. They identified themselves as the Muslim Brigade."

"Never heard of them," Dmitry stated.

Rabin shrugged. "A ragtag drug smuggling Hezbollah cell in Tijuana gave itself a name."

"What are their demands?" Lebedev asked.

"They demand the release of several Arab mass murderers, as usual. My government will be ever so grateful if you exert pressure on the Syrian and Iranian regimes. Hezbollah takes its orders from those governments. Russia's intercession coupled with pressure from the United States could very well save the lives of Ari Ben Ora and also the American who was taken at the same time."

"Mr. Ambassador, it will be my pleasure to help you secure the release of Ari Ben Ora and for Hezbollah's sake, they better release the American alive and unhurt as well."

Rabin liked what he heard. Dmitry glanced at his watch. The meeting was over.

"Mr. President, thank you so much for the pleasure of your company." They shook hands and Rabin returned to his embassy, a ticklish task well done.

Chapter 18

LOS ANGELES

Shimon managed a couple of good blocks of sleep on the flight from Paris to Los Angeles. Some good sleep because the flight took just short of twelve hours. Blocks of sleep because in the nature of things with long-distance air travel, he would have something or someone wake him from his slumber at odd times and for odd reasons. Still, he felt fairly refreshed when he arrived in the City of Angels.

He had little in the way of baggage and a diplomatic passport so he slid through customs and the security belt with little effort. He quickly spotted an old colleague waiting for him. Gideon Asher was a fit and trim forty years old, still had most of his hair, and had a warm smile for Shimon when he spotted him. His intelligent gray eyes looked pleased to reside in a face blessed by the Southern California sun and kept smooth by golf, body surfing, and weekly fiercely competitive handball games.

"Welcome to La La Land Shimon," Gideon said as they clasped hands.

"Gideon, it is good to see you again. You look like a film star. This duty seems to suit you very well."

"This is your first time to L.A., or so they tell me, Shimon. Too bad it has to be because of such a dire event."

"Yes, and yes. My first time in the land of the magic lantern, the Beach

Boys and Mickey Mouse. I hope we can get Ben Ora back quickly and safely. Do you like it here?"

As they talked they walked through the huge terminal to find the baggage claim carousels and collect the single bag Shimon had checked.

"I like it very much. L.A. has a unique culture with the beaches and Hollywood, the music industry, and all that. What I like about L.A. is that it is a very 'Jewish' town, the entertainment industry having loads of Jews at all levels. But I am on the downhill slope. In six months my tour will end and I will be off to sunny Madrid, land of olives, bullfights, museums, and dour churchmen."

"I haven't been much in Spain. I guess Madrid is not a 'Jewish' town?" Shimon grabbed for his bag but Gideon snapped it up first. The two men headed out into the bright L.A. Sunshine.

"I got it, Shimon. Madrid used to be a 'Jewish' city, back before the Inquisition or so I am told," Asher noted sarcastically.

"The embassy car is right here at the curb. We can park anywhere with our diplomatic license plates. It is very convenient. We can stop for coffee or lunch if you want to eat. One thing we have here is authentic Jewish delicatessens in abundance. People still move out here from the Bronx and I don't blame them. Living in Los Angeles must seem like heaven after the East Coast."

"That's a great idea. I am starving. They don't give you much on flights these days and what they do give you is pretty poor fodder, if you ask me. I have been in Paris for a while and I am afraid that I have been badly spoiled in the food department. The French sure can put out a plate that will make your taste buds dance. But what time do we have to be in San Diego?"

"We have about an hour and a half to spare, plenty of time to eat." They took a few seconds to gaze around at the balmy, hazy Southern California day. Shimon, glad to be free after twelve hours in the crowded belly of the aluminum tube, gazed at the sky, felt the sun on his face, and smiled. Just before slipping into the back seat of the car, he put on a pair of mirrored aviator sunglasses. He thought he looked cool in them.

When they had settled in, Gideon told the embassy driver where to take them for lunch.

"Nate and Al's on Beverly," Benjamin Lutz, the burly driver/bodyguard repeated and off they went.

Gideon took on a tour guide's manner. "Shimon, Nate, and Al's is a famous deli, at least here in L.A. Some of the Hollywood crowd hangs out there. We might see some celebrities or at least some wannabe celebrities. The food is first-rate too, comfort food for Jews. Nate and Al's has catered to Hollywood sorts for five decades now. Otto Preminger used to eat here regularly."

Shimon had only a dim and hazy notion of which Hollywood producer had done what in the nineteen fifties and didn't care much one way or another. He hadn't come all this way because he was some starry-eyed move fan.

"Enough about the rich and famous already. Please, Gideon, tell me what we know about Ari's kidnapping, will you?"

"Sure, not that we know all that much, I'm afraid. The FBI will brief us at their office. Since you were first to make contact with the abductors, they will want to interrogate you right off." Gideon grinned. "I would like to watch that, the FBI trying to pry information out of you."

Ben interrupted from the driver's seat. "Guys, if we do not run into any traffic problems, we should be at Nate and Al's in less than half an hour. We hit the 405 Interstate and north to Highway 55. From there we merge to Santa Monica Boulevard."

"OK, thanks, Ben," Gideon replied. Then he turned back to Shimon. "So, how are the kids getting along?"

"They're OK," Shimon replied shortly.

"Are they alright with the divorce?"

"They seem to be."

"How about you? Are you seeing anybody?"

Shimon seemed uncomfortable with this question. He did not reply immediately, thinking over the answer. "I am not sure. It is complicated."

On the flight, Shimon had thought about Michelle, thought about her a great deal, in fact. French women were very expressive, and her body language was unmistakable-as were her kisses. She did say her relationship with Andre had been strained. It was indeed complicated.

"You want to talk about it?"

"Not right now. But you tell me, Gideon, what about your wife and kids?"

"Well, they have settled down very nicely in LA. This is a great, sunny place to be a kid," Gideon replied.

Ben never quite came to a full stop when they came to the Santa Monica Boulevard intersection but suddenly slammed on his brakes to avoid piling into three careless pedestrians. The three J walkers glanced at the embassy car. Their expressions changed from disdain to hostility when they saw the small Israeli flag mounted by the headlight. One of the trio offered the single-finger salute and a nasty scowl.

"Fuck Israel!" The guy shouted. "Long live Palestine." He stopped in front of the car, blocking their progress.

Ben lowered the window and shouted back at the man. "Clear the road or I will call the police to clear you off."

"Fuck you too." The man kept waving his middle finger but he grudgingly gave ground. When the J walkers cleared the way, Ben made his right turn.

"Gideon, you told me LA Was a Jewish town. That reminded me of Paris," Shimon said.

"It is mostly in pockets here and there. On the campuses too often there is a virulent Boycott, Divestment and Sanction, BDS, movement. That is a constant source of anti-Israel and anti-Semitic propaganda. It works too, with some people. That guy looked like a druggie to me, some loser that at some level blames his problems on Jews. Jews are always handy, aren't we?" Gideon suggested with what kindness he could muster.

"You don't have to be a rocket scientist or even sane to throw a brick through a delicatessen window or to light a fire at a synagogue," Shimon replied.

"Here we are." Gideon announced.

Ben slid the car smoothly but illegally into the curb signed and painted to be the reserve and domain of the taxi cab fleet.

"Here you go, gents, right in front. An embassy license plate gets you a parking place no matter where you go," Ben boastfully revealed.

Inside a lady greeted them with a smile and a stack of menus. She looked about seventy but had the shape of a thirty-year-old. Her hair had the color and brittleness of stable straw at the end of a hot summer's day. Her skin looked like an aged oak wine barrel, darkly tan but with all the usual wrinkles pulled taught, and smooth. She had great teeth, movie star teeth, bright and white. Her eyes matched her smile like she really did feel some happiness that they had stopped into her place to eat. Perhaps she did.

"Do you handsome young boys want a table or a booth?" She opened with a full broadside of professional bombast. She made it seem genuine.

"How about that booth over there in the corner?" Gideon directed.

"Sure boys, right this way."

On the way over they heard the two couples who followed them bantering among themselves but loudly. From their apparent age, they might be talking loudly as a matter of habit, people with failing hearing often did that. Loud conversation attempted to make up for diminished acuteness in the ear department.

"Harold, do you see those three men, the three young guys over there?" One of the women asked.

"Yeah, I see um, Marcia. Are they famous or something? Are they movie people?"

"They are from the Israeli embassy, Harold," Marcia incorrectly informed her husband.

"The embassy sits in the capital of the host nation. In LA, Israel maintains a consulate, Harold revealed to Marcia.

"They have a Star of David flag on their car. Harold, they parked right in the taxi zone. They get curbside parking for free."

"They also have diplomatic immunity so they can't get towed. But those guys are not Moshe Dayan. Lenny and I remember Moshe Dayan. Now there was a real Jewish hero. I saw him at Nate and Al's once. I remember that better than when I saw John Lennon in New York, right on the street one time."

"Harold, where was I?" Marcia asked turbulently.

"You were still in High School then. I hadn't met you yet. It was way back in the late 60s.

"Oh." She still seemed peeved.

"You know he wore that eye patch? He got his eye shot out fighting the French," Harold said.

"The French?" Lenny, the second man asked in astonishment. "Why the Hell was he fighting the French?"

"I don't really know. I read that somewhere. But things have changed. Beverly Hills was in love with Moshe Dayan and Israel after the Six Day War. What you see now on TV are Israelis evicting Palestinians from their homes and the crazy Haredi as they burn tires and throw stones at ordinary

Jews like us. And all because we drive-not walk mind you, just drive -on Saturday," Harold opined.

"Well, and some people eat bacon too," Lenny's wife Susan added with a knowing smirk.

"They don't like that either. People should mind their own business and not throw rocks at people who drive cars on Saturday," The Lenny added.

"You got that right, Lenny. I tell you, Israel went downhill when that terrorist Begin became prime minister back in the eighties. After Begin they elected Shamir, another terrorist from the Stern Gang. They were even worse than the Irgun. It's no wonder Queen Elizabeth and Prince Charles never visited Israel."

Then they passed out of hearing, even at their enhanced volume.

"Are you hearing them? Cripes!" Ben asked.

"You'd have to be deaf not to," Shimon responded.

"That guy is not altogether misinformed. Israel used to have broader support among the Jewish community, not just in LA but all over the US. I really don't think that "Exodus", blockbuster or not, could be made today. The media is too enamored with the Palestinian cause," Gideon added.

"Doesn't that asshole know the British reneged on pledges and closed Palestine to Jewish immigration when they were trying to escape the Nazis? The Brits caved into Arab pressure, and millions of Jews who couldn't leave Europe died in gas chambers. Even after the Jews were liberated from the German death camps, the Brits interned them in allied camps on the island of Cypress in order to keep them out of Palestine. No wonder Begin and Shamir attacked the British. They wanted them out of Palestine," Shimon continued.

"Shimon, not all the British were against us. Without Captain Wingate's dedication to the Zionist cause and training, the Haganah would not have been an effective fighting force," Gideon Asher gently corrected.

"Gideon's got a point. It was the British army and navy that kept Rommel out of Palestine," Ben recalled.

"You win, but I still think Harold and Lenny need a history lesson," Shimon countered, some of the heat leaving his voice.

"What would you tell them?" Ben had a tone of genuine interest in his question. Yes, what would you tell someone who did not understand how history had unfolded?

"I would say that they have not given Begin credit for having the courage to bomb Saddam Hussein's nuclear reactor, that's what I would tell them."

Gideon nodded that he understood and accepted that bit of wisdom, little known and little discussed in the modern century. "And you should tell those guys it was Begin who made peace with the Egyptians and returned the Sinai, land we conquered, for a promise of peace. It has been a cold peace for over forty years but it has still been a peace. Peace is better than a war with Egypt four times in twenty-five years."

Ben grinned. "I think you did. Harold is within earshot. He is glaring at us. I hope he paid attention. You rarely get a chance to hear a history lesson by real experts from the Israeli diplomatic corps." He winked at Gideon.

"Hello boys, would you like to order now?" The waitress asked. She looked nothing like the leathery old hostess who sat them. The waitress has twice the heft of the older woman, sparkling blue eyes in a bovine face and blonde braids like Heidi. Her friendly, overly intimate manner was the only connection she had to the other woman.

"Coffee, a number 2, a 3, and a 7," Gideon ordered, pointing to who got what as he spoke.

The waitress blazed a smile at him and jotted quickly as she said "You got it handsome."

A busboy slammed a plate of dill pickles onto the table and hurried away.

Gideon launched into his professional mode as soon as the boy vanished. He pitched his voice to reach only his tablemates and so it would not carry to Harold and Lenny. "We'll be meeting with Detective Ryan of the San Diego Police. He works out of the La Jolla station. Also FBI Special Agent Woods and the chief of police from Tijuana, Alberto Diaz. Our position, the position of the government of Israel is that the Muslim Brigade is a Hezbollah cell taking orders from Hezbollah in Lebanon. This provides Israel with a great opportunity to diplomatically isolate and devalue Hezbollah."

"Gideon, do you think the FBI may try to link this kidnapping to the taking of Andre Dubois in France?" Shimon asked.

Ben answered. He drove the car today as if he were just a driver but the mission was not too small to have someone who only did one small thing. He was a proper shu shu man, a trained member of the intelligence service. He was smart and deadly, not just a body for odd tasks

"In the Dubois case, the French have received no ransom demands or communications from the abductors in any form. Isn't that right Shimon? You just came from there."

"Yes, the profile is altogether different from Ari's abduction. The French have to identify the Serb or some Balkan type that they have marked as the perp. They think he stole the car used to kidnap Andre."

Two waitresses rushed to the table holding lunch plates and French fries. They slid the right order to the right customer with no talking and got it exactly right. Quick as a wink, their blue-eyed, pudgy waitress asked "How about some more coffee, fellas?"

"Yes, please," Gideon replied.

"Mustard and relish are behind the napkins," she said.

"The fries are delicious," Gideon said with a mouthful of pastrami.

Chapter 19

PARIS

"Michelle, I think you like Shimon." Lucille mentioned with a bit of a wicked glint in her eye, wicked but at the same time, happy.

"I do like him, Maman. But I feel guilty too. Andre left Israel because I refused to leave with him. I could have returned to France, but I didn't." Michelle answered with a frown on her face and a distinct disturbance in her heart.

"Don't feel guilty, sweetling. He wanted you to give up your dream. Andre would have still been kidnapped even if you had returned to Paris with him. Maybe you would have been taken with him. You did not kidnap Andre. The bad guys have the responsibility and the guilt for that terrible deed, not my baby girl." Lucille put her hand on her daughter's shoulder in comfort.

"Perhaps you are right, Maman."

Her mother looked straight at her and spoke in a strong clear voice, a voice that cut through Michelle's emotional haze. "Michelle, were you able to recapture what you had with Andre before? Did you love him in the old way when he left you behind?"

"Oh Maman, we tried, we really did. Andre lost me to Ari Davidson and I lost my Ari to senseless murder. The rotten bastard who shot him did not even shoot Ari in particular. He just wanted to kill a Jew, any Jew and my brilliant, handsome, kind Ari came in front of his gun. Three years ago, when we broke up, do you know what I said to Andre?"

"I think you will tell me."

"I told him 'We will always have Paris.'" Michelle said with a wistful smile of remembrance on her beautiful face.

"You didn't! That is what Humphrey Bogart said to Ingrid Bergman in 'Casablanca.' Her mother nearly sputtered, trying to control a laugh.

"I know, Maman, I know. And I also know that Andre was a fish out of water in Israel."

"Well, we should not be surprised at that. He lost his father because of an Israeli airstrike and lost you to your archaeologist, and Israeli by the way. He might have lost you to another Israeli if things with Shimon work out the way they seem to be going." She raised an eyebrow in mute inquiry. Mothers can do that with daughters.

"We must not forget that Andre was raised in a Catholic orphanage and that this is still France, with all that historical baggage," Lucille continued.

"Maman, you, Papa, and me, we are all French, as French as French can be. We do not and Papa did not think like Marshall Petain or Archbishop Marcel Lebevre. I don't remember you or Papa ever uttering a bad word toward Jews."

"God bless your father, and may he rest in peace. Now, sweetling, I have to tell you the rest of the story."

"Tell me what Maman? What story?"

"You already know that your father was born in Menton in 1947," Lucille began.

"Yes, of course. I know where Menton is, over on the other side of Nice, over almost to the Italian border."

"His parents moved to Menton to escape the Nazis in occupied Paris. Menton was in the Italian zone. Benito Mussolini resisted Hitler and would not permit Jewish deportations from the Italian zone, thank God. Still, many Jews in Europe converted to Catholicism, but Hitler deported converts with the same fervor and zeal. With Hitler, it was about bloodlines, not religion. Granny and Grandpa were Jewish. They converted to Catholicism in 1942. When your father was born, he was baptized into the church. They never told your father, and Granny and Grandpa took the secret to their graves."

"Papa was Jewish!" Michelle exclaimed and gathered her thoughts. "How did you find out?"

"Grandpa had an older brother from Strasbourg, Alfred. In June of 1940, Alfred was deported by the Germans and sent to Dachau. He survived and in 1945 he was liberated by the Americans but was interned in Germany until Israel became a state. Alfred settled in Tel Aviv, married, and had three children. He was a paratrooper in the 1956 Suez campaign and died fighting the Egyptians. We know this because Alfred's son Nathan showed up one day. I think you were ten at the time, three years before your father was diagnosed with pancreatic cancer. Nathan had family pictures, and we received confirmation from church records."

"So Papa knew. Why did you keep this from me for so long, Maman? We have family in Israel."

"I didn't tell you because your father wanted it that way. I think if he were alive today, he would want me to tell you."

"This is all very sudden and shocking, Maman. I have to think."

Chapter 20

SAN DIEGO

They left Nate and Al's. Ben weaved through the streets of Beverly Hills and eventually made it onto Interstate 5. Over an hour later they passed through the pristine swath of unspoiled land in the enormous Marine base of Camp Pendleton. Shimon looked out the car window and watched in awe as the orange California sun descended on the horizon like a caress, spawning pastel colors across the skyline and the Pacific. Gorgeous tangerine, lavender, and maroon tones stretched across the sky delighting the eye and the soul.

But near the Carlsbad exit traffic slowed to a standstill and didn't ease up until after the second La Jolla exit. By the time they made it to downtown and found the FBI office, it was a little after six PM.

"Sorry to be a little late," Gideon apologized to the officers of the law. "We got caught in traffic. We aren't as used to the ebb and flow of the freeways as native Californians." He gave an apologetic little smile.

"Better late today than early tomorrow," Special Agent Woods quipped. "Let me introduce you all to Detective Ryan from the La Jolla precinct and Chief Alberto Diaz from the Tijuana Police Department."

The men exchanged polite greetings and handshakes and took seats around a circular table. On one side of the table, staff had stacked current newspapers. In the center of the table, within easy reach, they had placed a water pitcher and glasses on little paper doilies. Notepads and pencils sat close at hand at each person's station. With his right hand, Woods raised the pile of newspapers. "This is three days' worth of papers, and the Ora and Miller kidnappings are still the front-page story. Three days, gentlemen, and we have not found the stolen men. The press has noticed."

"Talk radio is full of the same thing," Ryan added.

"We listened to a few stations on the way down," Gideon concurred. "It seemed like all they could do was speculate and criticize."

"Alright gentlemen, what I expect from you and the Israeli government is co-operation, nothing less."

"Of course," Gideon replied, nodding his agreement.

"Special Agent Woods, you have my complete cooperation and that of my department as well. This kind of publicity does not do my city a bit of good," Chief Diaz noted.

Woods continued his recitation.

"Here are the facts as we know them at this moment. Approximately an hour and a half after the kidnappings, a security camera captured a brown 1992 Toyota Corolla crossing into Tijuana. The time stamp on the crossing stood at 5:14 PM. The car had four passengers, two in the front seat including the driver, and two in the back seat. We identified Ari Ben Ora as one of the men in the back seat. We could not identify the other three men but they have the looks of people of Middle Eastern descent."

"The California license plate number revealed that the car belongs to a Pastor Paul Roberts of the Church of the Holy Redeemer, a Pentecostal Church in El Cajon." He looked at the Israelis and added for their benefit "El Cajon is a companion community to San Diego, just west of San Diego proper."

"The pastor is currently at a church convention in Sacramento. We believe that someone stole his car from the church parking lot while he attended the gathering in Sacramento. We have no reason to believe he is involved beyond the fact that his car was stolen from him."

"They seemed to have planned this caper very well," Gideon commented. "The kidnappers obviously knew the preacher had an out-of-town event on his calendar. They picked his car because the theft might not be discovered until he returned from the convention. Do you think so too?"

"Yes, it looks that way to me. For that matter, his entire congregation knew the pastor would be away for several days. He did not make it a secret, not at all," Woods added.

"Does the church have a caretaker or a janitor, someone like that who might have been around to notice something?" Shimon queried, voicing a concern for the first time.

Detective Ryan nodded in the affirmative. "Yes. We had one of our detectives interview him. He claims that he was not on the church campus, it is a big church, when we think the criminals took the car. He has a verified alibi."

Woods distributed photographs of the Corolla taken from the front and back. The car was about as nondescript as you could get. Aside from the good shot of Ben Ora which made for easy identification, the car had nothing to draw the attention of anyone. It was just a smallish brown car, not even especially dirty, either unattractive or pretty, just dull and functional.

"What about Eric Miller, the American?" Shimon piped up again with a question.

"Glad you asked," Special Agent Woods replied. "You can see him in these photographs, also from the security cameras at the border crossing. Here is a series that starts with a timestamp of 5:04 PM, just a few minutes before the pastor's stolen Corolla crossed into Mexico. Our security cameras caught two men wearing baseball caps shouldering a third man who appeared drunk. We believe the third man is Eric Miller."

"They probably drugged him," noted Shimon.

"Ari Ben Ora rented a black 2009 Prius. We found it at the parking lot on the American side of the border. The Criminals had wiped the car clean. We found no usable prints," Woods reported after checking his notes.

"Senor Diaz, what can you tell us about the Muslim Brigade?" Gideon asked the Mexican police chief.

"We think the Muslim Brigade is a tentacle of Hezbollah. As far as we know, the members are mostly Shiite Lebanese expatriates. The Brigade recruited them from the lawless tri-border region of Paraguay, Argentina, and Brazil. These Arabs are savvy criminals. They traffic in illegal drugs and weapons and smuggle contraband into the United States from northern Mexico. They have infiltrated Juarez and Tijuana. They seem to rely on many of the same document and transport handles as the Mexican drug lords." Diaz looked like he had something bad tasting in his mouth. He didn't like to admit that such a nasty bunch could do business in his territory, but here it was for all to see. He didn't like it.

"Can you identify their leaders?" Woods asked.

"No, not yet anyway, Senior Woods. I assure you that we are trying every day. You see, until now they have thrived by being low key and that is why this alleged and daring foray into California strikes me as a loco thing for them to do. The kidnappings bring unwanted political and law enforcement attention to northern Mexico. I am certain the drug kingpins are not happy about these developments. For years now the cartel bosses purposely avoided kidnapping Americans not of Mexican descent. They don't want the blowback," Diaz said.

"Ari Ben Ora was an easy target. He had no security detail. And he is famous worldwide and of course of great fame and interest in Israel. Nonetheless, nobody believed that Hezbollah would dare pull off this sort of caper in the United States. Poor Miller just happened to be at the wrong place at the wrong time when the kidnappers struck," Detective Ryan gave his input.

Woods added "We have a few of our FBI analysts in D.C. examining any possible connections to the Andre Dubois kidnapping in Paris."

"Other than a similar timeline, we don't see any connection," Gideon responded.

"Both of them served in the same team of astronauts on the ISS at the same time. Both of them survived the landing in the same escape capsule. Those are similarities," Woods offered.

"There are two other astronauts on the same mission, a Russian and an Indian. Neither of them has been abducted. The Russian lives in Israel and we keep a close eye on him right now. The Indian spaceman is keeping a low profile, as we hear. But no troubles so far for either of them," Shimon interjected.

"Chief Diaz will update me with any leads he gets from resources within his department or from his wide range of informants," Woods added.

Diaz responded "Senores, we have a country-wide alert for the Corolla. We think it is still somewhere in Tijuana. Time is not on the side of the criminals and driving deeper into Mexico is not without risk for them. As you know, Mexico is a poor country and regrettable highway bandits are everywhere, even police officials are susceptible to bribes and extortion."

The American and Israeli agents had the grace to not make any comment on the policeman's observation. But not one of them thought that in the proper circumstances, Diaz could not make a profitable accommodation with the criminal element. The slogan 'Plata o Plomo,' that is, silver or lead, meant that police had a choice. They could take a bribe, Plata, or they and often enough their wives and children would receive Plomo, 55 grains of lead at a time. Mexico is a very dangerous place, even for cops.

"Cars can also be stolen in Israel. They usually get driven by the car thieves to the Palestinian controlled territories," Shimon added. No country was crime-free.

Diaz was intrigued. "How do they get through the checkpoints?" he asked.

"Bribes and favors, just like in your country, Senior Diaz. Some things are universal."

Diaz gave a thin smile but then his expression changed. "To my Israeli Senores, do not attempt to infiltrate Mexico with your agents. Mexico is not Uganda or Argentina. We will not tolerate the likes of an Entebbe raid or the Eichmann snatch as you did in Argentina."

Gideon was not disturbed by this outburst. "Of course, we understand, Chief Diaz." he replied mildly.

"OK, gentlemen, I think we can wrap this meeting up," Woods said.

Congregating on the steps of the FBI offices was an on-the-spot Channel 10 news team. Shimon, Ben, and Gideon hid under sunglasses, never mind that the sun had set long before. They completely ignored the reporter's constant barrage of questions. To a man, they despised the press.

Chapter 21

TIJUANA

Had it been two days or three days, Eric wondered? They had taken his watch, along with his wallet and his shoes. He felt his whiskers. More like three days, he thought. He had two emotions fighting in his innards, like a hawk chasing a bunny. One emotion, the most prevalent at the moment, was just plain garden variety boredom. He had nothing to do and all day to do it. The other emotion, the hawk, was fear, stark, straight-up fear.

He had seen the faces of his captors. He had watched enough cop shows to think the kidnappers could not afford to let him go. He might leave this room only to go to a shallow grave out in the Mexican desert.

But Rashid tried to keep his morale up. He brought Eric American sports magazines and the scandalous People sort of grocery store check-out-line magazines like it. He kept up on the lives of movie stars and speculation on the chances the Cubs had of ever seeing another World Series.

His captors allowed him to use a shower. He had a lamp to read by and an adjoining bathroom with a toilet that flushed, Hallelujah for that. Rashid had brought him a towel, soap, and tooth things. He kept clean. The whole thing made him feel like a child with adults bringing him clean undies to put on.

He ate food that he imagined came from Mexican food carts on the street. He avoided the peppers that came with each meal, like pickles in America. One bite one time had been plenty. Rashid provided bottled water so he didn't have to drink from the tap. Hallelujah once again. He knew he was in Mexico and that the tap water would likely give him the squirts. Captive was bad enough, thank you, captive with the squirts did not bear thinking about. He remembered crossing the border but as if through a fog. He knew they had drugged him.

He had some small hope that they would not kill him. What would they gain by his death? What could they suffer if he lived? He reasoned that he had been at the wrong place at the wrong time. They wanted Ari, not him. He thought mostly of Bette and Z and regretted missing her graduation. All that work, all those A grades and missed parties for her, and now her graduation would forever be washed away by his kidnapping. It didn't seem fair. And less fair if he would die and spend eternity under some Mexican cactus.

Rashid entered.

"Good morning Eric. You look terrible. Just for your database, Eric, the window is locked and secured by iron bars on the outside. This is common in Tijuana to keep burglars out. So if you have any ideas about escaping, forget them. Try to think this through logically, Eric. If we just wanted to kill a witness, we could have done it at the car park, no problemo, no?" He smiled in what he thought was a reassuring way.

"Eric, this will all end well, and I mean that for all of us. The Muslim Brigade will trade you and Ari Ben Ora for some of our prisoners held in Israeli prisons. We will, as part of the deal, be granted immunity from prosecution and Israel will fly us to Lebanon. When we get home, we will be treated like heroes." He smiled happily at the prospect. Eric kept as straight a face as he could. He didn't know very much about how Israel dealt with things like this but he did remember that Israeli commandos had flown all the way into the middle of Africa somewhere to rescue some hijacked passengers and had killed every single one of the hijackers. But let Rashid dream on if he would let Eric go.

"In the meantime, we see to your needs, no? What else can I get for you to pass the time?"

"A television," Miller shot back, quick and thoughtless.

"No, no TV, but I can get you a deck of cards. How about that?" Rashid was in a mood to accommodate this morning.

"I would rather play chess than solitaire."

"Me too, but I don't have time to play."

"At home I play on a computerized chessboard."

"How well do you play?"

"It depends on the degree of difficulty I select."

"At what level do you win?" Rashid asked more pointedly. Playing was one thing but winning was quite another.

"I can and have won games at any level but not from a better strategy but by daring and chance."

"Many things in life are that way," Rashid noted with a grim smile and a little nod. Indeed.

"Like my being here," Miller quipped.

"I'll try to find you a computerized chess set. Tijuana is not exactly Century City Plaza. Oh, just in case you are wondering, Miller, the door is locked automatically when I close it." With a very businesslike glance and with eyes so cold that Eric shivered, Rashid left the room.

Eric rested the back of his head on the pillow. Rashid was too reassuring, there are always unintended consequences. Still, Eric wanted desperately to believe him. His father lived until age sixty-three and Eric was already sixty. He closed his eyes and saw his father standing at the edge of the bluff, watching the Ogunquit River merge into the waves of the Atlantic.

Life seemed to be filled with great expectations and a sense of family renewal when Eric arrived in Ogunquit that long-ago summer. Remembrances were both more pleasant and safer than speculation on his immediate future.

Summertime and girls filled his thoughts.

Chapter 22

LA JOLLA

In a swift evasive action, the three Israelis ditched the Channel Ten news van and zig-zagged through the San Diego side streets. Eventually, they stopped at Z's apartment near the main campus of UCSD back in La Jolla. Ben stayed posted with the embassy car. He smoked cigarettes and tried to seem casual. As if. He had the body language of a relaxing timber wolf if those creatures smoked cigarettes.

The door opened to their knock.

"Come in," Bette said. "Detective Ryan told us that you would be coming to see us." She ushered Gideon and Shimon into the small but tidy student apartment.

"I am Gideon Asher and this is Shimon Levi, Mrs. Miller. Thank you for seeing us. I hope this will not be too much of an intrusion."

She waved his concerns away. "You can call me Bette. This is our daughter Z. Can I offer you some pop?"

"Coke or Pepsi, if you have it," Gideon replied. "Thank you."

Shimon spoke. "Thank you, Bette. We are very sorry that your husband got pulled into this affair. Ari Ben Ora was the target. Hezbollah does not want to make enemies of the Americans, you Americans. I assure you that they will treat him well."

"Until they murder him, Mr. Asher," Bette replied, her voice flat and lifeless.

"That would be stupid for them to do and they know it, Bette. They are in a strong negotiating position and they know that too. Israel has swapped prisoners before. We don't like to but, realistically speaking we may have to. American pressure may be too much for us to bear," Gideon replied.

"What can you do to find my Dad" Z wanted to know, her young face showing her worry and her fear.

"We are working with the Mexican and American authorities, Z," Shimon replied with as much consolation in his voice as he could.

"Bette, do you have pictures of Eric that we can take with us? We will return them when he has safely returned to you," Shimon asked.

"We have family pictures on our website. Z can print you a few?"

Z nodded and in a minute or two she had her printer clacking away as it produced a series of fairly recent family photos.

"Thank you Z, that will help us a lot." Shimon said then turned to Bette "I understand that he works for a large mutual fund company?"

"Yes, he had planned to retire next year, but with the market crashing....."

"You are Jewish? I see a menorah on the bookcase," Gideon asked.

"We are and what scares me is that his kidnappers will find that out somehow," Bette said. She looked worried.

"Miller is traditionally an English name. Your husband could easily pass for a northern European. He has fair skin like your daughter, he is tall and light of hair. They may not assume he is Jewish and I hope he wouldn't reveal it," Gideon replied.

Shimon remained silent for a moment. He feared that the press, utterly careless of anything except their own careers, would nose around the private business of the kidnap victim, talking to his neighbors and workmates. They could easily discover the faith of Eric Miller. He knew that with a Jewish man taken by fanatic Muslims the members of the press would blast that news to the stars and if Miller lost his life as a result, well that was more and bloodier news to spread. Blood, death, and tragedy sell papers, the only goal of the free press.

More gently Shimon asked "Bette, what can you tell us about your husband?"

"What do you want to know?" She frowned at her answer.

"Is he emotionally tough? Where did he grow up? What kind of music does he like? Does he participate in sports? Is he outgoing? It all matters, it all helps us to find a way to help him."

"I don't know how strong he is. He comes from Portland, Maine, born there in 1947. He has an older brother and a younger sister."

"What are his interests?" Shimon continued.

"He likes to play tennis and chess," Bette responded

"OK, what about his parents?" Shimon continued.

"His father died from heart failure in 1973, too early in life. His mother lives in Orange County California and is battling Alzheimer's."

"Wow, that's tough. I am sorry to hear that. Did you meet in Portland?

"No, we met in Scottsdale in 1978. Eric left Ogunquit in 1974. He first took a job in Denver and then moved to Scottsdale. That happened in 1977."

"Where is Ogunquit?" Shimon looked puzzled at the obscure name.

"Just south of Kennebunkport," she informed him.

They all knew about the summer enclave of the Bush family, the sprawling, comfortable compound at Kennebunkport Maine. Prior to the national fame of that political dynasty, Ogunquit had been the more popular and better-known resort destination. But that picturesque area of wide blue vistas and sea spray was long in the past of Eric Miller. The three Israeli agents left Z's apartment and found a place to have dinner. They chose, on Z's recommendation, a small family-owned Italian restaurant in La Jolla, not more than a mile from the sea and Westfield Plaza.

After they settled in and ordered, Gideon began the conversation. "The Americans are using the Swiss and the Lebanese diplomats to demonstrate their displeasure with Iran and Hezbollah."

"The Iranians and Hezbollah are vehemently denying any involvement in Ari's kidnapping," Ben added.

"That's not so unusual. After the British, the Iranians are the next best liars," Shimon replied, the disdain that he held for both governments clear in his voice.

"We have only received one call from the kidnappers. And it was made on a disposable cell phone, not traceable. Shimon, you will need to go to Tijuana," Gideon asserted.

"Gideon, you heard what the Mexican cop said. He made it very clear that he doesn't want us mucking about on his turf," Shimon responded just as strongly.

"For all we know, Diaz has both hands out, taking money from the drug cartels. It would be a miracle if he didn't have his hands out. Most, if not every single one, of the cops in Mexico take the drug money. So, fuck Diaz, fuck his horse, fuck Mexico and fuck all crooked cops everywhere. If I have to stage an Entebbe raid in Tijuana, that is exactly what I will do," Gideon declared after putting down his wine glass.

"Who will be my contact?" Shimon wanted to know. He also did not give a farthing for the prickly pride of some foreign cop, bent or not. He would have his citizen returned, safe and unharmed. If a part of Mexico got wrecked in the doing, so what?

"I don't know yet. To find out you will have to go to Las Vegas tomorrow."

Shimon gave Gideon a look. "You know that Las Vegas is not on my itinerary," he responded, his tone dry as a mummy.

Gideon smiled like the Cheshire Cat. "You need to pay a visit to Izzy Rothstein. I am sure you two will get along famously."

"Are you crazy, Gideon? Izzy has been convicted of drug trafficking, he headed a notorious gang of drug smugglers. We can't trust a guy like him. He's a stinking crook."

"The Yanks have him in jail awaiting his sentence. You will find him at the detention center in Las Vegas. He will be easy to find. He isn't going anywhere." Gideon was enjoying himself.

Shimon was not enjoying himself. Quite the contrary, in fact. Rothstein had a bad reputation, even for a drug smuggler. Well, to be fair, drug smuggler, reputed killer, and counterfeiter. He supposedly at one point in his storied career paid off a Burmese heroin trafficker in bogus British pounds. And lived to laugh about it. He asked, not off point at all, "What do you expect him to do for us?"

"Rothstein has contacts in Tijuana. For years he ran a flourishing 'ecstasy' business in Vegas. His supply came through Tijuana. We need him to give you some reliable contact across the border." Gideon came across as just a hair short of smugness.

"Ok, I'll bite." Shimon could see the way this conversation headed.

Gideon had gotten ahead of him, he had planned this out but kept it back. "What makes you think he will want to help us, even if he can?"

"He is still an Israeli."

"For what that might be worth to a man like that. We will have to offer him something in return. He will not likely help us just from a delayed sense of patriotism, now will he?" Ben asked with perfect reason.

"Even the Israeli prosecutors don't want him in Israel," Shimon declared.

"With good reason, they rightly fear that their witnesses will disappear. And that is why Israel waived our extradition rights," Ben added.

"Augh, we are on television," Shimon exclaimed.

Their focus shifted to the TV monitor over the bar.

"There is no volume, I wonder what the reporters are saying," Gideon added.

Ali Chaboun of the San Diego cell clearly heard the reporters and watched the Israelis duck the shrill members of the press. Ali sent a text to Ibrahim in Tijuana who in turn sent a text to the Hezbollah operations chief in Beirut. The following day, Ibrahim received by fax a photograph of Shimon Levi, a one-paragraph biography, and a dictum to place operatives at all the major airport terminals between LA and Tijuana. The Israeli was to be followed and, at the right time and at the right place, to be taken alive.

Chapter 23

LAS VEGAS

Shimon took the earliest flight the next morning from San Diego's Lindbergh Field to Sin City, Las Vegas herself. He would see the painted lady in all her fake glitter and gloss with his own eyes in just a few hours. The eight AM Southwest Airlines flight wouldn't give him any badly needed coffee until they leveled out. He had already ascended into the air, looking out the window at the ridges of Point Loma and wondering if even the steep climb would allow them to clear the hills when the designated operative from Hezbollah arrived at the terminal. The spotter would have a fruitless day. The pigeon had already flown the coop.

With no sudden crash into Point Loma, Shimon settled into his flight, his single suitcase snug in the bin above him. He had about an hour and fifteen minutes of airtime. He willed the aircraft to come to the proper heading, wing low in a turn to the North East. The turn gave him a splendid view of Mission Bay, La Jolla, and points further to the East as the plane gained altitude. The chime announced that the 'Remain Seated' sign turned off. The attendants stirred. Coffee would soon come forth.

More awake an hour and something later they touched down in the high desert of America's gambling Mecca. Shimon rolled his one suitcase through a terminal littered with mesmerized gamblers. The ones leaving

Vegas poured the last of their change into the greedy mouths of the one-armed bandits. The new arrivals made the first of many donations to the economy of the city. He heard one of the blackjack machines loudly announce a winner, albeit a temporary one.

Shimon didn't gamble as a rule. His life and vocation seemed a gamble enough.

The taxi driver offered assistance, but Shimon declined and took his suitcase with him into the wide back seat of the Honda Accord.

"Where to, Mister?" The cab driver wanted to know. Miracle of miracles the driver was an obvious American from his look, sound, and bold, outgoing manner. He was hard used, however, with a red bulb of a nose, rummy eyes, and a general sad ambiance of an unreformed alcoholic.

"I'm going to the Las Vegas Correctional Center," Shimon replied.

"Will you be staying there?"

"You ask a lot of questions." Shimon shot back, peevish even with two cups of horrid airline coffee sloshing around. Caffeine alone did not improve his mood.

"Just trying to be friendly, Mister, this your first time in Vegas?"

"Yes."

"Want a good tip?"

"Sure."

"Don't spend too much time in the casinos. They're in business to take your money. If you get a hot streak at the tables, just walk away. I just took a nice couple and their twenty-one-year-old daughter to the airport. Their first time at the table and she lost a hundred and fifty bucks. She was upset because she was winning two hundred but couldn't quit. I told her a true story about a guy who drove here in an eighty thousand dollar Mercedes, went into the casino, and left town in a four hundred thousand dollar vehicle."

Shimon looked up sharply, a puzzled frown on his face. "What did he buy for four hundred thousand, a Bentley?"

"No, he sold his Mercedes to cover his casino debts and went home in a Greyhound bus." The driver smiled as he told the old yarn. True or not, it could be true and it made a good, strong impression.

"I bet she felt better after hearing that," Shimon said.

"She seemed to, yep, she seemed to. Those casinos, Mister, are very good at getting your money from you and they don't care about what it does to you, not a bit," the driver philosophized. He looked like he might know about casinos taking people's money.

A little later, inside the detention facility, the jail, in other words, an overweight corrections guard made an announcement to a convict. "Rothstein, you have a visitor."

"That's nice, a woman?" the con responded, more in jest than hope.

"Nah, some guy named Shimon Levi from Jerusalem. You'll have to make it fast, visiting hours end pretty soon."

"OK." Rothstein looked alert and interested.

"You know the drill, Rothstein," the guard said.

The beefy guard escorted the handcuffed prisoner to the visitors center. He seated Rothstein at a table across from Shimon and then stepped to the edge of the room to give the crook and his visitor their privacy.

"So, who the fuck are you, Shimon Levi?"

Shimon handed his business card across the table.

"Mr. Rothstein, you may be able to help us rescue Ari Ben Ora."

Chapter 24

LAS VEGAS

"**R**othstein gave me a contact." Shimon spoke into his cell phone. "He had to have asked for a favor," Gideon surmised on the other end of the call.

"Nope, not yet anyway. But you are right, he will want something."

"Who is your contact?"

"Somebody named Jaime Gonzales. I will find him in San Ysidro, just on the US side of the border down by Tijuana," Shimon reported.

"And you made plans to meet?"

"Yes. I will meet him the day after tomorrow in San Ysidro."

"Shimon, where are you right now?" Gideon wanted to know.

"I am in my room at the Venetian. Pretty swank, too, in a glitzy, overdone sort of way. When they do it up in Vegas, they do it up big."

"Avoid airports, Shimon. We've picked up some Arab internet chatter since our television coverage at the FBI office in San Diego."

"I'll keep a sharp eye out, Gideon. Thanks for the warning."

"US border security can be tight. Going into Mexico is a breeze. Coming out into the US can be tricky depending on circumstances," Gideon mentioned.

"My passport is in good order."

"You can rely on the Israeli consulate in Tijuana if you need to. It resides on the Avenida 16 de Septiembre. I will text you the phone number," Gideon added helpfully. Gideon had his stuff together.

"Thanks."

Shimon closed out the call and tossed his cell phone gently on the big Vegas hotel bed. Off came his clothes. He took a quick but refreshing shower. Any time spent outdoors in Vegas made frequent showers a necessity. As he dried off the cell phone rang again. He glanced at the caller ID before he answered.

"Michelle?" he asked in surprise.

"Shimon, it's me!" Her voice burst with excitement.

"How are you?" He asked in a warm but concerned voice. She had been under a lot of stress and he could not help her from so far away.

"Oh, I'm fine, I'm fine. I'm here, at the Las Vegas airport."

"What? My God, what are you doing in Las Vegas?"

"I came to visit you." She replied, her voice a happy burble.

"You knew I was in Vegas?" Shimon asked in confusion.

"Eshkol told me, but only after I threatened him that I would fly to the LA consulate and make a spectacle of myself."

Shimon laughed. "You are very convincing, Michelle."

She laughed with him. "But he didn't tell me where you are staying."

"That's because he didn't know."

"If you don't want to see me, I will take a flight back to Paris tomorrow. Tonight I will go to the Las Vegas strip."

"Not on my watch, Michelle Dumas. I am staying at the Venetian."

"As soon as I get my luggage I will take a cab there," Michelle replied. "Do you need me to book a room?"

"When did you become a jerk, Shimon?"

He laughed again. "I am in room 6620."

Chapter 25

REIMS

A conservatively dressed gentleman in his middle years walked into the cafe, glancing around, looking for his luncheon companion. Sitting in the small waiting area, Inspector Gallant met his eyes. "Monsieur Papillon?" Gallant asked.

"Ah, Inspector Gallant," replied the smiling bank manager

The inspector rose and shook the outstretched hand that Papillon offered.

The watching maitre d' escorted the pair to their seats in the cafe proper.

"I think you'll enjoy the cuisine at the Roma, inspector."

"Monsieur Papillon, I could eat Italian dishes every other day with Chinese in between, but of course, that would make me fat." He made a very French gesture that implied regret, resignation, and a childish joy at escaping adult responsibilities all at once. "So, my wife serves me fruit and salads with little or nothing at all in the way of dressing," he smiled.

"I should heed your wife's advice. I have been warned by my physician that I am overweight and need to exercise more. More? But to business. How can the manager of the Reims de Bank National be able to help an inspector from the Eighth Arrondissement? I must say that I have never had the pleasure of meeting a genuine inspector from the Paris Metropolitan Police until this very moment."

The waiter approached.

"Welcome to the Roma. Shall we begin with a bottle of Chianti?"

"Chianti?" Gallant glanced at Papillon for guidance. Papillon accepted the waiter's suggestion.

"Excellent," the waiter frothed and vanished to fetch a bottle.

Inspector Gallant got quickly to the point.

"I suspect that one of your depositors is involved with illegal activities and is funneling money into your bank. I need your help."

"What sort of illegal activities?"

"I am not at liberty to say." He made a moue, as if to say that he would gladly tell the bank manager everything, if only he could.

"I see. Are you able to tell me the name of my customer?"

"His name is Shai Tanger."

The waiter returned, interrupting their private conversation. He uncorked the bottle and poured each of them a dab of wine. He waited until both men had indicated that the wine would be acceptable, and filled the bulbous glasses to the halfway mark.

"Are you gentlemen ready to order?" he asked.

"Give us a few minutes," the inspector requested.

"Are you certain that he is a depositor at my bank?"

Gallant nodded. "Yes, I am."

"We have thousands of depositors. Do you have a warrant, inspector?"

"Not today, but very soon."

Papillon refilled his glass. Gallant's had hardly been touched.

"I can tell you this much, inspector. The depositor is no longer a customer at my bank. Yesterday he closed his account and transferred all of his funds out of the country."

That got Gallant's attention. "May I ask you for more details?"

"Regarding the specifics of the transfer, I am afraid not, Inspector Gallant. Without a warrant, I am obligated by French law to protect my customer's privacy."

"I understand. Tell me Monsieur Papillon, on an ordinary business day how many of the bank's depositors wire transfer funds?"

"It varies from day to day. There are never less than twenty and often over fifty transfers in a single day." He glanced to get the attention of the waiter. "I am afraid that I have said too much."

"On the contrary Monsieur Papillon, I think only enough to get my warrant approved."

Chapter 26

LAS VEGAS

She kissed him goodbye, a kiss filled with regret, longing, and most of all with promises of days, months, and years to come. Then she disappeared into the terminal. The night before had happened so fast, the phone call, the shower, the knock on the door, a kiss to his lips before he spoke, the embrace, a swift kick that shut the door, their waltz to the bed, the removal of her blouse, the feel of her firm breasts in his hand and the taste of her nipples. They fell on the bed, and he kissed her hard. She placed her hand on his hardening crotch. On her back, she kicked off her shoes and quickly removed her jeans. He kissed her inner thighs, slipped off her panties, and explored her private parts.

He stood up, unbuttoned his shirt, and tossed it on the chair, then off with his pants and underwear. Naked, she crawled under the sheets. Shimon removed the top sheet and gently entered her. Michelle climaxed first and then had another and then he had his. Locked into an embrace, neither spoke for what seemed like the longest time. Michelle finally relented.

"I'm famished." Shimon announced with a grin.

"OK, but you better order extra towels from room service."

"How many should I order?"

"Order enough for you to make love to me after dinner and tomorrow morning before I leave. I don't know when I'll see you again."

They had dinner at the Venetian. She shared with him her newly discovered secret. Her father had a Jewish bloodline. She had a plan to locate her Jewish relatives who had returned to Israel. In such a small country she felt confident that she could locate them and make some try at knitting familial ties.

Besides, her boyfriend was a spy. He could find anybody.

"What about Andre?" Of course, Shimon was curious about her ex, especially in his current situation.

She seemed very confident, strong, and determined in the direction she wanted to travel in her life. With him. Michelle was not a girl, tentative and hesitant. She was a woman and a French woman at that. She knew what she wanted and wonder of wonders, she wanted him.

"I want him to be found safe, but I am moving on with my life. I want us to have a chance, Shimon."

"I would like that too." He grabbed her hand under the table. "You still want to see a show?"

"No. I want us to go back to our room and make love again and again." He smiled at his agreement.

Then she asked, "When will you go back to Israel?"

"I don't know."

"Be careful. And call me."

The rest of the night passed in confusions of passion and eventually, of delightful exhaustion.

Shimon drove to San Ysidro to avoid the watchers from Hezbollah that he knew had the airports staked out. It took him a little over six hours with stops, gazing at the vast stretches of America, so different from his homeland. The long trip offered him plenty of time for reflection. And recovery. He smiled. Michelle was a force of nature.

His meeting with a man he would call Gonzales would occur at a Denny's restaurant at 10:45 the next morning. Gonzales instructed him to watch for a man wearing a red baseball cap backwards. Shimon checked MapQuest and reserved a room at the Courtyard Inn.

Chapter 27

SAN YISIDRO

The morning after Vegas, Shimon walked across the parking lot to Denny's. A man sat on a stool near the far end of the counter. He looked Mexican, dark skin, hair, and eyes. He had a heft to him, heavy like he might be a guy who did a lot of physical labor, not tall but strong seeming. He didn't look like a gangster but just a guy, a manual worker, one of tens of thousands of similar-looking men in the border area. He displayed no tattoos, gold chains, or other indications of gang affiliation. He had watchful eyes and big, strong hands. Shimon took all this in at a glance.

The man had a red ball cap, bill reversed.

Shimon browsed past him. He took a seat two stools away.

"Jaime Gonzales, we spoke a few days ago," Shimon said quietly as he plucked a menu from a small chrome rack on the counter.

"Si, Senor Levi."

"What do you like on the menu?"

"I like the chorizo and eggs with corn tortillas."

Shimon looked at his companion's plate. Jaime seemed to have some kind of a scramble. He could identify eggs, some green leafy plant, meat, and onions. And cheese, he saw some bright orange cheese in the mix. The plate held a side of frijoles where most American breakfast plates would have hash-brown potatoes. Instead of toast, a small stack of corn tortillas sat on a smaller plate. Local comfort food, like mama used to make.

Shimon mentally shrugged. When in Rome, do as the Romans do. He decided to give the new dish a try. Jaime seemed to like it. When the waitress came up with a glass of water and her pad he pointed to the other man's meal.

"I'll have what he has and coffee, black."

He had a cup of coffee in front of him in a flash, just mass made American coffee and not the dark, rich brew served up when he ate at Lucille's flat in Paris. He quickly shook off those wandering thoughts. To business.

"I need your help to locate Ari Ben Ora."

"Everyone wants to locate Senor Ben Ora. The Mexican authorities have offered up a million pesos to anyone who can provide information on his whereabouts," Jaime informed Shimon. He had no trace of a Mexican accent.

"I am prepared to offer you more to be my ears and eyes." Shimon had a lavish, enormous, budget for this mission, all provided by four lifelong friends, very successful friends, who owned or at one time owned and cashed out from different high tech firms in the broad corners of the computer industry. He rather liked having the ability to say he could offer more of a reward than the Mexican government.

Jaime nodded as he used a tortilla to push food onto his fork.

"Senor Rothstein says we can trust you. I have known him for a long time. If he trusts you, then I will also."

Shimon sipped his hot coffee. Jaime continued.

"Senior, Levi, what year and model was the kidnapper's car?"

"They used a 1992 brown Toyota Corolla, we think it is probably being disassembled, if it hasn't been already."

"Maybe not," Gonzales opined.

"You don't think so?"

"I think it's too dangerous for the kidnappers to take the car apart. It would create a lot of noise and commotion, Senor Levi and there is also no incentive for the thief to peddle the auto parts, not when there is a big reward for someone to snitch. All the banging and cutting would attract attention. I don't think they would risk a regular chop shop. Those guys would drop the dime on the thieves in a hot minute."

"So, what do you think? Would they just give it a quick primer and a coat of paint of a different color?"

"Si, and maybe put on different bumpers to disguise the look of the car."

"If you had to guess, Jaime, what colors would they use?"

"I can't say for sure, you understand? Lots of cars in Mexico are green, red, and powder blue. They would attract the least attention, I think. I can put some guys around Tijuana. I will tell them to be on the lookout for Corollas of all colors and who knows, maybe we will get lucky." He shifted gears and asked, "How will you pay me, Senor Levi?"

"In cash."

"When, Senor?"

"Today is Friday. I have to get back to LA. We can transact someplace in San Diego on Monday. How does that sound?"

"That will work. There is a Tio Taco restaurant near the interstate where you get off to go to the airport. I will be there at the same time on Monday. Adios, amigo."

The waitress brought Shimon his novel breakfast. As Shimon looked at the tortillas she sashayed away and then back to refill his coffee. He paid close attention to the flavors and textures of his food. There were not many Mexican restaurants in Israel.

Chapter 28

PARIS

"**M**onsieur, I wish to converse with the honorable Juge d'instruction Adrian Goddard. If you please, let him know that Inspector Gallant of the Paris Metropolitan Police begs for a few moments of his valuable time."

"Only a moment, inspector. I will see if the magistrate can speak to you at this time. Hold the line, s'il vous plait." The line went from live to that electronic limbo that was neither open nor closed. Gallant could tell by the tone that the clerk had put him on hold. He waited patiently. He expected the call to go this way. The Judge after all had a flack to intercept his calls, which the flack did with polite if ruthless efficiency.

The Juge d'instruction combined some of the duties that in America a district attorney performed along with other duties that an American judge handled. Goddard came on the line, speaking quickly.

"Inspector, court convenes in two minutes. If this is another warrant request, the answer is no. The permission that I granted you to conduct phone surveillance on a French citizen based on circumstantial evidence produced no results."

"Your honor, that citizen closed his account at the Reims de National Bank."

"I would expect that he would. You told me he planned to immigrate to Israel, to join his co-religionists there."

"He has your honor but I have good reason to suspect that he was paid a huge financial settlement by parties unknown for unknown reasons. And considering that he is a mere waiter at a cafe this is very uncharacteristic," the inspector surmised.

"And what gives you a reason to suspect that Monsieur Tanger was paid a large sum of money? Wouldn't any honest citizen want to take his bank balance with him to start his new life in a new land? Why should you think he had some huge amount of money, an uncharacteristically large sum of money? Perhaps illegal money?"

"Because I interviewed the bank manager," Gallant answered.

"What, the manager volunteered this information, absent a warrant? This is a violation, inspector."

"No, your honor, not that. But I asked him on a typical day how many of his customers closed out their accounts at his branch."

"Get on with it, Jean. I have to go to court," the magistrate demanded. "Get to the point, and hurry."

"The manager told me that between fifty and a hundred depositors closed their accounts on a typical day. But then he brought up the name of our subject, Monsieur Tanger, not me. The manager told me that Tanger specifically had closed out his account."

"So what! Get to it, right now!" Goddard had clearly lost his patience.

"My point is simple, your honor. The bank manager recalled Monsieur Tanger closing his account and transferring his money elsewhere. One account out of dozens of accounts which closed every single day. Why would the manager know of this one account among many? Because of the amount of money involved, your honor, and for no other reason." Gallant finished his pitch with a flourish.

The judge paused for three seconds, seeking a way to thwart the policeman. Goddard had to go and wanted to finish the call quickly. "Or he might have known this Tanger personally."

"I didn't get that impression," the inspector quietly demurred, knowing he was close to his goal.

"Inspector, surely you have come across individuals who possess a photographic memory. Finish your thoughts, inspector, I am wanted in court."

"My predicament, your honor, is that I have three persons of interest who have left France and who could be connected to an unsolved murder and an unsolved kidnapping. If my suspicions are correct, Shai Tanger wired a significant amount of money out of Reims. And if I am right, your honor, we will soon know who and why."

"You will have your warrant by tomorrow, inspector, but only this one time and no more." The magistrate ended the call before the inspector could convey his respects and his gratitude.

Chapter 29

NEWPORT BEACH

S himon fiddled with his burner phone as he drove along the Pacific
Coast Highway, trying not to let the California drivers kill him.
When he had the number he wanted, he hit the button and waited
as it cycled and buzzed. When it connected he spoke loudly into the
mouthpiece to overcome the driving noise.

"What's a hundred thousand pesos Gideon?" he asked his colleague.

"Meh, eight thousand one hundred dollars, give or take," Gideon
replied.

"I need to pay Gonzales on Monday. Can you make arrangements?"

"Sure. Where are you now?"

"Ah, let's see. Dana Point, I think, or around Dana Point anyway."

"OK. Drive along the Pacific Coast Highway until you get to Newport
Beach. It is a beautiful little place with a beautiful view. Breathtaking,
actually. It is a nice, clean, upscale town. I want you to spend the weekend
there and just relax and enjoy yourself. We are still picking up Arab chatter
on the internet. Ben and I are confined to the consulate until further
notice. Stay away from LA and be as inconspicuous as you can. And
this is the hard part, for the time being, it is not a good idea to call your
girlfriend in Paris."

"Gideon, Michelle is not a problem."

"I know, but she has a mother and friends. Loose lips sink ships."

"She might make a fuss if she doesn't hear from me when she expects to. We parted the other day on very good terms. She will naturally expect and I hope she will want to speak with me often. You have seen movies of people in love, Gideon. We like to just hear each other's voice, no other reason, just that. If she doesn't hear from me, she will worry. She will think I am dead or something else bad. She will raise Cain until she finds me. Don't put a stick in that bear cage, Gideon, please don't."

"Good point, Romeo. How about if I have Eshkol give her a call and explain what's what? It won't be forever, I hope just a few days. Call me when you find a room. Just lay low and we will get the money to you early on Monday morning."

"OK, that should work. I'll call when I get somewhere," Shimon said and disconnected.

He continued his drive along the coast. The traffic kept him moving slowly enough that he could enjoy the landscape of some of the wealthiest and loveliest little beach towns in the world. He passed through Laguna Beach and Corona del Mar. He drove by beautiful beaches, pristine bluffs, and exquisite homes nestled behind gated fences and covered with glorious swaths of bright magenta-colored bougainvillea. Shortly after passing by Balboa Island, he reached Newport Beach and began to think about a place to stay.

To gather his thoughts and do some poking around, he turned in the huge Fashion Island shopping center. The gigantic outdoor mall had dozens of high-end shopping opportunities, fashionable boutiques, and what certainly looked like good restaurants. It also hosted one of the bookstores that were on Ari Ben Ora's book signing tour. He had visited this bookstore earlier on the day of his kidnapping. Fashion Island was a massive mall, built on the top of a cliff. It had the fake Spanish mode so common in California. Designed to form a delight for pedestrians, the vast space was filled with courtyards, flowers of every blazing color, and water fountains. It had a view of the wide Pacific ocean in all its glory that would pay the visitor for his trouble to stop by, even if the shops did not attract him. Fashion Island was the peak of California perfection, beautiful, casual, tasteful, and expensive beyond the ken of a normal man.

This Saturday brought waves of shoppers, including husbands and wives with their children. As he meandered along, looking at the stores, observed patrons as desperate as observant Muslim women clothed head to toe and accompanied by a male escort and other women of such high fashion and stilting along on such high and expensive heels that he thought they might be movie stars. He sort of wished he knew more about movie stars and starlets so he could brag later-'Yeah, I saw her, you know that movie with the monsters? Man, was she pretty in real life.' But no, they were just beautiful, very expensively wrapped women to him, not famous women.

When he found the bookstore, he strolled in. Ari had signed books at this store, met his public, and then motored down to another opulent mall in La Jolla only to be snatched by Middle Eastern terrorists. His books were still on front and center display.

More people would want to buy his book now that the newspapers had daily coverage of his kidnapping. People were like that, attracted to any excitement. Sort of like a painter whose work became more attractive after his passing or a rock n roller who sells more records after his spectacular car wreck than he ever did before.

The sun made its final descent of the day, gifting the shoppers with a sunset to be remembered. Shimon hung around Fashion Island and ate Chinese food. He reasoned that he could microwave any leftovers without a mess. Full, he took his carry out to the car and drove up the highway a couple of miles to Huntington Beach. He checked into a Comfort Inn on the side of the highway away from the beach. His paymaster should appreciate his frugality. An ocean view was an expensive luxury and the sun had gone down already.

He complimented himself on his thriftiness. Israel was small and needed to use her resources wisely if she was to survive. Even in laid-back, sunny, and beautiful California he never for a moment forgot who he was and what he was about.

Chapter 30

TIJUANA

A tall, well-built young man stood in a dirt courtyard behind a cinder-block and concrete one-bedroom house. Behind the house, a high wall topped with broken glass closed off the small courtyard from the eyes of the other denizens of Tijuana. The sixty-year-old house had iron bars on the windows, like many of her sisters across the wide swath of the third world. The house was typical, run-down, mean, and anonymous, not notable in any way. A gate made of corrugated metal connected the house with a dirt alley behind the building. There was no garage for the elderly auto parked in the tiny yard. For the good-looking young man, the last trait meant the most. For him and his fellows the small, mean home painted a chipped and faded electric blue served as a hideout, a refuge from their enemies and rivals. His neatly trimmed beard bobbed up and down as he spoke into a disposable cell phone.

"Ali, the Mexican police are pulling over all Corollas with American or Mexican plates," Ibrahim, the young man, spoke to his friend and boss via the disposable cell phone.

"Then, Ibrahim, be on the watch for Corollas with other plates."

"Other plates Ali? What do you mean?"

"And other colors too, Ibrahim. The car has undoubtedly been repainted. Especially be on the alert for Guatemalan and Panamanian plates. If you see a suspicious car cross the border, call Anwar in San Ysidro and give him the license plate number and the description of the car. You may cross the border into California if you find such a car. Follow it until Anwar sees you on the freeway and takes over. Got it?"

Ibrahim recalled the last time he phoned Anwar. He wanted him to tail a brown Honda with California plates. Anwar followed the car to the parking lot at SeaWorld in San Diego and watched a whole tribe of children come piling out of the car. A bust.

"Boss, the journalists said that a group identifying themselves as the Muslim Brigade are demanding the release of Marwan Barghouti, Bashar Seliman, and Jamil Khalid. The Israelis will never let any of them out of prison."

"Listen to me, Ibrahim. All of our Hezbollah agents have been strictly instructed not to kill any Americans unless Israel or the United States attacked Iran. I have never heard of the Muslim Brigade. Have you?"

"No, Ali. Do you think those idiots in Hamas have done this thing?"

"Maybe, they are not strategic thinkers. But whoever they are, they are not part of Hezbollah. But Hezbollah is getting the blame from everyone in the international community. Our spiritual leaders tell us over and over that we cannot kidnap Americans or Israelis in America. We don't do so. But Ibrahim, aren't the Americans encouraged to kill innocent Muslims every day in Afghanistan?"

"Yes, Ali, exactly right. The Americans have been getting away with murder any place they want because of 9/11." The beard stopped bobbing for a minute. The nice-looking young man shrugged his shoulders in resignation. "Inshallah. It is the way of the world, Ali. That's what I think."

"It is the same with our Muslim brothers in Hamas who can get away with kidnapping Israeli soldiers in the occupied lands. Public opinion considers it as legitimate resistance because the world believes that the Jews stole Arab land. You and I know that one day we will get our vengeance on the Americans."

"Ali, what if the kidnappers are not even Muslim?"

"I have thought about that, and considered that as a possibility. I think this has the markings of a covert Israeli operation. Think about it. The longer the book writer is held captive, the more Muslims get the blame for the kidnappings. You know that a Frenchman named Andre Dubois was on the same space station with Ari Ben Ora. A little before the Israeli got grabbed, someone grabbed this Infidel Frenchman in Paris. It just seems too neat and too beneficial for Israel to me. I don't see how even Hamas could be so stupid and I know for sure that it wasn't us in Hezbollah. It has been a great propaganda victory for Israel."

"So, do you think the Israelis kidnapped the Frenchman?" Ibrahim had never thought of that. It seemed so twisted, so convoluted that it might even be true.

"Does it seem logical to believe that both kidnappings were committed by Muslims? To what purpose? How does Hamas benefit? But we get the heat now. The Mexican cops have all their attention on us instead of on their bribes. Be watchful as you move around. The enemies of Islam will take your appearance as an Arab to be justification to harass you, maybe to arrest you for no reason."

"What are we going to do, boss?" Ibrahim asked.

"We need to flush out the real kidnappers. I can tell you this now. The Israelis have sent one of their agents here to find Ari Ben Ora. His name is Shimon Levi. I think he is part of the deception. I just sent his photo to your phone so you will know what he looks like. We need to get our hands on him, Ibrahim. We must take him alive and find out what he knows."

"I will watch for him, Ali. We will find him. We will not fail."

"With the help of Allah, we will catch him. Sooner or later."

Ali closed the call. Ibrahim put his phone away and went into the shabby little house looking worried.

Chapter 31

MONTMARTRE

Adjacent to the lofty village of Montmartre and situated on the Right Bank of the Seine, the imposing basilica of the Sacre Coeur towered above the city lights. A magnet for tourists, Montmartre is eclectic, artsy, laden with shops, gardens, stairwells, residences, fine restaurants, and literary dreamers.

One of the village's more popular restaurants is the Irish Pub. Inspector Jean Gallant arrived and was immediately seated. He lit a cigarette and only waited a few minutes for the mercurial vicar general Antoine de Gaulle to arrive. The vicar general gave his wet raincoat to the maitre d'.

"Bon jour Jean," Antoine began, full of faux friendship.

"Thank you for coming at such short notice," the inspector said politely.

Antoine nodded, acknowledging the comment. "You indicated urgency, and I was fortunately able to reschedule my calendar."

"I appreciate that. Can I buy you a beer, Antoine?"

"Whatever you order will be fine."

"Antoine, you are aware I am sure that we have not closed the case on Father Gauthier's death because there are too many unanswered questions surrounding his death. Suicide for a priest is just so unnatural, so strange and out of the ordinary.

"Yes, Jean, I know you still consider his death suspicious, but what does that have to do with me or with the church in general?"

"Well, perhaps nothing. But couple that with the unsolved kidnapping case of Andre Dubois and the murder of the man called Philippe and the mystery grows. Your priest identified this so-called Philippe as the man who drugged him and stole his car. That same car that persons unknown to us at this time used in the commission of the kidnapping. These things, two deaths and a kidnapping are all tangled up, Antoine. I want to untangle them."

"Our priest, as you call him, was exonerated. He had no connection to Andre's taking, nobody in the church did," Antoine said very forcefully.

Switching gears Gallant said "Antoine, do you know Shimon Levi, an Israeli who recently stayed for a time in Paris?" He immediately sensed the vicar general's discomfort.

"We have met," Antoine said and let it drop.

"You met the day after he arrived in Paris," the inspector added.

"Do the Metropolitan Police follow me around, Jean?"

"No, of course not, Antoine," Gallant responded to placate the churchman. "We have our eye on Shimon Levi. He is a man worth watching."

The waiter returned with two mugs of beer.

"The shepherd's pie," the inspector ordered.

"Nothing for me," Antoine said, touching his open hand to his middle, showing how full his tank was.

"Oh, Antoine, you should reconsider. The pie is really very good. If your hunger doesn't demand satisfaction right now, box it up and take it with you to the parish. You can enjoy it later. Please, my treat." Jean Gallant smiled his most charming smile at the churchman.

"Thank you, Jean. I will do just that."

"Antoine, if I may ask, what is your interest in Shimon Levi?"

"Inspector," now, so quickly, the man across the table became 'inspector' and not 'Jean'. "The proper question is what is your interest with this Jew?"

"He is a person of interest to the police. The day after you drove him around Paris, he took the train to Reims. Did you ask him to go to Reims?"

"I think so. Monsieur Levi asked me how the Cathedral at Reims compared with the Cathedral of Notre Dame. I told him the beauty is in the eyes of the beholder," Antoine smoothly lied with no hint of shame.

"You do not run in the same circles. How did you happen to meet?"

"We have a mutual friend at the Vatican embassy in Tel Aviv."

"I see." Gallant gave nothing away by tone of voice or facial expression that he either believed Antoine or disbelieved him. But he knew the churchman disseminated and wondered why. "Monsieur Levi also lunched out at the Cafe Voila in Reims. Are you familiar with the Cafe Voila, Antoine?"

"No"

"You should be. Father Gauthier dined there on the day of his death. The archbishops summoned him from the Cafe Voila. Father Gautier's server was Shai Tanger, a Moroccan Jew. Shimon Levi's server was also Shai Tanger. We followed the Israeli to Reims. Antoine, do you know Shai Tanger?"

A single twitch of an eyelid gave the vicar general away. "Now that you mention his name, I do indeed have a recollection. Archbishop Clement and I both considered it possible that Tanger poisoned Father Gauthier at the Cafe Voila before the archbishops arrived. Poison could explain his irrational behavior that led to his suicide," Antoine offered somewhat lamely.

"Unfortunately, your archbishops did not allow an autopsy. I have been troubled by that. Perhaps Archbishop Clement would reconsider?"

"You will need to ask him yourself, inspector. But if he was poisoned, the enemies of the Church could falsely accuse the archbishops of the crime, the murder of a priest. The noise of such a despicable charge alone would damage the reputation of the Catholic Church."

"Not necessarily. If traces of poison were found in the good father's digestive tract, Monsignor Tanger might also be a person of interest."

"And good luck with extraditing Tanger from Israel," Antoine blurted out.

"I never told you that Monsignor Tanger had taken himself to Israel, Antoine. How do you know the whereabouts of an obscure Jewish waiter? This becomes more and more curious, wouldn't you say?"

"Jean, I think we are done now. Thanks for the beer. I will leave the other shepherd's pie for you to enjoy tonight."

"Wait just a minute, Antoine. I have something to show you."

Inspector Gallant reached into his coat and produced an envelope from an inside pocket. He placed the envelope on the table. Antoine sat back down and reached for his reading glasses, adjusted them and picked up the envelope.

"We obtained a warrant to search Monsieur Tanger's bank account in Reims. We made a copy of it. It is in the envelope, please open it, Antoine."

"It is a photo-copy of a check," Antoine identified the paper.

"As you can see, one million euros was paid to Shai Tanger by the Vatican Bank. Unfortunately, this money is no longer in France. Several days ago Monsieur Tanger wired these funds to a Swiss bank. Because, as you have pointed out to me, he has flown the coop to Israel, I may not be able to interrogate him. Antoine, was Tanger blackmailing the Church? Are the allegations made by Andre Dubois, a kidnap victim, true?"

"Sometimes things are not what they appear to be. I am sure there is a logical explanation, inspector," de Gaulle replied lamely.

The vicar general rose from his chair and stiffly walked out.

Jean Gallant called after the departing churchman.

"You can tell that to the French media. The story will be in all the papers tomorrow morning. Have a pleasant day, Antoine."

Chapter 32

LE MONDE

Saturday, April 14, 2009 AM edition
Staff Writer: Henri Bettencourt
BANK OF THE VATICAN PAYS ONE
MILLION EUROS TO FRIEND OF
DECEASED PRIEST FATHER GAUTHIER

A Vatican payoff of one million euros to Shai Tanger added mystery to the two-year-old unresolved and suspicious suicide of Father Gauthier. The priest had breakfast at the Cafe Voila on the morning that he committed suicide. Monsieur Tanger was his server. Father Gauthier left the Cafe Voila with Archbishop Clement.

Until recently, Monsieur Tanger was an employee of Cafe Voila in Reims and a French citizen from Morocco. Soon after his financial bonanza, Monsieur Tanger moved his family to Israel.

According to Vatican sources, Gauthier had been assigned for relocation in Bolivia. En route to Charles de Gaulle airport, the archbishop's car stopped at Montmartre's Basilica of the Sacre Coeur. A television crew at the Basilica captured him as he ran to the precipice and jumped to his death. Andre Dubois, a close confidant of Father Gauthier alleged that his priest had sacrificed his own life to save many others. This reporter conducted an interview with Andre Dubois on March 27ᵗʰ prior to his kidnapping. The following is an excerpt from that interview.

"To those who conspired against Father Gauthier, they should know I will never give up until I can prove their culpability in his suicide."

"And when you find that proof, Monsieur Dubois, this reporter would appreciate being contacted."

Were any of Andre's allegations confirmed by any of his crewmates who served on the International Space Station? Not yet. Certainly not from Ari Ben Ora who was abducted outside a shopping mall near San Diego, Ca. two days after this reporter's interview with Andre. Authorities on both sides of the Atlantic had not established a link or connection between the kidnappings. Le Monde attempted to contact Andre's remaining crewmates and was rebuffed. Officials from the Israeli government still refused to acknowledge their possession of Andre's requisitioned laptop, and Le Monde has not been able to locate Shai Tanger in Israel.

Who benefited from Andre's silence? Was the Roman Church engaged in a cover-up?

Chapter 33

PARIS

Le Monde
Saturday, April 21, 2009 AM Edition
Staff Writer: Henri Bettencourt

Yesterday in Toulouse, vandals smashed several windows at the Abbey of St. Thomas. On Thursday gunshots fired at St. Agnes in Marseilles and St. Josephs in Lyon left shards of broken glass. On Wednesday in Le Havre, a note was hammered to the entry door at St. James. Contained in the note was a threat to burn St. James to the ground if Andre Dubois was not released by the end of the week. The police were unable to confirm if the vandalism was related. No arrests have been made.

And in Paris last Sunday priests walking from the Abbey of St. Victors were pummeled with eggs thrown by hooligans in a passing car. Tomorrow thousands of Parisians were expected to file down Champs Elysee and demand that the archbishop of Paris releases Andre Dubois. The archbishop's office emphatically denies any culpability, and no one has yet been charged with Andre's abduction.

There is an additional controversy. The inexplicable Vatican payoff to

Shai Tanger, a waiter at the cafe Viola in Reims, in the amount of one million Euros, will no doubt stoke new conspiracy theories.

For the record, Shai Tanger served Monsignor Gauthier his final breakfast at the Cafe Voila a few hours before the priest committed suicide at the Basilica of the Sacre Coeur in Montmarte. Shai Tanger recently relocated to Israel.

Henri's cell phone rang. He placed his burning cigarette in the ashtray.

"Henri Bettencourt."

"Henri, this is Antoine de Gaulle."

"You read my column?"

"I did and would like to personally invite you to a press conference at the archbishop's office Monday morning at 10:00 A.M. Of course, other media outlets will also be invited."

"To discuss the Shai Tanger controversy?" The reporter asked.

"His excellency will address the issue of compensation concerning Monsieur Tanger."

"I will be there," Henri affirmed.

Chapter 34

SAN YSIDRO

At first Anwar resisted the chime of his phone. He was in the middle of his business on the toilet. He cursed loudly in Arabic, angrily threw the newspaper to the floor, and ran as quickly as his underwear would allow his feet to move.

He snatched his phone off the end table. "Good morning."

"Anwar, this is Ibrahim. I want you to follow a Corolla that passed through Tijuana and headed north into the States. Look for a powder blue car with Canadian plates. It has a single driver, no passengers. The plate numbers are....."

"Wait, wait. I just got off the toilet." He scrambled around for a pen and paper. "All right, I'm ready. Go ahead."

"The Canadian plate number is 4ES2964, Province of Manitoba. I am following the car right now. I want you at the exit within five minutes."

"I am writing the numbers, 4ES2964, Canada, Manitoba. What if the car goes all the way back to Canada?"

"Consider it another adventure ride," Ibrahim chuckled.

"Don't be funny, Ibrahim."

"Follow the Corolla until you hear otherwise, Anwar. I'll see you at the exit."

Ibrahim quickly profiled the driver as either Latino or Middle Eastern. To avoid suspicion, he lagged a few cars behind.

At the exit, Anwar got a fix on a blue Corolla, followed by Ibrahim's white Taurus and merged onto the interstate. He moved ahead of Ibrahim's Taurus, keeping his Nissan between the other two cars. Ibrahim turned on his blinker and at the next exit, got off the freeway.

After about ten or twelve miles, the powder blue Corolla switched from the northbound lane of Interstate 5 and slid through the concrete spaghetti of the interchange to emerge on Interstate 8, heading east.

A few miles later, the shopping destination of Fashion Valley appeared. Anwar easily kept pace with the Corolla. The driver didn't seem to pay any attention to the possibility of a tail. The driver came up to the huge mall, drove around for a couple of minutes and found a parking place only about fifty yards from one of the entrances.

Anwar managed to stay with him even if he did almost lose the driver in the swirl of shoppers just at the entrance.

The quarry stopped at one of the map kiosks, the place that showed the location and brief description of each of the 147 shops in the mall. With plenty of other shoppers, Anwar easily kept the man in sight. His subject had a medium build and seemed to be in his middle years. Even inside the guy still had his sunglasses on. On closer examination, Anwar thought the subject might be Middle Eastern. Or Latino. He wasn't close enough to tell for sure and it didn't matter to him one way or the other, certainly not enough to come to the subject's attention. One good look and he was blown. With no back up, he couldn't take a chance of getting too close.

Keeping the guy in sight, he followed along at a distance. The subject came to an electronic game and toy store, filled with computer games, handheld games, and electronic gizmos of every possible kind and description. Anwar mentally shook his head. No wonder the decadent West was losing the battle between civilizations. American youth wasted their time on frivolity. Back home, the youths scrambled to survive and many of them trained for the coming battles.

Anwar grabbed a cup of not terrible coffee from a nearby coffee stand. He ordered an espresso, no creme, no whip, no nothing, from a barista so scantly and shamefully dressed that she would be stoned back home if she dared to show herself in public in such a state. But he did enjoy seeing her exposed limbs.

The subject exited the store after a few minutes, carrying a package. Still keeping a discreet distance, Anwar kept the guy in sight. Back at the parking area, he got into his Nissan. The powder blue Corolla was easy to keep in sight, standing out as it did.

As he followed, he hoped that the subject would return to Tijuana. Then the powder blue Corolla from Manitoba would become the problem of Ibrahim once again.

Chapter 35

OLD TOWN SAN DIEGO

The following morning Shimon received a casual hand-off on the Huntington Beach boardwalk from a courier from the Israeli consulate in Los Angeles. Bundled inside a copy of the LA Times he found a fat wad of US currency for Gonzales. After he got the package, Shimon drove all the way down to San Ysidro to meet his new best pal, Jaime Gonzales.

This time they met in a Tio Taco restaurant, one of many small chains of quasi-Mexican fast-food franchises in the Southwest. The whole swath of the US from East LA through Arizona and New Mexico, including South Texas but stopping when one got within gumbo distance of Louisiana, sometimes got the nomenclature of 'Mexi-America.' The cuisine reflected that cross border influence. On the other side of the line, you could find a Big Mac or something from Jack in the Box. Real Mexicans laughed at the food offered by Tio Taco but Americans wanted flavor, crisp taco shells and they wanted it fast, right now please, thank you so much. Volcanic peppers common just a few miles away were a hard sell to Yankees, no matter how fond of Mexican food they were.

Shimon walked to the back of the small fast food joint, found a table, left his jacket on the back of the booth to claim it and got in line behind another guy to order. Jaime Gonzales was the other guy in line.

"Just order a burger, amigo. The Mexican food here is horrible, an injustice to the ingredients." The solid, big-handed Mexican suggested.

"I think I'll just get something for the road. You can have my table." Gonzales made his order and then walked over to the soda machine and drew a Pepsi Cola. Then he walked back to the table where Shimon had left his jacket. He sat down to wait for his order to be called.

Shimon ordered a burger and fries to go and also drew a soda, fitting a spill-proof lid and piercing the center of the lid with a plastic straw. He watched Jaime claim his tray a couple of minutes later and return to his seat. In his turn, Shimon accepted his bag of food, paid, and departed for San Diego.

Gonzales ate like a guy with no conversation to distract him. He bit chewed, sipped his Pepsi, and repeated that series of acts, efficiently demolishing his cheeseburger and fries.

He picked up the abandoned jacket, feeling the chubby envelope in the inside pocket. He dropped his rubbish in the bin and walked out, full, happy with himself and with Shimon for their solid tradecraft. He hummed a bit of a cheerful Ranchero song and went on his way.

Gonzales was delighted to receive the money. For the minor crime boss, he would make good money and no one would shoot him or arrest him. Doing some small chores for the Israelis was safe, easy, and profitable.

Back on the road, Shimon called Gideon on a one-punch speed dial.

"Shimon, we got you a room for a week in a residential hotel in Old Town in San Diego."

"Old Town?"

"Yes, the historic center of the old Spanish town. The hotel is over a hundred years old and now caters to pensioners of limited means. You will have access to the police and FBI, should you need to deal with them as we go forward. And it is much closer to Tijuana and San Ysidro for contacts with your guy, Gonzales. There are a half dozen restaurants within walking distance, several of them very up-to-date craft eateries that you might enjoy. You can explore the old San Diego mission that goes back to the days of Zorro. In a mile, you can be on the freeway and off North or South, as your needs demand."

By late afternoon, Shimon had checked into the small hotel room. In Europe that hotel might be called a pension, a place for pensioners to live.

Here, they called it a residential hotel. The ancient room sparkled with fresh paint and modern furniture. He had a TV and a shower but not a lot of room to spread out. For dinner, he strolled around until he found a hippy-dippy little cafe. He ate a delicious chicken wrap and had a couple of glasses of wine that came from a town called Fallbrook, just north of San Diego. The Californians seemed to take their wine seriously. The sample he had of a Chardonnay from some label he had never heard of and would not likely taste again had a good nose and pleased his pallet. Not that he was an oenophile but he did enjoy a glass of wine.

On the way back he watched a couple of old guys playing chess on a concrete bench and chessboard thoughtfully erected by the city for the pensioners. San Diego seemed like a kind city, even to the oldsters and not just for the sun-burned young beachgoers.

Just as he returned to his room, his cell phone chimed.

"Hello, Senior Levi. This is Jaime. We might have a lead for you. My people followed a blue Corolla out of Tijuana this morning. It had Canadian license plates. It was an older model from the early nineties. My guys tailed it to San Diego to the Fashion Valley shopping center. He bought a chess game, not the kind with men to move around but an electric game, the kind that lets you play yourself if you don't have an opponent. He returned to his car after the single purchase, just in and out of the mall."

"A chess game?" Shimon pondered.

"Si Senor Levi, we also attached a magnetic GPS above his tire. And when he drove out of the parking lot in his Corolla, my men pulled the window washing routine on him at the stop sign and saw the chess set in the back seat. In case he looked in his rear view mirror my men remained at the stop sign to wash a couple more cars. Senor Levi, the next driver screamed in Arabic after we squirted water on his windshield, almost ran over one of my men. He drove a white Taurus. We also stuck a GPS tracker above his tire, and got his plate number, too."

"You can track these guys?"

"Si, Senor Levi, on my computer. I will email you both plate numbers and photos of the men. Right now both cars are heading north on the LA Freeway. Wait, the gray Nissan just turned south again."

"Can your men describe what the first driver looked like, Jaime?"

"They said he was middle aged and looked Middleeastern."

"Good surveillance, Jaime." Shimon broke the connection. Then he received the emails and called Gideon.

"Gideon, we may have a lead here, a blue Corolla, early nineties model, with a Canadian license plate, 4ES2964."

"I'll check it out," Gideon replied.

"Thanks, and check one more plate, a gray Nissan, older model with California plate, 36KL672."

"OK, what have you got?"

"The driver of the Corolla drove from Tijuana to Fashion Valley Shopping Center in San Diego and purchased a chess set. He is described as likely Middleeastern. The driver of the Taurus was an Arab tailing the Corolla. I'll send you pictures, Gideon."

Chapter 36

PARIS

Print journalists, electronic journalists, journalists from all corners of France and more from Europe and across the world squeezed into the too-small auditorium like so many sardines. Men, women, cameras, tripods, and microphones crowded against each other in a claustrophobic mass of eager, questing humanity. But this meant nothing to Henri Bettencourt. He held the position of senior reporter for Le Monde and no one denied him his front-row seat for whatever show the Catholic Church would present here today. The show, after all, would never happen if Henri had not spread the Church's secrets across the front page of his paper.

The noisy, pushy news people began to quiet down when a Vatican spokesperson approached the podium and introduced the featured speaker of the day, Archbishop Clement. After testing the microphone and clearing his throat Clement began to read from a prepared text.

"In 1858 in Bologna, Italy, agents of the Roman Inquisition kidnapped a six-year-old Jewish boy, Edguardo Perez, and physically removed him from his Jewish family. These kidnappers had learned Edguardo had been secretly baptized with the connivance of his nursemaid. A young teen herself, the nursemaid feared the sickly boy would descend into Hell if he wasn't baptized. Under unambiguous Papal canon law, non-Christians were not allowed to

raise a Christian child. Edguardo remained under the protection of the Vatican and was raised a Catholic. His father spent years trying to get his son back, and all appeals to the Church to return the child to his family were rebuffed. His parents were occasionally allowed to see him but never alone. Church authorities told the boy's parents that they could have the boy back if the family converted to Catholicism. They refused."

"Now one must remember the incident happened before the nation of Italy was formed, and well past a hundred years before the Second Vatican Council. The Church's relationship with the Jewish people is very different today and much better. The incident was very embarrassing to Pope Pius IX in 1858. The Church was criticized in many quarters locally and abroad for taking this boy away from his family."

"When Edguardo was nineteen and no longer a minor he declared himself a Roman Catholic and entered the Augustinian Order in France and became a priest at the age of twenty-three. Although his father had died, he kept in touch with his mother and his siblings for most of his life. Edguardo died in 1940."

"I am certain that you are wondering what this bit of unfortunate history has to do with Shai Tanger and the one million Euros paid to him from the Vatican bank. Quite simply, the money is compensation for the kidnapping of Edguardo Perez in the spirit of cooperation and to avoid long and costly litigation. Monsieur Tanger is the last blood relative of Edguardo Perez."

Clement picked out the raised hand from a BBC reporter and called upon him.

"Your Excellency, the misdeed occurred over one hundred and fifty years ago. How do you explain Monsignor Gauthier's relationship with Monsieur Tanger?"

The archbishop now departed from his prepared speech and answered this one question.

"Well, they knew each other from the Cafe Voila. It is only through the efforts of Monsignor Gauthier that this matter came to the attention of the Church at all. That is all I have for you, ladies and gentlemen. Thank you, all of you members of the press. May God bless you all."

Chapter 37

RIVE GAUCHE, LEFT BANK

The door squeaked as someone unseen opened it.

Andre Dubois heard some footsteps that he had not heard before, steps that seemed shorter and quicker. He shouted out a complaint. "I am out of food."

A strange voice shouted back "You won't need any more food, Andre."

Andre didn't like this idea. He wondered if he would be allowed to starve to death. Better to have his captors shoot him or give him a poisoned chalice. Death by starvation had no appeal whatsoever.

Two men approached wearing gloves, dark sunglasses, berets, and ordinary clothes. Neither of them wore the Franciscan robes that Andre had seen before. One of the men shined a powerful handheld light in his face, blinding and distracting him. Andre squinted and put a hand out to shade his eyes. He could not make out any particular details of either man.

"Are you going to kill me?" Andre asked. He thought he got the phrase out bravely enough. His voice sounded calm and manly, quite the opposite of what he felt inside. At least he would not disgrace himself in his last moments.

The man chuckled. "Oh no, Andre, we will let you go free very soon."

"I can really go?" Andre asked, confused at the change in direction of his thoughts. Freedom? He could leave?

The second man tossed a knapsack onto the bed while the spokesman kept the light in Andre's face.

"Put your clothes on, Andre. The key to unlock your ankle bracelets is in the zippered side pocket."

Andre rifled through the knapsack pocket and unshackled himself. He shed his captive clothing and slipped into clean underwear, trousers, shirt, and socks. He recognized his own clothes, the same ensemble he wore on the day of his kidnapping, freshly laundered. Lastly, he stepped into his loafers.

"Sit down on the bed and take a look at this."

The man snapped off his spotlight and handed Andre a photograph. Andre turned on his own penlight to examine the photo. It showed Andre, asleep and shirtless, cuddled up next to an older man under the top sheet in a bed.

"What the fuck is this shit?" Andre stridently demanded. He had not felt such vocalized anger at the kidnapping as he did at this false attack on his manhood, his sense of self.

"It seems, Andre, that you had a little tryst with Father Martel."

"I don't sleep with men. You drugged me. You set me up."

"And who will believe you when these photos are published in the newspaper?"

"The people will believe me." Andre almost shouted in his outrage.

The spokesman responded in calm, measured tones as if stating the obvious to a child. "Perhaps, perhaps those who know you well will believe you. But enough of the general public will believe their own eyes, don't you think? Let me fill in some missing details for you. Another man was identified in the same room with Father Martel. The police found him dead, floating in the Seine. The police are still trying to identify him because his fingers were cut off. No fingerprints, you see? Andre, after we publish the photos, and there are more, who will the police have as their prime suspect? You know how they are, Andre. If they have someone to focus on, they will and not bother to look further. They will look at you, Andre."

Deflated, Andre said, "What do you want from me?"

"We don't have to release these pictures. When questioned by the police or anyone else, you just say nothing. You will never mention the Society of Saint Pius X. You will deny any Vatican linkage to Father Gauthier's death. When asked, you will admit your conspiracy theories were baseless and a result of your emotional pain and suffering."

"My reputation will be ruined."

"Andre, I think that is a very small price to pay for your life."

At the exit, the visitors activated the fire alarm and locked the door from the outside.

Chapter 38

RIVE GAUCHE, LEFT BANK

The control alarm panel signaled the location of the fire alarm. Within minutes the firemen arrived, snipped off the chain and lock and blow torched the metal door open. They entered the warehouse. There was no fire but they found Andre.

Inspector Gallant was immediately notified. Within the hour he and his team arrived and began combing the warehouse for physical evidence. Inspector Gallant and Detective Blanc immediately took Andre to the station for questioning.

Andre was first cleared by a physician, and taken to the interrogation room. After he was seated, Andre asked to go to the bathroom. Inspector Gallant knocked on the door to get the guard's attention, which he needed to do as the man leaned against the wall outside the interrogation room, his eyes closed, upright but in some middle place between wakefulness and slumber. He was not alert.

The guard stuck his head into the room and looked at Gallant in inquiry.

"Take Monsieur Dubois to the toilet." the inspector ordered with a weary briskness. He shook it off, like a water dog clearing his head. One could not expect rocket scientists to become men who escorted prisoners from here to there in a police station.

As Andre departed, Desjardin, the crime scene lead investigator, popped in, smiling.

"We did a title search on the warehouse. Inspector, you'll never guess who once owned the empty warehouse: Nate Gottschalk."

"The Jewish gun runner?" Gallant asked, clearly taken by surprise.

"Oui. Nate is serving year five of a six-year stretch for illegal gun-running," Desjardin replied, pleased with himself.

"Who owns the building now? Have you discovered that?" The inspector asked.

Desjardin's grin spread even further. He had a face like a garden gnome, a happy one just now. He pointed at himself and at Gallant.

"We do, you and me, the taxpayers of Paris. After the people in their exercise of justice put Gottschalk away, the city confiscated the property. The city managers intend to dedicate the building to some future civic project, but naturally enough they haven't gotten around to it yet. It just sits there. You have to wonder why they don't just auction it off, get the thing out of their hair and put it to some taxable use, no?"

Gallant made a very Gallic shrug and accompanying expression. Expecting too much from the mediocre clerks who actually ran Paris was a fool's game.

"Road trip" Blanc snapped out with a sense of glee. "We should get out of the city and see Nate in the centre pénitencier. It will get us out of town for a few hours in the sweet air and sunshine of the country and Nate will be glad of the visit. I bet he is bored out of his skull with no criminal schemes to concoct." He referred to what in America would be called a 'medium-security prison or penitentiary, a place for simple crooks to serve their time, not a place to hold dangerous killers.

Desjardin interjected a comment, ignoring Blanc entirely.

"Inspector, have you considered the possibility that Dubois staged his own kidnapping?"

"Naturally, but as I see it, he would have very little to gain and much credibility to lose. If caught out, his reputation would suffer beyond recovery. And why do it?"

Andre returned to the interrogation chamber, looking somewhat refreshed. After being reseated, Inspector Gallant began the interrogation.

"Andre, what can you tell us about your kidnappers?

"Not much, they wore masks."

"How many were there?"

"Three, maybe four."

"Did they speak with an accent, perhaps foreign?"

"No, Parisian French," Andre replied.

"Andre, did you know Zoran Coldovic?" Gallant asked.

"No."

"You do know Ari Ben Ora." That was not a question but rather a statement.

163

"You know that I do, very well as men would know one another after spending months in a tin can in outer space."

"He was kidnapped two days after you in La Jolla California. A radical Muslim group has claimed responsibility. Did you know about this?"

Andre looked shocked. "No, I hope the authorities will find him alive and well."

"Can you think of any reason why Ari might suffer the same fate as you?"

Andre shook his head in the negative. "Inspector, I don't even know why I was taken. Now, will you permit me to go home, to get on with my life?"

"Did you know Michelle came to Paris with Shimon Levi?"

"Is she still here, in Paris?" Andre asked with hopeful excitement.

"No, she flew to be with him in Las Vegas." He gestured to his minion. "Blanc, get the pictures on my desk if you would?"

Blanc returned with two photographs.

"When the cat's away, the mice will play. In Paris, I know they were kissing for the camera, but in Vegas, I'm sure he fucked her good and plenty," the inspector said with vicious speculation.

"Fuck you!" Andre shouted and spit at Gallant.

The inspector calmly pulled out a handkerchief and wiped the spittle off his face.

"If it is any consolation to you, Andre, they are both persons of interest.

Unfortunately, Shimon is in America and we are not sure where Michelle is. You must wonder if they had something to do with your circumstances."

"I have nothing more to say. I know my rights. If you continue to hold me without evidence, I will retain a lawyer."

Chapter 39

OLD TOWN, SAN DIEGO

Shimon's cell phone buzzed to announce the arrival of a text. Eshkol sent it.

"Andre found, unhurt, now in police custody."

Shimon stopped eating his Kung Pao Chicken. He sat in a Chinese place that might have sold Kung Pao Chicken in this spot for a hundred years. The guy who sat on a tall stool behind the cash register might have been there for the entire time. They had taken centuries to perfect at least this dish. Shimon had never had any better. But this news could not wait. He called Michelle.

The phone on the other side of the world clicked and rang, and rang but she did not pick up. He left a message.

"Michelle, Andre has been found. He is unhurt and is being questioned by the police. Call me soon. I yearn for you like a lost baby caribou for his mother."

He had just put his phone down and picked up his chopsticks when it rang.

"Hola, Senior Gonzales," he spoke, reading the caller ID.

"Senior Levi, we tracked the Corolla to a residential district in Woodland Hills, 12223 N. Canyon Road."

"Slow down. I am writing the address on a restaurant napkin. This is very good for us. Do you have anything on the Nissa?"

"Currently southbound on Interstate 5, just below San Diego," Gonzales replied, crisply giving the fact and nothing else.

"Great work. Stay in touch." He terminated the connection and hit the speed dial for Gideon.

"Gideon, can you do a title search for 12223 N. Canyon Road in Woodland Hills?"

"Sure, just give me a little time. Does this have anything to do with the blue Corolla?"

"Yes. Can you get a camera on that location right away? I want to see who comes and who goes. It may be important, or not, who knows? Good to cover that base, as the Americans say."

"A sports reference, I think." Gideon replied. "I'll get right on it. Ari has the highest priority here at the consulate. I'll let you know when I have it in place."

165

"Hold on Shimon, I have something coming in right now. I'll read it as it comes up. The blue Corolla is registered to Amir Delshad of Vancouver, British Columbia. And next, the 2002 Nissan is registered to Anwar Saba of 85 Monte Vista Drive, San Ysidro, Apartment 333. Who is Anwar Saba of San Ysidro? He is not in our database and neither is Amir Delshad. Do you want me to try the FBI, Shimon?"

"Not just yet. I will call Woods," Shimon replied.

"Will you also mention Delshad to Woods?"

"No, only Saba."

"I see. Because Amir can be a Jewish name and Delshad could be an Iranian name?" Gideon qualified.

"I think it would be best if you checked him out first, Gideon. We may find out something that we do not want to get out there. Once the data bit bird flies, it can never come all the way back. You know how it goes." Shimon instructed.

"Got it."

"By the way, I told you Delshad purchased a chess game at Fashion Valley in San Diego."

"You did. It makes sense. The Persians invented the game."

"Our missing American also played chess, Gideon. Do you think there could be a connection?" Shimon asked.

"Who knows? I play. You play. Who doesn't play chess, especially if you are Iranian?"

"Call coming in. Talk later." Shimon disconnected one call and took the other.

He heard Gonzales' voice. "Senior Levi, we have a location for you in San Ysidro."

After getting the update, he went back to his meal. Even now that the food was only warm, it still had a flavor he could enjoy.

Chapter 40

PARIS

Disgusted but unable to charge Andre, Inspector Jean Gallant released Andre the following afternoon. Andre's one permitted call was to his friend, Louis Major.

"Going back to get sloppy seconds," Detective Blanc snickered.

Andre's primal impulse was to strike Blanc, to hurt him, to wipe that nasty snicker right off his face with his fists. He wanted to do just that, very badly. He figured that he could, Blanc might be a cop but he didn't look like he had maintained his fitness. Andre knew he could take the older man. But he controlled himself, content with the thought rather than the deed. Besides, Blanc might have wanted to provoke him into assaulting a police officer, a serious offense.

Instead, he ignored the vile words and walked out of the precinct door. He found Louis Major waiting for him. Andre planned to stay with Louis until he could talk to Michelle. She might be in Paris at her mother's, at her mother's where the photos of her kissing Shimon were taken. Or she might have gone back to her work in Israel. He thought about that as they motored to Louis' place. She did drop everything and rushed to Paris when she found out about the kidnapping. That must mean something. He could forgive her for straying if indeed she did. That is if she would have him back if she would care if he forgave her or not, not a certain thing at all. He would call her.

He did but she did not pick up. Deflated, he did not leave a message. He told himself he would try again in a couple of hours.

"Louis, do you have anything to drink? I haven't had a drop in over ten days and I could use something strong."

His friend smiled. "Of course. I have an unopened bottle of four-star cognac I keep for celebrations, like the release of a friend from durance vile. Will that do?"

Andre offered the ghost of a smile and nodded.

"What's your plan now, chief?" Blanc asked his boss. Each of them had just let the disappointment of Andre's failure to rise to the bait roll off them. Some things worked, others didn't. It was the way of things.

"Now we go to talk to Nate Ghottschalk. You never know what will pop up. He is at the Fresnes, not so far to go."

The Fresnes Prison marred the landscape of the suburbs just to the South of Paris. It wasn't all that far as the crow flies but French roads and traffic made it an irritating journey for the two detectives. They had called ahead to warn the prison authorities of their coming and their desire to interview one of their prisoners. They parked, entered the grim building complex, registered, and gave up their weapons. In a surprising show of government efficiency, a guard quickly escorted them to an austere but quite secure interview room. Only a few moments later, Nate Gottschalk entered the room, closely followed by a beefy guard.

Gallant examined the prisoner. Gottschalk wore the full rig for moving prisoners about within the confines of the facility. He had on a washed-out gray jumpsuit, short leg chains which caused him to shuffle, and handcuffs. He did not have an imposing presence. He had too many years, nearing sixty, and too much weight. Fat criminals did not inspire either fear or confidence. Gallant thought the overweight crook might have spent some of his last four years doing push ups and so on, but no. He had short gray hair going to male pattern baldness at a rapid rate. He hadn't bothered to shave for several days and so he had an untidy stubble poking out all over his double chin. The guard sat him down.

Gallant didn't think the prisoner looked like much of anything at all. Blanc just looked blank and impassive.

"Monsieur Gottschalk, I am Inspector Gallant and this is Detective Blanc. You once owned a warehouse in the Sixth Arrondissement?"

"That was many years ago. The warehouse and my life currently belong to the French State. I am afraid you have wasted your time in coming to see me."

"Who else had a key to your property?" Gallant asked.

"Didn't the idiot bureaucrats change the locks?" Gottschalk asked, incredulous at such sloppy work, even from the government.

"Apparently not," the inspector replied with a wry twist of his lips.

"Every realtor in Paris had access to the key. I had the property listed for sale. Every realtor would have access to the key and the lockbox that held it. That doesn't cut down on the number of suspects, does it?" Gottschalk asked.

"Did you know your warehouse is now a crime scene?"

"Of course. We see the news on television."

"You know that Andre Dubois was discovered in your warehouse?"

"Inspector, it is not my warehouse. It has not been mine for years now. Do you think the actual kidnappers might have wanted to implicate me somehow? To muddy the trail, so to speak? Or just to harm me. I do have many enemies. Or maybe the kidnappers selected it because nobody bothers to show it anymore."

"The city owns it and they do not have it on the market any longer. And I have witnesses who will attest that I have been in prison for the last four years, just in case you want to pin this on me," Gottschalk dismissively laughed.

"Monsieur Gottschalk, did you know Zoran Coldevic?"

"Yes, I did. And I even know where he was a day before he died," the crook replied with a smug expression.

"Well, tell us," Blanc demanded.

"Oh no, not unless I get something. I have a year left on my sentence. Shorten it, a lot."

"It would be my pleasure to save taxpayer money spent on feeding scum like you," the inspector responded.

"I will take you at your word, inspector. Before his death, Zoran was spotted walking in the jewelry district in La Place Vendome."

"The Place Vendome is the location of Cleef & Arpels, Boucheron and

Cartier," Blanc noted, a bit proud that he knew where these grand luxury emporiums resided.

"Yes, and many smaller jewelers," Gallant added.

"Who gave you this information?" Blanc demanded.

"I have my sources," Gottschalk responded coyly.

"Monsieur Gottschalk, we can easily verify all your communications."

"Not on the inside you can't. It will be simpler, not easy but simple, to look at camera video feeds from the jewelry stores. Every one of them has a camera, even the smallest. Look, I gave you a lead that you didn't have. Are we finished?"

Gallant nodded and tapped on the door for the guard.

On the way out of the prison, he said to Blanc "Well Blanc, it seems that Zoran might have been trying to fence some gems."

Quman Caves, Israel

Michelle, back at work with her team of archaeologists, examined remnants of bones and fragments of pottery from the Hasmonean era. This ancient burial site dated from about fifty BCE. The cave was situated beneath the famous Qumran Plateau.

At dusk, the archaeologists emerged from the caves below, dusty troglodytes, tired but pleased with their efforts. Michelle checked her phone for messages. She saw that her first message was from Shimon. She smiled as she walked to her car, listening to his voice. Shimon's message stopped as her phone shattered from the impact of a bullet that deflected into her skull. She fell to the ground and did not move again.

Chapter 41

WOODLAND HILLS

U nder the cover of a converted pest control van, staffers from the Israeli Consulate in Los Angeles installed a camera across the street from the target home. From his office, Gideon monitored the video in real time. Just before nine AM, the electric garage door opened and a blue Corolla with Canadian plates slowly backed out. Before the door closed Gideon spotted a second car inside, covered from top to bottom with a protective drape, the kind one could buy at any auto parts store or even Wal-Mart. Gideon immediately quickly dialed Shimon to report.

"Did you get a visual of the driver?" Shimon wanted to know first off.

"Yes. The driver is Amir Delshad."

"I need to make sure Gonzales is watching him. I'll get back to you in a few, Gideon." Shimon cut the call with Gideon and dialed Gonzales.

"Good morning, Senior Levi," the Mexican criminal answered cheerily enough.

Shimon didn't beat around the bush. "The Corolla is on the move. Why didn't you call me?"

"Oh no, Senior Levi. The Corolla we tagged is still in the garage, right where it has been since it first parked there. It has not moved an inch."

"It just backed out of the garage. Your tracking device must have been discovered and disconnected," Shimon contradicted.

"No, no, Senior Levi. The device we used is motion sensitive and there has been no motion. The Corolla you caught moving is not the same Corolla. If the people we watch had disabled the tracker, we would have gotten a ping to let us know. The tracker remains in place, it remains in operation, I assure you."

"It has the same Canadian Plates." Shimon was not giving up.

"Senior, the plates come off, the plates go on, they are easy to switch. If this new Corolla returns to Tijuana, we will find him. I will station one of my men at the border. The rest of my men are watching the gray Nissan from the convenience store."

"OK, stay on it," Shimon disconnected and dialed Gideon again.

"Amir pulled a switch on us. What you saw driving out is a copycat Corolla. The draped car in the garage was the Corolla that Gonzales tagged yesterday."

"We should break in." Gideon seemed enthusiastic for that action.

"No, an illegal search is too risky. What if something goes wrong and you get caught? I would lose you and your men. You would all be headed home by sundown and I would not have you to back me up. Plus, it would cause all kinds of bad press, which we do not need. We can use what we have for now. You have a camera on the house and a tracker on the car. I think there is no doubt that the draped car is the one used to kidnap Ari."

"They painted it blue and slapped Canadian plates on it to get it out of Mexico?" Gideon speculated.

"Yes, that is the way it looks now," Shimon said.

"Hold on Shimon. I just got a teletype from our embassy in Ottawa. The L.A. House is owned by a Canadian businessman named Meyer Baker. Let me read....He is a Russian Jewish emigre born to a one time Communist boss named Ivan Berovsky. The family immigrated to Canada twenty years ago, changed their name to Baker and thrived. Ivan accumulated a fortune in currency and commodity arbitrage. Allegedly, he has ties to the Russian mob. Amir could be driving to Canada even as we speak. Whew, I didn't expect that." Gideon finished his report.

"There is no motive, no ransom here. I don't believe Delshad is driving to Canada just yet. He has a chess set to deliver to someone in Tijuana."

"You think the chess set is for Miller?"

"It looks like it to me. Delshad came back to the US to switch the kidnap Corolla with the clean Corolla and picked up the chess set on the way, a side trip."

"Shimon, I never considered the kidnappers might be Jewish mobsters, not for a second."

"Gideon, you might be right but let's not get ahead of ourselves. I can't imagine a motive, lacking a ransom. Can you?"

"No. This is getting weird. I can't understand any of it."

"Too true."

A very thoughtful Shimon cut the connection.

Chapter 42

TIJUANA

A stinking cloud of self generated cigarette smoke enveloped, obscured and clung to Farouk, the designated spotter. He sat in a Ford pickup near a Circle K in Tijuana, bored out of his skull but still watching for a blue Corolla with Canadian plates. For hours he had covered for the Sunni asshole Anwar who told their boss Ibrahim Anwar lost sight of the blue corolla because he had been pulled over by a California Highway Patrol for switching lanes without signaling. Anwar, the liar, offered no proof of a ticket or citation.

A blue Corolla with Canadian license plates passed him, causing him to jerk himself into a greater state of alertness. He grabbed his cell and called Ibrahim. He read out the license numbers.

"Stay with it," Ibrahim commanded brusquely and hung up.

Farouk cranked up the engine and followed the Corolla into the Circle K. Deploying his cell phone camera, he photographed Amir at the gas pump and again when Amir finished and walked into the Circle K, carrying a burlap bag.

Farouk slowly drove his pickup past the Corolla. He saw a copy of "The Palestine Exchange," on the front seat, Ari Ben Ora's novel. Farouk photographed it and parked his vehicle at the next available gas pump.

Inside the Circle K, Amir exchanged burlap bags with Rashid. Rashid left the store and mounted his motorcycle. Farouk never saw the exchange.

Amir returned to his car, started the engine and drove away. Farouk dropped his gas cap and got a late start. Driving faster than he probably should have, he caught up with the Corolla. He called Ibrahim.

"Ibrahim, I followed the Corolla to a Circle K. On the front seat I saw a copy of "The Palestine Exchange." It has to be the book the American bought."

"Did you get a photograph of the driver?"

"Yes, on my cell phone camera."

"Was the Corolla repainted blue?"

"I am sorry, Ibrahim. I had no time to scrape the paint. It looked normal to me, just a blue car," Farouk replied.

"What did the driver look like?"

"He was almost six feet tall, had olive skin, straight black hair and had dark eyes. He wore a red polo shirt, tan slacks and sandals with socks. I'll send you the picture right away, as soon as I stop somewhere."

173

"OK, good job. Stay on it and keep me informed."

Farouk followed at a safe distance. He watched his quarry turn into the driveway at a small one level stucco house. The house was small and wore its orange tile roof like a jaunty cap. The Corolla pulled into an attached carport. The driver used a key to open the front door and enter the house.

Farouk called Ibrahim to report.

"He stopped at a house at 552 Luna de Valle."

"Keep watch and stay out of sight. Faisal, Karim and Yasser will join me. Update me every half hour or sooner if necessary."

"Do you want to take him alive?"

"Yes, after I smoke him out," Ibrahim replied and broke the connection.

As a matter of routine, Farouk took cursory looks into this rear view mirror. Fortunately, it would soon be dark enough for him to go out of the car to urinate. By the time full dark arrived, he badly needed to. He left the car as soon as he thought he safely could and ducked into an alley and relieved himself. He returned to the car, feeling much better but realized that he had hunger but no food. He silently admonished himself for his lack of foresight. He did have his cigarettes however and lit one up. When he burned that one down to his fingers, he tossed the butt out the window and lit another. And again. Each time he fired up another cigarette, the match flared in the dark confines of the pick up truck.

Amir took notice. After a while and during his stalker's urination, he quickly removed the Canadian license plates and placed them in the bicycle basket then peddled along an alley behind the little house, away into the dark.

Chapter 43

SAN DIEGO, OLD TOWN

Every time his phone rang was a reminder that Michelle hadn't called or e-mailed. This time, Agent Woods from the San Diego office of the FBI was the caller.

"Anwar Saba is a twenty-eight-year-old Palestinian from Hebron on an expired visa. Two years ago he came to Boston for medical treatment. Shortly after his medical treatment finished up, Immigration lost track of him, surprise, surprise. Thanks to you, FBI agents are on their way right now to pick him up."

"I'll go with you, if you let me?" Shimon asked.

"I am afraid it is out of the question, quite wrong under our rules to let that happen. I know you would like to be there and I know why. I sympathize. But no. If he is involved with the kidnappings we will find out," Special Agent Woods replied, not sounding like he was particularly sympathetic.

"Sure, I get it. Thanks for the heads up." Shimon disconnected and called Gideon.

"Get me everything you can on Anwar Saba, twenty-eight, from Hebron. His visa expired. I'm on my way to San Ysidro."

"I'll get right on it," Gideon answered.

Shimon stuffed a Jericho 941 semi-automatic, nine-millimeter, double-action pistol inside his jeans. On the run he phoned Gonzales.

"Senior Levi, always a financial pleasure to speak with you," Gonzales quipped.

"Jaime, can you lure Anwar away from his apartment? The FBI is on the way to pick him up."

"What should I do with him?" Now Gonzales was all business.

"Take him to a place where I can interrogate him."

"I have an amigo who owns a bar in San Ysidro called Julio's Barrio. I will take him there."

"Good. I'll meet you there in a couple of hours." Shimon disconnected. This will be some close timed work, to get Anwar away before the guys from Fumble, Bumble and Incompetent show up to arrest him.

Shimon started his car and waited for a minute for the oil to warm up. Preserving an expensive piece of machinery came second nature to him, even if it was not his car. Letting the car run for a minute or so would let the oil warm and give all the moving parts a nice slippery coat. His phone rang.

"Hello," he answered.

"Shimon, this is Lucille."

"Hello Lucille, is everything OK?"

"No. Michelle is at Hadassah Hospital in Jerusalem. She is in critical condition. She suffered a gunshot wound to her head."

"Oh my God! When?"

"Yesterday, at the Qumran Caves where she is working. A Palestinian from a nearby village shot her. He also wounded two others, but not as seriously. I am at the airport. My flight to Israel leaves in two hours."

"Michelle is a fighter. She will survive," Shimon reassured her and held back his rage, but only with the focus of his entire force of will.

"I know she is, Shimon," Lucille answered gently. "I will call you from Israel."

Then she broke the connection as she had broken his heart.

Chapter 44

TIJUANA

Rashid walked in, holding a chess set he removed from the burlap bag.

"Thanks, Rashid," the captive said politely.

"Would you like to play against me, Miller?"

"Yes, I would like that. It will pass the time and who knows? I might beat you." Miller grinned. He didn't care if he lost. Having something different to do would be enough.

"I wouldn't bet on it." Rashid grinned back.

Rashid heard his phone go off. He listened for a few seconds.

"Some other time, Miller. I must go." He ran from the room.

Eric heard a motorcycle engine cough into life. The deep buzzing sound of the motor gradually faded into the distance, into nothing.

San Ysidro

Anwar heard the glass break followed seconds later by the car alarm. He peered through the kitchen window. Mexicans were trying to steal his car. He couldn't believe their audacity. He cursed in elaborate Arabic and grabbed his gun. He opened the door, intending to chase the thieves away.

Instead, he saw a strongly built Mexican standing right at the open door. The Mexican held a pistol, steady as a rock and aimed directly at his face at a distance of perhaps a foot. The unexpected sight sent a thrill of fear right down to his toes.

"Very slowly, hand me the gun, Senior. Just hand it over, handle first, por favor. No need for me to kill you, none at all."

Anwar did exactly as he was told.

"Gracias. Now put on this sombrero, keep your head down and walk." Gonzales walked Anwar and put him in the front passenger seat. Gonzales sat directly behind Anwar with a gun on him. Gonzales tapped the barrel of the gun against Anwar's head a few times, just a light tap tap tap to let him know the gun was there, inches away.

One of the criminals slipped into the driver's seat, another joined Gonzales in the back. Under instruction, Anwar put his hands behind his head, under the sombrero. The whole operation had taken no more than two minutes from the first breaking of glass until the car and captive departed.

Off to Julio' Barrio they went.

Fifteen minutes later three FBI men kicked in the door of Anwar's apartment and discovered nothing of value. They banged on the adjacent apartment doors until one of the dwellers revealed to Special Agent Johnson what he had seen. Johnson called Special Agent Woods.

"The subject left in a black Honda Accord approximately fifteen minutes before our arrival. Our witness said that the subject had three companions of Mexican extraction." Johnson reported. "A gray Nissan belonging to the subject has been vandalized. The witness reported hearing the sound of the car alarm shortly before the men departed the premises. He didn't get a plate number on the Honda."

"Mexicans, my ass, Johnson. I'll bet you money that it was the Israelis." Woods spat back into the phone. Woods was not pleased.

Shimon entered Julio's Barrio through the kitchen door and walked into the office cramped next to the freezer. Gonzales and his two henchmen, Manuel and Pablo were also seated at the round table with the unfortunate Anwar Saba. Shimon pulled up a chair and made himself comfortable.

"Anwar Saba from Hebron. Your father is Sammy the Plumber. Your mother is Abeer. Your idiot brother Assim is a member of Hamas. Your sister Latifa is a student at the university branch right in Hebron."

"I see you have done your homework, Shimon Levi," Saba responded, quite calmly under the circumstances.

"Very good, Mr. Saba, I am impressed. Anwar, I will let you choose your poison. You will not like any of the choices I have for you but you may pick the least poisonous of the options available to you. Will it be your mother and father, or your sister and brother who are accused of collaborating with the Israelis? We can plant incriminating evidence and we can wire suspicious amounts of money to their bank accounts in Hebron. It will barely be an inconvenience for us. You just go right ahead and pick." Shimon did not bluster or threaten. Anwar Saba knew exactly what would happen to his family members if Shimon chose to put them in a frame. Arrests by the security police in any nation between Turkey and Japan would not go well, something that Saba knew quite well. He had seen it.

"What do you want from me?" he asked, a sheen of sweat showing on his forehead.

"Where is Ari Ben Ora?"

"I don't know, Shimon Levi. I could ask you the same question."

Gonzales opened and closed his big hands suggestively on the top of the table. "Senior Levi, I can make him tell us the truth. I shouldn't take long. But I should ask if you want him to survive the questioning?" Gonzales offered.

"Not just yet, Jaime." Shimon turned again to Anwar. "Mr. Saba, who or what is the Muslim Brigade?"

"I don't know. The Tijuana Arabs that I know think you kidnapped Ari ben Ora and the American so we would be blamed and discriminated against by the Mexican authorities."

"Anwar, you followed a blue Corolla with Canadian plates."

"Yes, I follow a lot of Corollas. I am looking for the kidnappers too. I will tell you the driver of that blue Corolla is at a house in Tijuana. The Tijuana Arabs are going to hit that house tonight and smoke them out. Hopefully, that is where Ari Ben Ora and the American hostage are. They can be released and we Arabs will be the heroes."

"Do you know the location and the time?" Shimon asked.

"They wouldn't tell me the location, but they said the time would be around eight in the evening."

"What makes you think that Ari Ben Ora is in the house?"

"On the front seat of that Corolla I spotted a copy of Ari Ben Ora's book, "The Palestine Exchange.

"Give me some names of your buddies, Anwar."

"Look, my only contact is Ibrahim Assad."

"And Ibrahim, where does he come from? I want to know about your friends, Anwar."

"Sidon, Lebanon."

"How many Tijuana Arabs are there? What kind of scale are we talking about here?"

"I am not sure, a half dozen, and maybe a few more." Anwar certainly looked like he was thinking hard. He should. Having the security police arrest his loved ones could not be contemplated. Even bogus evidence would be enough to put them in the cells. If they came out at all, not a sure thing, they would never be the same. To think of his mother or sister in the cells made him frantic. He really did want to give Shimon all the facts he had.

"More names."

"Farouk Hassan."

"Who do you report to?" Shimon leaned into the question to further intimidate his prisoner.

"Ali Chaboun in San Diego," Anwar quickly replied. He seemed to hold nothing back.

"Where does your Ali come from?"

"Beirut."

"Write down his contact information with this pen on the napkin. Anwer, your visa has expired. Even as we speak, the FBI is at your apartment waiting to deport you."

"What? I have broken no other laws," Anwar replied in a panicky voice.

"Jaime, let me have a word with you in private."

"Si, Senor Levi."

"How is it that your people didn't spot the Corolla in Tijuana?"

"I don't know, Senor Levi. Perhaps the driver didn't cross at Tijuana? Maybe he crossed at Mexicali or Tecate and drove west to Tijuana. Maybe he took the long way around because it made him feel safer. It could happen, no?"

Shimon's phone rang. He checked the caller ID. He ignored the call. He had not the least interest in talking to Special Agent Woods, not right now.

"What can you do, Senor Levi? You don't know the location of theis house in Tijuana. You don't know if Are and the American are in that house either." He held up first one of his big fingers and then another to mark his points. Then he shrugged. And smiled. "We will get there, Senior. Are you hungry? I am. Do you like good Mexican food Senior Levi? And tequila?"

"Sure." Levi responded, thrown off a bit by the sudden change of direction.

"Julio's Barrio is the best. Let's eat. We will feel better and maybe we will think of something."

"OK, good idea. Will you order for me?"

"Si, Senor Levi."

Shimon thought of Michelle. He wished he could be at her side right at this moment. He had seen too many gunshot victims with head wounds. Most did not survive. And when they did, they were never the same. He called Gideon.

"The Arab could be lying. It could be a trap," Gideon speculated.

"If it were a trap, I think I would have an address."

180

"Well, that makes sense. OK, not a trap. There is still a chance that Anwar can get an address, all he has to do is call his contacts."

"They don't trust him completely. Anwar is a Sunni. The others are Lebanese Shiites."

"He may be playing you, Shimon."

"I have interrogated a lot of men. I don't think so. He knows his family in Hebron could go down. He is straight with me."

"Maybe we'll know something after 8," Gideon opined.

Chapter 45

PARIS

"Louis, this is Lucille. Something terrible has happened. An Arab shot Michelle in Israel yesterday. She is in a bad way. I am waiting for my cab to drive me to the airport."

"Oh my God Lucille! Is there anything I can do for you?"

"Pray for her Louis, just pray for her."

"Was that Lucille?" Andre asked.

"Yes. Andre, an Arab, shot Michelle yesterday." Louis just passed on the horrid news. He had no way in the world to cushion the blow for his friend.

"Shot? Where? How? What hospital is she in?" Andre asked rapid-fire, clearly panicked.

"I don't know any of the details. Everything I know, you know," Louis answered.

Andre grabbed the phone and dialed Lucille's landline. No one answered.

"She doesn't answer," he announced, his eyes wild.

"Andre, she told me she was headed to Charles de Gaulle airport. Her cab must have come to pick her up."

"Did she say what airline, what time?"

"No, Andre, she did not say. She said what I told you and no more than that."

Andre shook his head as if to clear it. "No wonder Michelle didn't return my messages. Louis, can you drive me to the airport? I need to get to her somehow."

"Of course. What airline?"

"Whichever one can take me. If I have to, I'll go standby. I have to get to Michelle."

"Inspector, half the department has spent the whole day reviewing the video feeds from Van Cleef & Arpels, Boucheron, and Cartier along with all the other jewelry stores on Le Place Vendome. No one has so far spotted Zoran in any of the footage," Blanc reported to his boss.

Gallant looked judiciously at his detective. "Be more specific, Blanc."

"We reviewed videos beginning on the day of the Father Martel incident and each subsequent day until we fished Zoran out of the river with no fingers."

182

"Blanc, you will have to go further back. Go back two weeks, look at everything. Did you get the footage from the little stores, not just the famous?"

"Yes, we did all the stores, big and small. We will go back for two weeks. Who knows, maybe something will show up? I'm on it, boss."

Andre stepped up to the Air France counter.

"Monsieur, your passport please."

"A one-way ticket to Ben Gurion, please."

"When will you be returning to France, Monsieur Dubois?"

"I am not certain. Ashkelon is where I have been living with my fiancee."

"I regret to say, Monsieur Dubois, that your passport to Israel has been revoked."

"What? Revoked? That is unacceptable. My fiancee is dying in a Jerusalem hospital. I am Andre Dubois, the astronaut. I fought off the Russians. You can't do this to me!"

"Security, security, we have a situation at the check-in counter. Passenger in distress."

Chapter 46

TIJUANA

Mounted on motorcycles, engines revving, Rashid, and his men Gamal and Sammy lined up next to the other motorcycles parked at Jalapenos bar and lounge, a biker hang out. Amir arrived, puffing, on a bicycle, out of breath and disgusted that he had such a primitive and totally uncool mode of transportation.

The same burlap bag that held Eric Miller's chess set also held a special cell phone. Rashid handed off to Gamal. He tucked it safely into an inside jacket pocket. Then Gamal roared off without another word. No words were needed. Their plan was set.

Thanks to the careful work that Amir had done on the Corolla in LA, four pounds of C-4 plastic explosive rested quietly in the glove compartment of the car. A clever little remote-controlled trigger device came with the block of explosives. It could be detonated by a call from a cell phone. This technology, so very common in Iraq during the US occupation, had by now spread everywhere in the world. The phone that Gamal had in his pocket was ready to send a signal to detonate the explosives in the glove box with a single push of a button.

"Heading to my destination," Gamal said cryptically into a BlueTooth microphone attached to his helmet. Modern technology allowed easy speech while keeping both hands on the handlebars of the bike. Safety first.

He approached the Luna de Valle house from the west side and immediately caught sight of the pickup truck with a guy in it. The pickup was parked across and down the street from the target, innocuously between him and the Corolla which was parked at the target house. Still at a safe distance from the target, Gamal cut his light and engine. Then he rolled the bike from the street up and over a curb and parked the machine under a tree so desiccated that it didn't look like anyone had bothered to water it in this decade.

He could see the glowing flickers of cigarette light grow and fade in rhythm as the guy in the pickup smoked. He probably shouldn't do that, Gamal thought. Bad tradecraft, but these guys were like that. He smiled grimly to himself. That carelessness or bad training would cost them.

At 8:05 PM, two cars approached from the east side, cruised past the Corolla house and stopped behind the red pickup truck. The chain smoker stayed in the truck, watching and not alarmed. The new arrivals comprised the nucleus of Tijuana's Hezbollah cell. They left their cars and crossed the street to the target house. Gamal touched his Blue Tooth and said "Roll."

Rashid drove his motorcycle with Sammy behind him. More quietly if more slowly, Amir pedaled his bicycle for all he was worth to arrive not too far behind the others. When he got to the alley behind the house, Rashid and Sammy were already in place on the street side. Sammy hopped off the motorcycle. Rashid revved up the engine, making a loud distraction.

Hearing the noise, Ibrahim shouted "Take cover. Something is up."

They gathered behind the bulk of the Corolla, alarmed and cautious but not yet in battle mode. Their hands went near to their weapons but did not pull them out. Not yet. They faced in the direction of Rashid and his noisy bike and away from Gamal at the opposite end of the street.

Gamal started walking along the path where a sidewalk would be in a more prosperous part of town. He reached into his jacket and found the phone. As soon as he had it in hand, he touched the button that sent a signal to the detonator. A ferociously loud explosion came from the passenger side of the Corolla.

He released the cell phone and used the same hand to draw a small automatic pistol from under his jacket. He moved quickly but not at a run.

He zigged into the street, coming up behind the smoker by the driver's side of the red pickup truck. Farouk never saw him coming. Farouk watched big-eyed as the men around the exploded Corolla fell screaming.

Gamal put two quick rounds into Farouk's cranium and Farouk knew no more. Gamal changed direction and headed back for his motorcycle.

The explosion shattered the Corolla's windows, blew out the doors, shoved the engine forward through the grill, and in general, came apart in a spectacular and dangerous way. Chunks of glass and metal blasted into the men grouped around the car, tearing through their fragile flesh. Some of Ibrahim's men died right then and there. Others fell, bleeding and screaming out their last moments. Ibrahim was lucky to have one of his men directly between the blast and himself. The man, now quite dead, absorbed most of the fragments that would have shredded Ibrahim. Ibrahim took a few small bits of something in his left leg, terribly painful but not immediately life-threatening.

Quickly deciding that he could do nothing to help his dead or dying men, Ibrahim hobbled as best he could around the side of the house. He didn't know how badly he was hurt but the pain was at a level that he could tolerate, for the moment at least. He could get to the alley behind the house and find a way to get out of the immediate area. That was the first thing, getaway.

As soon as Ibrahim hit the alley, he saw Amir, waiting with a pistol in his hand. Amir raised the gun, as calm as he would be at the firing range. Two shots into the center of mass put Ibrahim down for the count. One bullet tore through the pulmonary artery causing a catastrophic loss in blood pressure. The shock caused Ibrahim to turn slightly. The next shot traveled diagonally through his torso. That shot clipped both lungs and his heart. The first bullet would have killed him in a minute, no more. The second bullet made the first bullet superfluous. It killed Ibrahim in seconds.

Seeing no more leakers come his way, Amir called Gamal. Gamal swung into the alley on his bike and picked up Amir. The pair of them took off in one direction. Sammy and Rashid headed away in a different direction. Both pairs of men stopped at the Tijuana slough but just long enough to toss their weapons into the disgusting water.

"Captain Diaz, this looks like a drug deal that went very bad. We found cocaine in the house." Lieutenant Raul Mendoza reported.

"Have you been able to ID any of the dead men yet, lieutenant?"

"Si, captain, Arabs by name, according to their driver's licenses. The explosion in the Corolla did kill most of them." He pointed across the street to a red pickup truck. "There is another victim in the truck. He caught a couple of bullets in the head. We found another body around the back. That one left a trail of blood from the site of the explosion to the alley. Someone found him there and shot him to death."

Diaz nodded to show he followed Mendoza's report but did not interrupt.

"Captain Diaz, the forensic people have just begun their work but they already told me that this was an older model brown Toyota Corolla that someone had recently re-painted blue." Mendoza gestured in the direction of Ortiz, the crime scene investigator.

Diaz called out to Ortiz.

"Senior Ortiz, was this pile of crap the car used to kidnap Ari Ben Ora?"

"Yes sir, I think so. We will know more when we know more, but it looks likely to me."

"Any evidence that the American or Ari Ben Ora was in the house?"

"Nothing yet sir, but we are just getting started."

Chapter 47

PARIS

Officer Beauregard broke the news.

"We have a video of Zoran."

Excited, the detectives convened in the video room, voluble as schoolgirls.

Beauregard took the lead in explaining what the detectives would see. "Quiet down you idiots. Let me talk." The hubbub stopped after a few seconds and he continued. "This is a video from Rothschild's Jewelers on Tuesday, three days before Zoran stole the kidnap car. At 10:33 AM Zoran left Rothschild's Jewelers, as you can see right here. He comes out, turns left and out of the shot. That is all we have."

Gallant spoke as soon as the short bit of tape ended. "Keep looking. This is good work, good detective work Beauregard. Now that we have a time established, we can check stores with cameras that focus on the sidewalk or street. Carry on now." He glanced at his chief henchman. "Blanc, please come into my office."

The two men entered the head detective's office and closed the door.

"OK Blanc, I can see you have something else. What did you not want the others to know about?"

"We found Zoran's apartment," Blanc revealed.

"Good work. Did he own a vehicle, even a scooter?"

"Not that we could find and nothing that we have a record of at the license bureau."

"How about a bank account? Sometimes even crooks have bank accounts."

"Yes. With the permission of the court, I located his bank account. He had approximately five hundred euros at the Banque Populaire branch just a five-minute walk from his apartment," Blanc reported after glancing at his notebook to make sure he had his facts straight in his mind.

"Blanc, we need to know why Zoran went to Rothschild's two days before he stole the priest's car."

"Yes sir. If whoever hired him paid him off in gems, even diamonds, he might want to get an appraisal to confirm their value. I don't think that would be out of the question," Blanc surmised. "I don't think that taking a criminal pay off in jewels to a legitimate jeweler for evaluation would be a smart thing to do, but he might have done it."

Gallant pondered. Zoran might have done such a thing. Zoran and criminals, in general, were not often the masterminds depicted in the cinema.

"Blanc, put yourself in his shoes. After you walked out of Rothschild's and turned left, what would you do? Where would you go? Would you take a cab?"

"No, not if I carried money or jewels. The cab driver would know he had business with jewelers and might have valuables on him. A crooked driver might pull a gun on him and take his goods or cash."

"We know things like that have happened, Blanc. That is a rational and logical assessment. The cabbies wait in their lines which makes it easy to see who comes in and out of these high-end jewelry stores. So, no cab. Would you take the metro?"

"Not from the Place Vendome. I could be followed."

"Well then, Blanc, what would you do?"

"I would want to get rid of my load, to get it somewhere safe. Carrying a load of valuable jewelry around in the neighborhoods where Zoran moves would just ask for trouble."

"Precisely the right answer, Blanc. How?"

Blanc brightened at his boss's approval. "I would walk to the closest bank and get a safe deposit box for my valuables."

"Yes. I would too. And then what?"

"I would walk to a cafe for a coffee and a small bite. Then, fortified, I would go into a department store in one entrance and out of another. Then grab the first cab I saw and have him drop me at the main metro station. I would get lost in the crowd and spend a pleasant hour riding here and there all over Paris, changing trains at each stop. When I felt that no one could possibly still have me under surveillance, I would go home to a well-deserved rest."

Blanc looked smug as he took in his boss's smiling expression.

Chapter 48

TIJUANA

Miller heard the garage door open and close. The cyclist had returned to the house where Miller had been kept, frightened and bored. In a few minutes Rashid walked into the room. He seemed distracted, perhaps wound up but keeping his disquiet under control. Miller did not like this at all. He could think of several reasons why Rashid might be disturbed and none of them boded well for him.

"We're leaving," Rashid announced with no preamble.

"Where are we going?" Miller asked, tucking the chess set under his arm.

"Leave the chess set." Rashid ordered. "You won't need it anymore."

Miller received this news like a blow to the gut. Eric knew the sort of place that would not accommodate a game of chess, even a solo game on an electronic chess set. A grave or some abandoned rock pit would not allow a rigorous game of chess. Rashid took Eric to the garage. Sammy, Jamal and one other person stood by their motorcycles.

"Miller, listen very carefully. You were rescued this morning from the trunk of a car. You saw nothing. Your Arab kidnappers blindfolded you and dumped you into the trunk of a car and drove away. You think you were in the trunk for several hours. Do you understand, Miller?"

"No, of course not. I hear your words, Rashid, I hear them clearly. I can remember them exactly, as I think you wish me to do?"

"Yes. Keep listening. You heard shots followed by an explosion and when it was over, you banged your feet on the inside of the trunk. Someone rescued you, someone speaking fluent Spanish, several men. They dropped you off at the American Consulate."

Rashid waited until Miller responded by nodding.

"When you get to the American consulate, they will ask you to identify some dead Arabs. You will tell them that four of them were the ones who kidnapped you in La Jolla. Do you have any questions? Can you remember all this without fail?"

"No, yes. I can remember the story, no problem at all. I can stick to it. I have seen the TV cop shows where the police ask the same questions over and over, trying to trip up a witness or extract more information. I know what to do. Stick to the story and only the story." He gave a rueful smile. "It is a short story and I really do not know much of anything, do I?"

"Good." Rashid said. Then he went over the story again with Miller. Then he went over the story again. Then he made Miller recite the story twice more. "OK, I think you have it perfectly, Miller. It will be well."

"I will do exactly as you say."

"I hope so, Miller. Don't forget for a moment that I know where you live." He gave Miller an ominous look.

"You can count on me, Rashid. You have my word."

"I believe you. I am sorry that we have to do this to you, Miller. You are innocent, just caught up in something that was none of your own doing." With that, he smacked Eric across the face, very hard, as hard as Eric had ever been hit. Rashid used an open hand which still hurt like Hell and broke the skin. Blood leaked slowly from a break in the skin.

Miller rocked back in pain and sunrise.

"You need to show some physical wear and tear for you to make a credible witness," Jamal added.

Sammy delivered a quick kick to Miller's lower leg. Miller grimaced.

Finally, Jamal slipped a rope around first one ankle and then the other. He pulled the rope back and forth a few times producing a very authentic- and painful-rope burn.

"Sit down and relax," Rashid ordered. Sammy opened a bottle of water for Miller and handed it over. Praying the beating had finished, Miller drank the water.

"Your bruises will turn black and blue in a few minutes," Rashid told him. "Have you ever been on a motorcycle, Miller?"

"No."

They blindfolded Eric Miller and put sunglasses on him to disguise the fact. He listened as Rashid gave him the last set of instructions.

"Hold on to me and always lean forward. The ride to the American Consulate takes about twenty minutes. When I tell you to get off the bike, get off on the right side. As you face away from the street, the consulate will be on your right. You will be a free man. Remember, you were always blindfolded except when you were in the bedroom. Got it?"

His heart racing, Miller just said, "I understand."

Chapter 49

TIJUANA

"**S**top," a consulate guard commanded. He drew his gun.
Eric stopped as ordered.
"Hands in the air. Identify yourself."

"Eric Miller." Eric said in as aloud a voice as he could manage. He didn't want to get shot by his own side after coming this close to freedom.

"Down on the ground."

Miller went face down on the cement sidewalk. The guard frisked him with swift efficiency, then helped Eric to his feet. Two other guards arrived, each grabbing an arm. They marched Eric into the building.

One of them reported to the greeter. "This man claims that his name is Eric Miller. Inform the counselor general."

When Rashid returned to the hostage house, Jamal had collected the trash, any odds and ends left around, and anything really that someone might have used or touched. He had put the whole mess into big plastic trash bags for disposal. Amir moved methodically through the house with a bucket of bleach and a sponge. He wiped every surface he could reach with a mixture of bleach and water. This not only wiped away any fingerprints left by any of them but also destroyed any lingering DNA evidence. He made sure to hit doorknobs, the handles on the toilet and the sinks in the house, knobs on kitchen cabinets. The place stank of cleanliness before he was half-finished.

They took the trash bags and put them into a trash container and wheeled the bin out to the curb for pick-up.

Satisfied, Rashid packed the chess game into his knapsack, a souvenir of sorts. Then the four men climbed onto two motorcycles and putted away. They headed for Tecate, a Mexican border town about twenty-eight miles to the east of Tijuana. They would arrive at the relative safety of the much smaller town in less than an hour. Their assignment with the kidnapped American had ended satisfactorily for them and Rashid supposed, to a degree for Miller as well. He still had his life, not a sure thing when this started, at least in Eric Miller's mind.

"Special Agent Woods, Eric Miller, the kidnapped victim, walked into our consulate in Tijuana a few minutes ago." The duty special agent, a guy named Derek, reported to Woods by phone.

Woods paused for several seconds to take it all in.

"Have any of our people interviewed him yet?" Woods meant any FBI people.

"Not yet. We have a special agent at the consulate but he has to wait for a physician to check Miller over and see if he has anything life-threatening going on. Our guy said Miller was bruised and battered a little bit but it didn't look serious to him. That was just from a glance at Miller. Of course, he could have injuries that didn't show in just a quick look."

"I'm on my way, Derek." Woods rang off.

While driving into the San Diego field office, Woods used his hands-free bluetooth to make some calls. He first made an exceedingly brief call to the FBI director followed by calls to Detective Ryan at the La Jolla station of the San Diego police department. Finally, he spoke to the Chief Alberto Diaz of the Tijuana Police Department.

Last on his shortlist, he called Shimon. Shimon had spent the night at Julio's Barrio. A few minutes after the explosion in Tijuana, Gonzales got a call, his men reporting in. Throughout the night he received regular updates. Gonzales' men on the ground informed them that members of a Hezbollah cell had perished in the explosion.

Shimon's phone chimed. His caller ID told him who was on the line.

"Good morning, Special Agent Woods." He spoke in a cheerful voice, in spite of the lack of sleep and uncomfortable half- slumber in a chair.

"Miller walked into the American consulate in Tijuana," Woods announced with no preamble.

"Good news for sure, but Ari Ben Ora is still missing."

"So is Anwar Saba. What have you done with him, Shimon?"

"Anwar joined me for dinner last night. He drank too many margaritas, as can happen to anyone. Before he fell asleep on the couch, he gave up his contacts. I'll be happy to share with you if you like."

Woods made no attempt to disguise his irritation.

"Where are you, Shimon?"

"I am at Julio's Barrio, a bar in San Ysidro," replied the Israeli.

"I will be there within the hour with additional FBI Special Agents. You will hand over Saba, do you understand?"

"You have my full cooperation. With your permission, Special Agent, I would very much like to interrogate Miller."

"You can have him after we are finished with him. I don't know how long that will take," Woods cautioned.

Chapter 50

PARIS

Armed with a court order, Inspector Gallant and Detective Blanc canvassed all the banks within a two-mile radius of the jewelry district. They hit pay dirt at the Credit Agricole branch just a few blocks from the jewelry district.

"And that my young apprentice is how we do detective work." Gallant snarked at Blanc. "We use our brains and our shoe leather to find a clue. Our work is difficult and sometimes dangerous but not too complicated."

Blanc just looked at his boss in resigned disgust. He had begun his work as a detective a decade ago and knew very well about shoe leather, patience, and the assembling of clues. This clue was the signature of Zoran Coldevic on the sign-in sheet for a safe deposit box. He visited the bank just one day before his body was found floating in the Seine.

It took another two hours to get the proper legal permission from a magistrate to open the box. Then they went back to the bank where the cooperative bankers helped them into the safe deposit box. The bank had one key but the other lock had to be drilled out by the custodian.

"Well well, Blanc, what have we here?" Gallant asked, still happy and full of himself that they had followed a trail of clues and suppositions to this place and time. They found a pouch with a clutch of small diamonds with value enough to be useful without being a fortune.

They also found a handwritten note.

My last will and testament

If someone is reading this letter then I am dead, murdered by Sasha Andreev. Sasha approached me at the Serbian Orthodox Church on Rue Vincent and offered ten thousand euros in small diamonds if I drugged an old gay man and stole his car. I insisted that he pay me in advance and Sasha did.

Sasha told me that the old man would be at the Cafe Rousseau on Saturday night, March 28th. My job would be to pretend to seduce him, to lure him to the Hotel Valee. Once we were in the hotel room, I poured him a drink of wine and slipped a drug into it, a drug provided by Sasha. Whatever the drug was, it worked immediately. When the old man fell asleep, I took his keys from his pocket. I looked in this wallet and it was only then that I discovered that I had drugged a priest.

I was ashamed of myself but I was also too afraid to back out. So I took the priest's car and drove it to a meeting place. Sasha waited for me there. I handed him the keys to the 2005 dark blue Renault.

I had no idea that this Renault would be used to kidnap and blackmail Andre Dubois. Two days later my picture was all over the news. I knew it would be a matter of time before the police got to me. I was more afraid that Sasha would get to me first. I plan to leave for Serbia and lay low there until things settle down. I hope no one reads this letter.

Zoran Coldevic
March 31, 2010

The bank video confirmed Zoran's presence in the lobby at 11;12 AM on Thursday, March 25th and again on the following Tuesday, March 31st. On his last visit to the bank, Zoran had colored his hair and applied a fake mustache to hide his identity.

The detectives returned to the station and made multiple copies of the will. Then they placed the diamonds and the last will and testament into the evidence locker for safekeeping.

After a pleasant lunch, the two detectives drove to the Serbian Orthodox Church for some more detective work. They thought they had made good progress in the case.

Chapter 51

―――――――――――――― ·•◈◍◈•· ――――――――――――――

TIJUANA

Julio's Barrio, where Shimon had spent the night, had an address in San Ysidro. San Ysidro sat right on the border, just a short drive from Tijuana. Shimon, with his diplomatic passport, had no problem crossing into Mexico on his way to the American Consulate. He found Special Agent Woods there ahead of him, waiting.

"Miller's not here," Woods announced flatley, not in a helpful, friendly way.

"Where is he?" Shimon responded, using all of his tact and restraint.

"Diaz and Deceptive Ryan took him to the morgue."

Shimon raised an eyebrow in silent interrogative. Woods picked it up.

"It is just a formality, Shimon. Miller has already identified four of the dead guys from photographs. The others, he didn't know about."

"Did the FBI match the facial scans with those photographs? Did you get any hits on the fingerprints yet? Any identification on the bodies?" He smiled in a rueful way. "Anything easy?"

That caught Woods off guard. He noted the professional interest in Shimon Levi, secret agent for Israel. He gave a little smile back, pro to pro. "Nope. The faces suffered a good deal of damage from flying glass and chunks of the car. One guy got popped in the noggin while sitting in

215

a truck. He looks OK but no hits on him yet. The prints will go through the Mexican system and sometime today Chief Diaz will have them faxed to Washington where we will send them through our system."

"You might send them on to Israel. We might have something on one of these guys."

"Now that is a good idea, Shimon. Let's do that too."

Shimon made a circling motion. "Hit all the bases. It can't hurt."

Woods nodded.

"But Miller could make a positive ID on four of them?"

"Not in the sense that he knew who they were. Just that he recognized them as his captors. It is helpful, just not very useful."

Now Shimon nodded.

"Have you interviewed Miller yet?"

"Yes, I did." Woods answered.

"Did you ask him about Ari?"

"Yes, naturally. He never saw Ari after the both of them got snatched in La Jolla. He got tossed into a different car from Ari, and that was that as far as seeing Ari was concerned. The Mexican police dusted the bomb car and three other vehicles at the scene that they think belonged to the gang. No prints from Ari or Miller on any of them. The same for the house on Valle de Luna. No prints of the kidnap victims."

"Have they found any witnesses?"

"Not yet, maybe not ever. Chief Diaz thinks the neighbors are afraid to talk."

"What do you think happened, Special Agent?" Shimon asked with gentle tact. FBI men named themselves Special Agents to differentiate themselves from other federal agents who were just 'agents.' Everyone outside of the FBI snickered when it came up, but not in front of the Fibbies. The Fibbies took it very seriously. All part of their reputation for having prickly pride and a stick up their butts.

"I don't have a feel for this one, Shimon. Miller's testimony is flimsy. He said he heard shots, then Spanish speaking men pulled him from the trunk, still blindfolded. They put him in another car and drove him to a place unknown. They dumped him and aimed him at the American Consulate. That's all, folks. It isn't much."

"It's a beginning," Shimon replied.

"The problem is there are no dead Mexicans. Think about it. Shots were fired, a bomb detonated and blew a car to pieces, and all we have are dead Arabs and one live healthy American hostage. Surpassing strange, wouldn't you say?" Woods analyzed.

"I see what you mean," Shimon nodded.

All for pretense. Shimon feigned his lack of information on the case. But he understood a few things that Woods didn't. He knew that this was a well planned operation to eliminate a Tijuana based Hezbollah terrorist cell. The operation was under the guiding hand of Amir Delshad. Shimon doubted that Miller had ever been at the scene of the bombing, much less in the Corolla. He looked at Woods as he posed a question.

"Special Agent Woods, do you know who owns that house? We may find a thread to follow with the owner."

"Technically, a bank owns this house and one other in Tijuana but owns it for the benefit of an outfit called Helene Realty. According to Chief Diaz, both houses are officially vacant."

"I'd bet that whoever used this house knew about it's status. They knew that they were not going to be disturbed."

"Obviously," Woods agreed.

"What is Helene Realty and where is it? Do we know that yet?"

"Yes. It is legally domiciled in the Cayman Islands. Under Mexican law, foreigners and foreign corporations are required to utilize a real estate trust to hold property in Mexico. And they must use a Mexican bank to act on their behalf. The bank legally owes the property but the beneficiary acquires the use and enjoyment. Helene Realty is also the beneficiary to four other houses in Northern Mexico. Two houses are in Tecate and two others are in Mexicali." His phone buzzed and he waved off Shimon as he took the call. He listened for a minute and then broke the connection.

"That was Chief Diaz. He gave me the address for the second house. Diaz and Miller are on the way back here to the consulate. I am going to check out the second house. Do you want to stay here and interview Miller or go to the second house and have a look?"

"I can interview Miller later. Let's get to the second house before Diaz does. Who knows what we will find? I'll follow your squad car.

Woods and Levi conducted a cursory examination of Helene Realty's second house in Tijuana. The FBI agent strolled to the kitchen to take another call from Diaz. Shimon wandered through the house, checking out chairs, mattresses and bed frames.

In the third bedroom, Shimon discovered a magnetic chess piece underneath the bed and pocketed it. He had proof now that Miller had been at this house, or so he surmised. Perhaps Ari would be in one of the other houses in Tecate or Mexicali. He ventured into the garage and turned on the lights. Oil droppings covered the floor, the smell of gasoline permeated the close atmosphere.

"That was Chief Diaz with an update. Helene Realty is controlled by Helena Valenzuela, the wife of Fernando Valenzuela. She lives in Barcelona, Spain," Woods revealed.

"Who is Fernando Valenzuela? I don't know the name."

"He is the leader of the Tijuana drug cartel. The Mexicans caught him a year ago. He was tried and convicted in Mexican courts. He now resides in La Mesa Penitentiary on a life stretch. Diaz sent me a text. Valenzuela wants a deal, his freedom for Ari Ben Ora's release. He promised that he can deliver Ari to the Israeli consulate in Tijuana within the hour." Woods seemed to think this over, to see where the new information fit into what he already knew. "How about that for a switcheroo?"

"It makes sense to me, I believe him. Let's talk to him," Shimon responded.

"Valenzuela doesn't speak English. Chief Diaz will translate."

"Do you trust Diaz?"

Woods made a face. "Shimon, we are the FBI. Chief Diaz is the head of one of the most corrupt police agencies in the world." Woods let it go at that.

"If it helps, I know a little Spanish from my time in Argentina."

"I forgot about that. It was in your profile."

"You have a profile on me?" Shimon pretended to be shocked.

Woods now cracked a big smile.

"Of course. We are the FBI."

Chapter 52

PARIS

The two detectives pulled up and parked across the street from the Serbian Orthodox Church. They crossed the street and entered the nave. Waiting for them, alerted by a telephone call, stood a big man, over six feet tall. He wore the black robes of an Orthodox priest, complete with headdress which made him even taller. His girth matched his height. His ferocious beard added to make him a formidable sight.

"Hello, gentlemen, may I help you?" The visage asked.

"We phoned ahead to meet with Bishop Nikolai Debrojovic. We are with the Metro Police," the inspector said. "Can you take us to him?"

"I am he," Debrojovic responded calmly.

"Bonjour Bishop Debrojovic, I am Chief Inspector Gallant and my colleague here is detective Blanc."

"May I see your police badges?"

Both the detectives reached for their credentials folders and showed their badges.

Satisfied, the bishop asked politely "How can I help you, detectives?"

"We are looking for Sasha Andreev. We have reason to believe that he attends your church," said the inspector.

"When Sasha is in Paris, he often does. I hope he's not in trouble."

Gallant shook his head in the negative.

"No trouble, we just wanted to ask him a few questions about a person of interest. You mentioned 'when he is in town'. Does he live elsewhere?"

"Sasha works as a flight attendant on Jat airlines. He travels often, as you might think. I should have a local address for him. If you can spare a few minutes, I will search my membership files on the computer. Why don't you come with me, detectives?"

The policemen followed the archbishop into his office after passing through the big, empty hall of the church.

"Please give my best to Sasha when you see him," Debrojovic said as he fired up his computer.

"We surely will, bishop."

"Ah, here we are. We have two addresses. Do you want to write this down? Sasha lives at the Bastille at 20 rue Godfrey, apartment number 334. He also has an address in Moscow.

At the cafe across the street from his apartment building, Sasha savored his meal and finished his second glass of Pinot Noir. He gazed through the window to his apartment building. Raindrops continued to fall on the window pane, slightly blurring his view. A flicker of motion attracted his attention.

A plain car a few years old pulled up and parked in the loading zone, quite against regulations. Two men jumped out and rushed to Sasha's building. The concierge of the building, merely a custodian and rent taker in spite of his lofty title, met them at the door.

No time to process his charge card now, Sasha immediately placed some euros on the table. Raindrops accumulated on the window, making it somewhat opaque. It was not enough to hide the view of the lights going on in his apartment. He stood up.

"A check, Monsieur?" The waiter asked.

"No, the payment is on the table. I have a problem." He grimaced, as if in pain. "You see, my ex-wife just entered my apartment building across the street. May I live through the kitchen?"

"Follow me, Monsieur." The waiter did not bat an eye. Helping a patron out of a jam fell well within his duties, as he saw them.

Sasha followed the waiter back through the swinging doors and out the back into the alley. Sasha passed rows of garbage cans on his way to the metro station.

Chapter 53

JULY 19, 2007

Moscow Command Center

Igor paced the floor of the windowless tech center, nerves on edge. His cell phone rang. He checked the caller ID.

"Hello Boris. We didn't have time to block the network news. Of course, they know the priest died. He killed himself on TV. Nobody could miss his death. The Frenchman, Andre Dubois, is already receiving emails of condolence from his friends at the academy. I let those emails through because I don't want to arouse suspicion on the ISS. He hasn't replied to any so far. Dubois may or may not know that his fellow astronaut Alex's brother Yuri has been arrested in Moscow. But he knows Father Gauthier has died very spectacularly. He may be suspicious and come clean with the others about the email he intercepted and forwarded to him. Dubois may have even figured out his priest couldn't have replied to his email. The priest was already dead when the email supposedly from him was sent. Boris, we will have to monitor everyone's actions on the ISS very carefully."

Igor inhaled and exhaled the cigarette smoke. Only three days until the supply ship was scheduled to arrive at the ISS docking station. An explosive device embedded in the wall of the visiting shuttle was set to detonate when the shuttle locked into the station. Both would then be blown to smithereens along with the people on board. More space junk would circle Earth more or less forever, for many years in any case. Igor took another puff. He hoped the shuttle launch would not be unnecessarily delayed due to bad weather.

"Igor," Ivan went on, "a new email is coming from the Israeli on the ISS, sent to his wife." Igor walked over to Ian's station.

Dearest Rachel,

I am so looking forward to seeing you and the children. Is the baby kicking? The supply ship is scheduled to dock on Friday and depart on Sunday to Russia. You may have heard about the French priest who committed suicide on national television.

He was Andre's priest. They were very close. Andre is grieving but doesn't want to talk about it right now. Most of the time I am bedridden from the radiation exposure, but occasionally I have spurts of energy.

Rachel, I have been listening to Sanjay's mp3 player. I would like to suggest that your father finally replace some of the Sinatra, Bennett and Dean Martin recordings on his jukebox at the restaurant and replace them with these songs, more contemporary for the patrons.................

I am very sorry I can't call David on his birthday tomorrow. The phones are still down. Wish him a happy birthday. And Rachel, if for some reason I don't make it back to you, please scatter my ashes in the Negev. Otherwise, I will see you in Shdema.

Love,
Ari

"So, he wants to email his wife 'Jumpin Jack Flash is a gas, gas, gas.' Ivan, did I ever tell you that I saw the Stones perform in Moscow in 1998? They were great." Boris gave a big smile at the remembrance.

"Should I let it through?" Ivan asked.

"Sure, the Israeli and I like some of the same music. He'll be a dead man soon. Send it through; it's harmless."

July 20, 2007

At 2 AM Ivan had just poured himself yet another cup of coal-black coffee, the better to keep himself awake even if the foul stuff riled his stomach after so many others. He slouched into his swivel chair, exhaustion battling with irritation. He had only one more hour before his relief showed up to free him. He kept an eye on the satellite feeds that poured onto his monitor from the ISS. The feeds never stopped, coming in a flood, all day, every day, 23/7.

"Igor, do you see the Frenchman spacewalking and performing unscheduled maintenance on the escape capsule?"

"I do see him. He is checking the heat shield. The ISS just sent a wire."

Attention Command Center

The ISS has been hit by space junk that punctuated a hole nearly three centimeters wide....

Life support systems aboard are unstable.....will rely on spacesuits until normal systems are restored... man outside trying to fix the problem.

Sanjay

"Ivan, I have a gut feeling they are planning to ditch the ISS and escape on the emergency capsule."

"Don't worry Igor, the escape capsule is programmed to fly to Russia."

"But they can easily disengage that program and land elsewhere. Where would they go, Ivan?"

"The Israeli mentioned Shdema in the email to his wife," Ivan recalled. He immediately typed Shdema into the search engine.

"Where is Shdema?" Igor asked.

"In the Negev. It is an Israeli missile site."

Enraged, Igor threw his cigarette on the floor and uttered a few profanities. He stepped hard on the burning butt.

"Igor, the music titles in the email might be a code. Should we alert Boris?"

"God no, not yet. Who knows how pissed he will be at us. We should not worry him yet. First, run a check of the titles." Igor stalled because he knew Boris would certainly demote him if he discovered that Ari's email had been a coded message. It was still only 3 AM. There was time to think and observe, Igor calculated. Igor lit another cigarette, his eyes riveted on the monitors. His head began to throb, the beginning of another migraine. He popped two aspirin and closed his eyes for a few minutes. He fell asleep, but only briefly.

"Igor, the music titles are sequential. Did you know the Beatles tune 'Rain' has the same four letters as Iran?"

"What else did you find?" Igor asked, his face suddenly pale.

"The song titles are code for an Iranian nuclear test and an immediate departure from the ISS. Boris needs to be notified," Ivan emphasized.

"You know the routine, Ivan. Write up your report first, and I'll sign it."

Igor received a second wire from the ISS.
Attention Command Center

Unable to repair breach.....shutting down all systems.... entire crew will disengage and board space capsule for 6 AM departure.......expected arrival at Russian landing strip 9 AM.

Sanjay

"Ivan, do you want a fresh cup?"

"Yes, I could use another cup."

Igor hated to do it but reasoned that he had to do it to prevent Ivan's report from reaching Boris. With a slight of hind, Igor furtively dispensed the fatal dosage of tasteless poison in Ivan's coffee. His KGB training came in handy after all.

Working diligently on the report, Ivan ingested the poison diluted in his coffee and in seconds lost consciousness. Igor called the medics. They quickly arrived and placed Ivan on a gurney and whisked him to the infirmary. Igor quickly deleted Ari's coded email and Ivan's half-prepared report. Satisfied that all incriminating evidence was purged, he called Boris.

"Hello Boris.......Of course, I am aware that they're preparing to leave the ISS. Look, I've lost Ivan.....I don't know. He passed out. The medics are working on him...........what's my assessment? ....reprogram the escape capsule flight to Kazakhstan."

Boris replied "Igor, I can't kill them even if they land in Kazakhstan. It's too risky."

"Destroy them in space, Boris. Doesn't their flight over Kazakhstan take them over Pakistan?"

"It does."

"A well-timed Pakistani test launch into the atmosphere, and the escape capsule will be nuked."

"Yes, Igor, yes it will."

Chapter 54

TIJUANA

A pair of Mexican corrections officers took the visitors to an interrogation room deep in the foul bowels of the La Mesa Penitentiary. Penitentiary meant a place where sinners might contemplate their sins and do 'penance.' Woods and Shimon Levi glanced at each other, for once they were on the same page. This dark place was not a place of penance.

Chief Diaz stood up when they entered the shabby concrete room with the added and peeling institutional green paint.

"May I offer you gentlemen some coffee?" Diaz asked hospitably.

"I'm good," Shimon answered, shaking his head at the same time.

Woods accepted with more politeness "Black for me, thank you." He would work with the Mexican police chief again and again in the future. Unless he couldn't solve this case. In that event, he would no doubt find himself posted to Shishmaref, a tiny Eskimo village on the edge of the Arctic Ocean in Alaska. No one in the agency knew if there actually was an FBI post in such a remote place but it served as a name for a place of career-ending exile. He had heard that it gets to 80 degrees below zero there and the village had six months of darkness.

He vowed to himself that he would solve the case, keep good relations with Chief Diaz and continue to enjoy San Diego, the American city with the best weather and best beaches.

Woods was just sipping his excellent cup of coffee when two guards, one on each elbow, brought in Prisoner 54. The guards plopped the handcuffed prisoner in a chair across from the visitors. Chief Diez shooed the guards out of the room and turned on a tape recorder. They would now begin to question Valenzuela, crime lord, killer, Narco Traficante and with any luck, a man would help them to find the missing astronaut before his abductors tired of the whole thing and just killed him.

After some preliminary questions Valenzuela said "My men knew the Muslim Brigade was coming to Helena's house in Valle Luna."

"How did you know all of that?" Shimon asked in his accented Spanish."

"We infiltrated the Muslim Brigade. We had been watching these Arabs for a while and doing some business with them. We traded some of our drugs for some of their weapons, nothing serious, just a little contact from time to time. Some of the cartel leaders decided that these Arabs would be bad for business if the United States or Israel attacked Iran's nuclear facilities."

He continued, seemingly at ease. "The cartel leaders reasoned that Arab cells in Latin America would attack Jews in Mexico and in The United States and possibly other Americans. The cartel leaders decided it would be bad for their business."

"You said you can release Ari Ben Ora. How did you find him?" Shimon asked.

"My informant knew where he was being held. The Arabs left him to starve to death."

That got a reaction from Special Agent Woods. "Did your men rescue Miller in front of the house on Valle de Luna, and the following day drop him at the consulate?"

"Si, Señor."

"And you couldn't extend the same courtesy to Ari Ben Ora?" Shimon interjected with some heat.

"No, Senor. This Israeli is too valuable. I want to trade his life for mine. Free me, and he will be freed. Get me a pardon and I will give you Ari Ben Ora."

"I am not in a position to grant you a pardon, Senor Valenzuela," Chief Diaz clarified.

"Then why are we talking?"

"Your best chance for freedom is a reduced sentence. Give us Ari Ben Ora alive and unhurt, and I promise you President Calderon will hear about your cooperation," Diaz said.

"The director of the FBI has the ear of the American president," Woods added.

"A sentence reduced from life to thirty years, when I'm old and stooped over, no thank you. No deal. Take me back to my cell."

"It can be less than thirty years, maybe ten. Be cooperative Senor Valenzuela. Time goes by more easily when you are eating better food and having sex with women occasionally. Think it over, Valenzuela," Diaz advised.

Chapter 55

PARIS

The apartment manager did not want to challenge the policemen about the legal rights of tenants. That would not do well in Paris. French law valued the rights of the state over the rights of the citizens in the best of cases and it never paid to get sideways with the flics. But, to his credit, he insisted that he be present in the apartment while the officer perused and examined Andreev's personal belongings. The flics went through the closet and drawers. Blanc lifted a worn shirt on the chair and discovered Andreev's calendar. He looked at his boss.

"Inspector, Sasha is scheduled to fly out tomorrow on the noon flight to Dubrovnik."

Gallant nodded to show he heard his minion and understood the import of the clue. He picked up a photo from the bureau. He held it up to the concierge.

"This looks like a recent family photograph. Which one in the picture is Andreev?"

"This one," the manager replied as he pointed out his tenant in the photo.

Antoine let the anger he felt burst forth into his voice.

"I told you never to call me on this phone."

"Don't worry, don't worry. I am on a disposable cell. Look, Antoine, I am in trouble. The police are at my apartment waiting for me. They probably know by now that I am supposed to fly out of Charles de Gaulle airport tomorrow." Sasha pleaded.

Antoine paused in thought for a few beats of his heart. "We need to get you out of France."

"Yes, yes, right away."

"You will need a fake passport, ID, and sufficient euros to travel with and to tide you over for a while. I will see to it."

"Thank you, Antoine." Sasha sounded relieved.

"We will need to meet."

"Yes."

"At 9 PM at St. James Oratory on Rue Renee, go to the first empty pew and sit as far to the right as you can."

"I'll be there."

The line disconnected. Sasha looked at his watch. The time showed as 7:40 PM. St. James was on the other side of Paris. The metro would take him there in no more than forty minutes with only one connection. He had time to make it.

Chapter 56

JULY 20, 2007

Moscow Space Command Center

Out of cigarettes, Igor found a pack of menthol in Ivan's desk. Menthols were not his favorite but they would do. He inhaled, choked out the smoke and answered his beeping phone.

Boris spoke in his ear. "Igor, Andre manually overrode the capsule's flight path after mision control radioed in the alternative flight plan. But no matter where they land, they can't avoid the nuclear wind blast from Pakistan's nuclear launch. Relax and know that in approximately twenty-five minutes, the capsule will be vaporized. It's been a long night and it is already 8 AM. We connected your monitor to a spit feed so you can watch the missile launch."

Igor went into a coughing spasm.

"Are you all right? Not you too?" Boris asked.

"Yes, it's just these fucking menthols." He hawked up a loogie and spat into a trash can.

"Igor, the Iranian tanker sits in port waiting for clearance before setting out to sea. I wish I was a fly on the wall of the Israeli Knesset after Iran launches its first nuclear test missile."

"You know Boris, it is actually our Russian scientists that are preparing the launch and Pakistan that provided the nuclear weapon," Igor corrected his boss.

"Immaterial, Igor. Perception is everything. The whole world will see this as a fully Iranian effort. We want Ahmadinejad to get the credit for this and he will. Even if the truth leaks out in a few months, it still won't matter. Most people will not get caught up and will still think Iran can shoot nuclear missiles whenever they want."

Silently and mockingly, Igor laughed at Boris. Igor no longer harbored any doubts. Israeli intelligence had connected most of the dots from Ari's email. Iran would pay dearly. Igor didn't give a shit about the Iranians anyway and tossed the remaining menthols in the garbage can. He thought it over and retrieved the pack as the Pakistani launch process began. Engulfed by billows of rocket-fuel exhaust, the nuclear missile ascended straight up toward the blue sky above the surrounding desert, slowly at first and gradually picking up speed. He almost forgot that Boris was still on the phone.

"Igor, before I forget, the Kremlin wants me to start an audit of your department by next week. We'll need to review all your electronic correspondence. I also want to visit Ivan as well."

"Yes, of course. I look forward to your visit, Boris." He disconnected but another caller was on the line.

"This is Igor."

"This is Dr. Aaskov. I have good news. Ivan has regained consciousness, although he suffered a minor stroke. His memory is impaired and he has no recollection of passing out."

"Will his memory return?"

"Maybe some, maybe none, maybe all of it. The brain is a tricky place for us doctors," Aaskov replied.

"Thank you, Dr. Aaskov. Be sure to tell Ivan that I'll be over to see him."

"I will but please wait for a day or two and check with me first, alright?"

"Yes doctor, you know best for Ivan." Igor answered and hung up.

The poison must have deteriorated in the years that it sat in the back of his stash, Igor thought. What should have been a lethal dose just wasn't enough. But he had plenty left. All he needed was a chance to squirt a few drops into Igor's intravenous feed.

He would visit Igor just as soon as he could.

At 8:26 AM, Pakistan's nuclear missile reached its zenith of forty km and detonated with a yield of ten kilotons, the equivalent of ten thousands tons of TNT. The blast created an energy burst of blinding light, thermal heat and radiation. That event was followed instantly by a deafening sound, a huge fireball, and powerful winds. Ionizing radiation burst from the explosion and ranged for hundreds of miles through the atmosphere. The heat generated from the fireball spread outward and created a system of overexposure powerful enough to collapse concrete structures, had there been any forty kilometers high in the sky.

The explosion disrupted the command center's communication system. Monitors went blank, and lights went out. When the tech crew got the juice back on line, the capsule had disappeared from the screen.

Igor calculated the capsule's terminal velocity and the rate of its fall at nearly 17,000 miles per hour. That placed the capsule at approximately fifty miles above the burgeoning mushroom cloud. By his estimation, the capsule could not have escaped destruction. Simply peeling off a single heat resistant tile on the capsules underbelly would create a fire tomb for those inside.

But for the moment, Igor lacked certainty about the fate of the capsule and those aboard her. He felt cheated.

The atmospheric nuclear test done by Pakistan triggered a chain of electromagnetic pulses that crippled electronic systems through the Middle East and Asia. For nearly an hour, telephone and satellite communications came down. People went crazy, business and government stopped and people in the impacted area went into panic mode. Proof positive beyond a doubt just how humanity had allowed itself to be enslaved by its own technology.

Igor continued to stare into a monitor that looked more like a window to a Siberian snow storm. With eyes glued to the screen, Igor waited out the systematic paralysis. His phone rang, a good sign for improving systems availability. He glanced at the caller ID, knowing already who must be on the line.

"Hello Boris."

"Igor, against all odds, the escape capsule was sighted and seen floating on the Mediterranean Sea." Boris nearly shouted into the phone.

"Fuck! That is impossible!" Igor blurted.

"Calm down, we need to get a handle on this right away, while we still have some advantage. We have a Russian frigate close to their location. As we speak, the captain of our frigate has launched a hydrofoil and a helicopter to the capsule. If the crew is still alive-and they might already be dead Igor- the frigate crew will take them aboard and we will sink the capsule."

"What then? What will happen to the astronauts?"

"They will ingest radiation pills, Igor. The world will think they were dead on arrival. It will be a believable story."

"Boris, is the capsule near Israeli territorial waters?"

"It could be but we don't know exactly just yet. Our electronic eyes have been closed from the electromagnetic pulse. If they have a ship or visual from a low flying aircraft and get to the capsule first, then we go to plan B."

"And that is?"

"We scrub the Iranian nuclear launch, dissemble and disarm the missile and transport the warhead to our submarine."

"But the Israelis will know that Russia conspired." Igor feigned a protest, because the Israelis had very likely already been tipped off via the email code that Ari sent to his wife.

"So, what can they do, attack Russia? Boris mocked and laughed at the absurd idea of the mouse attacking the elephant.

Igor couldn't help himself. He started laughing too.

"You think that was funny too?" Boris sarcastically replied.

"Forgive me Boris, but this reminds me of a Hollywood chase scene with cops and robbers."

"Interesting observation, Igor, and who are the cops and who are the robbers?"

"We are the robbers, Boris. We tried to hijack an economy. Do you actually think Israel will cower to a nuclear Iran? Iran has no air force capable of penetrating Israeli airspace and no guarantee its missiles can either. On the other hand, Israel can launch nukes from submarines, from their aircraft and from their own missiles. What do you think will happen when Iran tests its first nuclear missile?"

"There will be total, regional war, and listen to me Igor, if Russia can't steal one economy, we can rebuild another that has been destroyed. That was always the plan. One way or the other, Russia's objective was to obtain profits and gain traditional influence in the area at the expense of America. Igor, I was just told that our Russian helicopter is right now circling above the capsule. Someone in the capsule is firing bullets at our chopper. Oh shit, Igor, Israeli helicopter gunships are closing in. Our hydrofoil and helicopter are returning to international waters."

"What now? What do we do?" Igor asked, an edge of panic in his voice.

"Igor, now this is a matter for the diplomats."

With the ISS crew falling into Israeli hands, the deals bagan to fall like dominoes, one hitting another. The following day, a Kremlin spokesman reported that negotiations with the Vatican concerning the return of church property had ended without significant progress. Two days later, at a news conference Russian and Pakistani ambassadors scrubbed the Russian nuclear assistance program. The reason given was political insatiability within Pakistan. A week later, a Russian submarine surreptitiously docked at the port city of Karachi and returned the Pakistani nuclear warhead.

Chapter 57

TIJUANA

"Hello Lucille, this is Shimon." Shimon spoke into his cell phone. "Where have you been, Shimon? I left you messages."

"I am so sorry. I was at a meeting and my phone was off."

"Shimon, Michelle went into a coma. Her doctors say she had a stroke."

"Oh my God, Lucille! What can I do?"

"Come, Shimon. Come now. Be at her bedside. Hold her hand. When she opens her eyes, she should see you." Lucille had no doubt about what Shimon should do.

"You are right. I will return to Israel immediately."

"Please hurry, Shimon."

He phoned Gideon.

"Gideon, I have to return to Israel right away. Have your office arrange it."

"Why?" Gideon asked, not unreasonably.

"Michelle had a stroke, a complication from the head-shot wound."

"That's horrible, Shimon. I understand. You need to get to her as soon as you can. But you will have to stay in Tijuana a little longer. Something's coming down real soon. Our Ambassador in Mexico City cabled our Tijuana consulate. President Calderon is prepared to reduce Valenzuela's sentence from life to seven years. Valenzuela took the offer. Ari Ben Ora will be released into your custody later today."

"I just walked out of the prison. There was no deal on the table then. What the fuck is gong on Gideon?" Shimon demanded.

"The Mexicans granted Chief Diaz special authority to make a deal. They made the deal just a few minutes ago. Ari will see daylight in a few hours."

"Where is Ari now? Do we know?"

"Tecate, Mexico, less than thirty miles from where you are now," Gideon replied.

"I am on my way. What address?"

"Diaz doesn't want you, Shimon. Special Agent Woods will go with Diaz and pick up Ari. They will take him to the local airstrip where a helicopter will fly him to the Israeli consulate in Tijuana. OK?"

"Not OK, but OK. Will there be a news conference at the airstrip?," Shimon inquired.

"Likely, which is why I want you at the consulate, not on Mexican TV."

Woods was glued to his cell phone. In front and behind the car he sat in, police cruisers provided more security.

"I have an update," Gideon continued. Ari should be at the Israeli consulate within the hour. I want you to be there for him."

"Where is the Israeli Consulate?"

"It is in the Zona Centro district in a small, secure building. You need to go there now. Emilio Rosenberg is waiting for you."

"Who is he?"

"Emilio is Israel's Mexican legal counsel and will represent Ari during questioning to make sure his rights are not violated."

"I am on my way."

Chapter 58

PARIS

Sasha arrived a few minutes early. He smoked his cigarette down to the filter before flicking the butt into the gutter. He cautiously walked into the Saint James Oratory.

It comforted him a little to see a woman lighting candles at the far left of the knave. A man in tattered clothes knelt head down in a pew farther down. He would not sojourn in the church alone, good for his safety.

Sasha passed the man on his way to the fourth pew. He sat to the far right and picked up a prayer book. The man in tattered clothes slowly, cautiously re-positioned himself behind Sasha.

"Don't talk or turn your head. Take this prayer book over your right shoulder," the man instructed Sasha.

With his left hand, Sasha reached over his right shoulder for the prayer book. Inside he found an envelope containing his fake identity papers and ten thousand euros.

"I was expecting somebody else," Sasha muttered.

"He couldn't make it. Don't talk."

"I recognize your voice. You were in on it with me and Zoran. I thought you went back to Russia."

"You talk too much," Igor complained.

"You tell Antoine that I will call him when I get settled."

Igor had enough. It had a prickly feel but the needle penetrated through Sasha's shirt and delivered a nerve toxin into the flesh of his shoulder. It immediately caused a general and escalating paralysis. One by one, his organs shut down, including his ability to use his vocal cords. Igor propped him up, lifted his billfold and portable cell phone. He left the fake passport but took the cash. Waste not, want not was a rule Igor lived by. And now a million rubles just didn't seem enough.

He crossed himself before he fled.

Eventually, the weight and tilt of Sasha's body caused him to slouch.

Father Beaulieu walked past him once and thought the man might have had too much to drink or even that he had fallen asleep. Both happened from time to time. When the other parishioners had all left the church, the man still lay in the pew. Father Beaulieu nudged him, but there was no response. Concerned that the man had stopped breathing, the priest tried to find the man's pulse. On the man's lap was an envelope. In the envelope were a passport and a driver's license. A glance at the passport identified the man as Sergey Cohen of Brussels, Belgium. Father Beaulieu felt perplexed. Cohen was the most Jewish of names. He locked the doors to St. James and made the call.

"I am Father Beaulieu at the St. James Church. I am calling to report an unresponsive and unconscious man in my pew. He is not breathing and I find no pulse. I can see no visible wounds, about forty years old, I would guess. His name is Sergey Cohen according to his passport. It says he is from Brussels, Belgium."

Igor disappeared into the Parisian streets. He wiped the syringe clean and dropped it in a garbage can in front of a corner store, awaiting the trash man. A few weeks earlier, he had arrived in Paris to be part of the trio that kidnapped Andre Dubois. He had been ordered to kill Zoran after his photo showed up in the papers. Sasha on the other hand was not supposed to be killed. He would get money and documents to get him safely out of France. But Sasha was loose with his mouth. He could implicate Igor as Ivan maybe could have a couple of years earlier at Moscow's command station. Now they were both dead. Igor knew how to cover his tracks. Igor recalled the phone call he received from Boris before his flight to Paris.

Hello, Igor. It's been a couple of years. How's retirement?

Good, Boris. No complaints.

Always sad when I think of Ivan passing away at such a young age.

Me, too.

Remember Andre, the Frenchman on the ISS?"

How could I forget?

How would you like to fly to Paris and play with Andre's head? Nobody gets hurt, he's blindfolded and released in a few days. I'll send you the details with a contact in Paris. He will pay you a million rubles.

I'm interested.

Chapter 59

TIJUANA

Besides the foreign consulates, the Zona Centro had all things for the American tourists. For daytime use craft shops, souvenir shops, taco carts, and restaurants in all their color and noise vied for the American dollar. By night, bars served underage high school kids, sailors, and indeed anyone with the cash to buy a drink. And whores of every conceivable size, shape, and price range plucked what they could from the ever-renewing crop.

The Israeli consulate rested within the vibrant, chaotic eight-block enclave of lawless commerce. Wisely, the consulate had a tall concrete block fence encircling it, topped with another two feet of razor wire to discourage any enemies or the always present common criminals. Shimon used his Google locator app on his phone and had no trouble finding the consulate, for once Goofball worked perfectly.

"I am here to see Emilio Rosenberg," Shimon informed the receptionist, a strikingly beautiful young woman dressed in rather severe business attire. She gave him a blinding smile. Visitors to the consulate would begin their visit on a very positive note.

"Senor Rosenberg and our counsel, Zeev Shamir, are expecting you,

Senor Levi. Go to the first room on the right and place the magnetic card on the sensor. That will allow you to open the door."

She told him as she handed him a credit card-sized bit of plastic and a lanyard with large letters spelling out the word 'Visitor' in Hebrew, Spanish and English.

"Thank you."

The sensor, magnetic card, and doorknob all worked as expected. Shimon entered the room.

"You must be Shimon: I am Zeev," a handsome man of medium height greeted Shimon. He had enough lines on his face to show his experience along with a strong dusting of gray in his hair. He wore a professional smile with ease and grace. Shimon had no doubt that the man was very good at his job. Even his handshake seemed an authentic and genuine expression of welcome.

"Hello Zeev. I was told that Emilio Rosenberg would meet me here?" His tone made the statement into a question.

"He is upstairs but we will take the elevator." Zeev swiped a different electronic card and the elevator door opened up.

"Three floors." Shimon noted, holding up three fingers for clarity.

"Four if you count the underground garage. I live on the top floor. The offices where our real work goes on are on the first and second floor." Zeev did not mention the partial sub-basement under the garage which held other, more dangerous, and sensitive items, nor the small dorm-style rooms where the security staff lived to the rear of the second floor.

The elevator door opened to an undersized, unkempt, living room. The room held two large plasma video screens, telephones, a tangle of wires running here and there, and three overstuffed chairs. On the left, Shimon could see a small kitchen area. Someone stood there, pouring coffee from the pot into a mug. That someone was Ari Ben Ora.

Shimon broke into a face shattering grin and hugged the astronaut while the two of them laughed, one in relief and the other in general release of his secret.

"Thank God, you are safe, Ari. When did you get here?"

"I have always been here. I came directly to the consulate from La Jolla." He waved to include the untidy room.

"Who is riding with Woods and Diaz in the helicopter if it wasn't you?"

"Someone who looked like me," Ari answered.

"Are you telling me that your kidnapping was staged?" Shimon demanded, astonished.

"Yes."

"So, Amir Delshad is on our side," Shimon asked.

"Yes, he was part of our plan."

"Why wasn't I brought in on it?" Shimon seemed a little miffed.

"Your bosses believed that our chances of success would be greater if you were kept in the dark. We flushed out the Hezbollah operatives from Tijuana and destroyed them," Zeev explained.

"Why take the American, Miller?"

"Bad luck. He was just in the wrong place at the wrong time. He was never in danger, but we had to let this play out. The American and Mexican Directors of National Intelligence were also read in on the plan," Zeev told Shimon.

"If you flushed out Hezbollah in Tijuana, this could only mean one thing. Israel is going to hit Iran," Shimon suggested.

Zeev just smiled. "And for the record, there is no Emilio Rosenberg," Zeev added and brought over coffee and corn muffins for the two newcomers.

"You guessed right, Shimon. We will hit Iran before the mullahs receive the Russian S300 surface-to-air missiles. I've got a consulate car and driver waiting to take you and Ari to LAX. Ari will finish filling you in on all the details. It is a long flight home."

Chapter 60

TECATE

As soon as the convoy left the city limits, Diaz had his officers turn off their sirens and flashing lights. He wanted to diminish the attention the string of cars would bring in the rural areas as they sped along the highway. Special agent Woods watched Diaz, wondering how this would all play out, and mentally critiqued his control of the convoy. Not for one minute did he buy into Miller's or Valenzuela's explanation of events. As to Diaz's thoughts, Woods didn't bother to ask. The squad cars eventually approached the Valenzuela owned house in Tecate, the purported location of Ari Ben Ora after his rescue from the Mexican Arabs.

The Valenzuela owned house sat in a residential section of the town at 56 Cora Street. Diaz ordered two of his officers to block the street at each ingress and egress. He and Woods had been told that two men would walk out the front door, Ari Ben Ora and Rashid, a Valenzuela associate. Two men walked out, but Woods knew instantly that neither was Ari Ben Ora. He drew his pistol on the men. Diaz followed suit.

"Stop right there, hands up, identify yourself," Woods barked.

"Rashid Din; My Canadian passport is in my back pocket." A man shouted across the lifeless lawn.

"Amir Delshad, Canadian citizen; my passport is in my pants pocket." The second man shouted.

"Where is Ari Ben Ora?" Diaz yelled in anger and frustration.

"Perhaps I can explain," a third man spoke loudly as he stepped out of the house.

"Director Brown!" Woods exclaimed in surprise. "Diaz, holster your gun. He is the director of the FBI."

"Gentlemen, on the way to the Tecate airport, I will explain. We have a helicopter awaiting our arrival." Director Brown and the two Canadians slid into the back seat. Woods slipped into the passenger seat, crowding in next to Diaz.

"Please save your questions until I am finished," Brown instructed, cutting off any inquiry. "The kidnapping of Ari Ben Ora was committed with his full knowledge and consent. This operation had the full approval of the U.S. Director of National Intelligence, Israeli intelligence and the president of Mexico. This was a covert operation. As director of the FBI, I was not even informed until several days after the fact.

"The American, Eric Miller, was not part of the operation. He was at the wrong place at the wrong time, but we believed his life was never in danger. The men beside me, Rashid and Amir, helped to engineer the kidnapping of Ben Ora and Miller as part of this covert operation."

"On the day of the kidnappings, Ari Ben Ora was taken to the Israeli consulate in Tijuana. Even as we speak, he has crossed the border to the United States and will soon board a non-stop flight to Israel. Amir, who is the same height and complexion as Ari will stand in for him in case we run into photographers. We have immediate clearance to take off at the heliport. Amir is to be surrounded by the five of us until he boards the helicopter." The director rattled off in quick, short bursts. He didn't ask for follow up questions, and gave no indication that he would welcome them.

"Special Agent Woods, may I lend your sunglasses to Amir?" The director asked.

Chapter 61

TIJUANA

"**A**nd Rachel knew all along," Shimon said, moving his head from side to side and smiling at how easily he, and the Hezbollah cell and the whole world had bought the tale, hook line and sinker.

"Yes." Ari matched his grin. "My wife is a team player; you recall how she tricked the Russians and decoded my email from the ISS and alerted Israeli intelligence."

"Ari, don't forget I discovered your manuscript on the escape capsule, and now your novel is on the top ten list in the New York Times. No doubt interest in your book spiked with your abduction."

"No doubt," Ari affirmed, his grin getting even bigger.

"Ari, what about Andre? Was his kidnapping and reappearance a Mossad operation?"

"No, not that I am aware of. Not that they would tell me, of course. But I have no knowledge of such an operation and I can't think of any reason why they would do it."

"It is weird but the French cops have me as a person of interest in Andre's kidnapping. The inspector in charge has concocted a love triangle with me as one of the parties," Shimon revealed.

"But I hear that you really are in love?"

"It happened. Michelle and I just came together. Now she is in Israel fighting for her life. You didn't know?"

"No. What happened?"

"A Palestinian sniper shot her while she was doing her thing, working at an archeological dig."

"I am so sorry. I hope she will come through all right."

"She is alive and she is a fighter. We can talk more about her on the plane to Israel. Why don't you fill me in on the details of your operation?" Shimon continued.

"Sure, Izzy Rothstein worked on this plan with the U.S. DNI to set up my kidnapping in order to deflect blame on the Hezbollah cell in Tijuana and draw them out. They wanted to get this done before the impending air strike on Iran's nuclear facilities. An active terror cell so close to San Diego could easily be activated in response to the strike."

"I met with Izzy. He gave me a contact," Shimon admitted.

"He was part of the plan."

"But you couldn't tell me, could you?"

"Well, you know how it goes. It would be better for you if we kept some things quiet in case anything went wrong. Things might have gone wrong in any number of places," Ari told him.

"Did Gideon know?"

"No, not him either. We kept it as close as we could."

"So you had somebody drive a Corolla with Canadian plates around Tijuana." Shimon stated.

"Yes, exactly, we expected that the Arabs would take the bait. We bought the second Corolla in Canada, repainted it blue, and drove all over Tijuana. In case we got pulled over by the Mexican police we'd have proper registration."

"Who was this guy, Amir Delshad?"

"He is a Canadian. Rothstein got help from Ivan Berovsky in Manitoba. I didn't ask if Delshad was an employee of the Berovsky gang or not. It didn't matter for our operation but I would say that yes, he is a made guy for Berovsky."

"What did Berovsky get out of the deal?"

"He owed Rothstein a favor. Now the favor has been paid. Izzy will be transferred to Israel by the end of the month to be retried there," Ari added.

"You know he will never be convicted in Israel. Witnesses will disappear or be bribed. Some might even wind up suddenly dead."

"All of that is very possible but it isn't our problem, Shimon. We couldn't exactly say 'no' to the U.S. Director of National Intelligence, could we?"

Chapter 62

MOSCOW

At the Moscow Airport Inspector Gallant and Detective Blanc and several members of the Moscow police force joined forces. The Russians took them swiftly through the necessary procedures to enter the country and immediately drove them to Sasha's apartment in a neighborhood of ghastly communist concrete high rises near Gorky Park.

Waiting for them at the door, they met Alexei, Sasha's roommate.

"Alexei, do you speak French or English?" Gallant asked.

"I have a bit of French but my English is much better. More practice at the airline, you understand?"

"Why am I not surprised?" Blanc said as he rolled his eyes.

In Russian one of the Moscow police officials said "They have come from Paris to investigate the suspicious murder of your roommate Sasha Andreev."

Alexei looked somber but stayed quiet.

Gallant took up the thread, in English. "Two nights ago, Sasha was killed in the pew of a Catholic church in Paris. On his person we found a fake passport issued in the name of Sergey Cohen, from Brussels, with Sasha's photo. An autopsy that our people performed on him found that someone had injected him with enough atropine to cause his immediate death," Inspector Gallant informed the roommate.

"Alexi, you are also an airline steward. Were you in a relationship with Sasha?"

"No, not at all. I am straight. We were just roommates. Sasha and I aren't, weren't I guess now, even friends, really, just roommates. With our different schedules, we did not spend much time together."

"I see. Did he ever talk about his friends?"

"No, but he must have had a rich friend because Sasha often dressed in the most expensive clothes and shoes. On his salary, he could not afford to buy clothes like that. I know I can't. He also kept the flat in Paris, another very large expense for him."

"We saw his wardrobe in his Paris apartment. Did he mention restaurants or did you ever see emails or recall a phone conversation?"

"Sasha usually left the apartment to talk on his cell. He would go to an internet cafe to chat on the internet. So, no. I can't help you with that."

"Does he have any family or friends in Moscow?" Blanc bluntly entered the conversation.

"Not that I know about. He did tell me that his mother and sister live in Belgrade. Oh, I almost forgot. He kept their letters in the bottom drawer of his dresser."

Gallant held up one finger as he checked his buzzing phone. "Excuse me, I have to take this overseas call."

"Inspector, this is Christian Doucet, Jerusalem reporter for Le Monde. Henri Bettencourt asked me to call you. Shimon Levi and Ari Ben Ora have just deplaned in Israel."

Gallant nodded his understanding into the phone, as if Doucet was in the room with him.

"Thank you, Christian. I appreciate you notifying me."

"Inspector, if you can go to CNN International?"

"Yes, thank you." Gallant cut the connection.

"Blanc, log in to CNN International. Ari Ben Ora and Shimon Levi have just landed in Israel."

Blanc looked to Alexi for permission, got the nod, and started to work the computer.

"Alexi, everything is in Russian. It might as well be Greek to me. Can you bring up CNN so we can check the news?"

Alexi smiled and said, "Yes, of course. It won't take a minute."

Chapter 63

JERUSALEM

Ari and Shimon separated in the terminal. Journalists assembled in a segregated area and waited for Ari. They took pictures and fired off rounds of non-stop questions. Ari waved off reporters as he entered a vehicle. Unnoticed, Shimon waved down a taxi who rushed him to the ICU at the Jerusalem hospital. An Israeli spokesman from the prime minister's office fielded questions from the reporters.

"Lucille, I am on my way to the hospital. It is a miracle she has come out of the coma.g" Shimon spoke into his cell in the car.

"It is God's will."

"Thank God for the anti-seizure medications," Simon said.

"The doctors have been so wonderful."

"Has she spoken?"

"Not yet. They took the breathing tube out of her nose, gave her a tracheotomy, and put a feeding tube through her throat. That will let her speak when she wakes up. The doctors have reason to hope or they wouldn't do that."

"So she is breathing on her own now?"

"Yes. But Shimon, parts of her skull had to be removed to compensate for brain swelling."

"They can replace those parts later," Shimon advised her.

"There were also embedded fragments of her cell phone that they surgically removed. They are concerned about permanent damage, especially with speech and movement."

"No bullet fragments?"

"The sniper's bullet passed all the way through from her left forehead and out the back of her skull. Michelle was very fortunate."

"Can she move her fingers and open her eyes?"

"Yes. She moved her fingers and today she opened her eyes for a few minutes."

Shimon found the right place to be in the big hospital. He hugged Lucille. The medicos rigged him up in a blue suit from feet to hair and let him quietly enter the ICU where Michelle was. He pulled up a chair next to the bed and held Michelle's hand in his. She responded to his voice, squeezed his hand ever so slightly, and opened her eyes.

Chapter 64

———⁕~⁕~⁕———

PARIS

Inspector Gallant took the call.

"Henri, it has been a while: How are you?"

"Fine Jean. I received a text from Christian, Le Monde's Jerusalem correspondent. Michelle Dumas is scheduled to return to Paris for occupational therapy tomorrow. She will be at Le Clair Rehab. I called to let you know before we publish."

"Thank you, Henri, that is very thoughtful of you. Can you tell me how she is doing? I know the poor woman was shot in the head by an Arab sniper, but not much else."

"After six months, I understand that she has regained some of her cognitive functions. So, how is your investigation progressing?"

"Our trail got cold in Moscow."

"You and Napoleon both," Henri quipped.

"I appreciate your humor, Henri. I still believe that we will find the key to solving the murders in some connection between the two kidnappings."

"Help me with this, Jean. I think I know that Arabs in Mexico kidnapped the Israeli but I don't know of any Muslim connection to Andre. Am I right?"

"Yes, you are. Instead, I found Jews connected to both kidnappings. I can indirectly connect Izzy Rothstein to the Mexican drug lord Valenzuela. The Mexicans reduced Valenzuela's life sentence because he allegedly assisted the authorities. And shortly after this collaboration, Rothstein received an American 'get out of jail free card'."

"Maybe that is not enough of a connection, Jean. The Israelis will have a retrial for Rothstein when he gets to Israel."

"Yes, yes, Henri, I know. But he may well achieve an acquittal in Israel. The Americans had a rock-solid case against him. Rothstein was the major ecstasy supplier in Las Vegas, the perfect place in the world for that particular party drug. In Israel, Rothstein can bribe witnesses. For one reason or another, bribery, sudden death, witnesses can not testify, or not testify truthfully. By the way, did you know that Shimon Levi visited Izzy Rothstein at the Las Vegas prison only days before Ari Ben Ora was found? We got an anonymous tip. Odd that, don't you think?"

"No, I did not know that, but what does that have to do with the Dubois kidnapping in Paris? If anything?"

"Henri, who received a 'get out of jail free card' in Paris?"

"Oh, Jean, I see what you mean. Nate Gottschalk. In fact. You interceded on his behalf, I think?"

"I did. Was it a coincidence that Gottschalk once owned the warehouse where Andre was held prisoner? Was it just a coincidence that Gottschak led me to Zoran's letter which in turn led me to Sasha, but unfortunately not in time to prevent his murder? And who, Henri, I ask you, who was present immediately after both kidnappings, who was that Henri?"

"Shimon Levi." Henri seemed stunned at the connection.

"But wait, there is more. Levi met with Shai Tanger, also Jewish, and connected to Father Gauthier, Andre Dubois' mentor. There is no doubt at all that Tanger extorted a great deal of money from the Vatican. Levi seems to appear everywhere in both cases."

"I think you have found most of the missing pieces, Jean. You only need to put the pieces together to solve the puzzle."

"I wonder if Shimon Levi plans to accompany Michelle to Paris."

"I would think so," Henri replied.

"Why do you think so, Henri?"

"Two reasons, Jean. You told me the two of them were now lovers, so he would naturally be there for her as she recovers. And secondly, Andre Dubois is in Paris."

Chapter 65

PARIS

The couple deplaned at Charles de Gaulle. Down the ramp, Shimon gently pushed Michelle in her wheelchair. By her side, Lucille held her left hand. A porter transferred their luggage into the taxi that brought them to the Le Clair Rehabilitation Center.

"Is this Paris, Maman?"

"Yes, Michelle. We are back home."

The phone rang interrupting their dinner. Louis rudely answered "What?"

"I am Henri Bettencourt from Le Monde News. I have some interesting news for Andre."

"Whatever it is, it can wait. Monsieur Bettencourt. I am eating supper," an irascible Louis reprimanded the reporter.

"I thought you would like to know that your friend Michelle has returned to Paris. She checked into the Le Clair Rehabilitation Center a little while ago."

"OK, you have my attention."

Andre rested his fork on the plate and listened attentively.

"She is accompanied by her mother and Shimon Levi."

"Is that all, Monsieur Bettencourt?"

"Oui, that's all. Au revoir."

"What was that all about, Louis?" Andre asked.

"A reporter from Le Monde said that Michelle has checked into the Le Clair Rehabilitation clinic, here in Paris."

"What? She is in Paris?"

"We don't know, Andre. It might be a ruse, an excuse to get you out of the apartment and into the open. I don't trust the press."

"Me neither but that doesn't matter. I have not been hiding. The reporters on the sidewalk outside have all gone. And, while you are at work, I go to the grocery store to buy food and whatnot. No one has accosted me. I think I should call the rehab center."

"They can't give out names. It is against the privacy laws."

"Please drive me, Louis. Or I can call a cab."

"I can drive. She is also my friend. Bettencourt said she is accompanied by Lucille and Shimon Levi."

"Bettencourt is the reporter who interviewed me and published my story the day of my release from the kidnappers," Andre recalled.

"Andre, surely you can see that this reporter only wants a story, a showdown between you and Shimon. For the sake of Michelle and her mother, you do not want to create an incident. You have your plans and your new job in Montreal. You have your life, Andre, a new life."

"But Louis, now that Michelle has returned to Paris, I may not want to go to Montreal. I may still have a life here."

Louis looked gravely concerned at this rapid and irrational change of direction. "Andre, she is in a rehab center and maybe for months, years even, or forever. You cannot turn back the clock, my friend."

Andre shook off the advice. "I have to sort this out, Louis. I have to."

Chapter 66

PARIS

Andre donned his leather jacket and slipped his father's semi-automatic pistol into the inside pocket. The little .32 caliber Ruby was the smallest of that line and the easiest to conceal. How his father had come by the gun, he never knew. He did know that France had contracted with Spanish manufacturers during the Great War for many hundreds of thousands of them. He patted his jacket.

"I am ready, Louis."

Nearly an hour later, Louis passed the front of the rehabilitation center and pointed out the van with the logo for Le Monde news splashed across it.

"I told you. They set you up, Andre. They want to write about a fight between you and Shimon."

Andre just gave his friend a particular look. Louis drove around the corner and out of sight before looking for a place to park. Paris being Paris, it took them a while to find a place. They walked the three blocks and entered the center. The man in the van spotted them, double-checked his photos of the two men, and reached for his cell.

"Henri, it is Gigot. Andre and Louis have arrived and entered the Le Clair center, just as you expected."

"Stay with them and see what develops, h" Henri ordered.

Louis and Andre approached the receptionist.

"We are friends of Michellel Dumas. May we see her?" Louis inquired politely.

"If you and your companion will sit there for a moment, Monsieur, I will be happy to check for you. Do you have identification for my log?" She picked up the desk phone as the men handed over their ID cards.

"I am sorry to disturb you, Madame. There are two men requesting a visitation. One is Andre Dubois and the other is Louis Major."

"Oh, they are friends. Please have them wait for five minutes and send them up."

"Oui," the receptionist replied. She turned to the pair. "If you give them five minutes to tidy up, I will send you to her room on the third floor."

Lucille said to Shimon. "Louis and Andre will be here in a few minutes. You must go."

"Did you call them?" Shimon asked with a touch of anger to his voice.

"No, Shimon, I did not."

"OK, I will go down to the cafeteria downstairs and wait."

"That is a good idea. I will call you when they have gone."

Shimon kissed Michelle on her forehead and took the stairs. She smiled.

A few minutes later the elevator opened to Andre and Louis. Lucille was waiting.

"Lucille," exclaimed Louis happily

"Louis, Andre." She returned his smile. Hugs and kisses followed in the French tradition: A kiss on the right cheek followed by a kiss on the left and then another kiss on the right.

"Michelle," Andre kneeled next to her wheelchair and kissed her hand and cheek.

"Louis, how did you know Michelle and I were here?"

"A reporter called to let me know. He had interviewed me in the past."

"Andre, it has been a …..…time," Michelle struggled for the word but quickly forgot because her attention had switched to Louis. "Is that you, Louis?"

"Oui, may I have a big hug and kiss?"

"Come." Andre made room for Louis to kneel and get close.

"Where is Shimon?" Andre asked Lucille as he stood up.

"Andre, do not start trouble for us," Lucille responded.

Andre put his hand on his heart. "I give you my word that there will be no trouble, but I must speak to him."

Lucille looked hard at Andre while she thought this over for a moment. "He is in the cafeteria in the basement."

Shimon sat at a table with a cup of hospital coffee in front of him, bitter and black like his mood. He stood up as he saw Andre headed toward him. He extended his hand in a gesture of, if not friendship, at least peace.

"Andre, I am so glad to see you in one piece."

"I ought to shoot you dead," Andre said without preliminary words.

Shimon withdrew his hand and sat back down. He placed his left hand in the pocket of his sport coat where a very small, five-shot, semi-automatic pistol rested in concealment. He picked up his coffee with his right hand and took a sip, awaiting events and ready for anything.

"We have a lot to discuss. Please sit down, Andre."

Andre sat. "OK, I am seated. Now what?"

"Look, Michelle and I just happened. She thought you could be dead. I didn't intend to get involved with her. It just happened. Look, I love her too, but now you have the advantage. She came back to Paris. You live in Paris, I don't. My life is in Israel, my kids are in Israel. Michelle requires therapy, love, and encouragement to overcome her challenges. I am happy you and Louis are here to help her get through this." Shimon got it all out in one long spew of words.

"Did you have me kidnapped?" Andre demanded.

"Fuck no! I had nothing to do with it, and I don't know who did. Now, why the fuck did you leave Michelle anyway and return to France and stir up such a hornets' nest? You gave me your word that you weren't going to talk to the press."

"You forget that I gave my word conditionally. It was only good until Alexander's brother got himself away from the Russian gulag. When Yuri and his mother arrived in Israel, our deal ended. Those responsible for Father Gauthier's suicide needed to be held accountable. They still do."

"Andre, this is bigger than you or your priest. Middle East peace hangs in the balance. Because the stakes are so high, I cannot tell you that

Mossad had no hand in it. Others had a reason for shutting you up. The Russians have skin in this game. The Vatican also has important interests involved here, as you know."

"If they wanted to shut me up, why didn't they just kill me? I am alive and I am still capable of stirring up a hornets' nest." Now some of the anger had left Andre. He seemed genuinely interested in the opinion of Shimon, the government agent, not Shimon, his rival in romance.

"So Andre, why don't you do some stirring?"

He gave a very Gallic shrug. "I don't have any credibility anymore. Too many Parisians now believe that I arranged my own kidnapping."

"Andre, I don't know who kidnapped you but Ari Ben Ora was kidnapped too, a few days after you were."

"Yes, I heard about that."

"He is free now. You are free now. It could have turned out worse, much much worse. Other men were killed, both here in Paris in connection with your abduction but also in Mexico."

"OK Shimon, what can you tell me about my kidnapping? What do you know and what do you suspect?"

"I know you were kidnapped in front of Le Monde's office by three men in a Renault. They stole the car from a priest. I don't think that was a coincidence. Maybe the kidnappers wanted to muddy the waters by trying to make a connection between you and the Catholic Church. Of course, the priest had no involvement and was cleared right away. That's all I know." His phone buzzed.

"I am sorry, Andre, I have to take this call." He got up and stepped away from the table, turning his back for a bit of privacy.

"Shalom."

"Welcome to Paris. It is Eshkol."

"I know it is, what do you want?" Shimon asked.

"I need you at the embassy. I will send a car for you. Wait in front of the center."

Shimon turned back to Andre.

"I have to go to the embassy for what I don't know," Shimon told Andre.

"Wait, before you leave I need to reveal some information. Other than my friend Louis, no one else in Paris knows. I have accepted a position with the Canadian government. I will go to Montreal to assist and help train Canadian astronauts for space travel, for shuttle missions. So you see, Shimon, regarding Michelle, I now cede my home-court advantage."

"This is news. When are you leaving?"

"Next week. I have to get on with my life. More importantly, I have to get out of France. Too much has gone wrong for me to stay here."

"I understand."

"I will tell Lucille today about my moving to Canada. So you can stay longer in Paris and be with Michelle."

Shimon looked thoughtful and asked "Andre, how did you know I was in Paris?"

"A reporter from Le Monde called and told me. They have a news van in front of the center. They must think that something newsworthy will come of Michelle, you and I all being here at the same time."

"Well, too bad for them. I was afraid that this would turn into a media circus. I had better leave through the kitchen. Tell Lucille I will call her later. Goodbye Andre, you will do well in Montreal."

They shook hands. Shimon dialed Eshkol as he walked into the kitchen, getting funny looks from the staff.

The reporter, Gigot, had followed Andre to the cafeteria but sat several tables away to avoid suspicion. He was not nearly close enough to eavesdrop on their conversation. His dilemma was who to follow when they separated. Andre walked to the elevator. Gigot decided to follow the Israeli.

Shimon spoke into his cell phone. "Eshkol, the press is watching the clinic. Have your driver meet me behind the center. I will be near the dumpster."

The salad maker stopped him. "You cannot enter, staff only, Monsieur."

"Do you speak English?" Shimon asked the man to put away his phone and pulled out his wallet. He placed a fifty euro bill onto a vacant plate.

"Yes, enough."

"And you will not let anyone into the kitchen from the press, will you?"

The man pocketed the bill and replied "Certainly not. The press is not allowed in the kitchen."

Shimon exited the kitchen via the delivery door.

Gigot attempted to gain entry to the kitchen, but the salad maker blocked his entrance. Gigot pulled out his Le Monde press badge. The salad maker held his ground, keeping the reporter at bay. Frustrated, Gigot uttered a profanity at him and retreated to the elevator.

"Did you talk to Shimon?" Lucille asked when Andre walked into Michelle's room.

"I did. He was called to the embassy. He said he'd call you."

"Oh, Andre. Please find him and give him the key to my apartment." Andre took the key and dashed back out.

The elevator door opened, Gigot entered and pushed the close button only to see Andre run down the stairs and bolt through the kitchen door. Too late, the elevator door closed. Gigot tried to pry the elevator door open, with no success. The elevator went up to the third floor.

Shimon waited in the alleyway behind the center. He heard the sound of a slowly moving car entering the alley. Expecting Eshkol, he looked at the car. He didn't recognize the older model Citroen. When the passenger side window rolled down, he faced the barrel of a semi-automatic pistol.

A rough-looking guy about sixty years old held the gun.

"You got Izzy Rothstein out of prison, you mother fucker. Get in the back seat now and keep your hands in the air."

"Up yours," Shimon replied. "I'm not going anywhere with you." He reached into his pocket for his own pistol. He wasn't fast enough.

Gottschalk fired. A bullet tore into Shimon's right leg. The leg collapsed like wet paper mache and dropped Shimon to the filthy pavement.

Andre hurried through the kitchen. Seeing his haste and determination, none of the employees, even the salad maker, impeded his progress. He blew through the back door just in time to see a guy fire through the open window of an old Citroen. He grabbed his own gun.

It took only seconds to aim and fire his weapon. His aim was true. Gottschalk got a small bullet just above his right eyebrow. The bullet passed through Gottschalk's head, blowing blood and brains all over the driver and passing out the driver's side window, shattering the glass. Gottschalk slumped forward. The driver hit the gas and peeled out of the alley as fast as the little car could go, leaving a trail of burnt rubber on the alley and the scent of escape in the air.

Right behind the departing Citroen, the embassy car came into the alley. Eshkol drew a gun on Andre.

"Drop it," Eshkol commanded.

Shimon had both hands squeezing hard on this leg wound. "No, Eshkol, Andre saved my life."

Eshkol and Andre put their guns away. Together, they lifted Shimon into the back seat.

"Jump in, Andre. You had better come with us. You don't want to be here when the flicks show up." Andre nodded and jumped into the car. The embassy driver took off.

Gigot just missed seeing the embassy car vanish into general traffic. He saw fresh blood on the pavement. A couple of kitchen workers opened the door to see what the commotion was all about. Gigot got out his pad and started asking questions.

In the back seat of the embassy car, Eshkol and Andre applied a dressing to Shimon's leg from the first aid kit under the front seat.

"It looks like a clean wound, Shimon, just an in and out. We won't know if the bullet nicked a bone until we can get it looked at. It doesn't look too serious."

"It hurts like a bitch, Eshkol. It doesn't look too serious because you aren't the one with a hole in him leaking blood all over."

"Don't be a baby. It isn't like you haven't been shot before."

"Yeah, that makes all the difference, right?" Shimon grimaced in pain. Now I need to find out who shot me and how they knew I'd be waiting by the dumpster? Somebody who hates Izzy Rothstein. Any idea who, Eshkol?"

"Yeah, word on the street is there is bad blood between Nate Gottschalk and Izzy Rothstein."

Shimon switched gears. "Andre, you saved my life."

"I didn't think Shimon, I just reacted. If I had thought about it, I might have gone back inside and let things play out." Andre's face revealed a slight, wry, smile.

"Shimon, why would Gottschalk want to kill you?" Eshkol asked. "What did you do to piss him off that bad?"

"Maybe Gottschalk held me responsible for getting Rothstein out of prison back in the USA. That's all I can think of. Maybe when this stops hurting, I will think of something else."

Andre piped up. "Were you the one who got Rothstein out of jail?"

"During the time I saw him in prison I knew he had connections in Mexico that might help us get Ari back alive. But I had no power to release him."

"You will be considered a suspect, Andre. We have diplomatic immunity. Give me your gun," Eshkol demanded.

"No, not a chance. This is a family heirloom. It belonged to my father and I think to his father before him, all the way back to the Great War. I'll keep it."

"For now, Andre, I'll keep it for you at the Israeli embassy. I promise to keep it safe and return it to you when this blows over."

Andre reluctantly handed over the pistol to Eshkol.

"The authorities will search your apartment. Do you have ammunition in your apartment?" Eshkol asked.

"Yes, I have a box of cartridges in a drawer in the foyer."

"We must stop at your apartment first." He looked down at Shimon who was draped across both Eshkol and Andre. "We stopped the bleeding for now, Shimon. We will get you to the embassy doc as soon as we can. But we can't let your savior go to prison for saving your life, can we?"

"I get it. But hurry will you, this hurts like you cannot believe?"

"Andre, you will bring down the box of ammunition and give it to us. Then take all of your clothes and put them in the wash, I mean right now. You want any blood spatter or gun powder residue to go right down the drain. The same for you. As soon as you turn on the washing machine, you get into the shower. Give all your exposed skin, especially your hands and face, an extra good scrubbing. Wash everything two or three times to be sure you get it all. Even a speck of residue will give up the game to the cops. OK?"

"I got it. Are you a spy too, like Shimon?"

Eshkol glanced at Shimon who just rolled his eyes.

"We have to get our stories straight, Andre. Why were you in the alley?" Eshkol quizzed Andre.

"Lucille asked me to give Shimon her apartment key."

"I was supposed to crash at her place tonight." Shimon continued.

"That will do. The police may never know that Gottschalk was in the alley. And they will not find my DNA in their system, so there will be no link there. They have no weapon, no body, no DNA, and no prints. All they have is a report of gunfire and my blood on the pavement. So, Andre, keep it simple. You followed me to the alley and gave me the key. The embassy car arrived and you asked for a ride to your apartment. Neither of us witnessed a shooting or heard any gunshots."

"What if someone saw me shoot Gottschalk?"

"Even if a witness comes forward, without a weapon they have nothing, no security cameras and the alley is not well lit. The shade from the buildings puts you in a dark shadow. If a witness comes forward, he will be able to testify that he saw 'someone' fire a shot, not a particular someone, not you. Besides, even if they find out that Gottschalk was killed in the alley, he was a Jewish gangster, not Mother Teresa," Eshkol finished up.

"Andre, continue with your life as if nothing strange happened. Visit Michelle tomorrow. Tell Lucille about your plans to move to Montreal." Shimon grunted out through his clenched teeth.

Andre looked at Shimon and appraised his situation.

"You might end up in a wheelchair for a while, Shimon, or at least crutches."

Shimon gave more of a grimace than a grin. "That could happen when one slips on a bar of soap in the shower," Shimon responded.

At Andre's apartment, Eshkol went with Andre. He returned in a couple of minutes with a lump in his jacket pocket, the ammo. The driver started up and headed for the embassy. Eshkol phoned ahead so the embassy doctor would meet them.

"Eshkol, Gottschalk knew my exact location," Shimon reiterated.

Eshkol nodded and responded in a whisper of his own. "Right."

"Who else at the embassy knew my pickup location?"

"Debra, the comms girl and our driver here, that's all."

"Eshkol, we may have a security leak. This should not have happened."

Inspector Gallant ordered the Le Clair Rehabilitation center into a lock-down. He dispatched investigators to the crime scene, or what they were treating as a crime scene for the moment. The crime scene investigators discovered one shell casing near the kitchen door and two bullet fragments. One bullet they found across the alley stuck into a brick wall. It was a small-caliber bullet, much deformed but with visible blood and 'matter' on it. It seemed like the bullet had traveled through a human head. They dug the second bullet out of the pavement. Even a little bit of blood would be discovered back at the lab. But at least one person was struck, Gallant knew that much already.

Gallant and Blanc began to interrogate the kitchen employees.

Gigot, the reporter, spoke quietly into his phone, reporting to Henri as things happened. He stood well away from the action, trying to be inconspicuous. The cops would shoo him away from the scene if they discovered who he was.

"Did any of you see either of these two men earlier today?" The inspector asked the gathered kitchen workers. Blanc distributed photographs of Shimon Levi and Andre Dubois.

"This one left the building through the kitchen, and then the other man followed him a few minutes later," the salad maker revealed. He of course said nothing of the fifty euro bribe that Shimon had given him.

"When did you hear the gunshots?"

The chef answered for all of them. "The shots came just after the second man left the kitchen and entered the alley."

"Do you mean Andre Dubois when you say 'the second man?'" Gallant prompted.

"Yes, the man in the photograph," the chef pointed.

"Did any of you go to the alleyway after you heard the gunshots?"

"No, detective. We thought it would be dangerous. We talked about going, but no one left the kitchen," the chef continued

"We need each of you to write a statement telling us what happened. The officer there will have pens and paper for you. Nothing elaborate, just the facts as you remember them." He pointed to a uniformed officer with a bundle of paper and pens.

"So, no eyewitnesses," Detective Blanc commented to his boss.

"Not yet, but we haven't yet questioned Shimon or Andre."

"Maybe the love triangle got out of hand and they shot each other?" Blanc offered.

"We will see. Let's go up and talk to their mutual girlfriend, Michelle Dumas."

At the door to Michelle's room, the two detectives presented their badges. Lucille and Louis quietly left Michelle to engage the detectives in the hallway.

"What is going on with all the sirens?" Lucille wanted to know.

"Madam, there was a shooting behind the kitchen."

"Oh my God, where is Andre?"

"We don't know. We have reason to believe that both he and Shimon Levi were in the alleyway when the gunshots were fired. There is blood in the alley," the inspector told them, watching carefully for their reaction.

"I must call them to make sure they are safe." Lucille blurted out, clearly anxious. "I sent Andre downstairs to give Shimon my apartment key, but he didn't return. Louis, call Andre," she ordered. "I will call Shimon on his cell."

She dialed her phone as Louis did the same on his.

"Shimon?" Lucille nearly shouted into the phone.

"Hello, Lucille. I apologize for leaving, but I was called to the embassy." He could sense her nervousness.

Inspector Gallant motioned for her to give him her phone. She did.

"Monsieur Levi, this is Inspector Gallant of the Metropolitan Police. I have a few questions. Are you at the Israeli embassy?"

"Yes, I am."

"Do you know where Andre Dubois is currently?"

"I couldn't say, inspector."

"Have you seen him today?"

"Yes, I saw him at the Le Clair center. First we talked in the cafeteria, and then a little later he met me in the alley behind the kitchen. He gave me the key to Lucille Dumas' apartment. Then our driver took him to his apartment. I last saw him leave the car, with the intent of going to his flat. The car then took me to the embassy. I have not heard from him since that time."

"How long ago was this, Monsieur Levy?"

"I don't know exactly, I didn't note the time. It was a little while ago, detective, but less than an hour."

The inspector cupped the phone, suspecting a stall from Shimon.

"Blanc, call for a warrant to search Andre's apartment."

Louis piped up. "Andre isn't answering. Should I leave a message for him to call me?"

"Yes," Gallant ordered. He resumed his call with Shimon.

"Monsieur Levi, did you hear the sound of gunshots when you were in the alley?"

"No, why?"

"Did you or Andre fire a weapon in the alley?"

"No. What is this about? Has someone been shot?"

"Were you or Andre fired upon?"

"No."

"Did you not find it strange that Andre would leave without telling Louis or Lucille that he was departing?"

"How would I know he didn't tell them he was going to leave? I did not interrogate him, inspector."

Blanc took a call and signaled with a thumbs up to the inspector. The warrant had been approved. Blanc left to pick it up.

"Monsieur Levi, I have a written affidavit from the Le Clair kitchen staff that placed you and Andre in the alley, at the time the gunshots were heard."

"Did they witness what they allege they heard?" Shimon replied.

"Shots were fired. We have ample evidence, a pool of fresh blood on the pavement, bullet fragments and tire tracks," the inspector continued, pointedly not answering Shimon's direct question.

Louis' phone rang. Andre was on the line.

"Andre, are you OK?" Louis nearly shouted into the phone.

"Monsieur Levi, I will talk with you again." The inspector returned her phone to Lucille and turned his attention to Louis.

Louis spoke into his phone. "Why did you leave without telling us?"

"I needed time to think."

"Think about what?" Louis wanted to know.

The inspector gently removed the phone from Louis' grip.

"Andre, this is Inspector Gallant."

"What, Inspector Gallant?" Andre did a good job of faking surprise.

"Have you been involved in a shooting? We know you were in the alleyway behind the Le Clair center when gunshots were fired."

"I don't know what you are talking about."

"Are you at your apartment?"

"I am."

"Do you require medical services?"

"No, of course not."

"The magistrate has issued a warrant for us to search your apartment."

"Inspector, come on ahead. I have nothing to hide."

"We will see. In fact, I will see you very soon Andre. Goodbye."

"Lucille, I never got a chance to see Michelle," the inspector said as he gave Louis back his phone.

"She gets better every day, for which we are very happy and grateful."

"May I greet her?"

"Perhaps another time, Inspector Gallant. I think it would be too much for her now."

"Perhaps another day would be better. Please give her my best wishes."

Somewhat later while Gallant was en-route to Louis' apartment, Blanc provided the inspector with an update on the search of the apartment.

"We are going through the apartment with a fine-tooth comb. We have examined Andre for body wounds and bullet residue. He is clean, too clean. He had already showered prior to our arrival and began a machine wash of his clothing," Blanc reported.

"Stop the machine and separate his clothing. Test for blood, residue, whatever you can, and check the building's dumpsters. I am on my way."

Chapter 67

PARIS

The embassy guards suspended the perfunctory security checks. At the portal, medics stood ready and equipped to help the injured Shimon Levi. Eshkol and two of the embassy guards lifted Shimon from the car and into a wheelchair.

For at least the next hour, Sol, the embassy driver that had brought Shimon from Le Clair to the embassy, disappeared from the sight of anyone connected with the diplomatic mission. While no one paid attention to him, he drove to the Charles de Gaulle airport and parked in the huge parking garage there. Then he went to the taxi stand in front of the terminal building and waited patiently, politely for an available cab.

Inspector Gallant took a call while he poked around in the apartment of Andre Dubois.

"Inspector, we have one DNA match off the bullet fragment in the wall," the lab technician told him.

"Excellent work, Dani. I didn't expect such a fast turnaround. A million thanks," Gallant gushed. Truly, often enough the lab work might take weeks. The lab people were on the ball this time.

"Well, I would like to take all the credit but it is really a new technology.

We have the hottest new microchip in a portable scanner. It is another gift of the American's bent for ingenuity and innovation, to my regret. We French should be more aggressive in inventing useful things, no?"

"Of course, Dani, but what did you find out?"

"The DNA belonged to Nate Gottschalk. So did the traces of brain matter. Someone blew his brains out, Chief."

"Ah, there we are, Dani, positive proof that there is justice in the universe. What about the blood on the pavement?"

"Sorry, inspector, there is no match on that sample."

"Thanks Dani, good work. Goodbye for now." Gallant broke the connection. Then he put his hands behind his back and paced around the apartment, thinking and not touching a thing. After a while of ambulatory pondering, he sought out Andre Dubois.

"Andre, we have discovered that Nate Gottschalk took a bullet through his head. Someone killed him deader than disco. For which blessed event I am truly thankful. This is wonderful news for Parisians, for us to be utterly rid of a vile and dangerous ethnic criminal. Whoever killed him will be lauded as a hero. So how did it happen? We know you were there. Why did you kill him?"

"Slow down there, inspector. I didn't shoot anyone. I don't even own a handgun," Andre shot back, waving his hands at the same time in a warding off motion.

"But as an astronaut, you had weapons training. We both know that guns can easily be purchased on the black market. Look, Andre, I know you are not a killer. If you shot Gottschalk, I am sure it was in self-defense. I am grateful, as are the people of Paris. But more importantly, the judges and magistrates are grateful. Think this over, Andre, and call me."

The inspector placed his card by the telephone. He and Blanc exited the apartment.

"What next?" Blanc asked.

"Let's go to the Israeli embassy and have a talk with Shimon Levi."

At the embassy, in the well-equipped clinic, the staff doctor examined an x-ray image.

"The x-ray shows a clean flesh wound with no bone fragments," Dr. Davidson pointed for Shimon to see. "You just need to take it easy for a bit and you will be as good as new."

"Now that is good news, doctor," Eshkol said, smiling at Shimon.

Dr. Davidson spoke to Shimon. "We will want to keep you in bed for a few days. We'll put a cast on your leg to keep it from moving around. I am afraid that you will be on crutches for a while, but not too long," he assured his patient.

Eshkol's phone buzzed.

"Excuse me, Doctor Davidson, Shimon. I have to take this." The security office was on the other end of the call.

"Eshkol, I have two policemen here, an Inspector Gallant and a Detective Blanc. They have come to see Shimon Levi.".

"Tell them Levi is not available today."

Chapter 68

PARIS

few minutes after 6 PM, on their way home to their wives, the
detectives received a radio message from another squad car. An
eye witness to the shootings had walked into the station. The
detectives turned around and headed back to work.

Somewhat later, back at the station, Gallant and Blanc perused
Solomon Marcus' passport and Israeli embassy ID card. The inspector
seemed to fondle this identification.

"Monsieur Marcus, so as to be clear for the record, you witnessed
a shooting in an alleyway behind the Le Clair Rehabilitation Center at
approximately 17:00 hours? We will record your statement to ensure the
accuracy of our records," Gallant explained.

"I understand. Technically, inspector, I didn't see the shootings but
I witnessed one of the persons shot. I will be happy to share the details."
He paused and glanced at the policemen. "But first, we need to agree on
certain rules and conditions." He looked at them to see their reaction.

"What did you have in mind, Monsieur?" Gallant asked, succeeding in
hiding his irritation. People in French police stations did not customarily
try to make bargains.

"I want immunity from state prosecution and witness protection," Sol explained.

"We are capable of providing you with these safeguards, unless we find that you were a participant or accessory to the shootings," the inspector qualified.

"I assure you that I am neither a participant nor an accessory to the shootings."

"Then you have no reason to fear us, Monsieur."

"Do we have a deal?"

"I can call the magistrate. What is your phone number?"

"You can't reach me. I lost my cell phone, and I am on the run."

"I see. So you are seeking witness protection from your own people?"

"Yes. I left the embassy car at the airport parking lot and took a taxi here."

"Before I call the magistrate, tell us who got shot."

"An Israeli staying at the embassy," Sol answered.

"Shimon Levi?"

"Yes."

"Who shot him?"

"I was told it might be Nate Gottschalk, but I didn't see the shooting."

"What did you see?"

"I saw Andre Dubois holding a gun. I saw Shimon Levi with a bullet in his leg. We got them into the embassy car and drove Dubois to his apartment. Then we took Shimon to the embassy where our medical people took charge of him."

"Who shot Levi?" the inspector asked.

"Gottschalk, Andre said."

"So, Andre fired the gun that killed Gottschalk," Blanc confirmed.

Within the hour the inspector received a signed fax authorization for immunity and witness protection for Solomon Marcus, eyewitness.

"Monsieur Marcus, your request has been approved. Here are your copies, Monsieur. As you see, you will receive immunity subject to your full cooperation, disclosure, and candor. Witness protection will commence if and when the state prosecutor decides to file criminal charges."

"Good. Where will I stay in the meantime?"

"Wherever you like. For your safety, we recommend that you stay right here, at the precinct. Here, you will have a bed, shower facility, and use of the cafeteria. I presume you have some money for food and drink?"

"I have some money," Sol admitted.

"Did Andre know Gottschalk?" the inspector asked.

"No, I don't think so. He was in the alley to give a key to Levi."

"You say Andre Dubois shot Gottschalk. According to our records, he is not a registered gun owner."

"The gun belonged to his father and grandfather before that, a family heirloom. We took the gun to the embassy for safekeeping," Sol told them.

Blanc and Gallant looked at one another in disappointment.

"We're fucked," Gallant said. "We can't subpoena the Israeli embassy."

"And we have no DNA match on the pavement blood," Blanc added.

"No, because it is Shimon Levi's blood, and you don't have his DNA in your system," Sol revealed.

Blanc snorted and Gallant shook his head in a negative way.

"Tell us, Monsieur Marcus, why do you think Gottschalk wanted to kill Shimon Levi?" the inspector asked. "I doubt that their paths have crossed."

"Sure. I think it goes back to the feud between Gottschalk and Rothstein. They have some dispute, like Mafia dons, I don't know why. But they hate each other with a murderous hate. I think Gottschalk wanted to shoot Levi to send a message to Rothstein. The word is that Levi helped to get Rothstein out of jail in the USA."

"We were informed that Shimon Levi helped secure Rothstein's release," Gallant added.

You know because I called it in," Sol revealed.

Gallant looked perplexed.

"You seem to be very well informed, Marcus. I am not so interested in Israeli oddsmakers as I am in the part you played. And I warn you again, anything but the truth and you forfeit both immunity and witness protection. We will prosecute you to the full extent of the law," Gallant admonished the driver.

"Yes, yes, I understand the conditions, inspection. You don't have to threaten me every five minutes. You have me over a barrel and we both know it."

"How did the late Monsieur Gottschalk find out that Shimon Levi would be alone in the alleyway waiting for you to pick him up"

"Gottschalk knew because I texted him."

"You texted him?" Blanc repeated in disbelief. "Why?"

"Gottschalk gave me money. I had accumulated some serious gambling debts. He should have killed Shimon with the first shot. If he had done that as he should have, and if Andre hadn't shown up just in the nick of time, Gottschalk would still be alive and I would not be here with you, my life a ruin and a wreck."

"You would still be here. They would have figured it out. Do you think Gottschalk meant to shoot to wound? Why would he do that?" Blanc asked.

"Gottschalk was a nasty piece of work, detective. I bet he wanted Levi to suffer for a while before he finished him off. Nate does have a reputation for that sort of thing."

"Well, too bad for him that he tried to get fancy and now he is dead. What do you think, Blanc? Does this make any sense to you?"

"Inspector, I don't see how we have a legal case. Shimon and Eshkol have diplomatic immunity. We have no weapons. We have no body, and I don't think we will ever see the body. We got a big fat zero when we tossed the Dubois apartment. We have the witness of Marcus here but nothing more than that. I think we are...., well, at a dead end. At least for now." Blanc summed it up.

"I agree with your assessment, Detective Blanc. Even if we had the gun Andre Dubois used, he fired it to prevent a murder. No, I don't see a case for us either."

"So, where does that leave me?" Sol asked.

"You stay here for now. My guess is your embassy has recovered your phone and will find the text message that implicates you. Instead of running, you could have thrown the phone into the river and maintained your cover."

"I was about to be considered their prime suspect. It was my time to leave. Let them find the phone and think I fled the country."

"One more question, please?" Gallant asked. "Who was responsible for the Dubois kidnapping?"

"Honestly, I don't know, inspector. It is a mess with the gangsters, and the Catholic Church all tangled up but with not enough evidence to pin it on one or the other of them. I wish you luck in solving it. But there is one bit of information that might interest you. Dubois will soon take up a new life in Montreal."

"You are certain?"

"Yes."

"You are going to be fine, Shimon," Eshkol assured his friend, giving him an easy smile.

"At least it doesn't hurt anymore, not with the happy juice they gave me. In fact, I feel very good right now. But I don't see how I will sleep with my leg elevated in this shithole cast. And now that I think about it, what was so urgent yesterday that you needed me to rush to the embassy, getting shot along the way?"

"I'll explain. It's about a cell phone we recovered that cost us more than a few shekels, but well worth the price.""

Eshkol's phone buzzed. "But I have to take this first."

He listened and heard a voice say "Eshkol, this is Ephraim. Sol is missing. We tracked his car on GPS. It is in a parking garage at Charles de Gaulle."

"Did you call him?"

"Every five minutes, but he is not picking up."

"Did you GPS his cell?"

"Yes, it is also at the airport," Ephraim replied.

"What is going on?" Shimon whined.

Eshkol closed the phone. "Sol is the mole."

Chapter 69

PARIS

The following morning Louis drove Andre to the Le Clair Rehabilitation Center. The crime scene investigators puttered mysteriously here and there, trying to extract some last bit of evidence with little success. They had roped off the alleyway save for a narrow lane reserved for food and medical deliveries to the center. Andre pitied the poor, diligent police technicians. Some of them looked like they had been there all night.

He didn't pity them enough to confess, which would allow them to head for home.

Louis never questioned Andre about his kidnapping or yesterday's shooting allegations. Louis wanted to talk about both events the previous evening, but Andre raised his finger to his lips as a signal that the apartment might be bugged. He motioned his friend outside where Louis could speak freely. He did.

"Don't change your mind, Andre. Get the Hell out of France as soon as you can."

"Don't worry, Louis. I will do just that. I am done with France and France is done with me. Quits, I call it."

They spoke of these things no more.

The next morning at the rehab center gift shop, Andre bought some flowers and the morning paper. The headline on the newspaper read:

Nate Gottschalk believed dead. Gangster's DNA found on bullet

Absorbed, Andre was oblivious to the man who stepped up next to him.

"Good morning, Andre. What wonderful weather we have in Paris this spring. It isn't anything like Montreal," offered Inspector Gallant as he bought his own copy of Le Monde.

Andre said nothing and scarcely gave Gallant a glance. He went straight up to Michele's room.

"Bon matin, Andre. What lovely flowers. Thank you." Lucille smiled, accepted the flowers, and offered greeting kisses in the usual manner. Michelle was napping so they stepped into the hallway.

"How is she today?" Andre asked.

"The staff had her singing 'Michelle' earlier. It was very nice."

"The Beatles tune? Did she remember all the words?" Andre asked.

"Not all, but most. She is a work in progress. The important thing is that we have progressed a lot, Andre. She gets better every day but it will take a while, I think. But sometimes there is a breakthrough that speeds the process up, so the doctors tell me. In the meantime, I try to be patient. Humming Beatles songs helps." She smiled at him again.

They meandered to the end of the hall where Andre ushered her into the stairwell.

"Well, we are private here. What is it, Andre?"

"The police are all over the place. They might even have bugged the room. This gangster Nate Gottschalk that the cops think was killed in the alley last night? They put me on the list of suspects just because I happened to be in the alley at about the same time. I went there to give Shimon your apartment key, as you know. They came to my flat and tore everything up, looking for God knows what." He handed Lucille the newspaper, showing the headline about the shooting.

"Andre, the important thing is that you were not hurt. I couldn't stand that."

"Lucille, I will very soon leave for a new start in Montreal."

Lucille looked concerned. "Why, Andre?"

"I have no life in Paris anymore. I have accepted a position with the

Canadian Space Agency. I will be helping with some things that I have special expertise in."

Lucille covered her mouth with her hand to disguise an involuntary chuckle.

"Oh, I am sorry Andre. I just didn't know that Canada had a Space Agency."

"Lucille, Canada is a real country. They have astronauts to train. Someday, Canadians will be among the crew of the International Space Station."

"I never thought about it, Andre, but I am sure you are right. But you said you would leave very soon. What does that mean?"

"Next week."

She looked stricken. Lucille was not good at hiding her emotions and truly, didn't try very hard to hide them. She touched his face gently. "I understand Andre. Now I must return to Michelle. She could wake up any time and I should be there."

"I can stay until she wakes up."

"Maybe it is better that you go."

"I can return later."

"No, I am so sorry Andre, really I am, but too much has happened to you and continues to happen. My main, my only concern, is Michelle, her recovery, and her safety."

Subdued, Andre sighed. He said his goodbyes and hugged Lucille, perhaps for the last time. He left, caught up in his own thoughts, he got on the Metro and more or less at random headed for Montmartre, the iconic village where he and Michelle had met quite by accident only a few years before. That meeting now seemed like an eternity ago.

He looked out the window at nothing and tried to imagine what living in Canada would be like. Cold, he thought, but at least new to him. He wondered how the inspector had found out about his travel plans.

"Do you have any good news?" Eshkol whispered from the seat behind him.

Andre instantly recognized the voice.

"Why are you following me?"

"I came to tell you something, some not-so-good news. We have a mole."

"Who knew of my plans to move to Montreal?"

"I am afraid so. But don't worry. The police have no cards to play. They have no corpse, no gun and no real evidence to tie you to the supposed crime. You are in the clear."

"But they have a witness who can identify me, don't they?"

"Not exactly. He didn't see you pull the trigger. He just saw you in the alley. It isn't enough. If they had enough evidence, they would have arrested you today at the rehab center. You should make a point of enjoying Montreal; it is a great city."

The metro slowed to a stop, the doors opened and Eshkol unobtrusively exited as other passengers entered.

Andre closed his eyes and recalled that fateful day when he saw her at the Italian restaurant in Montmartre. And celebrating with friends about his selection as the first French astronaut assigned to the International Space Station. At that time, Michelle was an archaeology student at the University de Paris. She and her friends were at a nearby table. They met and began a wonderful, confusing, delightful whirlwind romance, interrupted when she left to continue her education in Israel.

He didn't shed a tear but the memory was sharp, biting deep into his soul. That was the best time of his life.

And then came the bombshell. Michelle broke off their relationship. She fell in love with an Israeli archaeologist. A despondent Andre completed his training and went up in the space shuttle to the ISS. He joined crew-mates Israeli Ari Ben Ora, Russian Alexander and from India, Sanjay.

Andre fast-forwarded his memories to the escape capsule's tumultuous landing on the Mediterranean Sea. No doubt his skilled piloting of the escape capsule and his courage to fire Ari's Uzi at the hovering Russian helicopter saved all their lives.

And during his recuperation at the Haifa hospital, with the help of an investigator named Shimon Levi, Andre and Michelle had been reunited. She had lost her Israeli lover near the Lebanese border. He died in a terrorist attack, one of many lives lost over the years in more or less random events. The Muslim terrorists seemed content to kill any Jew, any age or sex whenever they could. It was a story that went back to the life and time of Mohammad. Jews were then and are now the enemies of Islam, made so by the Muslims themselves.

Shimon had convinced Andre to maintain silence about the Russian attempt to murder him and his fellow astronauts. In a conversation that completed just moments before a French policeman entered Andre's hospital room, Andre agreed to keep quiet. Silence would buy the freedom for Alex's brother, languishing in a Russian prison, as well as family members. The French cop had the death of Father Gauthier under investigation. He got nothing from Andre.

Because of Andre keeping silent, Alexander's family eventually resettled in Israel. So did Andre, for a while. But the death of Father Gauthier wore on him until he could take no more. Gauthier was in a way the second father of the orphan Andre. He considered that his part of the bargain was over. He returned to Paris and used his celebrity status to rail against the Catholic hierarchy for alleged involvement in an international plot that resulted in the suicide of Father Gauthier, his friend, and mentor.

Andre could not prove his accusations. As he explained when asked, the proof resided in a series of email correspondences contained in the hard drive of his laptop which had been taken out of the escape capsule by the Israelis. Proof of the emails was also on the laptop that belonged to the late Father Gauthier. That laptop could not be found. Andre felt strongly that the Father's laptop had been picked up by the Catholic prelates in Paris. The original email on the computer used by Alexander's brother Yuri now was the property of the Russian state. A perfect trifecta of a cover-up. The proof existed in three computers. Each computer was in the hands of powerful forces that would be badly harmed if the truth ever emerged. Andre was stymied and frustrated.

Andre exited the metro at the Montmartre station. The sun shined brightly, a light breeze cooled him. On this perfect Paris day, he decided to return to the Italian restaurant where he had first met Michelle. To his horror, he found not his special place but a Japanese restaurant, an affirmation if he needed one, that not everything in life was meant to last. He moved on and found a French cafe. He sat outside in the sunshine, ordered a quiche and a delicious glass of Beaujolais. He settled down with the paper to distract his wandering thoughts. On the second page of Le Monde, a headline blared out at him.

VATICAN SYNOD:
JEWS ARE NOT CHOSEN
AND HAVE NO PROMISED LAND

Shocking statements from a Vatican Synod seem likely to set back Jewish-Catholic relations to pre-Vatican II times. The synod denied the Jewish connection to the land of Israel.

The Holy Scriptures can not be justified to endorse the return of Jews to Israel at the expense of Palestinians. The notion of a "promised land" for a "chosen people, the Jews was nullified by Christ.

Andre could have scripted the Vatican statement. He had been told as a child that the Jews were the enemy of the Catholic Church. He blamed them collectively after the Israeli air strike leveled the French-built nuclear reactor in Baghdad. The attack killed only one person, a French scientist who was also Andre's father. Andre would never forget, could never forget the 1981 raid. Nor could he forgive.

But Andre's religiousness leaning became less important than bringing to justice the church prelates who had responsibility for the suicide of Father Gauthier. The selfless act of the priest saved Andre's life and the lives of all of his crewmates on the ISS.

As for the Palestinians, Andre's empathy for their plight plummeted after a Palestinian sniper nearly killed Michelle. The attempted murder of his former lover, an archaeologist, left her in a brain-damaged state. His once unshakable convictions morphed into a self-absorbed paranoia that focused on self-survival. Even his father's semi-automatic pistol that he had entrusted to Eshkol for safekeeping might still have his fingerprints on it somewhere. Those prints could be used against him by the Paris Metro Police.

He flipped through the pages of the newspaper. One column caught his attention.

U.S. Casts only veto (with regret) against Palestinian resolution to sanction Israel for constructing apartments in E. Jerusalem, land the international community wants for a future Palestinian state.

Paraguay, Brazil, Venezuela, Uruguay and Chile recognize the right to a Palestinian state based on the 1967 borders with Israel.

Andre speculated that Europe and the US were poised to break Israel's grip even though Israel had no borders in 1967, only a temporary armistice line. Israel had conquered territory in defending against a multi-nation attack by the adjoining Arab states. She later ceded much of the conquered land in exchange for an ephemeral and elusive quest for peace.

He turned the page again. The next article really got his attention.

Vicar General Selected As
New Assistant Secretary of State

An invitation-only gala event will be held Saturday evening at the Palace of Versailles hosted by Archbishop Clement of Paris to celebrate the soon to be outgoing vicar general Antoine de Gaulle.

Yesterday, the Vatican Secretary of State Lajolo announced that the vicar general will replace the retiring assistant secretary Salvatore Amato.

Andre had not forgotten that Archbishop Clement had witnessed the suicide of his beloved Father Gauthier at the Basilica de Sacre-Coeur in Montmartre. He suspected both the archbishop and vicar general of plotting the cover-up. Saturday was also an important day on Andre's calendar. He had a ticket for that day on Air France to travel from Paris to Montreal.

Chapter 70

―――――――――⚜――――――――――

THE PALACE AT VERSAILLES

Antoine gazed admiringly in the mirror within the confines of his private suites at Versailles. An aide stood on a step stool and adoringly placed the silver chain and oversized crucifix around the vicar general's neck. The cross rested on a clerical robe of burgundy silk, costly enough to pay a priest in Africa for a year.

A figurative who's who of Paris had come to attend the evening's dinner at Versailles and to celebrate Antoine's appointment as the chief assistant to the Secretary of the Vatican. Included among the invitees were the mayor of Paris, the French ambassador to the Vatican, Archbishop Clement, other Catholic prelates, distinguished politicians and the inevitable members of the press. French and Italian cuisine, spirits, wines with names known to oenophiles across the globe waited to delight the taste buds of the guests as they listened to a tuxedoed ensemble gently play Handel's 'Water Music.'

The hundred or so guests reveled in the glory of the famous Hall of Mirrors.

Steeped in centuries of French history and power, the Palace of Versailles had been home to King Louis XVI and Marie Antoinette. The Treaty of Versailles that ended the Great War had seen the signers gathered in this very room. Perhaps no place in France has the historical, cultural, and architectural grandeur and meaning as the Hall of Mirrors.

Antoine's cell phone buzzed. Antoine fixated on getting his hair to part and dismissed the call. As he looked in the mirror, he reflected on the Jewish push back as a result of the Vatican Curia's synod. It had been relentless, but this would be his day, his and no others. He would insist upon that. Again his phone vibrated like an electric bumblebee. This time he glanced at the caller ID.

The call was from Sasha's cell phone. But that could not be! Not only was Sasha dead, but his phone had been destroyed after his murder, so he was informed. Immediately, Antoine's complexion turned wan.

"Out," Antoine brusquely told his aide. He took a deep breath to calm himself and answered the phone.

"Hello."

"May I congratulate you on your promotion to the office of Secretary of state. I know I am not the first, but I hope I will not be the last." The caller deliberately confused the promotion.

263

Antoine would become the assistant to the Secretary of State, not the secretary himself. But the caller knew, as did anyone in the Vatican, that the man who held the more lofty title was only a decorative figurehead, a distinguished-looking figure to carry on the public tasks of the office. The real work, and the power, would go to Antoine.

"Who is this?"

"Shimon Levi, your Excellency. You are confused because I am calling you on a certain phone."

"Say no more."

"We have to meet tonight, Antoine."

"Call me tomorrow."

"Tomorrow is too late," Shimon insisted.

"Impossible. I am the guest of honor at a private party tonight."

"See that I am on the invitation list."

"Is this your idea of a joke?" Antoine snapped back.

"Absolutely not. Versailles is blessed with acres of lush gardens, ponds, and walking paths. We can find a quiet place to speak for a moment or two. You do not want to refuse me." The threat hung heavy behind the words.

"How can I explain your presence to the archbishop? His eminence has approved of all the guests that we invited."

"Tell him I'm a cousin to Baron de Rothschild," Shimon quipped.

"Nonsense, Archbishop Clement already knows who you are."

"And he will find me easily; I am on crutches."

Chapter 71

MONTREAL

Considering the three hour time change and the seven hour long flight, Andre landed in Montreal at 4:20 in the afternoon. He wasted another half hour of his life clearing Canadian customs. To his surprise, he spotted an attractive woman holding up a sign with his name on it in big letters. He had not expected to be met by anyone so lovely. He enthusiastically waved at her. He headed her way and when he got close, he thrust out his hand. She smiled and extended her hand in turn and gave him a warm handshake.

"Bon jour. May I call you Andre?"

"I insist. And you are?"

"Mylène Douchette. Please allow me to help you with your luggage."

"If you can just take my laptop?" He handed her the device. "Jonathan mentioned that somebody would be waiting for me at my arrival. I just assumed that it would be one of the agency's chauffeurs."

"What makes you think that I am not, Andre?" She asked playfully. She looked at him like a woman looks at a man, not in a way that a fellow employee would look at another wage slave.

"You didn't strike me as a chauffeur, that's all. So, tell me, who is Mylene Douchette?"

Still smiling, still playful she replied "She is a financial analyst for the Canadian Space Agency and works on the agency's annual budget that we must present to the Canadian Parliament."

Smiling back at her, he could not help but return her friendly, coquettish smile, he asked "Why does a financial analyst volunteer her Saturday afternoon to chauffeur a stranger from a strange land into the warm embrace of Canada?"

"Jonathan asked me to pick you up and drive you to the Old Port Marriott. It is only a forty-minute drive. The night has not yet begun. I will join my friends for dinner after I take you to where you need to go."

"That sounds like a plan." He responded. He wondered if she might invite him to join her and her friends for dinner. He suddenly was not so tired from his flight.

"Have you been to Montreal before?"

"No, this is my first time. So far, I am quite pleased with the place."

"Five minutes at the airport?"

He laughed and pointed at her. "No, you. I think it was very charitable of you to make a foreigner feel so welcome."

"Not at all, and since you are French and this is Montreal, I can't think of you as a foreigner. But there is my car, a black Audi 4." Marlene popped the trunk and he loaded his two suitcases."

"Nice wheels," he said in genuine admiration.

"Thanks. Just put your laptop in the back seat." She gave him an appraising glance as he slipped into the passenger seat. "You travel light for someone who is starting a new life in Canada."

"I used to be an astronaut. I pack light."

"And may I add, a man of mystery."

Andre offered no reply. Mylene started the car and drove to the toll booth at the edge of the parking area. Andre went for his wallet.

"No, Andre. Jonathan insisted the agency pay."

"OK. Thanks. So, you are from Montreal?" He asked.

"Yes, I grew up near Saint-Denis, in the Plateau."

Andre had no idea what this meant. He tried again. "Did you attend a university in Montreal, or elsewhere?"

"Oui, right here. I did my undergrad studies at the University of Montreal. My graduate degree in finance and business analysis I took at

McGill. You will love the Old Port section at night. It is like New Orleans is supposed to be, all cobblestone streets, quaint but excellent shops, and wonderful eateries. The view of the Saint Lawrence River is breathtaking and even interesting for someone like me, trade ships going by, and so on. The area is close to the downtown shopping of Saint Catherine Street and Sherbrooke."

"Now that you mention food, I am a little hungry," he prompted, hopefully. "These days we don't get much on the airlines, even Air France."

"You are welcome to join me and my friends tonight." Her smile went up a few degrees.

"Thank you for the offer, but I like to shower first and change. It was a long flight. I could always grab something at the hotel to ward off starvation." He decided to play coy, but only momentarily.

"Andre, you are used to long flights. Do not disappoint me," she rejoined.

"Touche. So tell me something about Montreal that I don't know."

"OK, Andre. Did you know that in Montreal we have many immigrants from Asia? Montreal has Muslims, Jews from North Africa and Europe, and Africans. We are very multicultural and secular despite a preponderance of French Catholicism."

"What you describe is similar to Paris," Andre noted.

"Andre, Montreal's Chinatown is a short walk from the Old Port. The city is very safe to walk at night. Pubs and restaurants are nearly on every street corner, and most of them remain open through the very late hours."

"Good to know. What else can you tell me?" He liked to watch her lips as she spoke.

"In the northeast section is Montreal's Little Italy. The Sicilian and Calabrian Mafia have declared war on each other. So you want to stay out of that zone. But good Italian food is available all over Montreal, especially in the Old Port."

"Tonight I will meet my friends at a restaurant where the menu is printed only in French. Most restaurants have their menus printed in English too, but only after the French is displayed. The restaurant we are going to is like being in a medieval French castle with French armor hanging on its walls and minstrels singing victory songs over the Saracens. Of course, the patrons sing along and drink beer in mugs."

"I am intrigued," Andre admitted.

"The best part is the food preparation. The main course is served piping hot on a metal platter laden with cooked hen, boar, ham, potatoes and prepared to simulate a successful hunt in the French medieval forest. No forks or spoons are provided, only knives and one's fingers." She gave him a quick, playful glance as she drove. "And nobody is supposed to speak English."

"So, what happens if an American group patronizes the restaurant?"

"This is very funny. Last summer, an American, a friend of a friend, joined us and began speaking English. From the other side of the restaurant, one of the two minstrels singing French songs picked up on it. He came over to the table and demanded to know if the American was an Anglo-Saxon. And that caught the attention of the patrons, all in good fun. You have arrived at your destination, Andre Dubois. Here is my card with my cell number."

"Thank you so much, and it was a pleasure for me to meet you, Mylene Doucett."

The bellhop took the luggage. She shifted the Audi into gear. As she drove away from the hotel, her cell phone rang. She picked up the call.

"Do I have time to shower before dinner?" Andre coyly asked.

Chapter 72

THE PALACE AT VERSAILLES

"**A**rchbishop, I have an urgent situation that requires your immediate presence. Can you come to the Palace now? Antoine appealed.

"Within the hour," Clement replied.

"Thank you, your Excellency." Antoine waited for the archbishop to disconnect. Then he called for his aide.

"You called for me, Antoine?"

"Aidan, please inform security to add Shimon Levi to the invitational list and communicate his arrival to the kitchen staff."

"It's not even a good fit," Shimon argued.

"Stop complaining. The dinner jacket is a bit big for you because the pants have to be large enough to cover your cast." Eshkol explained.

"I am ready, I guess," Shimon said with a bit of a disgruntled tone still in his voice.

"Got everything, the photographs, and the cell phones?" Eshkol double-checked.

"Yes."

"There will be a security check. You may be required to remove your dinner jacket," Eshkol advised.

"I have the photographs in an envelope taped securely to my cast. I am good to go."

Archbishop Clement knocked twice.

"Your excellency, please come in. A glass of whiskey? Just this morning I received a single bottle of Elijah Craig, an eighteen-year-old Bourbon."

"Yes, thank you. Who sent this elixir to you?"

"A very old friend is now the bishop in Lexington, Kentucky. He gets a case every year from an admirer. The thoughtful man heard of my new posting and sent it to me to help celebrate."

"I must say that I have never tasted finer, not that I am all that familiar with American whiskey. It is delicious, Antoine. Thank you."

Antoine turned up the volume on the TV set in the room and moved to stand very close to the archbishop. He wanted no one to overhear their conversation. He touched his glass to the other.

"An hour ago Shimon Levi called me on Sasha Andreev's disposable cell," Antoine revealed.

"But you said the cell was destroyed after..."

"The Israelis were on to Sasha. Somewhere that night they had to have switched phones with him. Or maybe Igor pulled a fast one, who knows? Shimon Levi insisted on meeting tonight and I invited him to come to the celebration. I had no choice, really, but I wanted you to know."

"You could be sent to prison for the rest of your life," he whispered into Antoine's ear.

"We have done business with the Jews before. This is about business," Antoine countered.

The archbishop downed the last of the elegant whiskey and put the glass down on the table.

"Antoine, have you already forgotten the Vatican Synod result that officially stated that God did not promise Israel to the Jews? Put yourself in their place. The vicars of Christ two thousand years after the Crucifixion have told this generation of Jews that they have no right to their homeland, even after Hitler exterminated a third of them. On the issue, we are unwittingly bedfellows with the Muslim world and the political far left. Antoine, try not to be seen with him in the banquet room."

The musicians began to warm up and played the opening bars of the La Marseillaise, the stirring French national anthem. The first guests to arrive were Baron de Rothschild and his wife. The Baron Rothschild was scion to the centuries-old banking and wine family dating back to the European political machinations of the Napoleonic Wars. The baron and his wife proudly displayed their name tags. Church prelates and Mayor Broussard formed a greeting line and extended a warm welcome to each new arrival.

Within minutes, scores of other guests arrived, including Henri Bettencourt from Le Monde and Inspector Gallant of the Metropolitan Police. Like the others, they went to the security line, and placed their phones and other electronic devices in a tray to be scanned. The line formed, and one by one the announcer greeted the guests by name, rather like a herald at the court of a monarch.

A man hobbled up to the security post on crutches.

"Monsieur, you have two portable phones, one of which is prepaid and disposable. May I ask why?" inquired the security guard.

"One I use when I speak to my wife, the other is for speaking to my lover," Shimon lied smoothly, with a sly grin to the guard.

"May I see your identification?" The guard examined the ID. "Monsieur Levi, you may be unpleasantly surprised. Wives often know more than you think. But go ahead. Just head for the table to the left." The guard gestured in the proper direction.

Inspector Gallant and Henri Bettencourt showed some surprise at seeing Levi hobble into the room. Eyes always busy, Gallant noticed that Antoine, the guest of honor, swiftly and with little commotion exited from the room.

"I can't believe my eyes," Henri said to Gallant.

"Scotch on the rocks," the inspector said to a passing server, not responding to Henri's comment.

"Vodka for me," Henri tasked the waiter.

Shimon found his table and took a seat to rest his injured leg. A waiter came over and offered him a choice of wine or spirits. Shimon ordered a glass of Merlot.

"Don't trash the napkin," Aidan whispered and moved on to other guests. Shimon notices some writing on the napkin and stuffed it into his pocket without reading it. Two men with drinks in their hands approached him.

"Bonjour, Monsieur Levi, we meet again," the inspector smiled.

"Hello, inspector," Levi responded neutrally.

"Have you met Monsieur Bettencourt, from Le Monde?"

"No, but I have read and admired many of your columns," Levi addressed Bettencourt.

"Merci," Henri acknowledged with a bob of his head.

"May I ask what happened to your leg?" Inspector Gallant asked.

"I had an accident, nothing serious."

"I call that good news. One never knows what damage a bullet can cause. I know you took a bullet, Shimon. Sol Marcus, your embassy driver told me. I believe it was the late, unlamented, Nate Gottschalk who shot you. Then your rival in love, Andre Dubois plugged Gottschalk. Funny that he should be your savior, no?"

"How is Sol doing? He is a disgruntled employee. I hope you have some evidence to support your bellicose claims?"

"We have blood samples, but unfortunately, your DNA is not on file."

"The Merlot is from the Rothschild collection. I recommend it. Excuse me, gentlemen, I am going to sample the hors d' oeuvres."

Shimon intentionally placed the empty wine glass on the table and hobbled across the room. The inspector broke the seal to a tissue box and carefully picked up the wine glass that Shimon had used. He carefully touched only the flat base of the wineglass to disturb neither any fingerprints or the traces of DNA on the rim of the glass where lips had met with glass." He put the glass into his jacket pocket with care.

"Was he taunting or helping?" Henri asked.

"Taunting. Shimon still has diplomatic immunity."

Shimon read the instructions on the napkin while he sampled the appetizers. On the first of the three calls for dinner seating, his instructions told him to take the elevator downstairs and drive the golf cart on the pathway to the second cluster of trees on the left, by the fountains.

"I'll be back in a few minutes. Watch him for me, would you, Henri?"

"That shouldn't be difficult. He is seated at our table," Henri replied.

The inspector left the Hall of Mirrors to secure the wine glass in his police car. The musicians took a short respite and the conductor announced the first dinner call. Scores of elegantly dressed guests headed to their assigned tables. Shimon nonchalantly grabbed his crutches and stole away. Henri followed. He called the inspector, but only got his voicemail. Shimon wobbled to the elevator and pressed the down button. Henri redialed, the inspector answered this time.

"He had taken the elevator down," Henri reported.

"That will take him to the pool and gardens. Take the stairs, Henri. I'll be there in a minute. I had to go through fucking security again."

Henri descended one flight of stairs to the area of the reflecting pool. He spotted Shimon buzzing along the pathway to the fountains and gardens, driving a golf cart. Sounds of footsteps on the steps announced the arrival of Inspector Gallant.

"Can you see him, inspector? The golf cart must have been placed here, waiting for him." The glow of the full moon gave them plenty of light to spy by. They watched the cart turn off the pathway toward a cluster of trees.

"Henri, go back to our table or your colleagues will get suspicious. This is a police matter now."

"Be careful," Henri cautioned. The inspector began a slow jog, trying to be both quick and quiet.

Shimon stopped at the fountain. The entire area was surrounded by eucalyptus trees. The sound of the water made a soothing noise that provided excellent cover for potential eavesdroppers. From the opposite direction another cart appeared and abruptly stopped.

"You have ten minutes of my time," Antoine tersely stated.

"Antoine, I have proof that implicates you in a murder, and I don't want to send you to prison. Instead, I want you to reset the calculus." Shimon reached underneath his pant leg for the envelope.

"Be careful Shimon, with your accusations. Reset what calculus?"

"The understanding between the Vatican and Israel. Please take the pictures: I have copies."

"What pictures could you have from Sasha's disposable phone?"

"It was not disposable," Shimon replied.

Antoine perused the old photographs from weekends he spent with Sasha in Saint Laurent. The photographs revealed intimate moments they shared on a beach blanket.

"Last week, your Vatican newspaper, the Vatican Curia, published a synod finding that rejected Jewish claims to our homeland. The publication is a lighting rod for the European elites of the Left and Muslim leaders that work so hard and so diligently with the UN to de-legitimatize Israel. This is not good, and I told my superiors that you can do something about this."

"Both Archbishop Clement and myself are on record that we opposed the synod."

"I know, and that should make it easier for you. We recovered salacious details from deleted calls on Sasha's cell. Shall I replay some of your conversations?"

"No."

"Sasha called you for help, he said the police had his scent and were looking for him. He needed money and forged papers to get out of France. You agreed to meet him at the church. He went to the church and got murdered in the pews. This will be a great story as I am sure the members of the French press would agree."

"I didn't kill Sasha. I loved him. The Russians killed Sasha and Zoran," Antoine reeled as he sobbed. "I never meant for him to die this way."

"But you set him up, them up, both of them."

"Yes, I had to protect myself and the Church. My superiors were so worried about Andre that they reached out to the Russians for help. They hatched a plan to kidnap Andre. The plan had no one getting hurt, let alone die, not Zoran and not Sasha. Of course Andre would not suffer any harm. He would be out of circulation for a while and then he would go free."

"Why?"

"We set him up. We, that is the Russians, drugged him and placed him in bed next to Father Martel, also well drugged up. They took photographs of the pair in bed and threatened to release them unless Andre shut up. He shut up. The whole idea had Andre intimidated by the loss of his credibility, not to hurt him or anyone else. But when Zoran's picture hit the papers, all bets were off. The Russians went into panic mode."

"How did Sasha get involved?"

"Sasha and Zoran went to the same church. We needed a young, good looking gay or bi-sexual male, fluent in French to seduce a gay man, and steal his car. Zoran fit the bill. But Zoran didn't know his gay victim would be a priest dressed in ordinary clothes."

"A brilliant strategy," Shimon complemented.

"I did what was necessary to survive and to preserve our agreement."

"That was a rather gratuitous response, Antone. Effective tomorrow, Israel no longer wants to be part of your quid pro quo. No longer does Israel want to be any part of your Vatican blackmail scheme against the Russian government."

"And, Antoine, no longer does Israel want to conceal your complicity with the Russians in their aborted attempt to destroy the ISS, kill innocents, and knowingly provide cover for an Iran seeking a nuclear option to wipe Israel off the map."

"Be careful with your threats. If you backstab the Kremlin, Ahmadinejad will receive the missile he needs to protect his nuclear sites," Antoine warned. He could play hardball too.

"Maybe, but the Russian people will not be kind to their Kremlin leaders when they learn their government tried to blow up their own space station. And how will your Catholic flock react when they realize this pope is no better than the Borgias?"

"The Iranians are on the cusp of producing weapons-grade uranium and a capable delivery system that can reach Tel Aviv. You are not that narcissistic, you are bluffing. You need to stay with the arrangement and keep the defensive missiles away from the Iranians."

Shimon just looked at Antoine for three heartbeats, then continued. "Antoine, do you know what can happen to a nuclear centrifuge when it spins uncontrollably and undetected?"

"No, I am not a nuclear expert. Please, tell me quickly. I have to go."

"It self-destructs. Imagine a computer worm, very hard to isolate and detect which spins the centrifuges out of control while at the same time sending false data to the monitors. A computer worm like that might set back the Iranian program for several years."

"If there is such a computer worm, I have never heard of it. You spin a fantasy."

"You will know by tomorrow. The worm is called STUXNET, and that means the military option is off the table for at least a few years, and maybe more if another computer worm comes into play. I think you get my point, Antoine."

"You are bluffing again."

"I assure you that I am not. And I am ready to return to the Hall of Mirrors and hand out these photographs to the reporters at the press table and to Inspector Gallant. I will gladly reveal the Vatican secrets that we share."

"Wait, not so fast here, Shimon. Let me assume for the moment that what you say is true. What do you expect me to do?"

"Convince the Secretary of the Vatican to acknowledge that Israel is the only democracy in the Middle East where Christians are safe from Islamist aggression. Israel needs Vatican legitimacy and your opposition to a unilateral Palestinian state. One more thing, Antoine, you are never to release the photos of Andre with Father Martel. If they are, I will give the inspector what he needs to put you in prison for the rest of your life, even if you become Pope."

"Why should you care about Andre? I am curious. You two are not friends, as I understand." Antoine wanted to know.

"He saved me, he saved my life when I stood helpless before a murderer with a gun in his hand. You should know something about being saved. Aren't you in the business of saving people? Don't forget your pictures." Shimon snarked and then buzzed away in his electric golf cart.

The enormous grounds at Versailles took some time for Gallant to cross, even at a trot that brought out what seemed like buckets of sweat pouring down his forehead. He had nearly lost all of his breath when he gained sight of the two men. One man left, his golf cart making a whirring sound. Gallant saw a light flicker in the darkness, followed by a much bigger flame. He crouched in the shadow of a tree, panted and watched.

He recognized Shimon as he drove right past his hiding place. He turned his full attention to Antoine.

Antoine put a flame to the photos. He held the paper as long as he could and then dropped the burning paper into the pond around one of the fountains. Then he took his golf cart and departed, hurrying back to the party.

His breath restored, the detective sprinted to the pond and salvaged a partially burnt photograph. He recognized the face on the waterlogged picture. Sasha, the dead man, murdered in a church, peered at him, wet but smiling. Gallant put the fragment away safely in his pocket.

Stephen Lewis and Andy McKinney

Minutes later, Antoine returned to the Hall of Mirrors and joined Archbishop Clement at the head table. The serving of the main meal had commenced.

"Antoine, you have sweat on your brow. When we get some privacy, you'll have to tell me what the Israeli wanted." The archbishop's phone beeped, indicating an incoming test. He pulled his phone out of his robe and read the text. He gave the phone to Antoine. The message read...

'A computer worm identified as STUXNET caused irreparable damage to Iran's nuclear centrifuges. Unable to confirm, but Vatican suspects Israel created STUXNET. This will lead the news tomorrow for Reuters, BBC and CNN International.'

"Not good news for Iran," the archbishop whispered.

"Or for us, Your Excellency."

Chapter 73

PARIS

The receptionist offered Shimon a wheelchair, but he politely declined and headed over to take the elevator up to Michelle's room.

Michelle had Nick, her personal trainer with her, helping her with some stretching exercises. Her face lit up when she saw her suitor.

"What happened to you?" Michelle asked, pointing to his cast.

"I slipped on a bar of soap in the shower," he fibbed, more interested in her improved sentence structure.

"You slipped in the shower?" Michelle giggled.

"I am a klutz." He smiled disarmingly.

"Can I write on your cast?"

"Please do. I will like that."

Michelle slightly favored her left side. Shimon sat down on her bed. Normally right-handed, she used her left hand today. Nick nodded. Part of the therapy included using her damaged side, working the left side of her body to help it get better. She painstakingly scripted 'Love Michelle' on his cast.

"I am the first to write on your cast," she said, a pleased smile on her face, almost childlike.

"Yes, I can see that."

"Yesterday, I swam in the pool."

"And she worked on strengthening her legs," Nick added.

"I am hungry, Nick. Please get me some breakfast," she asked her trainer.

"Will you watch her?" Nick addressed Shimon.

"Sure, of course I will."

"Shimon, you did not visit me yesterday or the day before."

"Because I hurt myself. I am sorry, Michelle."

"I forgive you," she answered, smiling brightly.

"Michelle, do you remember the day you were hurt in Israel?"

"I don't remember the day I was shot, not clearly. I really only know about it from what I learned later."

"What do you remember?" Shimon asked.

"I remember lots of things. I remember Las Vegas," she replied with a wanton leer overtaking her expression.

"You do?" Shimon asked, a little shocked but delighted.

"Yes! How I surprised you, your kiss and your....what is the word?"

"Intimacy," he replied.

"Oui, Shimon, you can kiss me in a moment." Michelle reached for a stick of gum on the table next to her bed. She chewed quickly a few times and threw it in the wastebasket. Shimon laughed."

"May I have a stick of gum, too?" he asked.

Shimon chewed the gum a few times, and deposited the gum in the same waste basket. He cut her laughter short by a gentle kiss.

"I love you, Shimon."

"I love you, Michelle. Will you spend the rest of your life with me?"

"You want to marry me, Shimon?"

"I do."

Shimon reflected. Through sickness and health, and good times or bad, he would be by her side.

Chapter 74

———— ❧ ————

MONTREAL

2011

Eric and Bette visited Z for a month in Montreal. She had postgraduate studies in Quebec and in the course of those studies had discovered a handsome young Frenchman, well French/Canadian. He suited her to a T. Her parents had come to help with the wedding.

They held the wedding in October. The very modern, very secular couple exchanged their vows at a pub in Montreal's Old Port, the very place where they had met. A modest crowd of friends and family from both the bride's side and the groom's side attended.

After the celebrations and festivities, the honeymooners headed off to be by themselves while the out of town guests, including her parents, scattered to the four winds. Eric and Bette stopped on the way to the airport at Dunn's Delicatessen for some refreshment for the long flight to Phoenix.

"I can't believe you told that story about playing those Frankie Valli songs to Z when she was too little to protect herself," Bette chuckled, shaking her head.

"Hey, she loved the Four Seasons. They made great songs too. "Candy

Girl," "Big Girls Don't Cry," and especially "Sherry," are all classic hits. Songs like that make me happy to be alive."

"You did tie it into the Broadway play "The Jersey Boys," but really, I think you were the one most interested in your words." She clutched his arm as they left the restaurant to show she still loved him, no matter his taste in wedding speeches.

Eric thought about that and decided that his wife was right. Weddings had something old but he realized that his little story was a Pyrrhic victory, old songs or not. In truth, no one at the wedding gave a shit about Frankie Valli and the Four Seasons. The wedding marked a generational change, from the older to the newer. And he knew that he and his generation would become even less relevant as time progressed. A small sigh escaped him, unnoticed by any save Bette, who gave his arm a comforting squeeze. She knew how he felt because she felt the same way.

After eating, it started to rain, cold and hard as it sometimes happens in the fall in Montreal. Eric, prepared, opened his umbrella against the weather and with he and Bette protected, heads down, they walked briskly to their rental car.

Like two ships passing in the night, two men who would have instantly recognized each other passed by unknowingly. With their heads hidden by the brollies, they went right by each other. Eric and Rashid had missed being in the same restaurant at the same time by just a couple of minutes but neither would ever know it.

Rashid stepped up to a man eating alone at a table, sampling his food as he read the daily Montreal newspaper.

"Excuse me Monsieur Dubois, do you have a moment?" Rashid asked politely.

"And you are?" Andre asked the man with the dripping umbrella.

The man showed a package the size of a large best seller, wrapped in heavy paper and tied up neatly with strong string.

"Shimon Levi asked me to give this to you. It belonged to your father." Andre accepted the package with a smile.

"Thank you. I have been waiting for this. Will you sit down, Monsieur?"

"For a few moments only," Rashid consented.

"May I buy you some coffee or a cup of tea? It is cold and blustery outside."

"Thank you, but no. I can't stay long."

"How is Shimon"

"Very well, happy and healthy. He has recovered entirely from his 'injury'."

"Do you know Michelle?"

"No, but they were married a few days ago." An awkward silence ensued.

Then Andre broke the silence.

"I didn't know. That is wonderful news. How is her recovery?"

"Very gradual but in the right direction, steady but not dramatic. Or so I am told." Rashid brightened with a smile. "I understand that you are soon to marry as well?"

"Yes, how did you know?"

"I live here. Andre, you of course remember Inspector Gallant?" Andre nodded. "He has retired and the word is out that he intends to publish a tell-all book about his investigations of Father Gauthier's suicide and your kidnapping."

"Interesting, I will look for it. Do you know the title?"

"J'accuse."

Andre frowned.

"So, he took the title of the historical letter that Emile Zola wrote in 1898 addressed to the French President that accused the highest ranking French generals of conspiring to falsely convict Captain Alfred Dreyfus on trumped-up charges of treason motivated by Anti Semitism."

"It isn't very original of him," Rashid responded.

"When will the book be released?"

"Not until March. I was able to read a pre-publication copy at the Paris Book Fair."

"Thank you, ah, I did not get your name?"

"Benjamin."

"Thank you Benjamin. Thank you for the news and thank you a thousand times for the package. Au revoir."

Rashid grabbed his umbrella and left the restaurant.

EPILOGUE

Paris Book Fair

Jean Gallant, retired police inspector, had reserved a small room at the March Paris Book Fair. He had invited a selection of literary agents and independent publishers to listen to his pitch. A curious few had taken him up. Most came out of curiosity and wanted a chance to read the manuscript of "J'accuse."

"Bonjour, thank you distinguished members of the literary community, for coming to hear me today. I hope you will be interested in my book," Jean opened his speech.

"Monsieur Gallant, who do you accuse and what do you accuse them of?" inquired French publisher Madame Machete, a striking looking older woman wearing what could only be designer clothes.

Gallant paused and sipped from his water glass, holding the attention of the room.

"I accuse Antoine de Gaulle, formerly vicar general to Archbishop Clement and current assistant to the Vatican Secretary of State, of willfully concealing information about his relationship to one of the deceased suspects in the Andre Dubois kidnapping case. The deceased suspect, Sasha Andreev was murdered in a pew of the Saint James Oratory."

"Do you accuse de Gaulle of doing the murder?" Asked a publicist named Louis Poulin, a prominent and familiar face in literary circles.

"Monsieur de Gaulle had an iron clad alibi of the night of the murder, but he remains a person of interest. As lead detective on the Andre Dubois kidnapping, I can tell you that the first victim was a man named Zoran Coldovic, also known as Philippe. Evidence suggested that Sasha Andreev recruited Coldovic as an accomplice in the kidnapping. You will remember that we found Coldovic floating in the Seine with his fingertips missing to obfuscate his identity."

"Do you believe Sasha killed Coldovic?" Madame Machete asked.

"Zoran Coldovic said so in his final testament that we discovered in his safe deposit box. The trail to the Dubois kidnapping led to Coldovic and Andreev. But the trail went cold before it could lead all the way to Antoine de Gaulle and possibly others."

"How did you discover Antoine's relationship with Sasha Andreev?" The proprietor of the Renaud Bookstore chain wanted to know.

"Purely by accident, Monsieur Renaud. I had been invited to a dinner at Versailles sponsored by Archbishop Clement to honor Antoine de Gaulle's appointment to the Vatican. On a hunch, I followed one of the guests, Shimon Levi, an Israeli intelligence officer, into the gardens of Versailles. He drove a golf cart, and I ran to keep pace. I hid behind a tree. The Israeli and Antoine, the guest of honor, had arranged to meet secretly in a glade by the pond and the fountains. Levi offered Antoine several photographs. Antoine looked at pictures and lit a match to each of them, dropping each of the charred remains into the pond. After they sped away in their golf carts, I used a tree branch and salvaged one partially burnt photograph. On the fragment I could see a clear picture of Shasta Andreev."

"My initial inclination was that this was attempted blackmail. Shimon had discovered what I discovered from the photographs. Antoine and Sasha were lovers. As to the nature of their conversation, I was unable to hear them. The running water in the fountains drowned out their conversation."

"After Sasha's murder, we discovered he had been a flight attendant, and we obtained his log. We tracked his locations between flights and days off. Detective Blanc and I flew to San Tropez and investigated. We showed their photographs to waiters and innkeepers. The pair were well known. Sasha Andreev and Antoine de Gaulle met frequently and intimately at various cozy inns and bed and breakfasts along the French Riviera."

"With all this evidence, why didn't you arrest Antoine de Gaulle?" asked the book publisher Jean La Roche.

"I couldn't arrest the vicar general, because I had no proof he had committed a crime. But I will say that he was not forthcoming with his information. By the time we returned from San Tropez, Antoine had taken up his residence in the Vatican. Unfortunately, French rights to extradite are hindered by Vatican law."

"Not so long ago, law enforcement officers from America were also hindered and failed to extradite the former Archbishop of Boston, Bernard Law. The archbishop fled from the United States to avoid possible criminal charges that he willingly and knowingly harbored priests with histories of sexual crimes committed against innocent children. Antoine de Gaulle remains just as untouchable."

"Let me now switch and talk about Shimon Levi. A few years ago, I flew to Israel to question Andre Dubois as part of my investigation of Father Gauthier's suicide. I had to clear my interview with Shimon Levi. He had in his hands Dubois' laptop. Politely, I asked him for access to the computer to assist me with my investigation. Levi denied me access to the computer. I will tell you that this Israeli agent got to Andre because Andre gave me nothing."

"When I learned that Levi came to Paris in the company of Andre Dubois' ex-girlfriend, I placed him under immediate surveillance. The following morning, the surveillance crew spotted a car from the archdiocese at the Israeli embassy. My officers photographed Antoine de Gaulle, the then vicar general, as he greeted his passenger. The passenger was the same Shimon Levi. The following day, one of my men followed Shimon Levi as he took the train from Paris to Reims. Levi took a taxi to the Cafe Voila. He was served by a Moroccan waiter named Shai Tanger."

"Who is Shai Tanger? The name sounds familiar somehow," asked Jean La Roche.

"Shai Tanger is famous for bilking the Vatican for a million euros. Last year, he relocated to Israel. Shai Tanger knew Father Gauthier. In fact, he was the last person to see him in Reims on the day that he killed himself." Gallant seemed to have the small crowd of literary people listening intently. He continued.

"You may also recall that Archbishop Clement had already held a news conference and explained the nature of the financial settlement awarded to Tanger," Gallant added.

"Do I remember correctly, detective, that this involved some preposterous tale about a child kidnapping in the nineteenth century?" La Roche asked.

"Indeed, you have it exactly right, Monsieur La Roche. In 1858, an eight-year-old Jewish boy in Bologna named Edgardo Perez was forcibly converted to Catholicism. The church kidnapped the child and, in defiance of international pressure even from the Rothschild banking family and others, Pope Pius IX kept the boy at the Vatican and refused to return him to his family. It made a famous and nasty story at the time, as you might well imagine."

"According to the archbishop, Monsieur Tanger was the only living relative of this 19th century boy, Perez. While Perez remained Catholic and eventually became a priest, his sibling's grandchildren relocated to France and perished in the Holocaust. Tanger supposedly came from a branch that moved to Morocco around 1900. You are all in the book business. What do you think?"

"I think this is interesting. Is this the stuff in your book?" La Roche wanted to know.

"Most definitely, Monsieur La Roche. Tanger received the one million euros only two days after Shimon Levi met with him at the Cafe Voila: a coincidence, I think not?" the inspector offered and then took another question.

"My question, Monsieur Gallant, is what service do you believe Antoine de Gaulle required from Shimon Levi, or was it the other way around?" Monsieur La Roche asked.

"A very thoughtful question, but I can only speculate. It is probable that Shimon Levi urged Shai to take the Vatican money and flee to Israel. Supporting this postulation is the fact that the Israelis placed Tanger and his family at the front of the Israeli immigration line. I know. I checked with the French immigration authorities. This was also in the interest of the Israelis."

"Why?" La Roche probed.

"Monsieur La Roche, what was Israel's most singular problem in 2010?"

"The Palestinians," he replied.

"The Palestinian crisis is one Israel always has with it, but it is not the most existential problem for Israel. Iran has that place of dishonor." He paused and then continued.

"Let me explain. In 2010 Iran expected to receive a delivery of Russian S-300 anti-missile/anti-aircraft missile systems, a very capable system from what experts have told me. They need a high-quality system to protect their atomic infrastructure, the reactors, centrifuges, and so on, all the nuclear sites. But they have never been delivered. Putin's stooges constantly apologize to the Iranians for delay after delay. Why would Putin forgo hundreds of millions of euros in payment? It does seem odd, doesn't it?" Gallant asked.

"Why?" La Roche asked.

"I suggest you reread the interview conducted by Henri Bettencourt with Andre Dubois for Le Monde newspaper which I quoted at length in my manuscript. My book dovetails with Andre Dubois' account. I can offer a brief summary for you right now."

He held up his first finger for drama and continued.

"This is what I believe happened. Israel, Russia, and the Vatican participated in a three-way quid pro quo. Israel extracted concessions from Russia and Israel extracted concessions from the Vatican in exchange for sitting tight on information that the Israelis gleaned from Andre Dubois' computer hard drive."

La Roche quickly responded. "What concessions did the Israelis extract from the Vatican? What hold could they possibly have over the Church?"

"Which two Popes were on the fast track to sainthood, Monsieur La Roche?" Gallant responded.

Nonplussed, La Roche replied "Pope John Paul and Pope Pius XII, but what does that have to do with anything?"

"Pope John Paul is still on track but Pope Pius XII's train to sainthood has been derailed. Why would the Vatican stall Pius XII's sainthood? Because it was part of the quid pro quo. His detractors refer to Pius as Hitler's Pope. Pius XII, as ruler of the independent state of Vatican City, became the first head of state to recognize Hitler and legitimize him in the 1930s, before the outbreak of WWII. Catholics in Germany who were taught that Hitler was sinful now received the instruction to obey the Fuhrer, and importantly to Israel, to look away when he began the systematic oppression of the Jews and Slavs. The Poles have not forgotten

Pius' silence during Hitler's brutal atrocities against Polish priests in 1940. But Pius has his defenders, too. Unfortunately, or very conveniently, the Vatican archives for Pius XII can be examined only up to 1939. No files after that date can be reached by outsiders. Curious, no?"

Gallant continued.

"One can only imagine the depth of anger inside the Vatican to have their internal affairs dictated to them by Jews. In any case, the Vatican foreign office has reliably echoed the sentiments of the EU and the Arabs, especially when the political climate turned more hostile to Israel. Let me give you a sample of the rhetoric coming from the Vatican."

"The Pope convened a conference where Catholic archbishops called for the return of Palestinian refugees and the nullification of Israel's Jewish character. They asserted that the Jews' right to their promised land, that is Israel, had been nullified by the arrival of Christ."

Monsieur Poulin asked "Did the Israeli ambassador to the Holy See have a reaction to this declaration?"

Gallant smiled widely. "Oh yes indeed, he did have a reaction, a vivid reaction. He accused the conference of opposing the teaching of the Second Vatican Council and of adopting a replacement and succession theology in its place. This amounts to a very pointed and direct criticism not simply of Vatican foreign policy but of theology as well, nearly unprecedented."

Now Gallant held up his finger again, emphasizing his words. "The following month, the Pope lifted the 1988 ex-communication of a traditionalist Catholic bishop who had denied the Holocaust and said that no Jews had been gassed during World War II. The Holy See claimed that had the Pope known the English Bishop's views, he never would have lifted the excommunication that the church imposed in 1988."

"This bishop had been consecrated without papal consent for membership into the traditionalist Society of Saint Pius X. This society within the Church rejected openly and loudly many of the teachings of Vatican II, including specifically the outreach to the Jews, contained in the 1960's Nostra Aetate." Gallant used his finger again to make his point. "Nonetheless, the Pope did not reverse the lifting of the ex-communication. How about that?"

"La Civilita Cattolica, the Vatican magazine reviewed by the Holy See secretary of state before publication opened with a shocking editorial on Palestinian refugees. Adopting the Islamist propagandist word 'Nakba,' that is 'the catastrophe,' the paper declared that the refugees are a consequence of 'ethnic cleansing' by Israel. The article goes on to say that the 'Zionists' cleverly exploited the Western sense of guilt for the Shoah to lay the foundations of the Jewish state. By the way, the mobs in Gaza used this same word, chanting it just this week as they sought to swarm into Israel to kill the Israeli soldiers guarding the border."

"So you might ask 'Why is Israel silent in this period of the Vatican bashing her?' Israel had no choice. The Vatican assessed the geopolitical situation and determined that Israel would not push back as long as the Russians held back on the delivery of the anti-missile missiles to Iran. Iran was and is the real and present danger to Israel's existence."

"Monsieur Gallant, are you aware that the Pope has just written a new book exonerating the Jews from killing Christ? I have just finished reading my advanced copy," Monsieur Renaud inquired of the detective.

"Oui, I am aware of this." Gallant answered.

"In his book, the Pope persuasively and cogently argues there is no basis in Scripture to hold the Jews collectively responsible for deicide. This is groundbreaking, Monsieur Gallant. Too many priests still hold Jews responsible for the death of our savior. We've all heard the deicide charge against the Jews. Now you have a Pope who has taken on Scripture to exonerate the Jews as a people and to prevent the future slaughter of Jews in the name of Christ. Perhaps you can explain the juxtaposition? It seems like the church is going in two directions simultaneously, no?"

The man continued before Gallant could take a breath to answer.

"Inspector Gallant, how is the same Pope simultaneously able to theologically defend and to plot against the Jews? Do we have a duality of purpose at the Vatican when it comes to policies regarding the Jews and the country of Israel?"

Gallant took a crack at explaining this seeming duality.

"Admittedly, the Pope's book of Jewish exoneration contradicted the vitriol spewed from the Vatican during the previous year. Catchy phrases like 'clever Zionists,' and a nullification of the Jewish character of Israel. Does antisemitic commentary from La Civilta Cattolica or a statement at a bishops' conference emanate without a Papal imprimatur? I don't think so.

"Let me explain the force of nature that men have compelled the Pope

314

to exonerate the Jews in his upcoming book. And it was not to save Antoine de Gaulle from his troubles. Believe me when I say that Antoine de Gaulle is not so important within the gates of the Vatican to effect such a radical change in Vatican policy. Monsieur Levi may have engineered a lobbyist for Israel in the Vatican, but that was the extent of that blackmail."

Gallant paused for effect and looked at his listeners for a few beats of his heart.

"The force of nature that forced the Vatican to fold its hand and change its policy on Israel and the Jews to a benign one was....STUXNET," Gallant triumphantly declared.

"STUXNET, the computer worm unleashed on the Iranians? You really have our attention, Monsieur Gallant. To the best of my knowledge, no country has ever admitted to creating STUXNET, although Israel is often cited as the creative source," La Rouche commented.

"It is not so important to prove or disprove who created STUXNET," Gallant opined. "One has only to follow the timeline. The morning following Antoine's party at Versailles, news of STUXNET went viral, no pun intended. The damage inflicted on the nuclear centrifuges in Iran by STUXNET even the Iranians had to acknowledge. Estimates vary, but experts claim that Iran's nuclear drive could be set back several years, which as this audience of sophisticated observers well knows, is an eternity in diplomatic circles."

"It could have been the Israelis working solo or even in comport with the Americans, but it matters less who created STUXNET than the importance of it. With Iran's centrifuges sabotaged and the threat of additional viruses booming, Iran was no longer the biggest threat to the Jewish state, for the moment."

"Israel needed a friendly Pope, spiritual leader to a billion Catholics worldwide, to provide the moral case for Israel, to challenge the shared view from the political left and the Arab street that Jews were never entitled to their own state. STUXNET provided Israel with their existential security. Israel no longer feared the export of the Russian missiles, and" Gallant held up his finger again, like a preacher getting to the point of his sermon, "Israel no longer feared the Vatican. On the contrary, the invention of STUXNET likely caused the Vatican to fear that Israel would retaliate against the Holy See and reveal Andre's emails and the cover-up."

"That is what I believe Antoine de Gaulle learned that night at the fountains in the gardens of Versailles. He had no choice but to be an Israeli pawn in a political chess game," Gallant concluded, finally.

"And that is your explanation as to why this Pope made nice and exonerated the Hebrews through the re-examination of scripture?" another of the literati asked.

"I do, you have it exactly," Gallant nodded.

"Monsieur Gallant, I am curious about Andre Dubois. What can you tell us?"

"To the best of my knowledge, he resides in Montreal, Canada. He has not been found guilty of any crime, or even charged."

"Were you able to connect him to Shai Tanger? Did they know each other?"

"No, there is no evidence that they knew each other."

"And what of the Israeli kidnapped in California soon after the Dubois kidnapping? Those two victims knew each other." La Roche recalled.

"Oui, Monsieur. They both served on the International Space Station. Living in the same tin can in space as they did, you might expect them to know each other very well, as you say. But the kidnappings were not related, purely coincidental. Arab affiliates of Hezbollah in Tijuana, Mexico, kidnapped Ari Ben Ora. They planned to bargain him for Arab prisoners held in Israeli jail cells, to swap an astronaut for murderers. If you remember, there was an American tourist who was also kidnapped at the same time, a simple bystander. Both kidnap victims achieved their release at the same time, released unharmed. It is a different set of circumstances and is not covered in my manuscript."

"And onto the subject of my manuscript, my colleague and friend Henri Bettencourt sitting at the end table will gladly distribute copies and set appointments. I am interested in acquiring a publisher either directly or through the services of a literary agent. I have reserved this room for the remainder of the afternoon."

"Monsieur Gallant?"

"And you are?"

"Barry Zwick, I review books for the Montreal Sun," the Canadian journalist replied.

"I wasn't aware Montreal had any."

"Sunshine or book reviewers?" Zwick parried.

"Touche. Monsieur Zwick. I see you registered only yesterday. I am pleased that you are covering this event from Montreal. And your question is...?"

"I believe you posited that kidnappings of Ari Ben Ora and the American, Eric Miller were not connected to the kidnapping of Andre Dubois."

"I discovered no evidence to prove any linkage, Monsieur Zwick. As a policeman, I must follow the evidence."

"Monsieur Gallant, every Saturday, the Montreal Sun covers one of our local eateries. Last October, our photographers did a photoshoot on a seven-decade-old family operated Montreal delicatessen. Only last week one of our editors happened to notice that Andre Dubois had been photographed in the delicatessen during that October shoot. He was alone and eating breakfast."

"Monsieur Zwick, every person in this room is aware that Andre Dubois has left France and resettled in Montreal. The fact that he ordered breakfast at a delicatessen is hardly a news event."

The Canadian journalist parried "Your point is well taken, Monsieur Gallant. However, at that photoshoot were a man and a woman who sat two tables from Andre. Our editor recognized the man but couldn't place him. That prompted her to conduct an internet search of Andre Dubois' kidnapping."

"The man photographed sitting with his wife at the delicatessen was the kidnapped American, Eric Miller. Monsieur Gallant, the population of the United States in over three hundred million souls. The population of Canada is over thirty million. I am no statistician, but the odds of Andre Dubois and Eric Miller dining at the same restaurant at the same time, just by coincidence, in Montreal Canada, must be totally off the charts."

"Only a few thousand Americans were in Montreal last October. They indeed could have been there by chance," Bettencourt concluded with prejudice after a quick and inconclusive internet search.

"You see, Monsieur Zwick, your statistics are grossly inflated. You have no photographs of the two of them together."

"You are correct, Monsieur Gallant. We don't know whether they communicated or not."

"If you have your newspaper with you, Monsieur Zwick, I would like to see the photograph," La Roche requested.

"I do, Monsieur."

"Monsieur La Roche, do not be deceived by this Zwick. His paper is a tabloid, a rag, specializing in sensational gossip and maybe even digital trickery." Gallant protested.

"We are a respected tabloid," Zwick quickly defended his paper.

"I would like to see the picture too," another of the literati interjected. Others joined the request in an excited hub-bub.

"In my opinion, Monsieur Gallant, the photograph is genuine. I see no evidence of photo-shopping. I recognize Andre Dubois, but I do not know what the Millers look like," La Roche said with finality.

"I have a copy of the 2009 San Diego newspaper with photographs of Eric and Mrs. Miller," Zwick revealed.

"Let me have a look, if you will." La Roche took the two newspapers and compared the photographs. He nodded his head.

"As a journalist, I think the readers deserve to know if a connection existed between Andre Dubois and Eric Miller. If so, you might possibly prove that the two kidnappings were not simply coincidence. Now that would be a book I would stand in line to purchase, Monsieur Gallant," Zwick attested.

'IF' is the biggest word in the dictionary. Had Rashid been photographed with Andre accepting a package and Andre by implication connected to Canadian mobsters, what a story that might have been at the Sun? Had Eric Miller waited for a refill of his coffee, he most certainly would have recognized Rashid. Would he have thought he was being followed and his family's life endangered? Would he have gone to the authorities?

These occurrences, if they had happened, may have triggered a police investigation on both sides of the pond, and cast doubt on the former inspector's version of events as depicted in his yet to be published manuscript, 'J'Accuse.' But unfortunately for would be author Jean Gallant, Barry Zwick had begun to sow seeds of doubt among the editors and book publishers that the book was not yet finished. What more was yet to be discovered?

"Monsieur Zwick, as a former investigator I can assure you there was no meeting. The fact that they were photographed at the same restaurant was purely happenstance. A more fluid location such as a metro station or some other less conspicuous place would have been more suitable had they intended to meet.

"There is no evidence to suggest they knew each other. Are there other questions or comments? Henri has manuscripts, and I will make myself available this afternoon for private consultations."

Madame Machete interjected "Inspector, as a book editor, I must say that notwithstanding your excellent research on this subject matter any you mastery of criminal deduction, most of today's book buyers are either mostly young readers of fictional wizards and vampires or women who purchase romance novels."

"I concur with Madame Machete," La Roche agreed. "No longer is the buying public intrigued by crusades of the Knights Templar or Vatican mysteries and codes. Although your subject matter is of personal interest to me, I do not believe I could make moncy publishing your book."

"Monsieur La Roche's assessment of the book business is not wrong. And to be honest, Monsieur Gallant, I am troubled with your conclusion dismissing the possibility that the two kidnappings had an as yet unknown connection," book agent Poulet added.

Standing at the lectern a sullen Gallant looked into the face of the bookseller, Renaud, but he rendered no opinion. The inspector's sullenness instantly morphed into a look of contempt beamed in laser-like fashion to his Canadian critic. Zwick deflected the glare and looked at his wrist watch.

"Monsieur Gallant and guests, I apologize, but I have other appointments scheduled, and I am pressed for time. I will leave business cards on the table if any of you would like to be in communication. Merci."

Barry Zwick grabbed a manuscript as he left. The other guests slowly filed out.

"Well, Jean, they all took a manuscript," Henri optimistically said, sensing the author's disappointment.

"Out of respect, Henri, out of respect: they are not interested."

"I know you had them all interested until Zwick shot off his mouth. I wish he had stayed in Canada."

"You are correct, my good friend. But the truth is that Andre and the American were in the same place at the same time and that in itself is not so easy to dismiss."

"Jean, maybe you should consider a re-title of 'J'accuse" and re-write your manuscript as a fictional novel based on these unsolved murders and kidnappings. What do you think?"

"I would likely have to self-publish. You heard what the experts said -wizards, vampires, and romance novels."

"So you self-publish. You have book signings, go on talk radio. You might be surprised. Engage Zwick. He might be able to help you promote the novel in Canada."

"Or I could try to solve this case on my own," the retired inspector added.

"That is a decision you'll have to make, Jean. Are you hungry?"

"Famished. I had no time to eat breakfast this morning."

"The cafe in the lobby," Henri said and placed his laptop in the carrying case. Jean took the remaining manuscripts. The two men sat where the host directed them to sit. A waiter appeared.

"Good morning, gentlemen. Espresso or cappuccino?" The waiter offered them a choice.

"Espressos and croissants," Henri ordered for both of them.

"My apologies, Monsieur, we are out of croissants. We do have some fresh English scones."

"Do we look like fucking Englishmen?" Gallant barked at the man, venting his built-up frustration.

"Jean," Henri cautioned his friend, making 'calm down' motions with his hands. Henri addressed the waiter. "What kind of scones do you have?"

"We have either mixed berries or chocolate chip scones," the waiter responded with a squeamish glance at the angry Jean Gallant.

Henri looked at Jean for approval of his order.

"Whatever."

"We'll take two mixed berries scones," Henri told the waiter.

"Would you like them baked or fried?" The waiter asked.

"Fried, Monsieur, French fried."

THE END

THE REAL BARRY ZWICK

1942-2010

The real Barry Zwick, on whom the investigative reporter in this story is based, was a prolific writer, a deep thinker, a broad reader, a sharp wit, and a dear friend. Though the world is left with writing across the spectrum of subjects-everything from book reviews to character studies-Barry loved to travel. He wrote nearly one hundred pieces of insightful, lively travel literature which was published in newspapers and magazines around the world. Barry earned his master's in journalism at Columbia University. He served on the staff of The Philadelphia Inquirer, The Detroit Free Press, and the Los Angeles Times. He wrote, edified, wrote, and connected the worlds of the newsroom and the composing room at the Times for thirty-seven years.

Always interested in history, Barry researched his wife's family history and discovered that Bobbie's family, and thus their children's, were rabbinical scholars. On his own side, he found a host of scholars, doctors, lawyers, engineers, and writers. Stephen Lewis met Barry Zwick through their mutual love of writing. Barry was passionate, articulate, and well organized: for years he ran a DNA group linking individuals to families and though several members tried to fulfill his role when that became necessary, no one could hold the group together the way Barry could. He traveled the world with Bobbie, and sometimes with the kids. He studied art history, drank good wine, rode his bike for miles, listened to opera, recited poetry, read multiple newspapers daily, took pictures, sang songs, learned foreign languages, and showed gratitude for the blessings of his life. Barry lived, in every sense of the word.

Most important to Barry, despite the glory inherent in seeing his name and these stories in print, and in being lauded by his friends and colleagues around the world for his work, was his family. He continued to write Bobbie love letters even after almost forty years of marriage. His daughter Natasha and his son Alex brought him pride and joy-and he made sure they knew. Barry Zwick has quite an impressive legacy in the form of hundreds of thousands of words (now available on a website his children maintain for his work). But his greatest legacy remains his love for his children, who both write, and who honor him in everything they do and are.

I count myself a lucky man to have had the privilege to call him friend.

POST SCRIPT

"French Fried" is a fictional story. However, certain events in the novel are factual. The following is a timeline intended to help the reader distinguish between fact and fiction.

1858: The kidnapping of Edgardo Mortara.
Http://www.amazon.com/Kidnapping-Edgardo-Mortara-David-Kertzer/dp/0679768173

1970: Society of Saint Pius X. SSPX
http://en.wikipedia.org/wiki/Society_of_St._Pius_X

2005: Sainthood of Pope Pius XII on hold until the archives of his papacy are opened to researchers in 2014.
http://en.wikipedia.org/wiki/Canonization_of_Pope_Pius_XII

2010: Pope Benedict revokes ex-communication of Holocaust denying bishop and member of the Society of Stain Pius X, SSPX.
http://topics.nytimes.com/top/reference/timestopics/people/w/richard williamson/index.html

2010: Vatican synod, "God's promise to Israel was nullified by Christ."
http://www.ncronline.org/2010/vatican

2010: Russia backtracks on S-300 missile system for Iran.
http://latimesblogs.latmes.com/babyonbeyond/2010/02/iran-russia-promises-to-provide-tehran- with-promised-s300

2011: Stuxnet, the computer worm.
http://nytimes.com/2011/01/16/world/middleeast/16stuxnet.html?pagewanted=all

http://www.pcworld.com/businesscenter/article/205827/was_stuxnet_built-to_attack_irans_nuclear_program.hml

2011: Pope Benedict XV exoneration of the Jews.

http://www.huffingtonpost.com/2011/03/02/pope-jews-jesus-death_n_830140.htm

CPSIA information can be obtained
at www.ICGtesting.com
Printed in the USA
JSHW042332120322
23655JS00006B/5